Twenty Years After

ALEXANDRE DUMAS

Twenty Years After

Book Three of the Musketeers Cycle

❦

EDITED AND TRANSLATED
BY LAWRENCE ELLSWORTH

PEGASUS BOOKS
NEW YORK LONDON

TWENTY YEARS AFTER

Pegasus Books Ltd.
148 West 37th Street, 13th Fl.
New York, NY 10018

Twenty Years After, by Alexandre Dumas, Translated by Lawrence Ellsworth
Translation and Original Material Copyright 2019 © by Lawrence Schick
Front cover art: Adolphe Alexandre Lesrel

First Pegasus Books hardcover edition October 2019

Interior design by Sabrina Plomitallo-González, Pegasus Books

ISBN: 978-1-64313-202-0

10 9 8 7 6 5 4 3 2 1

Printed in the United States of America
Distributed by W. W. Norton & Company, Inc.

CONTENTS

Introduction
by Lawrence Ellsworth

In 1844 Alexandre Dumas, then age forty-one, had been a successful writer for almost a decade and a half, having made his mark first in the theater with sensational contemporary and historical melodramas. The rise of the *feuilletons,* French weekly newspapers that published episodic novels in serial form, gave him the opportunity to turn the lessons he'd learned crafting crowd-pleasing plays to popular prose. Dumas's gifts were for engaging characters in plot-driven stories depicted with vivid scenes and crackling dialogue. More than that, he had a genuine feel for French history, and a knack for bringing it to life for his readers.

These virtues all came together in March 1844, when the first chapters of *The Three Musketeers* began appearing in the pages of *Le Siècle,* a Parisian weekly. The story was a runaway success, and the paper soon had to increase print runs to keep up with the demand. Once published in book form, *The Three Musketeers* was a global sensation, and Dumas was elevated from a mere successful writer to the ranks of history's greatest storytellers.

At that time a great many serial novels were being published on both sides of the English Channel. What was it about Dumas's novel that struck a chord with such a broad national, and then international, audience? For one thing, its fast-paced and sweeping drama took maximum advantage of Dumas's strengths as a writer, mentioned above. But beyond that, its quartet of quirky and charismatic heroes were immediately beloved by readers everywhere. Each musketeer expressed an aspect of Dumas's own outsized personality, his boundless enthusiasm for life, romance, and adventure: the bold and clever d'Artagnan, noble Athos, jovial Porthos, and sly Aramis were vivid and engaging incarnations of archetypal adventure heroes, familiar yet uniquely and individually themselves.

And with these four characters, Dumas had created a tight-knit team of disparate personalities that was durable, flexible, and expansive enough to enable him to address, through their exploits, what he saw as life's central challenge: how to find the courage to adhere to a personal code of honor despite the conflicting dictates of society and authority. How, in short, to do right.

The spectacular first Musketeers novel established Dumas's core characters and their all-important interrelationship, that comradeship and commitment that made the Inseparables a byword for devoted loyalty. "All for one and one for all." But the four musketeers were no Knights of the Round Table, no paragons of chivalry, they were recognizably real people with flaws as well as virtues, and when Dumas pitted them against the soldiers and assassins of repressive authority, the reader felt they were in genuine danger, at risk not just of failure, but of death. Against such enemies they had only their courage, their wits, and each other—and somehow, that had to be enough.

The serialization of *The Three Musketeers* concluded in July 1844, and was published in book form before the end of the year in both Brussels and Paris. By then readers and publishers were already clamoring for a sequel, and Dumas, after discussing it with his assistant Auguste Maquet, was ready to provide one. But when the first chapters of *Twenty Years After* began to appear in January 1845, it wasn't quite what anyone had expected.

The Three Musketeers, in which the heroes are all between the ages of eighteen and twenty-five, is profoundly a novel of youth, its protagonists exuberant, passionate, and energetic, overcoming obstacles by sheer audacity. Dumas could have written a second book set right after the first, simply expanding upon the formula of youthful heroics, but the author, by then approaching his mid-forties, was more interested in how his most popular characters would face life's complexities once they were past the simple moral clarity of youth. How would his heroes cope when confronted by the ambiguities and compromises of maturity? Excited by this idea, Dumas planned out what we would now call a character arc for each of his four archetypal heroes, a long saga set against the events of one of the most dramatic periods in French history, the rise of King Louis XIV. *Twenty Years After* was the first installment of this grand story, a tale that would run to over a million words, culminating at last in *The Man in the Iron Mask*. It was a bold and ambitious undertaking that took several years to complete, but *pardieu*! He pulled it off.

Back to the work at hand: at the end of *The Three Musketeers*, d'Artagnan has achieved his dream, an officer's rank in the elite company of the King's Musketeers—but he's also suffered tragedy by his failure to protect the woman he loved, who was murdered by his enemies, and this shadows his achievement. When his comrades one by one leave the musketeers to go their separate ways, d'Artagnan falls into the immemorial routines of the career military officer, and the years pass by. Though he serves with bravery, even distinction, so long as Monsieur de Tréville is still captain-lieutenant of the King's Musketeers, there's no path for d'Artagnan to advance without leaving the company, which to him is unthinkable. So, he marks time for twenty years, a trusty weapon going to rust, until the events of *Twenty Years After* rouse him from his daze and propel him back into action.

What has changed? For one thing, old Tréville has finally retired, leaving a vacancy at the head of his company. For another, the stable regime established by Cardinal Richelieu and enforced by him on the fractious French has been steadily unraveling since his death, and the dire inequities and long-suppressed rivalries in the fraying social order have erupted into a seething low-grade civil war, the Fronde. D'Artagnan's commonplace skills, those of a mid-level military officer, are little valued during ordinary times, but now opportunity knocks; it's only in times of trouble, when extraordinary measures are called for, that d'Artagnan can find expression for his unique talent for bold and unorthodox stratagems.

So as the factions arm for battle, d'Artagnan once again has the opportunity to perform extraordinary services for the queen, for her son the young king—and, of course, for himself. But the resources of the orthodox military he's served in for twenty years are of no use to him here, for he's at his best acting outside of hierarchy and unrestrained by convention. D'Artagnan summons up his all old energy and audacity and hurls himself at the complex challenges of the new regime.

And . . . he fails. D'Artagnan *fails*, because times are not what they were, and the virtues of youth, no matter how skillfully deployed, are no longer enough to master the situation. Life has become complicated, and simple solutions cannot succeed.

However, d'Artagnan knows the solution, or at least part of it: to find his old comrades, the Inseparables, Athos, Porthos, and Aramis, and reforge the bonds of comradeship and loyalty they formed when they were all youths. But they have grown apart from each other with the passing years, even as each one has grown to be more indelibly himself in the process. And they are on different sides in the French civil war of the Fronde. Pride, ambition, and sheer time have opened gaps between the old musketeers, and d'Artagnan will find it no easy thing to bridge those gaps and draw them back together.

And even if he does—for how long?

A Note on the Translation: The public appetite for a sequel to *The Three Musketeers* was so great that the first volumes of *Twenty Years After* were rushed into book publication before the serial had even finished running in *Le Siècle*. The first (and unauthorized) edition, published in Brussels in early 1845, was cobbled together by collecting the installments published in Paris and was so hastily compiled that it omitted an entire chapter: that of XXIX, "Good Councilor Broussel" (*"Le Bonhomme Broussel"*). This error was perpetuated in some later editions published in Paris, and as it was one of those editions that was used as the basis of the first English translations, that chapter has been absent from nearly every British and American version of the novel ever since. Though the four musketeers don't really appear in the "missing" chapter, it provides solid entertainment and context for the character and personalities of the leaders of the Fronde. It's good stuff, and we're pleased to restore it to the novel's continuity.

As the above example illustrates, the sources of the original French version of *Twenty Years After* are a jumble. Where there were inconsistencies, this editor usually relied on the Pléiade version edited by Gilbert

Sigaux in 1962, as well as the edition compiled and annotated by Charles Samaran that same year for Éditions Garnier. (Note that the "Good Councilor Broussel" chapter appears in *neither* of these "definitive" editions.)

The original 1846 English translation by William Robson was solid work and has proved so durable that there hasn't been a significant new version for readers of English in over a century—until now. The foremost original translators, Robson and William Barrow, did their work well, but they were writing for a Victorian-era audience that was uncomfortable with frank depictions of violence and sexuality. Moreover, they employed a style of elevated diction that was deemed appropriate for historical novels of the 19th century, but seems stiff, long-winded, and passive to today's readers. It also does a disservice to Dumas's writing style, which was quite dynamic for its time, fast paced and with sharp, naturalistic dialogue. This editor's new version attempts to restore Dumas's edge, aiming as well to recapture some of the bawdy humor lost in previous translations.

As noted above, *Twenty Years After* was the first long installment in Dumas's final million-word-plus character arc recounting the lives of his Four Musketeers. It's a big novel, considerably longer than the already-large *Three Musketeers*, big enough to be awkward and unwieldy in a single volume, and in fact, in the Victorian era it was often published in two parts. We have chosen to follow that tradition, dividing it into *Twenty Years After* (the current volume) and its conclusion, *The Son of Milady*. This will make reading it more manageable and convenient, and also acknowledges the realities of modern publishing and distribution, which cannot easily handle a novel the size of this one in a single volume. (Dumas's epic continuation, the titanic *Le Vicomte de Bragelonne*, which is three times the size of *Twenty Years After*, will appear in four volumes.)

Twenty Years After is a truly great novel, and it's been an absolute pleasure to prepare a modern version that honors the author's original intentions, and which I hope will help it find a new audience in the 21st century. I think you'll enjoy it.

Historical Character Note: The first time a notable character from history is mentioned in the text, their name is marked with an asterisk.* A brief paragraph describing that person appears in the **Dramatis Personae: Historical Characters** appendix at the end of the book.

Twenty Years After

I

Richelieu's Ghost

In a chamber of the Palais Cardinal, or Palais Royal[1] as it was now known, near a vermeil-gilded table stacked with books and papers, sat a man with his head resting on his hands.

Behind him was a vast fireplace, glowing with heat, with flaming embers crackling over large gilded andirons. The glow from the fireplace lit the dreamer's magnificent robes from behind, as the flickering light from a grand candelabra illuminated the front.

To see this crimson robe edged with intricate lace, this pale forehead bent in meditation in the solitude of his study, to hear the silence of its antechambers and the measured tread of the guards outside on the landing, one might have thought the shadow of Cardinal Richelieu* still haunted this room.

Alas! It was no more than the shadow of that great man. France badly weakened, the authority of the king disregarded, the Great Nobles once more strong and defiant, foreign enemies menacing the borders—all testified that Richelieu was no more.

But more than anything, the proof that this red-robed form was not that of the former cardinal was his isolation, which seemed, as we've said, more like that of a ghost than a living man. It was the halls devoid of courtiers; the courtyard bristling with guards; the air of disdain and derision blowing in through the windows from the streets, the breath of a whole city united against this minister; and finally, from near and far, the rattling of gunfire, not, fortunately, aimed with intent to injure, so much as to show the guards—the Swiss, the musketeers, and the soldiers stationed around the Palais Royal—that the people, too, had arms.

This ghost of Richelieu was Cardinal Mazarin.*

But Mazarin now stood alone and knew his weakness.

"*Foreigner!*" he muttered. "*Italian*! These are the words they use as curses. With these same words they assassinated and dismembered Concini²—and if I let them, they'd do the same to me, tear me limb from limb, though I've never done anything worse than just squeeze them a little. Fools! Unable to see that their enemy isn't this Italian who speaks poor French, but rather those lords who feed them fine words in a pure Parisian accent.

"Yes, yes," continued the minister, pale lips smiling a subtle and incongruous smile. "Yes, you tell yourselves that the fortunes of favorites are precarious—but you should know I'm no ordinary favorite! Though the Earl of Essex³ wore a splendid diamond-crusted ring given him by his royal mistress, and I wear only a simple ring engraved with a number and a date, *my* ring has been consecrated by a vow in the Palais Royal chapel.⁴ They won't break me to their will! Let them join their eternal call of 'Down with Mazarin!' to cries of 'Long live Monsieur de Beaufort!' or 'Long live Monsieur le Prince!' or even 'Long live the Parliament!' Well—Monsieur de Beaufort* is locked up in Vincennes, the Prince de Condé* may join him any day, and as for parliament . . ."⁵

Here the cardinal's smile twisted into an expression of hatred more virulent than seemed possible on such a mild face. "Well, as to parliament . . . parliament, too, will get what's coming to it. We have the royal strongholds of Orléans and Montargis. We have time. In time, all those who today shout, 'Down with Mazarin' will in their turn shout, 'Down with the princes.' Richelieu, whom they hated while he lived, but can't stop talking about now that he's dead—he had worse days than this, when he feared he'd be dismissed, or seemed actually forced out. But Queen Anne* will never dismiss *me*—and if the people force me out, she will go with me. Then we'll see how the rebels like having neither a king nor a queen! Oh, if only I wasn't a foreigner! If only I were French, and a nobleman!"

He fell back into his reverie.

Indeed, the situation was dire, and the day that had just ended had made it more complicated still. Mazarin, always driven by sordid avarice, was crushing the people with taxes. In the words of Advocate General Talon, the people had been left with nothing but their souls, and still had those only because they couldn't be sold at auction. The people had been advised to be patient, as great victories were in the offing, but since glory couldn't feed empty mouths, the people used their mouths for muttering their discontent.

But that wasn't all, because when it's only the people who complain, the Royal Court, insulated by the bourgeoisie and the gentry, doesn't hear it. However, Mazarin had been so reckless as to offend the magistrates! He had created offices for twelve newly made Judges of Requests and sold them, and as the existing judges had paid high prices for their positions, and the addition of twelve new colleagues could only dilute their value, the magistrates had united against him. They'd sworn on the Gospels to oppose these appointments and to resist all encroachments from the Court, promising each other that any member who lost his office by this rebellion would be reimbursed by the others.

Now, here's how the conflict played out:

On the seventh of January 1648, seven or eight hundred mutinous Parisian merchants had gathered to protest a new tax on business owners, sending ten delegates to talk to Prince Gaston, the Duc d'Orléans,* who had always been popular with them. The duke, receiving them, had been told they were determined not to pay this new tax, and were even willing to take up arms against anyone the king might send to collect it. The Duc d'Orléans listened politely to them, which gave them hope; he promised to speak to the queen about it and dismissed them with the usual response of princes: "We'll see."

For their part, on the ninth the Judges of Requests came before the cardinal, and their designated representative spoke so firmly and fearlessly the cardinal had been astonished. He gave them the same response the Duc d'Orléans had given the merchants: "We'll see."

So, in order to *see,* the King's Council had assembled and sent for d'Émery, the superintendent of finances.

This d'Émery was widely despised by the people, first of all because he was the superintendent of finances, and all superintendents of finances should be despised, and second because, it's fair to say, he deserved it.

He was the son of a banker of Lyon named Particelli who had, after filing for bankruptcy, changed his name to d'Émery. Cardinal Richelieu, who recognized his merits as a financier, had presented him to King Louis XIII* under this new name, recommending d'Émery for the position of superintendent of finances, and the king had agreed. "Excellent!" he'd said. "I'm glad to hear about this Monsieur d'Émery, as we need an honest man for the post. I'd thought you were going to sponsor that swindler Particelli for the job and was afraid you'd persuade me to agree."

"Sire!" replied the cardinal. "Don't worry, that Particelli you mentioned has been hanged."

"All the better!" said the king. "It's not for nothing that I'm known as Louis the Just." And he'd signed the appointment of Monsieur d'Émery.

It was this same Superintendent d'Émery who'd been sent for by Prime Minister Mazarin. He rushed in pale and frightened, saying his son had been nearly assassinated that day on the Place du Palais; a crowd had confronted him, complaining of the extravagance of his wife, who'd decorated their home with hangings of red velvet trimmed with gold fringe. She was the daughter of Nicolas Le Camus, who'd come to Paris with just twenty *livres,* but had by 1617 become royal secretary. His salary had been only forty thousand livres, but somehow his children had received an inheritance of nine million. D'Émery's son had barely avoided violent suffocation at the hands of the mob, which had threatened to squeeze all the stolen gold out of him. So, the council decided to take no action that day, as the superintendent was in no condition to think straight.

The following day, First President of Parliament Mathieu Molé, whose courage in these affairs, according to Cardinal de Retz, was equal to that of the Duc de Beaufort or of Monsieur le Prince de Condé—the two men who were considered the bravest in France—the next day, we say, the first president was attacked in his turn. The people threatened to take him to task for the ills they were suffering, but the first president, always unflappable and self-possessed, replied with his usual calm that if the malcontents didn't bend to the king's will, he would erect enough gallows in the squares to hang the lot of them. To which they replied that they asked nothing better than some new gibbets, as they would serve to hang those judges who bought favor from Court at the cost of the misery of the people.

There was more: on the eleventh, when the queen went to mass at Notre Dame, as she did every Saturday, she was met by over two hundred women crying out and demanding justice. They had no worse intention than that, wishing only to kneel before her to try to move her to pity, but the guards kept them back, and the queen, haughty and proud, passed without paying any attention to their cries.

That afternoon, the King's Council met again; it resolved to maintain the royal authority, and summoned parliament to convene on the following day, the twelfth.

That day, on the evening of which our story begins, started when King Louis XIV,* then ten years old and just recovered from smallpox, had gone to Notre Dame to give thanks for his deliverance. This gave him a pretext for calling out his troops—guards, Swiss, and musketeers—and posting them around the Palais Royal, on the Pont Neuf, and on his route along the quays. After hearing mass the king had made a surprise call on parliament, where he held an impromptu *lit de justice*, confirming all his previous tax edicts as well as issuing five or six new ones, each one, according to Cardinal de Retz, more ruinous than the last. The new measures were loudly opposed by President Blancmesnil[6] and Councilor Broussel.* Furthermore, the first president, who as we saw had supported the king only the day before, indignantly protested this high-handed method of bringing the king in person to impose the royal will on parliament.

These edicts decreed, the king returned to the Palais Royal. Crowds of people lined his way, but though they knew he came from parliament, they didn't know whether he'd gone to demand justice for the people or to oppress them further, so no cheers greeted his passing, and there were no felicitations on his return to health. Every face was anxious or gloomy, and some were even threatening.

Though the king had passed, the troops remained in position; it was feared there would be riots once word of the decrees at parliament got around—and indeed, at the merest rumor that, instead of rolling taxes back, the king had increased them, crowds began to gather. Soon a great clamor filled the streets, with shouts of "Down with Mazarin!" as well as "Long live Broussel" and "Long live Blancmesnil." The people knew that Broussel and Blancmesnil had spoken out on their behalf, and though their eloquence had been to no avail, it had won them the citizens' goodwill.

Attempts were made to dispel these crowds and silence their shouts, but as often happens, that served only to increase the throngs and redouble their cries. The Royal Guards and the Swiss were first ordered to stand firm, and then sent to patrol Rue Saint-Denis and Rue Saint-Martin, where the crowds seemed thickest and most animated.

At this point the merchants' provost appeared at the gates of the Palais Royal, and was immediately admitted. He came to say that if the troops weren't ordered to stand down, all of Paris would be under arms within two hours.

While the options were being debated, Lieutenant of the Guards Comminges* came in from the street, his clothes torn and his face bloodied. Seeing him, the queen cried out in surprise and asked what had happened. As the provost had predicted, the sight of the guards had inflamed the crowds. They had swarmed the belfries and rung the tocsin. Comminges had stood firm and arrested a man who appeared to be one of the leading agitators, and then, in order to make an example of him, ordered the man hanged from the Croix du Trahoir. The soldiers had moved to carry out this order but were attacked with stones and halberds by rioters from Les Halles. The rebel had taken advantage of the chaos to escape, reaching the Rue des Lombards, where he'd disappeared into a house.

Despite an aggressive search, they couldn't catch the culprit. Comminges had posted sentries in the street and then, with the rest of his detachment, returned to the Palais Royal to report these events to the queen. They were followed all the way back by threats and curses, several of his men were wounded by pikes and halberds, and he himself had been cracked over the eyebrow by a stone.

Comminges's report only confirmed the advice of the merchant's provost. The authorities were unprepared to withstand a serious revolt; the cardinal had the rumor spread among the people that the troops stationed along the quays and the Pont Neuf were there only for the ceremony and were being withdrawn. Indeed, by four in the afternoon they were all concentrated around the Palais Royal, with a detachment at the Barrière des Sergents, another at the Quinze-Vingts, and a third at the Butte Saint-Roch.[7] They filled the courtyards with Swiss Guards[8] and musketeers, and they waited.

This is where things stood when we introduced our readers to Cardinal Mazarin's study, which had once belonged to Cardinal Richelieu. We saw in what state of mind he heard the crowd noises and gunshots that echoed into his windows.

Suddenly he looked up with a determined expression, like a man who has made up his mind. He stared at a huge clock that was on the verge of striking ten, reached for a silvered whistle placed on the table within reach of his hand, and trilled on it twice.

A hidden door in a tapestry opened soundlessly, and a man dressed in black emerged and moved silently to stand behind the cardinal's chair.

"Bernouin,"* said the cardinal without turning, for having whistled twice he knew it was his valet, "which King's Musketeers[9] are guarding the palace?"

"The Black Musketeers, Monseigneur."

"Which company?"

"Tréville's."[10]

"Is there an officer of that company in the antechamber?"

"Lieutenant d'Artagnan."*

"He's a good one, I believe?"

"Yes, Monseigneur."

"Get me a musketeer's uniform and help me into it."

The valet went out as quietly as he'd entered, and returned a few moments later, carrying the requested outfit.

Silent and thoughtful, the cardinal began removing the ceremonial robes he'd worn to attend the session of parliament and then donned the military uniform, which he wore with a certain ease thanks to his time in the Italian campaigns. Once he was fully dressed, he said, "Get me Monsieur d'Artagnan."

And the valet, silent and mute as ever, went out through the antechamber door like a shadow.

Left alone, the cardinal regarded himself in the mirror with some satisfaction. He looked young for his forty-six years, and though a bit short, he still cut an elegant figure. His complexion was fair and smooth, his eyes expressive, his nose large but well-shaped, his brow broad and majestic. His chestnut hair curled slightly, and his beard, which was darker, took a curling iron well. He straightened his baldric, then looked complacently at his hands, which were handsome and of which he took great care. He removed the buckskin riding gauntlets from his belt and replaced them with simple gloves of silk.

At that moment the door opened. "Monsieur d'Artagnan," announced the valet.

An officer entered.

He was a man of thirty-nine or forty years, compact but lean and well made, with a sharp and clever eye, his goatee still black though his hair was touched with gray, as often happens when a man has lived too well or not well enough, especially if he's of dark complexion.

D'Artagnan stepped into the study, recalling that he'd come into it once before in Cardinal Richelieu's time, then stopped when he saw no one within but one of his company's musketeers. At a glance he recognized the cardinal under the uniform. He remained standing in a respectful but dignified pose, as befits a gentleman who has spent much of his life among the *Grands*.

The cardinal fixed him with a gaze more cunning than penetrating, looked him over carefully, and said after a few moments of silence, "You're Monsieur d'Artagnan?"

"Himself, Monseigneur," said the officer.

The cardinal considered for a moment that intelligent face and mobile expression restrained by years and experience; but d'Artagnan withstood the examination like a man who has been subjected to a far more piercing gaze.

"Monsieur," said the cardinal, "come with me—or rather, I'll go with you."

"I'm at your orders, Monseigneur," d'Artagnan replied.

"I'd like to personally inspect the guard posts around the Palais Royal. Do you think there's any danger?"

"Danger, Monseigneur?" asked d'Artagnan, astonished. "From where?"

"They say the people are in open revolt."

"The uniform of the King's Musketeers still commands respect, Monseigneur—and even if that weren't the case, I think with four of my men we could chase off a hundred of these clowns."

"Didn't you see what happened to Comminges?"

"Monsieur de Comminges is an officer of the guards, not the musketeers," d'Artagnan replied.

"In other words," said the cardinal, smiling, "the musketeers are better soldiers than the guards."[11]

"Everyone prefers his own uniform, Monseigneur."

"Except me, Monsieur," the cardinal said, still smiling. "As you see, I prefer yours to my own."

"*Peste*, Monseigneur," said d'Artagnan, "now that's modesty. As for me, I confess that, if I had one of Your Eminence's grand outfits, I wouldn't need any other."

"Perhaps, but to wear one of those out tonight might not be safe. Bernouin, my hat."

The valet returned, carrying a musketeer's broad-brimmed hat. The cardinal put it on, cocked it like a cavalier, and turned to d'Artagnan. "You have horses saddled in the stables, don't you?"

"Yes, Monseigneur."

"Very well! Let's go."

"With how many men, Monseigneur?"

"You said that with four men you could chase off a hundred of these rabble; we might meet two hundred, so bring eight."

"As Monseigneur wishes."

"I'll follow you. No, wait." The cardinal paused. "We'll go this way. Bernouin, a light."

The valet brought a candle; the cardinal took a small golden key from his desk and unlocked the door of a secret staircase. A few moments later they found themselves down in the side courtyard of the Palais Royal.

II

A Night Patrol

Ten minutes later, the little troop went out through the Rue des Bons-Enfants, behind the theater built by Cardinal Richelieu for the play *Mirame*, and in which Cardinal Mazarin, a patron more of music than of literature, had sponsored the production of one of the first operas performed in France.

The great city showed every evidence of turmoil: large crowds roamed the streets, and despite what d'Artagnan had said, stopped to watch the soldiers pass with a menacing air of mockery that showed the citizens had temporarily traded their usual deference for insulting belligerence. From time to time a commotion was heard from the markets of Les Halles. Gunfire rattled toward Rue Saint-Denis, and occasionally, for no apparent reason, church bells were rung.

D'Artagnan steered his course with the nonchalance of a man unimpressed by such nonsense. When a crowd blocked the middle of the street he rode his horse straight for them without a word of warning and, whether rebels or not, they seemed to see what manner of man they were dealing with and parted to let the patrol pass. The cardinal envied his composure, which he attributed to familiarity with danger, and he regarded the officer with the esteem the cautious accord to cool courage.

As they approached the detachment posted at the Barrière des Sergents, the sentry cried, "Who goes there?" D'Artagnan replied and, having asked the cardinal for the passwords, advanced at the order. The countersign was *Louis and Rocroi.*

The passwords acknowledged, d'Artagnan asked if Monsieur de Comminges wasn't commander of the post. The sentry indicated an officer on foot talking to another on a horse. D'Artagnan recognized him and returned to the cardinal, saying, "There is Monsieur de Comminges."

The cardinal urged his horse toward them while d'Artagnan held back discreetly. However, from the way the two officers removed their hats, he knew they'd recognized His Eminence.

"Bravo, Guitaut,"* said the cardinal to the mounted officer, "I see that despite your sixty-four years you're as alert and devoted as always. What were you telling this young man?"

"Monseigneur," replied Guitaut, "I was saying we live in unusual times, and that today looked a lot like things must have during the days of the Catholic League[12] I heard so much about as a youth. Do you know there's even talk of the mob throwing up barricades across Rue Saint-Denis and Rue Saint-Martin?"

"And what did your nephew Comminges have to say to that, *mon cher* Guitaut?"

"Monseigneur," Comminges replied, "I said that you can't make a League without the essential element of a Duc de Guise.[13] Besides, they won't repeat what they did before."

"No, this time they'll make a Fronde,[14] as they call it," said Guitaut.

"What's that you said? A Fronde?" asked Mazarin.

"Monseigneur, that's the name they've given their party."

"Where does it come from?"

"Apparently several days ago Councilor Bachaumont said at the Palais that all these rowdies in the alleys were like schoolboys slinging stones— *fronding*—ruffians who scatter when they see a constable, only to gather again once he's passed. The rebels picked up on the word *frond*, quick as a Brussels beggar, and started calling themselves *frondeurs*. Since yesterday, everything is the Fronde: Fronde hats, Fronde gloves, Fronde fans, even Fronde bread, and . . . well, just listen to that."

A window had opened, and a man stuck out his head and began to sing:

> *The Fronde wind blows*
> *So, let her in*
> *I think it goes*

Against Mazarin
If the Fronde wind blows
We'll let her in!

"Insolent wretch!" Guitaut growled.

"Monseigneur," said Comminges, whose injury had put him in a blood-thirsty mood, "shall I have that fellow shot to teach him a lesson about what to sing?" And he reached toward the holster on his uncle's horse.

"By no means!" cried Mazarin. "*Diavolo!* You'll spoil everything, my friend, and just when things are going so well! I know your Frenchmen as well as if I'd made them myself. If they sing the song, they'll pay the piper. During the days of the League that Guitaut was speaking of, they only sang the mass, and things ended badly for them. Come, Guitaut, let's see if they keep guard at the Quinze-Vingts as well as they do at the Barrière des Sergents."

And, with a salute to Comminges, he rejoined d'Artagnan, who assumed the lead of the little troop, followed immediately by Guitaut and the cardinal, with the rest as rear guard.

"That figures," Comminges muttered, watching them ride away. "I forgot that he's satisfied so long as everyone pays."

Along Rue Saint-Honoré the people were gathered in small groups discussing the new edicts. They pitied the young king, used as a tool to plunder the people unknowingly, and blamed Mazarin for everything. They talked of appealing to the Duc d'Orléans and Monsieur le Prince, and applauded Blancmesnil and Broussel.

D'Artagnan passed through these groups as inflexibly as if he and his horse were iron. Mazarin and Guitaut talked softly together, while the musketeers, who had finally recognized the cardinal, rode in silence.

They reached Rue Saint-Thomas-du-Louvre and the post at the Quinze-Vingts. Guitaut beckoned to a junior officer, who advanced to report.

"Well?" Guitaut asked.

"Ah! All is well on this side, *mon Capitaine,* but I think something is going on over there." And he pointed toward a beautiful hôtel, or mansion, on the spot where the Vaudeville Theater now stands.

"That's not just any mansion," said Guitaut. "That's the Hôtel de Rambouillet."[15]

"I don't know about any Rambouillet," said the officer. "All I know is I saw some pretty shady characters go in there."

"Bah!" said Guitaut, laughing. "Those are just poets."

"Bah yourself, Guitaut," said Mazarin. "I'll thank you not to speak of those gentlemen with such irreverence! Didn't you know I was a poet myself in my youth? I wrote verses in the style of Monsieur de Benserade."

"You, Monseigneur?"

"Yes, me. Shall I recite some of it?"

"Not on my account, Monseigneur! I don't know Italian."

"Yes, but you know French, don't you, my brave Guitaut?" replied Mazarin, laying his hand in a friendly way on the officer's shoulder. "And whatever order you're given in that language, you'll follow?"

"Of course, Monseigneur, as I always have—provided it comes from the queen."

"Ah, yes!" said Mazarin, biting his lips. "You're absolutely devoted to her."

"Well, I *have* been captain of her guards for more than twenty years."

"Onward, Monsieur d'Artagnan," the cardinal said. "All is well here."

D'Artagnan resumed the lead of the column without saying a word, displaying the unquestioning obedience that is the hallmark of an old soldier.

Passing through Rue de Richelieu and Rue Villedo, they arrived at Butte Saint-Roch, the third post. It was the most isolated, for it was just inside the walls, and the city was sparsely populated in this neighborhood. "Who is in command here?" asked the cardinal.

"Villequier," replied Guitaut.

"The devil!" said Mazarin. "You speak with him—you know I'm at odds with him since I charged you with the arrest of the Duc de Beaufort. He complained that he, as captain of the Royal Guard, should have had that honor."

"I know it, and I've told him a hundred times he was wrong. The king couldn't have given him that order, as he was barely four years old at the time."

"Yes, Guitaut, but I could have ordered him on the king's behalf, and I chose you instead."

Guitaut didn't reply, just urged his horse forward, and after being recognized by the sentry, called for Monsieur de Villequier.

He came out. "Ah! It's you, Guitaut. What the devil are you doing here?" he said, in his usual ill-humored tone.

"Just checking the situation in this direction."

"Why bother? There were shouts earlier of 'Long live the king!' and 'Down with Mazarin!'—but there's nothing new in that. We're used to it by now."

"And do you join in?" Guitaut replied, laughing.

"My faith, sometimes I'd like to! I think they're right, Guitaut. I'd give five years of my pay, which they don't pay me, if it would only make the king five years older."

"Really? And what would happen if the king were five years older?"

"He'd be at the age of majority and could give his orders himself. I'd much rather obey the grandson of King Henri IV than the son of Pietro Mazarini. Death of the devil! I'd kill for the king. But if I got killed on account of Mazarin, like your nephew nearly was today, there's nothing in heaven worthwhile enough to console me for it."

"All right, all right, Monsieur de Villequier," said Mazarin, coming up. "Rest assured, I'll report your devotion to the king." Then, turning to the escort: "Let's go, Messieurs—all is well here."

"So, Mazarin was there all along!" said Villequier. "So much the better, Guitaut—I've wanted to tell him that for a long time. You gave me the opportunity, and though I don't imagine you did it as a favor, I thank you." And turning on his heel, he returned to the guardhouse, whistling that tune of the Frondeurs.

Mazarin was thoughtful on their return. What he'd heard in succession from Comminges, Guitaut, and Villequier just confirmed his suspicion that, if it came to a crisis, he'd have nobody on his side but the queen. And yet the queen had so often abandoned her friends, it seemed to the minister that, despite his precautions, her support couldn't be counted upon.

During the whole of their nocturnal ride, that is, for an hour or so, the cardinal, while studying in turn Comminges, Guitaut, and Villequier, was keeping his eye on another man. This man, self-assured despite the angry populace, responding neither to Mazarin's wry remarks nor to the catcalls of the crowd—this man seemed to him above and beyond, a person well adapted to the events taking place, and even more suited for events yet to come.

The name of d'Artagnan wasn't completely unknown to Mazarin, although he hadn't come to France until around 1635—that is, seven or eight years after the events we related in *The Three Musketeers*. It seemed to the cardinal that he associated that name with a person said to be a model of courage, skill, and dedication.

He was so taken by this idea that he immediately wanted to learn all he could about d'Artagnan—but he couldn't exactly ask d'Artagnan about himself. From the few words he'd heard the lieutenant of musketeers say, he'd recognized the accent of Gascony, and the Italians and Gascons are too much alike, and know each other too well, to ever trust what any of them would say of themselves.

As they arrived at the walls that enclosed the Palais Royal gardens, the cardinal knocked at a small door right about where the Café de Foy stands now, and after thanking d'Artagnan and asking him to wait in the courtyard, he gestured to Guitaut to follow him. Both dismounted, handed the bridles of their horses to the lackey who'd opened the little door, and disappeared into the garden.

"My dear Guitaut," said the cardinal, leaning on the arm of the old captain of the guards, "you told me just now that you've been in the queen's service for twenty years?"

"Yes, that's the truth," Guitaut replied.

"Now, *mon cher* Guitaut," the cardinal continued, "I know that in addition to your courage, which is proven, and your loyalty, which is beyond question, that you have an excellent memory."

"You've noticed that, Monseigneur?" said the guard captain. "The devil! Too bad for me."

"What do you mean?"

"Beyond all doubt, the most important quality of a courtier is to know how to forget."

"But you're no courtier, Guitaut, you're a brave soldier, a veteran captain from the time of King Henri IV, one of the few who are still among us."

"Peste, Monseigneur! Did you ask me to come with you so you could cast my horoscope?"

"No," said Mazarin, laughing, "I brought you here to ask whether you noticed our lieutenant of musketeers."

"Monsieur d'Artagnan?"

"Yes."

"No need for me to notice him, Monseigneur—I've known him for a long time."

"What kind of man is he, then?"

"What kind?" said Guitaut, surprised. "Why, he's a Gascon!"

"Yes, I know that; what I want to know is if he's a man one could trust."

"Monsieur de Tréville holds him in high esteem—and Tréville, as you know, is a good friend of the queen."

"I need to know if this is a man who's proven his worth."

"If you're asking if he's a brave soldier, then yes. At the Siege of La Rochelle, at Susa Pass, at Perpignan,[16] it's said he did more than his duty."

"But you know, Guitaut, we poor ministers often need men who are more than just brave. We need people who are quick and capable. Wasn't this d'Artagnan, according to rumor, involved in some intrigue in Cardinal Richelieu's time that he managed to conclude quite cleverly?"

"As to that affair, Monseigneur," said Guitaut, who saw what the cardinal was getting at, "I have to tell Your Eminence that I don't know any more than what everyone knows. I never meddle in intrigues, and if I'm sometimes told things in confidence, since those secrets aren't mine to share, I'm sure Monseigneur won't mind if I keep them to myself."

"Upon my word," Mazarin said, shaking his head, "I've heard some ministers are actually lucky enough to get told what they need to know."

"Monseigneur," Guitaut replied, "those ministers don't weigh all men in the same balance. They ask men of war what they need to know about war, and intriguers about intrigue. Ask your questions of some intriguer of that period, and you'll find out what you want to know—for the right price, of course."

"Pay, by God!" said Mazarin, with the grimace he always made at the subject of payment. "Then we'll pay . . . if we must."

"Does Monseigneur seriously wish to know the name of a man who was involved in all the conspiracies of that time?"

"*Per Bacco!*" Mazarin swore, as he was growing impatient. "It takes an hour to get something through that iron head of yours."

"There's one man who can tell you everything you want to know—if he'll talk."

"That's *my* problem."

"Ah, Monseigneur! It's not always easy to get someone to tell you what they don't wish to say."

"Bah! With patience, I find, one gets results. And this man is . . . ?"

"The Comte de Rochefort."*

"The Comte de Rochefort!"

"Unfortunately, he disappeared four or five years ago, and I don't know what became of him."

"Ah, but I do, Guitaut," said Mazarin.

"Then why is Your Eminence complaining that he doesn't know anything?"

"So," Mazarin said, "you think that Rochefort . . ."

"He was Richelieu's demon twin, Monseigneur—but I warn you, this will cost you dearly. The old cardinal paid his creatures well."

"Yes, Guitaut," said Mazarin, "Richelieu was a great man, but he did have that tragic flaw. Thank you, Guitaut—I'll try to take advantage of your advice this very evening."

As they had arrived at the courtyard of the Palais Royal, the cardinal dismissed Guitaut with a salute; then, seeing an officer walking up and down the yard, he approached him.

It was d'Artagnan, who was awaiting the return of the cardinal, as ordered. "Come, Monsieur d'Artagnan," said Mazarin in his friendliest tone. "I have an order to give you."

D'Artagnan bowed, followed the cardinal up the secret staircase, and a moment later found himself in the office from which they'd departed. The cardinal sat down at his desk and wrote a few lines on a sheet of paper.

D'Artagnan stood, impassive, waiting with neither impatience nor curiosity. He seemed like a military automaton, a clockwork soldier.

The cardinal folded the letter and sealed it with his ring. "Monsieur d'Artagnan," he said, "you will carry this dispatch to the Bastille[17] and return with the person who's named in it. Take a carriage and escort, and guard the prisoner carefully."

D'Artagnan took the letter, touched his hand to his hat, turned on his heel like a drill sergeant, and a moment later could be heard ordering in his curt monotone: "An escort of four men, a carriage, and my horse."

Five minutes later came the sound of carriage wheels and the ringing of horseshoes on the pavement of the courtyard.

III

Two Old Enemies

D'Artagnan arrived at the Bastille just as the clocks were striking half past eight. He was announced to the governor who, when he heard the visitor came with an order from the cardinal, came out to meet him on the steps.

At that time the governor of the Bastille was Monsieur du Tremblay,* brother of the famous Capuchin monk known as Father Joseph,[18] that terrible servant of Richelieu who had been called His Gray Eminence.

When Marshal Bassompierre[19] was in the Bastille, where he stayed for twelve years all told, and heard his fellow prisoners say, when dreaming of liberty, "I'll be released at such-and-such a time," or "I'll soon be free of this place," Bassompierre would say, "As for me, Messieurs, I'll leave when Monsieur du Tremblay leaves"—by which he meant that when the old cardinal died, du Tremblay would lose his post as governor, and Bassompierre would be freed to resume his place at Court.

But his prediction failed to come true, because to Bassompierre's surprise, when the cardinal died things just went on as before: Monsieur du Tremblay didn't leave, and neither did Bassompierre.

Du Tremblay was therefore still governor of the Bastille when d'Artagnan presented himself with the minister's order. He was received with great courtesy, and as the governor was about to dine, he invited d'Artagnan to join him.

"I would accept with pleasure," said d'Artagnan, "but unless I'm mistaken, the envelope of this letter is marked *Urgent*."

"Quite so," said Monsieur du Tremblay. "Ho there, Major! Send down Number 256."

Upon entering the Bastille, one ceased to be a man and became nothing more than a number.

D'Artagnan shuddered at the sound of the keys. Still in the saddle, he looked around at the ironbound doors and barred windows; he had no desire to dismount inside these thick walls that he'd always seen from the other side of the moat, and which he'd learned to fear twenty years before.

A bell rang. "I must go," said Monsieur du Tremblay. "They're calling for me to sign the release of the prisoner. I hope to see you again, Monsieur d'Artagnan."

"Devil take me if I share *that* hope," d'Artagnan murmured from behind a gracious smile. "Only five minutes in here, and I'm sick of it already. Let's go—I'd rather die penniless in a shack than be a rich governor of the Bastille, even if it paid ten thousand a year."

He'd scarcely finished this monologue when the prisoner appeared. Seeing him, d'Artagnan started with surprise, a movement he quickly suppressed. The prisoner entered the carriage without appearing to recognize d'Artagnan.

"Messieurs," d'Artagnan said to his four musketeers, "I was ordered to keep an eye on the prisoner, and since the carriage doors have no locks, I'm going to ride with him. Monsieur de Lillebonne, be so kind as to lead my horse by the bridle."

"Of course, Lieutenant."

D'Artagnan dismounted, handed his horse's bridle to the musketeer, and entered the carriage. He sat next to the prisoner, then ordered, in a voice that showed no emotion, "To the Palais Royal, at the trot."

The carriage moved, and as it passed under the gatehouse, d'Artagnan took advantage of the shadow it cast to grip the prisoner in an embrace. "Rochefort!" he cried. "It's really you!"

"D'Artagnan!" cried Rochefort, astonished.

"Ah, my poor friend!" d'Artagnan said. "I haven't seen you for four or five years, and feared you were dead."

"*Ma foi,*" said Rochefort, "there's not much difference between being dead and being buried—and they buried me deep."

"And for what crime were you in the Bastille?"

"Do you want to know the truth?"

"Yes."

"Well, then—I have no idea."

"Are you serious, Rochefort?"

"I'm serious, faith of a gentleman! At any rate, it can't be for the crime they accused me of."

"What was that?"

"Petty theft."

"You, a petty thief? Are you kidding me?"

"I wish I was. You want the whole story?"

"I'll say I do."

"Well, here's what happened. One evening, after roistering at Reinard's in the Tuileries with the Duc d'Harcourt, Fontrailles, de Rieux, and some others, d'Harcourt proposed we go cloak-snatching on the Pont Neuf.[20] As you know, that sort of prank had been made quite fashionable by the Duc d'Orléans."

"What, at your age? Were you crazy, Rochefort?"

"No, just drunk. But it didn't sound like fun, so I told the Chevalier de Rieux we should just watch rather than take part—and to get the best view, we should climb onto King Henri's bronze horse.[21] No sooner said than done! We used the royal spurs as stirrups and sat on the king's crupper. Perched there, we could see everything. Already four or five cloaks had been snatched with great flair, from victims who hadn't dared say a word in protest, until one fool, less patient than the others, called out, 'Guards! Guards!' which got the attention of a patrol of archers. D'Harcourt, Fontrailles, and the others ran for it, and de Rieux wanted to do the same, but I remember telling him they'd never see us where we were.

"But he wouldn't listen to me. He put his foot on the spur to climb down, the spur broke off, he fell, broke his leg, and instead of keeping quiet about it, began to howl like a hanged man. I tried to jump down in my turn, but too late: I jumped right into the arms of the archers. They took me to the Châtelet, where I slept soundly enough, as I was sure I'd be out the next day. But the next day passed, then another, and then a whole week, so I wrote to the cardinal. That same day they came for me and took me to the Bastille, where I spent the next five years. Do you think that was for committing the sacrilege of riding pillion behind Henri IV?"

"No, you're right, my dear Rochefort, it can't be for that. But you're probably about to learn what it *was* for."

"Ah, yes, I forgot to ask—where are you taking me?"

"To the cardinal."

"What does he want?"

"I don't know, since I didn't even know it was you I was going to get."

"Impossible. A favorite like you?"

"Me, a favorite?" d'Artagnan cried. "My dear Count! I was a cadet from Gascony when I met you at Meung[22] twenty-two years ago, and I'm still not much more than that!" He finished with a deep sigh.

"But you're leading a command, aren't you?"

"Because I happened to be the one in the antechamber when the cardinal called. But I'm still just a lieutenant of musketeers, as I've been for the last twenty years."

"Well, at least nothing bad has happened to you."

"What could happen to me? To quote some Latin verse I've mostly forgotten, or rather never knew, 'Lightning doesn't strike the valley'—and I'm a valley, my dear Rochefort, the deepest around."

"And Mazarin is still Mazarin?"

"More than ever! They say he's secretly married to the queen."

"Married!"

"If he's not her husband, he's certainly her lover."

"So, she resisted Buckingham but gave in to Mazarin!"

"Women!" said d'Artagnan, philosophically.

"Not just a woman, but a queen!"

"*Mon Dieu,* queens are just women twice over."

"And Monsieur de Beaufort, is he still in prison?"

"Indeed. Why?"

"It's just that he thinks well of me and might get me out of this."

"You're probably closer to being free than he is, and will have to get *him* out of it."

"Then, the war . . ."

"Oh, we'll have a war."

"With the Spanish?"

"No, with Paris."

"What do you mean?"

"Don't you hear that gunfire?"

"Yes. What is it?"

"That's the citizens getting warmed up before the game!"

"And you think these civilians mean business?"

"*Mais oui,* if they can find a good leader to pull them together."

"What a rotten time to get out of prison."

"Good God, cheer up! If Mazarin sent for you, it's because he needs you, and if he needs you—well, my compliments! He hasn't needed me in years, and you see where I am."

"Then speak up about it! That's my advice."

"Listen, Rochefort—let's make a deal."

"What's that?"

"We've been good friends to each other."

"Pardieu! I've got three sword wounds to prove it."

"Well, if you get back in favor, don't forget about me."

"On the honor of a Rochefort—but you must do the same for me."

"Deal! Here's my hand. So, the first chance you get to put in a word for me . . ."

"I'll speak up. And you?"

"I'll do the same."

"And what about your old friends? Are they included?"

"Which friends?"

"Athos,* Porthos,* and Aramis*—have you forgotten?"

"Just about."

"What's become of them?"

"I don't know."

"Really?"

"Good Lord, yes! We parted, as you know; I sometimes hear indirect news, so I know they're still alive, but that's all. But where in the world they might be, devil take me if I know. Upon my honor, the only friend I have is you, Rochefort."

"And your illustrious . . . what did you call that lad who made sergeant in the Piedmont Regiment?"

"Planchet?"

"Yes, that's it. And the illustrious Planchet,²³ what happened to him?"

"He married the owner of a confectioner's shop in the Rue des Lombards . . . he always did have a sweet tooth. So, he's a merchant of Paris, and probably leading the riots. It's funny, but he'll probably make alderman before I make captain."

"Come, my dear d'Artagnan, buck up! It's when you're at the bottom of the wheel that it turns you back to the top. Your fate may change this very evening."

"Amen to that!" said d'Artagnan, halting the carriage.

"What are you doing?" asked Rochefort.

"We're nearly there, so I'm getting out. It shouldn't look like we know each other."

"Quite right. *Adieu!*"

"*Au revoir;* remember your promise." And d'Artagnan mounted his horse and took over lead of the escort.

Five minutes later they entered the courtyard of the Palais Royal.

D'Artagnan led the prisoner up the grand stair, across the antechamber, and along a corridor. At the door of Mazarin's study, he was about to have himself announced when Rochefort laid his hand on his shoulder. "D'Artagnan," said Rochefort with a smile, "do you want to know what I was thinking as we rode along that route, passing those angry mobs that watched you and your four men with flaming eyes?"

"What?" said d'Artagnan.

"Just that all I had to do was shout for help and they'd have torn you to pieces, you and your escort—and I'd have been free."

"Why didn't you do it, then?" said d'Artagnan.

"Come now!" Rochefort replied. "What of our sworn friendship? Now, if it had been someone other than you who was taking me, I don't say . . ."

D'Artagnan saluted him—and said to himself, "Has Rochefort become a better man than I?"

And he had himself announced to the minister.

"Bring in Monsieur de Rochefort," came Mazarin's impatient voice, as soon as he heard the names, "but ask Monsieur d'Artagnan to wait—I've not yet finished with him."

At these words d'Artagnan withdrew happily. As he'd said, it was a long time since anyone had needed him, and this directive from Mazarin seemed a good omen.

As for Rochefort, the summons had no effect on him other than to put him on his guard. He entered the study and found Mazarin seated at his desk in his usual attire, that of a prelate of the Church—similar to the robes of an abbot of the period, but with stockings and mantle of purple.

As the doors closed, Rochefort glanced at Mazarin from the side of his eye, and saw the minister sizing him up from the side of his own.

The minister was the same as always: curled, primped, perfumed, and thanks to this grooming, looking less than his age. As for Rochefort, that was something else; five years in prison had aged Richelieu's worthy aide, turning his black hair white and changing his healthy complexion to a wan pallor. Seeing him, Mazarin shook his head slightly with a look that said, "Here's a man without much use left in him."

After a silence that stretched out for what seemed to Rochefort an age, Mazarin took a letter from a pile of papers, showed it to him, and said, "I see here a letter in which you request your freedom, Monsieur de Rochefort. Are you in prison, then?"

Rochefort trembled at this question. "But," he said, "it seems to me Your Eminence ought to know that better than anyone."

"Me? Not at all! There's still a crowd of prisoners in the Bastille who've been there since Monsieur de Richelieu's time, and I don't know all their names."

"Oh, but me, Monseigneur, that's another thing entirely! You knew my name, since it was by Your Eminence's order that I was taken from the Châtelet to the Bastille."

"You think so?"

"I'm sure of it."

"Yes—I think I do remember it. Didn't you, at the time, refuse a mission to Brussels on the queen's behalf?"

"Ah," said Rochefort, "so that's the real reason? I've been wondering for five years. Fool that I am, not to have seen it!"

"I don't say that's the cause of your arrest, I'm just asking a question, that's all. So, listen: did you not refuse to go to Brussels on the queen's service, after you'd gone there on the service of the old cardinal?"

"It's precisely because I'd gone there in service to the cardinal that I couldn't go back in service to the queen. I'd left Brussels in terrible danger. I'd gone during the Chalais conspiracy to intercept the correspondence between Chalais and the archduke, and when I was recognized, I was nearly torn to pieces. How was I supposed to go back after that? Instead of serving the queen, I'd have been lost to her."

"Well, here we see, my dear Monsieur de Rochefort, how even the best of intentions can be misconstrued. When you declined to go, the queen saw it as insubordination. Her Majesty still bore a grudge about some of your services to the late cardinal!"

Rochefort smiled sourly. "Now that he's dead, the fact that I served Cardinal Richelieu against the queen is exactly why I would serve you, Monseigneur, against all the world."

"Unlike Cardinal Richelieu, Monsieur de Rochefort," said Mazarin, "I am far from all-powerful. I'm just a minister who, as servant to the queen, needs no servants of his own. But Her Majesty is very sensitive; having heard of your refusal, she took it as a declaration of war, and since you were a capable man and therefore dangerous, Monsieur de Rochefort, she ordered me to . . . attend to you. Which is how you found yourself in the Bastille."

"Well, Monseigneur," said Rochefort, "it seems to me that if I was in the Bastille by mistake . . ."

"Yes, yes," Mazarin replied, "I'm sure this can all be worked out. You're a man who understands how tangled affairs can become, and how to untangle them—by whatever means."

"That was what Cardinal Richelieu thought, and I'll admire that great man all the more if you tell me you share his opinion."

"It's true," said Mazarin, "Monsieur de Richelieu was a great politician, a much greater man than I, who am simple and straightforward. That's what holds me back, that frankness so entirely French."

Rochefort had to bite his lips to suppress a smile.

"So, I'll come to the point. I need good friends and faithful servants— when I say *I need*, of course I mean the *queen* needs. I do nothing except at the orders of the queen, is that clear? I'm not like Cardinal Richelieu, who followed his own whims. No, I'll never be a great man like him; but at least I can be a good man, Monsieur de Rochefort, and I hope to prove it to you."

Rochefort remembered well that silky voice, which sometimes slipped into sibilants like the hiss of a viper. "I'm quite prepared to believe that, Monseigneur," he said, "though for my part, I've seen little proof till now of that good nature Your Eminence speaks of. Remember, Monseigneur," he continued quickly, seeing the minister's expression, "remember that I spent the last five years in the Bastille, and nothing darkens a man's vision like seeing things through prison bars."

"Ah, but Monsieur de Rochefort, I already told you it wasn't my idea to put you in prison. The queen . . . well, the anger of a woman, and moreover a princess, what would you have? But it goes as quickly as it comes and is soon forgotten."

"I understand, Monseigneur, how five years at the Palais Royal, amid gallants and gaiety, might make one forget—but I, who passed them in the Bastille . . ."

"My God, Monsieur, do you think life at the Palais Royal is all parties and fun? Not at all! We have here, too, our trials and troubles. But let's say no more about it. I'll lay my cards on the table, Monsieur de Rochefort. Now tell me, are you with us?"

"Please understand, Monseigneur, I ask nothing better—but I have no idea of the state of affairs. At the Bastille, one talks politics only with soldiers and jailers, and you have no idea how little such people know about what's really going on. I've always been a partisan of Monsieur de Bassompierre myself—is he still one of the Seventeen Seigneurs?"[24]

"He is dead, Monsieur, and it's a great loss. He was a man devoted to the queen, and men so loyal are rare these days."

"*Parbleu!* Quite so," said Rochefort, "especially once you've sent them to the Bastille."

"Very well, then," said Mazarin, "how would you measure devotion?"

"By action," said Rochefort.

"Indeed—by action," said the minister thoughtfully. "But where does one find men of action?"

Rochefort shook his head. "There's no shortage of them, Monseigneur—if you know how to look for them."

"I don't know how to look for them? What are you saying, Monsieur de Rochefort? Kindly instruct me. You were close to Monseigneur le Cardinal and must have learned a lot. Ah! What a great man he was!"

"Monseigneur won't take offense if I lecture a bit?"

"Me? Never! As you know, I listen to everyone. I want to be loved, not feared."

"Well, Monseigneur, on the wall of my prison cell, scratched in with a nail, is a proverb."

"And what is this proverb?" asked Mazarin.

"Just this, Monseigneur: *Like master . . .*"

"... *Like manservant.* I know it."

"No: *like retainer.* It's a minor change made by those devoted followers I was speaking of."

"*Eh bien.* So, what does this proverb mean?"

"It means Monsieur de Richelieu knew how to attract loyal retainers by the dozen."

"He, the target of every assassin! He, who spent his life warding off attack after attack!"

"But he did ward them off, despite their number. Because though he had many enemies, he had just as many friends."

"But that's all I ask!"

"I've known people," continued Rochefort, thinking it was time to put in a word for d'Artagnan, "people so capable they were even able to foil the cardinal, with all his guards and his spies—people without rank, without money, and without support who nonetheless saved a crowned head her crown, and made the cardinal cry mercy."

"But these people you speak of," said Mazarin, smiling to himself at maneuvering Rochefort into bringing up the very subject he wished to discuss, "these people weren't devoted to the cardinal, since they fought against him."

"No, though they would have been better off if they had been. But they had the bad luck to be devoted to this same queen for whom you were just now trying to find servants."

"But how is it you know all this?"

"I know this because, at the time, these people were my enemies; because they were pitted against me, and though I did them all the harm I could, they got the better of me; because one of them, my particular nemesis, gave me three sword wounds, the last one seven years ago ... and that settled our old account."

"Ah!" said Mazarin, with good-natured longing. "If only I knew such men."

"Well, Monseigneur, you've had one of them standing outside your door for the last six years, and you haven't seen fit to do anything with him."

"But who?"

"Monsieur d'Artagnan."

"That Gascon?" cried Mazarin, in a perfect imitation of surprise.

"That Gascon saved a queen, and in skill, courage, and wit made Monsieur de Richelieu look like a schoolboy in comparison."

"Really?"

"It's exactly as I have the honor to tell Your Eminence."

"Tell me the whole story, my dear Monsieur de Rochefort."

"That's rather difficult, Monseigneur," said the count, smiling.

"He'll tell me himself, then."

"I doubt it, Monseigneur."

"And why is that?"

"Because the secret is not his to tell—because, as I've said, it's the secret of a great queen."

"And he alone accomplished such a feat?"

"No, Monseigneur, he had three friends, three brave men who backed him up, just the sort of loyal companions you said you were looking for."

"And these four men worked together, you say?"

"As if they weren't four men but one; as if four hearts beat in one chest. What they've done together, those four!"

"My dear Monsieur de Rochefort, you pique my curiosity, truly you do. Are you sure you can't share their story?"

"No, but I can tell you a tale—a true fairy tale, as it were, Monseigneur."

"Then tell me, Monsieur de Rochefort! I do so love a good story."

"You're sure that's what you want, Monseigneur?" said Rochefort, trying to understand the cardinal's motive in all this.

"Yes."

"Well then, listen! Once upon a time there was a queen . . . not just any queen, but the queen of one of the greatest kingdoms of the world, a queen whom a great minister wished to harm because once he'd loved her too well. No point in trying to guess who I mean, Monseigneur, as all this took place long before you came into the queen's kingdom.

"Now there came to Court a brave ambassador, so rich and so elegant, that all the women lost their hearts to him. Even the queen was taken with him, and doubtless because of how diplomatically he conducted himself, she had the imprudence to present him with some royal ornaments so remarkable and unique that they were irreplaceable. Now as these ornaments had been given to her by the king, the minister persuaded His Majesty that she should wear them at an upcoming ball. Needless to say, Monseigneur, the minister was well aware that these ornaments had left with the ambassador and were now far across the sea. Alas, the great queen was lost—doomed to fall from her high estate to below the lowest of her subjects!"

"Really!" said Mazarin.

"Yes, Monseigneur! But four men resolved to save her. Now these four men were not princes, nor dukes, nor peers, nor even men of wealth—they were just four soldiers with bold spirits, strong arms, and quick swords. So, they went to recover the necklace. But the minister knew of their departure and had placed men along their road to prevent them from reaching their goal. Waylaid by numerous assailants, three of them were brought low, but one fought through to the port, killed or wounded those who tried to stop him, crossed the sea, and returned the ornaments to the great queen. She wore them proudly to the ball on the appointed day, and the minister was nearly ruined as a result. And what do you say to that deed, Monseigneur?"

"It was magnificent!" said Mazarin, in wonder.

"Well, I could tell ten more such tales."

Mazarin didn't reply. He was thinking.

Five or six minutes passed.

"Have you anything more to ask of me, Monseigneur?" said Rochefort.

"So that's it. And d'Artagnan was one of these four men, you say?"

"It was he who took the lead."

"And the others, who were they?"

"Monseigneur, allow me to let d'Artagnan name them to you. They were his friends, not mine, and only he would have any influence over them. I never even knew them under their true names."

"I see you still don't trust me, Monsieur de Rochefort. Well, I will continue to be frank: I need him—and you—and all of them!"

"Then start with me, Monseigneur, since you sent for me, and here I am. I'm sure it will come as no surprise that after five years in prison, I'm curious to know what plans you have for me."

"You, my dear Monsieur de Rochefort, will be in charge of security; you will go to Vincennes, where Monsieur de Beaufort is imprisoned, and keep him under careful guard. Well! What do you think?"

"I'm afraid the position you offer me is impossible," said Rochefort, shaking his head ruefully.

"Impossible? How can it be impossible?"

"Because Monsieur de Beaufort is one of my friends, or rather, I'm one of his. Have you forgotten, Monseigneur, that he's the one who sponsored me to the queen?"

"Since then, Monsieur de Beaufort has become an enemy of the State."

"Yes, Monseigneur, that may be. But since I'm neither king, nor queen, nor minister, he's no enemy to me, and I can't accept what you offer me."

"So, this is what you call devotion? Good luck with that. Such devotion won't get you very far, Monsieur de Rochefort."

"But Monseigneur," Rochefort replied, "to come out of the Bastille only to go to Vincennes, for me that's just changing one prison for another."

"Just be honest: you're really on Monsieur de Beaufort's side, aren't you?"

"Monseigneur, I was locked up so long I'm not allied to any party, except the party of fresh air. Assign me anywhere else, send me on a mission, give me anything to do so long as it's active!"

"My dear Monsieur de Rochefort," said Mazarin archly, "your zeal is admirable, and though I'm sure you have the heart for it, in you the fire of youth has gone out. Trust me, what you need now is rest, and plenty of it. Hey, there, outside!"

"You're not sure what to do with me, then, Monseigneur?"

"On the contrary, I've decided." Bernouin entered. "Call a bailiff for me," Mazarin said to him in a low voice, "and stay nearby."

An officer was summoned. Mazarin wrote a brief note and handed it to him, then nodded. "Adieu, Monsieur de Rochefort," he said.

Rochefort said, "I see, Monseigneur, that you're sending me back to the Bastille."

"Clever man."

"I'll go, Monseigneur, but I say again, it's a mistake not to make use of me."

"You, the friend of my enemies!"

"What would you have? I didn't make them your enemies. I could still be on your side."

"Do you think you're the only one for that post, Monsieur de Rochefort? Believe me, I'll find others just as good."

"Then it is my turn to wish you luck, Monseigneur."

"All right, off with you. And by the way, don't bother to write me any more letters, Monsieur de Rochefort, as I'm afraid they'll just go astray."

"Well, I got played for a fool that time," Rochefort muttered on his way out. "But if d'Artagnan isn't satisfied with that little tribute I gave him, he's a hard man to please. Wait a minute, where the devil are they taking me?"

In fact, they took Rochefort out by the secret staircase, instead of passing through the antechamber where d'Artagnan was waiting. In the side courtyard he found the carriage and four-man escort waiting for him, but his friend was nowhere to be seen.

"Oh ho!" Rochefort said to himself. "That changes everything. If the mob still crowds the streets, then by God, we'll show Mazarin we're still good for something more than just guarding a prisoner."

And he leapt into the carriage as lightly as if he were no older than twenty-five.

IV

Anne of Austria at Age Forty-Six

Left alone with Bernouin, Mazarin paused a moment, thinking. He'd learned a lot, but he needed to know more. As Brienne has informed us, Mazarin was a card cheat, which he called just taking advantage of his opportunities. He resolved not to commence the game with d'Artagnan until he knew all of his opponent's cards.

"Would Monseigneur like anything?" Bernouin asked.

"I would," Mazarin replied. "Light the way; I'm going to see the queen."

Bernouin took a candlestick and led the way.

There was a secret passage[25] that connected Mazarin's suite with the queen's apartments; the cardinal could use that corridor to visit Anne of Austria at all hours.

Arriving in the bedchamber at the end of the passage, Bernouin met Madame Beauvais; he and she were the confidants of this pair of aging lovers. Madame Beauvais went ahead to announce the cardinal to Anne of Austria, who was in her oratory with the young Louis XIV.

Anne of Austria, seated in a grand armchair, elbow leaning on a table and head resting on her hand, watched the royal child as he lay on the carpet, leafing through a big book of battles. Anne of Austria was a queen who knew how to waste her time without losing her dignity; she sometimes spent hours idling in her bedchamber or oratory, neither reading nor praying.

As for the king's choice of reading matter, it was an edition of Quinte Curce's *History of Alexander*[26] profusely illustrated with engravings.

Madame Beauvais appeared at the door of the oratory and announced Cardinal Mazarin. The child got up on one knee, frowning, and asked his mother, "Why does he just come right in without asking for an audience?"

Anne colored slightly. "In times like these," she replied, "it's important for a prime minister to be able to report what's happening to the queen at any time of day, without exciting the curiosity or commentary of the whole Court."

"But it seems to me Monsieur de Richelieu didn't barge in like that," replied the child, unappeased.

"How would you know how Monsieur de Richelieu behaved? You were too young to remember."

"I don't remember it—I asked about it, and they told me."

"Who told you that?" asked Anne of Austria, with poorly disguised irritation.

"I know better than to tell on those who answer my questions," replied the child. "If I tell, they'll stop answering and I won't learn anything."

At that moment Mazarin entered. The king stood, picked up his book, put it on a table, and stood next to it, which compelled Mazarin to remain standing as well.

Mazarin took in the scene with a thoughtful eye, giving the queen an inquiring look. He bowed respectfully to Her Majesty and deeply to the king, who replied with a rather cavalier salute—but at a reproachful look from his mother Louis XIV swallowed the hatred he'd felt toward the cardinal since infancy and greeted the minister with a forced smile.

Anne of Austria tried to guess the reason for this unexpected visit from Mazarin's expression, as the cardinal usually didn't come in to her until everyone else had retired. The minister nodded slightly toward the door, and the queen said, "Madame Beauvais, it's time for the king to go to bed. Call La Porte."*

The queen had already told young Louis two or three times that it was time to retire, and the child had fondly insisted on staying with her—but this time he made no reply, just pursed his lips and turned pale. La Porte appeared at the door, and the child went straight to him without embracing his mother. "Louis," Anne said, "aren't you going to kiss me good night?"

"I thought you were mad at me, Madame, since you send me away."

"I'm not sending you away, but you're just recovering from the smallpox, and I don't want you to get overly tired."

"You weren't worried about that today when you sent me to parliament to issue those nasty edicts the people are complaining about."

"Sire," said La Porte, trying to distract him, "who would Your Majesty like to carry your candlestick tonight?"

"Anybody, La Porte," the child answered, then added, raising his voice, "so long as it's not Mancini." Mancini was one of Mazarin's nephews whom the cardinal had made a child-of-honor to the king, and whom Louis XIV treated with a measure of the disdain he felt for his minister.

And the king marched out without kissing his mother or bowing to the cardinal.

"Excellent!" said Mazarin. "I'm delighted to see His Majesty being brought up to abhor deceit."

"Why do you say that?" asked the queen, almost timidly.

"It seems to me the king's exit makes that quite clear. His Majesty doesn't even try to hide how little affection he has for me—which doesn't prevent me, however, from being entirely devoted to his service, and to that of Your Majesty."

"I beg your pardon on his behalf, Cardinal," said the queen. "The child is too young to understand all the obligations and duties you have."

The cardinal smiled.

"But you must have some important reason for coming," the queen continued. "What is it?"

Mazarin sat, or rather lay back, on a large chaise, and said with a melancholy air, "It's just that, in all probability, we'll soon be forced to part, unless your devotion is such that you'd go with me back to Italy."

"And why is that?"

"Because," Mazarin said, "as they sang in the opera *Thisbe*,[27] 'The whole world conspires to come between us.'"

"You're jesting, Monsieur!" said the queen, trying to recover some of her former dignity.

"Alas, no, Madame!" said Mazarin. "It's no laughing matter. On the contrary, I'm trying my best not to weep. And when I say, 'The whole world conspires to come between us,' I have to say you're part of that world, a part of what's driving us apart."

"Cardinal!"

"No? Didn't I see you the other day smiling very agreeably at Monsieur, the Duc d'Orléans—or rather at what he said?"

"And what was it he said?"

"Madame, he told you, 'It's your Mazarin who's the stumbling block here—once he goes, all will be well.'"

"But what am I supposed to do?"

"What? Why ask me? You're the queen, it seems to me."

"Some monarch, disrespected by every scribbler in the Palais Royal, and every petty lord in the realm!"

"Nonetheless, you still have the power to banish from your presence anyone who displeases you."

"You mean to say, anyone who displeases *you*!" replied the queen.

"Me!"

"Yes! Who sent away Madame de Chevreuse,* after she'd been persecuted for twelve years under the old regime?"

"She was an intriguer who wanted to continue her conspiracies under Monsieur de Richelieu and turn them against me!"

"Who sent away Madame de Hautefort, that friend so loyal and good that she refused the king's good graces in order to stay in mine?"

"Bah: a prude who told you every night, as she helped you undress, that it was risking your soul to love a priest—as if being a cardinal makes one a priest!"

"Who arrested Monsieur de Beaufort?"

"A ruffian who boasted of nothing less than planning to have me assassinated!"

"You see, Cardinal," replied the queen, "that your enemies are made into mine."

"That's not enough, Madame—your friends must also be my friends."

"My friends, Monsieur?" The queen shook her head. "Alas! I no longer have any."

"How can you have so few friends in prosperity, when you had so many in adversity?"

"Because in prosperity, Monsieur, I've forgotten my old friends. Because I acted like Queen Marie de Médicis[28] who, upon returning from her first exile, turned her back on those who'd suffered it with her, so that when she was banished a second time, she died friendless in Cologne, abandoned by all the world, even her son."

"Then it's past time to try to repair the damage," said Mazarin. "Think back and recollect your oldest friends."

"What do you mean, Monsieur?"

"Just what I said: recollect."

"Looking around now, I seem to have little influence with anyone. Monsieur, the Duc d'Orléans, follows his current favorite around, as always— yesterday it was Choisy, today La Rivière, tomorrow someone else. Monsieur le Prince, Condé, is led around by Coadjutor de Retz,* who himself follows Madame de Guéménée."[29]

"Ah, Madame, I didn't say to consider your friends of today, but to recollect your friends of old."

"My friends of old?" said the queen.

"Yes, your oldest friends, those who aided you against Monsieur de Richelieu, and even vanquished him."

"What is he getting at?" the queen said to herself, looking anxiously at the cardinal.

"Yes," he continued, "under the right circumstances, that powerful will and determination that characterizes Your Majesty was able, with the help of friends, to repel your opponent's attacks."

"Me?" said the queen. "I just suffered through those times, that's all."

"Yes," said Mazarin, "as women suffer—by avenging themselves. To the point. Do you know Monsieur de Rochefort?"

"Monsieur de Rochefort was never one of my friends," said the queen, "quite the opposite. He was one of my bitterest enemies, an agent loyal to the old cardinal. I thought you knew that."

"I know it so well," said Mazarin, "that for you I had him put in the Bastille."

"Is . . . is he out?" asked the queen.

"No, never fear—he's still inside. I mention him only to bring up another. Do you know Monsieur d'Artagnan?" continued Mazarin, with a shrewd look at the queen.

For Anne of Austria, it was a blow to the heart. "Has the Gascon been indiscreet?" she muttered, then said aloud, "D'Artagnan! Wait a moment . . . yes, that name is familiar. D'Artagnan, a musketeer, who loved one of my women.[30] Poor little thing, she was poisoned because of me."

"That's all?" said Mazarin.

The queen looked at the cardinal in surprise. "Monsieur," she said, "are you subjecting me to an interrogation?"

"Even if I was," Mazarin said, with his soft voice and eternal smile, "you'd still give only such answers as suit you."

"Be direct with your questions, Monsieur, and then I'll be direct with my answers," said the queen, beginning to lose her patience.

"Well, Madame!" said Mazarin with a bow. "I want only to make your friends mine, so I can share with them what little talent and energy Providence has given me. The situation is serious and calls for active measures."

"What, again?" said the queen. "I thought we'd settled things when we dealt with Monsieur de Beaufort."

"Yes! We diverted a torrent that threatened to drown us, but now we're menaced from deeper pools. There's a proverb in France about still waters, I believe."

"Go on," said the queen.

"Well!" continued Mazarin. "Every day I suffer insults from your princes and your titled minions, all of them marionettes blind to the fact that I'm pulling the strings, nor do they see that, beneath my calm exterior, I'm sup-pressing the hollow laugh of the injured man who will one day prove their superior. True, we arrested Monsieur de Beaufort, but he may have been the least dangerous. There's still Monsieur le Prince . . ."

"The victor of Rocroi! Even he is on your mind?"

"Yes, Madame, and frequently—but *patienza,* as we Italians say. Then, after the Prince de Condé, there is Monsieur, the Duc d'Orléans."

"What are you saying? Gaston, the First Prince of the Blood, the king's own uncle!"

"Not the First Prince of the Blood, not the king's uncle, but the cowardly conspirator who, under the previous reign, driven by caprice and resent-ment, eaten up by envy and idle ambition, jealous of all those who were admired for loyalty and courage, disgusted with his own worthlessness, made himself the crier of every slander, the center of every cabal—he who encouraged good men who had the folly to take him at his royal word to conspire on his behalf, then disowned them as they mounted the scaffold! Not the First Prince of the Blood, I say, not the king's uncle, but the assassin of Chalais, of Montmorency, and of Cinq-Mars,[31] who is now trying to play the same game again, and imagines that this time he'll win because he has a new opponent, a man who doesn't threaten but instead . . . smiles. But he is mistaken. He has lost by losing Monsieur de Richelieu, as I have no interest in keeping near to the queen this agent of discord whom the late cardinal used for twenty years to make the king's blood boil."

Anne blushed and hid her face in her hands.

"I will not have Your Majesty humiliated," said Mazarin, regaining his calm tone, though beneath it was an unusual firmness. "I want people to respect the queen, and to respect her minister, since in the eyes of the world I am no more than that. Your Majesty knows that, despite what they say, I'm not just some Italian dancing monkey. The rest of the world must know me as Your Majesty knows me."

"Well, then, what should I do?" said Anne of Austria, submissive before this domineering voice.

"You must search your memory for the names of those loyal and devoted men who crossed the sea despite Monsieur de Richelieu, spilling their blood along the road, to bring back to Your Majesty certain jewels you'd given to the Duke of Buckingham."

Anne rose, angry and majestic, as if stiffened by a steel spring, and regarded the cardinal with that hauteur and dignity that had made her so admired in the days of her youth. "You insult me, Monsieur!"

"I want you, at long last," continued Mazarin, finishing the speech interrupted by the queen, "I want you to do today for your husband what you once did for your lover."

"That old slander once again!" cried the queen. "I thought it was finally dead and buried, something you've spared me until now . . . but you bring it up at last. Fine! We'll settle this between us, and it will be over and done, do you hear me?"

"But, Madame," said Mazarin, taken aback by this show of strength, "I'm not asking you to tell me everything."

"But I want to tell you everything," said Anne of Austria. "So, listen. I want to tell you, Monsieur, that there were indeed at that time four faithful hearts, four loyal spirits, four devoted swords who saved more than my life—for they saved my honor."

"Ah! You admit it," said Mazarin.

"Is it only the guilty whose honor may be at stake, Monsieur, and can't a person, especially a woman, be dishonored by appearances? Yes, appearances were against me, and my honor was at risk—and yet, I swear, I wasn't guilty. I swear by . . ."

The queen looked around for something holy she could swear on, pushed aside a tapestry to reveal a cabinet, and drew from it a small, rosewood box chased with silver. Laying it on her altar, she said, "I swear upon these sacred relics that though I loved the Duke of Buckingham, the Duke of Buckingham was not my lover!"

"And what are these relics upon which you take this oath, Madame?" Mazarin said, smiling. "For I warn you, in my capacity as a Catholic prelate I know when a relic is a relic."

The queen detached a small golden key from a necklace and handed it to the cardinal. "Open it, Monsieur, and see for yourself."

Mazarin, astonished, took the key and opened the coffer, in which he found a rusted knife and two letters, one of them stained with blood. "What's this?" he asked.

"What's this, Monsieur?" said Anne of Austria with a queenly gesture, taking the coffer in her arms, still beautiful despite the years, and holding it open. "I'll tell you. These two letters are the only letters I ever wrote to him. And this knife is the one with which Felton killed him. Read these letters, Monsieur, and see if I speak the truth."

But despite being given permission, Mazarin hesitated to read the letters, and instead took up the knife that Buckingham, dying, had torn from his wound and sent by La Porte to the queen. The blade was all corroded, for the blood had become rust, and after a moment's examination, during which the queen turned as white as the altar cloth she was leaning on, he replaced it in the coffer with an involuntary shudder.

"It is well, Madame," he said, "and I accept your oath."

"No!" frowned the queen. "Read! I insist upon it. I want this settled between us so we never return to it. Do you think," she added, with a ghastly smile, "that I'm going to open this coffer for you at every accusation?"

Mazarin, daunted by this outburst, obeyed almost mechanically, and read the two letters. One was that by which the queen had asked Buckingham for the return of her diamond studs, the one d'Artagnan had brought him in the nick of time. The other was the one La Porte had borne to the duke in which the queen had warned him of his assassination, and which had come too late.

"It . . . is well, Madame," said Mazarin. "I have nothing more to say about it."

"If, Monsieur," said the queen, closing the coffer and resting her hand upon it, "I have anything still to answer for, it's that I've always been ungrateful to those men who saved me, and did everything they could to save . . . him. I gave nothing to that brave d'Artagnan, of whom you spoke just now, other than my hand to kiss, and this diamond."

The queen extended her beautiful hand toward the cardinal and showed him a marvelous stone that sparkled on her finger. "He sold it, it seems," she said, "in a moment of want; he sold it to save me a second time, because he needed to send a messenger to the duke to warn him of the assassination."

"So d'Artagnan knew of that?"

"He knew everything. How? I never learned. He sold this ring to Monsieur des Essarts,[32] on whose finger I saw it, and from whom I bought it back. But this diamond belongs to him, Monsieur, so return it to him for me—and since you're lucky enough to have such a man near at hand, try to make use of him."

"Thank you, Madame!" said Mazarin. "I'll follow your advice."

"And now," said the queen, brittle with emotion, "do you have anything else to ask of me?"

"Not a thing, Madame," said the cardinal, in his most soothing voice, "except to beg you to forgive my unworthy suspicions. It's just that I love you so dearly, is it any wonder I'm jealous even of the past?"

An indescribable smile passed over the queen's lips. "Well, then, Monsieur," she said, "if you have nothing else to ask of me, you may go. You must understand that you've upset me, and I need some time to myself."

Mazarin bowed. "Then I retire, Madame," he said. "Will you allow me to return?"

"Yes, but tomorrow. That should give me enough time."

The cardinal took the hand of the queen and kissed it gallantly, and then withdrew.

He'd scarcely left before the queen went into her son's apartments, where she asked La Porte if the king had gone to bed. La Porte just pointed toward the sleeping child.

Anne of Austria went up the bed's steps, put her lips to her son's furrowed brow and gently kissed it. Then she retired as quietly as she'd come, only saying to the valet, "Try, my dear La Porte, to help the king appreciate Monsieur le Cardinal, whom he and I owe so much."

V

Gascon and Italian

Meanwhile the cardinal had returned to his study, where Bernouin waited at the door. Mazarin asked him if anything had happened, and if there was any news from outside; the valet shook his head, and the cardinal motioned him away.

Left alone, he went through the door to the corridor, then the one to the antechamber, where he found d'Artagnan on a bench, exhausted and asleep.

"Monsieur d'Artagnan!" he said softly.

D'Artagnan didn't flinch.

"Monsieur d'Artagnan!" he said louder.

D'Artagnan continued sleeping.

The cardinal approached him and touched a finger to his shoulder.

This time d'Artagnan started, awoke, and instantly stood like a soldier under arms. "I'm here," he said. "Who calls?"

"Me," said Mazarin, with his broadest smile.

"I beg Your Eminence's pardon," said d'Artagnan. "I was so tired . . ."

"Ask for no pardon, Monsieur," said Mazarin, "when you tire yourself in my service."

D'Artagnan had to admire the minister's gracious manner. "Oh ho," he said to himself. "What's that proverb about good things coming while one sleeps?"

"Come with me, Monsieur!" Mazarin said, returning to his study.

"Well, well," murmured d'Artagnan. "It looks like Rochefort kept his word. Only where the devil has he gotten to?" And he looked into every corner of the study without finding Rochefort.

"Monsieur d'Artagnan," said Mazarin, sitting comfortably in an armchair, "you've always seemed to me a brave and gallant man."

Perhaps so, thought d'Artagnan, *but he took his time in telling me.* That didn't stop him from bowing to the ground to acknowledge the compliment.

"Well," continued Mazarin, "now is the time to profit from your talents and worth!"

The officer's eyes flashed with a joy he immediately covered, for he didn't know where Mazarin was leading him. "Command me, Monseigneur," he said. "I'm at Your Eminence's orders."

"Monsieur d'Artagnan," Mazarin continued, "in the previous reign you distinguished yourself in several exploits."

"It's kind of Your Eminence to remember that. In fact, I think I fought with some success."

"I'm not speaking of your exploits in war," said Mazarin, "because, though commendable enough, there were others who did more."

D'Artagnan was astonished. "Well?" said Mazarin. "Have you nothing to say?"

"I'm waiting," d'Artagnan said, "for Monseigneur to tell me what exploits he's referring to."

"I speak of a certain adventure . . . you know which one I mean."

"Alas, Monseigneur, I don't," d'Artagnan replied, perplexed.

"I see you're discreet. Fine. I speak of the adventure of the queen's diamond studs, and that journey you made with your three friends."

Hello, thought the Gascon, *is this some kind of trap? Better play dumb.* And he adopted an expression so bewildered it would have been the envy of Mondori or Bellerose, the greatest comedians of the time.

"Very good!" said Mazarin, laughing. "Bravo! I knew you were the man I needed. So, how far are you willing to go for me?"

"As far as Your Eminence needs me to," said d'Artagnan.

"You'll act for me as you formerly did for a queen?"

Clearly, d'Artagnan thought, *he wants me to speak of it first. Devil take his cunning, but he's no Richelieu.* "For a queen, Monseigneur? I don't understand you."

"You don't understand that I need you—you and your three friends?"

"What friends do you mean, Monseigneur?"

"Your three friends of former days."

"In former days, Monseigneur," replied d'Artagnan, "I didn't have three friends, I had fifty. When you're twenty, you call everyone your friend."

"Come now, Monsieur Lieutenant," said Mazarin, "discretion is a fine thing—but you might regret being overly discreet."

"Monseigneur, Pythagoras made his students listen quietly for five years to teach them to be silent."

"And you've been silent for twenty years, Monsieur, which is fifteen years too long, even for a Pythagorean philosopher. Now speak, for the queen herself releases you from your oath."

"The queen!" said d'Artagnan, and this time his astonishment was unfeigned.

"Yes, the queen! And the proof that I speak on her behalf is that she told me to show you this diamond that you'll recognize, and which she bought from Monsieur des Essarts."

And Mazarin extended his hand toward the officer, who sighed as he recognized the ring the queen had given him on the night of the ball at the Hôtel de Ville.

"So, you see that I speak to you in her name. Answer me without any more comedy—for as I've said, and I repeat it, your fortune is at stake."

"*Ma foi*, Monseigneur! My fortune is long overdue—Your Eminence has long forgotten it!"

"It's but the work of a week to repair it. Now, here *you* are—but where are your friends?"

"I don't know, Monseigneur."

"You don't know?"

"No. All three have left the service, and it's been long since we separated."

"But you can find them again?"

"No matter where they are. That's my affair."

"Good! And you require . . . ?"

"Money, Monseigneur, is what this kind of business needs. I remember too many times when we were thwarted for lack of money. Without that diamond, which I had to sell, we would have failed entirely."

"The devil! Money, and in no small amount, I'll wager," said Mazarin. "You ask a great deal, Monsieur Lieutenant. Don't you know the king's coffers are empty?"

"Then do as I did, Monseigneur, and sell the crown jewels. Believe me, it does no good to be stingy; one can't do great things with meager means."

"Well!" said Mazarin. "I suppose we can accommodate you."

Richelieu, thought d'Artagnan, *would already have given me five hundred* pistoles[33] *in advance.*

"So, you're with me, then?" said Mazarin.

"Yes, if my friends are."

"But if they refuse, I can still count on you?"

"I've never been any good by myself," said d'Artagnan, shaking his head.

"Then see that you find them."

"What will I say to persuade them to serve Your Eminence?"

"You know better than I do. Persuade them according to their characters."

"What can I promise on your behalf?"

"If they serve me as they served the queen, the rewards will be lavish."

"And what are we to do?"

"Everything, since it seems you know how to do everything."

"Monseigneur, when one has confidence in people and wants them to return your trust, one is more forthcoming with information than Your Eminence is."

"When the time for action arrives," said Mazarin, "I assure you I'll tell you everything."

"But until then?"

"Await events—and go find your friends."

"Monseigneur, they might not be in Paris, in fact they probably aren't, which means I'll have to travel. I'm only a poor lieutenant of musketeers, and travel is expensive."

"I don't intend for you to travel with an entourage," said Mazarin. "My missions are covert and mustn't draw attention."

"Still, Monseigneur, I can't travel on my pay, which is already three months behind. And I can't travel on my savings, because after twenty-two years' service the only thing I've saved is debt."

Mazarin thought for a moment, as if struggling with himself. Then, going to a cabinet closed with a triple lock, he drew out a purse, weighed it two or three times in his hand, and then gave it d'Artagnan. "Use this," he said with a sigh, "to fund your travels."

Well! d'Artagnan thought. *If these are Spanish double-pistoles, or even gold crowns, we may be able to do business together.* He saluted the cardinal and stuffed the purse into his belt pouch.

"So, then," said the cardinal, "you're off."

"Yes, Monseigneur."

"Write to me daily to report the progress of your negotiations."

"I shall not fail, Monseigneur."

"Very good. By the way, what are the names of your friends?"

"The names of my friends?" said d'Artagnan, with a touch of anxiety.

"Yes—while you search on your side, I'll investigate on mine, and maybe I'll learn something."

"The Comte de La Fère, formerly known as Athos; Monsieur du Vallon, known as Porthos; and the Chevalier d'Herblay, now the Abbé d'Herblay, known as Aramis."

The cardinal smiled. "Younger sons," he said, "who joined the King's Musketeers under assumed names to avoid compromising their families. The usual thing: empty purses but long rapiers."

"If God wills these rapiers to join Your Eminence's service," d'Artagnan said, "I dare to hope Monseigneur's purse will become lighter and theirs heavier—because with these three men, and me, Your Eminence shall move all of France, and even Europe, if he so desires."

"These Gascons," Mazarin laughed, "almost match the Italians for bravado."

"In words," said d'Artagnan with a matching smile, "and we're even better with deeds."

And he left, after receiving an indefinite leave order signed by Mazarin himself.

Once outside in the courtyard, he went to a lantern to take a quick look into the purse. "Silver crowns!" he said with contempt. "I suspected as much. Ah, Mazarin, Mazarin! You still don't trust me. Too bad—that will bring you misfortune."

Meanwhile the cardinal was rubbing his hands. "A hundred pistoles!" he murmured. "For a hundred pistoles I bought a secret for which Monsieur de Richelieu would have paid twenty thousand crowns. And I got this diamond into the bargain," he said, looking lovingly at the ring he'd kept, instead of giving it to d'Artagnan. "Why, this diamond must be worth ten thousand livres."

And the cardinal retired to his chambers, delighted with an evening in which he'd made such a handsome profit. He placed the ring in a silk-lined jewel box filled with gems of every kind, for the cardinal had a taste for precious stones. Then he called Bernouin to undress him, without another thought for the distant shouts coming in through the windows, or the gunshots resounding across Paris, though it was eleven at night.

Meanwhile d'Artagnan was making his way toward the Rue Tiquetonne,[34] where he lived at the Hôtel de La Chevrette . . .

But let's say a few words about d'Artagnan's home and tell how he came to live there.

VI

D'Artagnan at Age Forty

Alas! In the time since we last saw him in *The Three Musketeers*, when d'Artagnan lived in the Rue des Fossoyeurs, many years had passed and much had gone with them.

D'Artagnan hadn't missed his opportunities, the opportunities had missed d'Artagnan. When his friends had surrounded him, d'Artagnan's youth and inventiveness had flourished; he had one of those open and ingenious natures that easily assimilate the qualities of others. Athos gave of his grandeur, Porthos his enthusiasm, and Aramis his elegance. If d'Artagnan had continued to abide with these three men, he would have become a truly superior man.

But Athos had left him first, to retire to the small estate he'd inherited near Blois; Porthos had gone second, to marry the prosecutor's widow; finally, Aramis, the third, to take his vows and become an abbot. From that moment, d'Artagnan, who seemed to have counted on a future that included his three friends, found himself alone and unsteady, lacking the drive to pursue a career in which he couldn't quite excel without the spiritual essence contributed by each of his friends.

Thus, though he continued as a lieutenant of musketeers, d'Artagnan found himself feeling isolated. He was not of sufficiently high rank, like Athos, for the *Grands* to open their houses to him; he wasn't vain enough, like Porthos, to feel entitled to mix with high society; and he wasn't well-bred enough, like Aramis, to get by on sheer elegance and sophistication, drawing on depths from within. For a while the memory of the charming Madame Bonacieux gave the young lieutenant a certain poetic melancholy; but like all things of this world, even this memory gradually faded. Life in a garrison is fatal to delicate sensibilities.

Of the two opposing sides that composed d'Artagnan's nature, the material side had gradually won out—and slowly, without even noticing it, d'Artagnan, always in garrison or in camp, had become what we call in our time a career soldier. It's not that d'Artagnan lost his native cleverness, but rather that he'd turned his innate finesse toward solving small problems rather than great ones, focusing on the soldier's mundane concerns of finding comfortable quarters, good food, and an accommodating hostess.

And d'Artagnan had found all three of these things six years before in Rue Tiquetonne, at the sign of La Chevrette.

In the early days of his stay there, the mistress of the boarding house, a fresh and pretty Flemish woman of twenty-five or twenty-six, had been quite taken with him, but their amorous intentions had been blocked by an inconvenient husband. After d'Artagnan had pantomimed running him through with his sword a few times, one fine morning this husband had disappeared forever, after selling the best bottles in the wine cellar and carrying off what money and jewelry he could. Everyone assumed he was dead—especially his wife who, fancying herself in the condition of a widow, boldly asserted his death. Eventually, after three years of a liaison that d'Artagnan had carefully maintained, finding his lodging and his mistress more agreeable every year, as the two went so well together, the mistress decided it was once more time to be a wife, and proposed that d'Artagnan should marry her.

"How so?" d'Artagnan replied. "That would be bigamy, my dear! Don't even think of it!"

"But I'm quite sure my husband's dead."

"He was a thoroughly inconsiderate fellow and would certainly return just to see us hanged."

"Well, if he comes back, you'll kill him—you're so brave and masterful!"

"Peste! That's just one more route to the hangman, my love."

"So, you reject my proposal?"

"Completely! That's not going to happen."

The pretty hostess was devastated. If she'd had her way, Monsieur d'Artagnan would have been not just her husband, but her deity—he was so very
handsome, and had such a proud mustache!

During the fourth year came the campaign in Franche-Comté.[35] D'Artagnan was given his orders and prepared to leave. There was agony, rivers of
tears, and solemn promises to remain faithful—though all from the hostess,
of course. D'Artagnan was too much the *grand seigneur* to make promises,
other than to promise to do what he could to add glory to his name.

There was no doubting d'Artagnan's courage: he conducted himself
admirably, and, charging at the head of his company, he took a ball in the
chest that laid him out at full length on the battlefield. Everyone saw him
fall from his horse, and no one saw him get up, so everyone assumed he
was dead—especially those who hoped to assume his position. From the
generals of the divisions who hope for the death of the commander in chief,
down to the private soldiers who dream of the deaths of their corporals,
everyone wants someone deceased.

But d'Artagnan wasn't the sort of man to be killed so easily as that. After
lying unconscious on the battlefield through the heat of the day, the cool
night air brought him around. He made his way to a village, knocked on
the door of the finest house, and was received as wounded Frenchmen are
always and everywhere: he was taken in, treated, cured, pampered even, and
restored to better health than ever. One morning he set off down the road
to France, once in France took the way to Paris, and once in Paris to the
Rue Tiquetonne.

But d'Artagnan found his room occupied by another man's wardrobe,
complete except for a sword. "He must have returned," he said to himself.
"Well, too bad, and all the better!"

D'Artagnan, of course, was thinking of the missing husband. He asked
the new servants where their mistress had gone and was told to the promenade.

"Alone?" asked d'Artagnan.

"With monsieur."

"Monsieur has come back, then?"

"He must have," the servant naïvely replied.

"If I had any money," d'Artagnan said to himself, "I'd leave—but since I don't, I'll just have to stay, take my hostess's advice, and put this conjugal ghost to rest."

He'd just completed this monologue, monologues being suited to all dramatic occasions, when the servant, who was waiting by the door, called out, "Look! Here comes madame now, returning with monsieur."

D'Artagan glanced up the street and saw, at the corner of the Rue Montmartre, the hostess returning on the arm of an enormous Swiss Guard, who swaggered with such airs that d'Artagnan was pleasantly reminded of his old friend Porthos.

"So that's monsieur?" said d'Artagnan. "He's grown a bit, I think." And he sat down in the parlor where he couldn't be missed.

The hostess entered first, and gasped when she saw d'Artagnan. By this, d'Artagnan knew he'd been recognized; he leapt up, ran to her, and kissed her tenderly.

The Swiss looked on, stupefied, while the hostess turned pale. "It's you, Monsieur! Wh-what do you want from me?" she asked, dismayed and flustered.

D'Artagnan, unabashed, said, "Monsieur here is your cousin? Or is he your brother?"

And without waiting for a reply, he embraced the huge Helvetian, who stiffened uncomfortably. "Who is this man?" the Swiss asked.

The hostess just choked, unable to speak.

"And who is this Swiss?" asked d'Artagnan.

"He's going to marry me," said the hostess, between gasps.

"Your husband's finally died, then?"

"Vhat you zay?" said the Swiss.

"I'll zay plenty," replied d'Artagnan. "I zay you may not marry madame without my permission, and I . . ."

"Und you . . . ?"

"And I . . . do not give it," said the musketeer.

At this, the Swiss turned red as a beet. He wore a gold-trimmed uniform, while d'Artagnan was wrapped in dull gray cloak; he was six feet tall, d'Artagnan was five and a half; he thought he was at home, and d'Artagnan was an intruder. "Vill you get out of here?" the Swiss demanded, stamping his foot like a man growing seriously angry.

"Me? Not likely!" said d'Artagnan.

"But he'll just throw you out," said the houseboy, who couldn't understand how any normal man could stand up to the huge Swiss.

"You," said d'Artagnan, beginning to lose his temper and taking the houseboy by the ear, "get out of the way and don't move unless I say so. As for you, illustrious descendant of William Tell, get your clothes out of my room and take them elsewhere—they annoy me."

The Swiss began to laugh loudly. "I, leave? Vhy vould I do zat?"

"Ah, so you do understand French," said d'Artagnan. "Come take a little walk with me, and I'll explain vhy."

The hostess, who knew d'Artagnan for a swordsman, began to cry and tear her hair. D'Artagnan turned and said, more gently, "You should send him away, Madame."

"Pah!" said the Swiss, who had needed a moment's thought to understand d'Artagnan's intentions. "Pah! Who are you, crazy one, to ask me to take a valk vith you?"

"I am a Lieutenant of the King's Musketeers," said d'Artagnan, "and therefore your superior in every way. However, this isn't a question of rank, just of the right to quarters—and you know the custom. You want them? Then let's take a walk. The one who returns gets the room."

And d'Artagnan led the Swiss away, despite the lamentations of the hostess. Deep down, she felt her heart yearn toward her old love—but since he'd insulted her by refusing her hand, she wouldn't be sorry if the proud musketeer was taught a lesson.

The two adversaries marched straight to the moat outside the Montmartre wall. It was dark by the time they arrived; d'Artagnan politely requested that the Swiss yield him the room and be on his way; the Swiss shook his head in refusal and drew his sword. "Then you'll sleep here instead," said d'Artagnan. "This is a wretched bed, but you chose it, and it's not my fault." And with these words he drew steel and crossed swords with his adversary.

His opponent had a strong wrist, but d'Artagnan far outmatched him in agility. The Swiss soldier's rapier never even found the musketeer's blade, and he took two wounds before he realized he'd been touched. He felt a chill, a sudden weakness, and was surprised to find he was sitting down, dizzy and bleeding.

"*Là!*" said d'Artagnan. "What did I tell you? That's the price of being stubborn. But you're strong, and you'll be good as new in a fortnight. Stay here, and I'll send the houseboy along with your clothes. Farewell . . . Oh, you'll need a place to stay: try the Chat Qui Pelote, on Rue Montorgueil. You'll be well fed there, if I know the hostess. Adieu!"

And with that he strutted all the way home. The houseboy was standing exactly where he'd left him; d'Artagnan sent him to take his clothes to the Swiss, who was still sitting there, dumbfounded by his opponent's coolness.

After that, the houseboy, the hostess, and the entire household regarded d'Artagnan as if Hercules had returned after completing his twelve labors. But once he was alone with the hostess, he said, "Now, fair Madeleine, you see the difference between a mere soldier and a gentleman. As for you, you've behaved like a tavern wench. More's the pity, because as a result you've lost my esteem and my lodging. I chased off the Swiss to teach you a lesson, but I'm not about to stay under such a low roof as this. Hey, houseboy! Carry my things to the Muid d'Amour, in the Rue des Bourdonnais. Adieu, Madame."

D'Artagnan said these words in a manner both moving and majestic. The hostess threw herself at his feet and begged his forgiveness, clinging to him tenderly. What can we say? The roast was turning on the spit, the stove was glowing, and beautiful Madeleine wept adoringly. Hunger, warmth, and love all spoke together; he forgave her, and having forgiven, he remained.

VII

In Which d'Artagnan Is Confounded, but Receives Aid from an Unexpected Quarter

From the Palais Royal, d'Artagnan made his way thoughtfully toward home, somewhat reassured by the purse given him by Cardinal Mazarin, but thinking of the beautiful diamond he'd seen sparkling for a moment on the prime minister's finger.

"If that diamond ever fell into my hands again," he said, "I'd instantly turn it into cash. I'd buy a few properties around my father's small château, which is a lovely house, but has very few outbuildings, and a garden plot no larger than the Cemetery of the Innocents.[36] Then it's probable some rich heiress, attracted by my nobility and good looks, would come and marry me. We'd have three boys: I'd make the first a *grand seigneur* like Athos, the second a handsome soldier like Porthos, and the third a refined abbot[37] like Aramis. *Ma foi!* It would be infinitely better than the life I lead now— but unfortunately Monsieur de Mazarin is a gutless rat who wouldn't give me that diamond."

What would d'Artagnan have said if he'd known the queen had entrusted the diamond to Mazarin to give it to him?

As he turned into Rue Tiquetonne, he found it in a tumult, with a large crowd outside his boarding house. "Oh ho!" he said. "Is there a fire at the Hôtel de La Chevrette, or has the husband of the beautiful Madeleine actually returned at last?"

As d'Artagnan approached he saw it was neither, as the crowd was in front of the house next door rather than the boarding house. Some of those gathered bore torches, and by their light d'Artagnan could see armed men in uniforms. He asked what was happening, and was told that a mob of twenty men, led by a bourgeois, had attacked a carriage escorted by some of the cardinal's musketeers, but when reinforcements had arrived the citizens had fled. Their leader had gone to ground in the house next to the hôtel, and the troops were searching the building.

In his younger days d'Artagnan would have run to join the men in uniform and aid them against the citizens, but his hot head had grown cooler over time. Besides, he had the cardinal's purse in his pocket, and didn't want to carry that into a riot. Formerly d'Artagnan had always wanted to know everything, but now he knew more than enough already. He went into the boarding house without asking any more questions.

Inside he found the beautiful Madeleine, who wasn't expecting to see him, as d'Artagnan had told her he'd be on duty that night at the Louvre. So, she used his unexpected return to propose a small celebration, hoping to engage him because she was worried about what was going on in the street, and had no burly Swiss Guard to protect her. She tried to draw him out as to what was going on outside, and with his own affairs, but d'Artagnan was in no mood for chat; he told her to send supper up to his room, along with a bottle of old Burgundy.

Pretty Madeleine had been trained to obey at a gesture, like an officer's valet. And this time around d'Artagnan had deigned to speak with her as well, so she obeyed twice as quickly.

D'Artagnan took his key and his candle and went upstairs. He was satisfied with a simple room on the fourth floor, leaving the better rooms for Madeleine to rent out. The respect we have for the truth compels us to admit his room was next to the gutter and just below the roof. Here was the tent of this latter-day Achilles. D'Artagnan would camp out alone in his room when he wished to punish fair Madeleine by his absence.

Once inside, his first act was to open an old desk with new locks and put away the purse full of coins, without even bothering to take the time to count them. A few moments later his supper arrived, along with the bottle of wine, and he dismissed the houseboy and sat down. Not to think, as one might assume, not yet: for d'Artagnan was a man who believed in doing each thing in its turn. He was hungry, so first he ate his supper, and when he was done he turned in. Nor was he one of those people who do their best thinking when abed; when d'Artagnan was in bed, he slept. In the morning, refreshed, was when his mind was clear and he had his best ideas. It had been a while since he'd had to think much about anything, but nonetheless he saved his thinking for the morning.

At daybreak he awoke, jumped out of bed like a soldier at reveille, and paced around his room, thinking. "In '43," he said, "six months or so before the death of the late cardinal, I had a letter from Athos. Where was I? Let's see . . . ah, yes, I was at the Siege of Besançon,[38] I remember. I was in the trenches. What was it he said? He was living on a small estate—yes, that's it, a small estate. But where? I'd read only that far when a gust of wind carried the letter off. When I was younger I would have gone after it, even if it meant running out of cover into a crossfire. My youth would have cost me a pretty price! So, I let the wind blow my letter away to the Spanish, who were too rude to return it to me. That was my last contact with Athos.

"On, then: Porthos. I last had a letter from him inviting me to his estate for a grand hunt in September of 1646. Unfortunately, I was in Béarn at the time due to my father's death, and though the letter followed me there, I was gone again by the time it arrived. They sent it after me to Montmédy, but once again it missed me. It finally caught up to me in April, but by then it was April 1647, and as the invitation had been for the previous September, I was out of luck. Now, where is this letter? It must be with my title deeds."

D'Artagnan went into a corner and opened an old trunk stuffed with parchments pertaining to the Artagnan estate, most of which had been out of the family for two hundred years. He searched through it, and finally he gave a cry of joy as he recognized the great looping handwriting of Porthos, followed by some spidery lines traced by the wrinkled fingers of his worthy wife. He remembered what it said, so d'Artagnan skipped through the body of the letter to get to the address: Château du Vallon.

Porthos had included no other information. In his pride he thought everyone knew the location of the château that bore his name. "Devil take him!" said d'Artagnan. "Still the same vainglorious lummox! However, it's nonetheless a good idea to find him first, as he can't be short of money, having inherited eight hundred thousand livres from Monsieur Coquenard. But the other two are bound to fail me. By now Athos will have pickled his brain from drinking, and Aramis will be worn thin from his devotions."

D'Artagnan took one more glance at the letter and noticed it contained this sentence as a postscript: *I write by this same courier to our worthy friend Aramis at his abbey.*

"At his abbey! Yes, but which abbey? There are two hundred in Paris and three thousand in France. And for all I know when he became an abbot he changed his name for the third time. If only I was learned in theology and remembered the subject of that thesis he discussed so earnestly at Crèvecœur with the curate of Montdidier and the superior of Jesuits![39] Then I might figure out which order he'd entered and which saint he'd taken as his patron.

"Maybe I should ask the cardinal for a safe-conduct that would enable me to inquire at all the abbeys—maybe even the convents? That's an idea . . . but it would be admitting right at the outset that I need help, and the cardinal would be finished with me. The great are only grateful when one does the impossible for them. 'If it was possible,' they say, 'I'd have done it myself.' And rightly so.

"But wait a minute—I recall I had a letter from my old friend, in which he asked a favor of me. Yes, I remember it! But where's this letter now?" D'Artagnan thought for a moment, then went into his dressing room and opened the wardrobe where he kept his old clothes. He was looking for the doublet he wore in early 1648, and as d'Artagnan was an orderly man, he found it hanging right where it belonged. He reached into its pocket and drew out a paper: it was the letter from Aramis.

> *Monsieur d'Artagnan,*
>
> *As you know, I've quarreled with a certain gentleman, and he's given me a rendezvous for this evening in the Place Royale. As I'm a member of the Church and it would reflect poorly if it were known I took part in a duel, I can ask only the most*

loyal and discreet friend to help me, so I'd like you to stand as my second.

Come in through the Rue Neuve Sainte-Catherine entrance and look for your opponent under the second lamppost on the right. I will be with mine under the third.

Entirely yours,
ARAMIS

This one lacked even a postscript. D'Artagnan remembered the affair: he'd gone to the rendezvous and met his opponent, a man he didn't know, and had given him a pretty thrust through the arm. Then he turned toward Aramis, who was already approaching, having finished with his man. "All done," said Aramis. "I think I've killed the insolent dog. Thank you, *cher ami,* and if you need me in the future, I'm entirely at your service." And Aramis had shaken his hand and disappeared under the arcades.

So, he had no more idea where Aramis was than Athos or Porthos. The embarrassment of it was just turning to irritation when he heard the sound of a window breaking in his bedchamber. He immediately thought of the money bag locked in his desk and ran to his room. He was right: as he came in the door, he could see a man entering through the window.

"Ah ha! Wretch!" snarled d'Artagnan, taking the man for a thief and grabbing his sword.

"Monsieur!" the man cried. "In heaven's name, leave your sword in its scabbard and hear me out! I'm not a thief, far from it! I'm an honest citizen, a local merchant, and I'm called . . . but wait! Aren't you Monsieur d'Artagnan?"

"And you—you're Planchet!" cried the lieutenant.

"At your service, Monsieur," said Planchet, smiling in delight and relief, "if I still can be."

"Maybe," said d'Artagnan, "but what the devil are you doing running over the roofs at seven in the morning in January?"

"Monsieur," said Planchet, "if you must know—but maybe you don't have to know."

"You think not?" said d'Artagnan. "Well, first put a towel over that broken window, and draw the curtains."

Planchet leapt to obey, and when he was done, d'Artagnan said, "Well?"

"First of all, Monsieur," said Planchet warily, "how do things stand between you and Monsieur de Rochefort?"

"Very well indeed. Didn't you know Rochefort's now one of my best friends?"

"Ah! All the better."

"But what does Rochefort have to do with the way you got into my room?"

"Ah, well, you see, Monsieur . . . I must inform you that Monsieur de Rochefort is . . ."

"Pardieu!" d'Artagnan said. "I know, he's in the Bastille."

"That is to say, he was," Planchet replied.

"What do you mean, he was?" d'Artagnan gasped. "Has he had the good luck to escape?"

"Ah, Monsieur!" gasped Planchet in his turn. "If you call that good luck, then all is well. You should know that yesterday guards were sent to take him back to the Bastille."

"Yes, by God! I should know that, since I was the one who'd fetched him out."

"But it wasn't you who took him back, fortunately for him. Because if I'd seen you were part of the escort, believe me, Monsieur, I have too much respect for you to—"

"Out with it, you animal! What happened?"

"Well! When the carriage carrying Monsieur de Rochefort got to the Rue de la Ferronnerie, it was blocked by a crowd of citizens, who started muttering at the sight of the guards. The prisoner thought the time was right and started shouting for help. I happened to be in the crowd and recognized the voice of Monsieur de Rochefort; after all, he was the one who got me appointed sergeant in the Piedmont Regiment. I shouted out that the prisoner was a friend of the Duc de Beaufort, and then there was a riot. The crowd surrounded the horses and pulled down the escort. Meanwhile I got to the door and opened it, and Monsieur de Rochefort jumped out and disappeared into the crowd. Unfortunately, just then a patrol came by, reinforced the guards, and charged us.

"I beat a retreat toward Rue Tiquetonne, but they were right behind me, so I ducked into the house next door to this one. They surrounded and then searched it, but in vain, as on the fifth floor I'd found a sympathetic person who hid me under a couple of mattresses. I stayed in my hiding place all night, but when day broke I thought they might resume their search, so I scrambled out across the gutters looking for some unguarded way into another house. That's my story, Monsieur, upon my honor, and it'll be terrible if you disapprove of it."

"No, *ma foi*," said d'Artagnan. "On the contrary, I'm very glad to hear Rochefort got away. But you realize, don't you, that if you fall into the hands of the king's men, you'll be hanged without delay?"

"By God, I know it!" said Planchet. "That's what I'm afraid of, and why I'm so glad I found you—because if you agree to help me escape, no one could do it better."

"True," said d'Artagnan, "and I ask nothing better, though I risk being stripped of my rank if anyone found out I'd given asylum to a rebel."

"Ah, Monsieur! You know I'd risk my life for you."

"You might even mention that you've already done so, Planchet, and more than once. I forget only those things I ought to forget—and that's something I'd rather remember. Sit down, then, and have a bite to eat, as I can see how you're making eyes at the remains of last night's supper."

"Thanks, Monsieur. Your neighbor's pantry wasn't very well stocked, and I haven't eaten since I had a slice of bread and jam at noon yesterday. I don't mind sweet things in their place, but that was rather a light meal to serve as both dinner and supper."

"Poor lad!" said d'Artagnan. "Well, put yourself around that."

"Ah, Monsieur, you've saved my life twice," said Planchet. And he sat down at the table, as happy with scraps as in the old days in the Rue des Fossoyeurs.

D'Artagnan began to pace up and down, trying to figure out what sort of advantage he could wring out of the unexpected appearance of Planchet. Meanwhile, Planchet worked to make up for lost time. Finally, he gave that sigh of satisfaction that shows when a hungry man is ready to take a break.

"Tell me," said d'Artagnan, who thought it was time to see what he could learn, "do you know where Athos is?"

"No, Monsieur," Planchet replied.

"The devil! What about Porthos?"

"Him neither."

"Two devils! And Aramis?"

"Nor him."

"Three devils! Curse it all!"

"But," said Planchet slyly, "I know where Bazin[40] is."

"What! You know how to find Bazin?"

"Yes, Monsieur."

"And where is he?"

"At Notre Dame."

"And what is he doing at Notre Dame?"

"He's a beadle."

"Bazin is a beadle at Notre Dame? Are you sure?"

"Absolutely: I saw him and spoke with him."

"He must know how to find his master."

"Without a doubt."

D'Artagnan thought for a moment, then took up his cloak and sword and prepared to go out. "Monsieur," said Planchet with a lamentable air, "you're not going to abandon me, are you? You're my only hope!"

"Oh, they won't look for you here," said d'Artagnan.

"Yes, but if you leave," said the prudent Planchet, "the folk of this house, who didn't see me come in with you, will think I'm a thief."

"Good point," said d'Artagnan. "Let's see—can you speak like a provincial?"

"I can do better than that, Monsieur," said Planchet, "I even know another language: I can speak Flemish."

"Where the devil did you learn that?"

"In Artois, where we fought for two years. Listen: *Goeden morgen, mynheer! Ith ben begeeray te weeten the gesond bects omstand.*"

"What does that mean?"

"Good morning, Monsieur! Be so kind as to tell me how you're feeling."

"You call that a language?" said d'Artagnan. "Never mind, that'll do perfectly." D'Artagnan went to the door, called for the houseboy, and told him to ask the fair Madeleine to come up.

"What are you doing, Monsieur?" Planchet said. "You're going to reveal our secret to a woman?"

"Don't worry, this one won't tip our hand."

At that moment the hostess entered. She came in smiling expectantly, thinking to find only d'Artagnan, but upon seeing Planchet, she stopped short, astonished.

"My dear hostess," said d'Artagnan, "may I present your brother, who's just arrived from Flanders, here to spend a few days in my service."

"My brother!" said the hostess, even more astonished.

"Say hello to your sister, Master Peter."

"*Vilkom, Zuster!*" said Planchet.

"*Goeden day, Broer!*" replied the bewildered hostess.

"Here's the situation," said d'Artagnan. "Monsieur is your brother, just come from Amsterdam, whom maybe you don't know, but I do. Get him dressed properly while I'm out, and when I return in, say, an hour, present him to me. Since I can refuse you nothing, I'll take him into my service on your recommendation, although he doesn't speak a word of French. Got that?"

"I've got enough of it to see what you're after, and that's all I need," Madeleine said.

"You're a precious gem, dear hostess, and I leave it to you."

Whereupon, with a wink to Planchet, d'Artagnan went out to go to Notre Dame.

VIII

The Differing Effects of a Half-*Pistole* When Bestowed upon a Beadle and a Choirboy

D'Artagnan crossed the Pont Neuf, congratulating himself on having found Planchet, because though it might seem as if he was doing the good fellow a favor, it was really Planchet who was helping him. At the moment, nothing could be more useful than to have a brave and intelligent lackey. It's true that Planchet probably couldn't stay in his service for long, but after hiding in his home, which had saved his life, or nearly so, when he returned to his home in Rue des Lombards, Planchet would still be in d'Artagnan's debt. D'Artagnan wasn't sorry to have friends among the bourgeoisie when they were preparing to make war on the Court. He would have an agent in the enemy's camp, and for a man as shrewd as d'Artagnan the smallest advantage could lead to great results.

So, it was in this frame of mind, pleased with his chance and how he'd seized it, that d'Artagnan arrived at Notre Dame. He mounted the steps, entered the church, and, addressing a sacristan who was sweeping the vestibule, asked him if he knew Monsieur Bazin.

"Monsieur Bazin the beadle?" said the sacristan.

"Himself."

"He's assisting at mass over there, in the Chapel of the Virgin."

D'Artagnan sighed with relief, for despite what Planchet had told him, he'd secretly feared he'd never find Bazin. But now he had hold of one end of the string, and just needed to follow it to the other.

He knelt in the front of the chapel so as not to lose sight of his man. Fortunately, it was Low Mass, and ending soon. D'Artagnan, who'd forgotten all his prayers, and had neglected to take up a prayer book, used the time to take a good look at Bazin.

It must be said, Bazin wore his vestments with majesty and beatitude. He had arrived at what was, as we know, the height of his ambitions, and the silver-chased virge he held up was as honorable to him as the commander's baton that Condé threw—or didn't throw—into the enemy's lines at the Battle of Fribourg.[41] His physique had undergone a change perfectly suited to his vestments, in that he was as round as the halo of a saint. Every angle had disappeared from his face: he still had a nose, but his cheeks had expanded to absorb the rest of his features, smoothing his chin into his throat. This swelling had nearly shut his eyes. His forehead, down to the wrinkles just above his eyes, was covered by his hair, which was cropped in ecclesiastical bangs. But Bazin's forehead, even when visible, had never been more than an inch and a half high.

The officiating priest finished the mass as d'Artagnan completed his survey: he pronounced the sacramental words and withdrew, giving his benediction—which everyone received kneeling, to d'Artagnan's astonishment. But then he recognized the celebrant as the "coadjutor" himself, the famous Jean-François de Gondy,* who, sensing the political moment, was currying favor with the devout among the populace. It was to feed this popularity that from time to time he led the morning masses, which were usually attended by just a few commoners.

D'Artagnan knelt like the others, received his blessing, and made the sign of the cross—but as Bazin passed humbly by, walking last with his eyes raised to heaven, d'Artagnan tugged at the hem of his robe. Bazin looked down and jumped as if he'd seen a snake. "Monsieur d'Artagnan!" he cried. "*Vade retro, Satanas!*"

D'Artagnan laughed. "So, my dear Bazin, is that how you receive an old friend?"

"Monsieur," Bazin replied, "a Christian's true friends are those who help him to salvation, not those who tempt him away."

"I don't understand you, Bazin," d'Artagnan said. "I fail to see how I can be any bar to your salvation."

"You forget, Monsieur," replied Bazin, "how you almost destroyed that of my master—that thanks to you he was nearly damned forever by staying a musketeer, when his vocation so clearly drew him to the Church."

"My dear Bazin," d'Artagnan said, "you can see, by where you've met me, that I'm a changed man. Age brings reverence—and as I'm sure your master is well on his way to salvation, just tell me where he is so I can get his advice on how to achieve my own."

"Say rather to drag him back with you into the world. Fortunately," Bazin added, "I don't know where he is, and since we're in a holy place, I wouldn't dare tell a lie."

"What?" cried d'Artagnan, crushed by disappointment. "You don't know where Aramis is?"

"First of all," said Bazin, "Aramis was his name of perdition. In *Aramis* one finds *Simara*, the name of a demon—but fortunately for him, he's left that name behind him forever."

"Right," said d'Artagnan, determined to show patience, "it's not Aramis I'm looking for, it's the Abbé d'Herblay. Come, my dear Bazin, tell me how to find him."

"Didn't you hear me say, Monsieur d'Artagnan, that I don't know?"

"Oh, I heard you say it; it's just impossible for me to believe it."

"It's the truth, Monsieur, the good Lord's honest truth."

D'Artagnan could see he wasn't going to get anything out of Bazin. He was obviously lying but was firm and persistent about sticking to it. "Very well, Bazin!" d'Artagnan said. "Since you don't know where your master is, we'll say no more about it. But let's part friends; here's a half-pistole to drink to my health."

"I do not drink, Monsieur," said Bazin, majestically pushing away the officer's hand. "Such things are for the laity."

"Incorruptible too!" murmured d'Artagnan. "Really, I'm off my game."

And since d'Artagnan, distracted by his thoughts, had let go of Bazin's hem, the beadle took advantage of his release to retreat to the sacristy, not thinking himself safe until he'd closed the door behind him.

D'Artagnan stayed where he was, thinking, his eyes fixed on the door that had put a barrier between him and Bazin, when he felt a fingertip touch him lightly on the shoulder.

He turned and was about to exclaim in surprise, when the one whose finger had touched him brought that finger to his lips to enjoin silence. So, he lowered his voice and said, "You, here, my dear Rochefort!"

"Quiet!" said Rochefort. "Did you know I was free?"

"I heard it firsthand."

"From who?"

"From Planchet."

"Planchet? How do you mean?"

"He was the one who freed you."

"So that was Planchet! I thought he looked familiar. Which just goes to show that no good deed is ever wasted."

"And what are you doing here?"

"I came to thank God for my joyous deliverance," said Rochefort.

"I know that can't be all. What else?"

"And then to ask for orders from the coadjutor, to see if there's some way we can outrage Mazarin."

"You're a bad egg, and you're going to end up back in the Bastille."

"Oh, don't be too sure about that! I'm enjoying this fresh air entirely too much. In fact," said Rochefort, taking a deep breath, "I'm of a mind to take a walk in the country, a tour of the provinces."

"Really!" said d'Artagnan. "I've had the same thought."

"Ah. And without prying, can one ask where you're going?"

"To look for my friends."

"Which friends?"

"The ones you asked me about yesterday."

"What, Athos, Porthos, and Aramis?"

"Yes."

"On your honor?"

"What's so surprising about that?"

"Oh, nothing. It's funny, that's all. And on whose behalf are you looking for them?"

"You can't have any doubts about that."

"True enough."

"Unfortunately, I have no idea where they are."

"And no way to find out? Just wait a week, and I'll tell you myself."

"A week is too long. I must find them within three days."

"Three days! That isn't long," said Rochefort, "and France is large."

"Never mind, you know the word *must*. We can do a lot once *must* is invoked."

"And how will you start your search?"

"I'm on it."

"Good luck, then!"

"And you, *bon voyage*!"

"Maybe we'll meet each other on the road."

"Not likely."

"Who knows? Chance is capricious."

"Adieu."

"*Au revoir.* And by the way, if Mazarin happens to mention me, tell him I said he'll soon see if, as he says, I'm too old for action."

Then Rochefort went off with one of those diabolical smiles that, once upon a time, had made d'Artagnan shudder. But d'Artagnan watched him go without anxiety, smiling on his part with a touch of that melancholy peculiar to him. "Go, old demon," he said to himself. "Do as you will, it doesn't matter to me—for there's no second Constance in the world!"

Turning, d'Artagnan saw that Bazin, having removed his ecclesiastical garb, was talking with the sacristan d'Artagnan had spoken with upon entering the church. Bazin was waving his short little arms around in lively gestures, probably, thought d'Artagnan, warning the lad against him in future. He took advantage of the two churchmen's preoccupation to slip out of the cathedral and take up a post on the corner of the Rue des Canettes from which he could watch the door unnoticed.

Five minutes later d'Artagnan saw Bazin appear on the steps. He looked all around to make sure he wasn't observed, but didn't see our officer, hidden around the corner of a house fifty paces away. Reassured, he set off along Rue Notre Dame. D'Artagnan darted from his hiding place and caught up just in time to see him turn down Rue de la Juiverie and then, on Rue de la Calandre, enter a boarding house of honest appearance. Our officer had no doubt it was the home of the worthy beadle. D'Artagnan was careful to keep his distance; if the house didn't have a concierge, there'd be no one to speak to, and if it did, she'd already have been warned. Instead he went into a small tavern on the corner of Rue Saint-Éloi and Rue de la Calandre, where he ordered a hippocras.[42] That drink would take a good half hour to prepare, giving d'Artagnan plenty of time to watch Bazin's house without arousing suspicion.

In the tavern, he noticed a young lad, aged twelve or so, whom he thought he recognized from having seen him twenty minutes earlier dressed as a chorister. He spoke with him, and as the apprentice sub-deacon had nothing to hide, d'Artagnan learned that he served from six to nine in the morning as a choir boy, and then from nine till midnight as a tavern boy. As he was talking to the lad, a horse, saddled and bridled, was led up to Bazin's front door, and a moment later, Bazin came down. "Look!" said the lad. "There goes our beadle, on his way again."

"And where is he off to?" asked d'Artagnan.

"*Dame*—blessed if I know!"

"There's a half-pistole in it," d'Artagnan said, "if you can find out."

"For me?" said the lad, eyes sparkling. "Oh, I'll find out where he's going. It won't be hard. You're not kidding?"

"No, faith of an officer. Look—here's the half-pistole." And he displayed the corrupting coin but kept hold of it.

"I'll ask him."

"That's the best way *not* to get the answer," said d'Artagnan. "Wait till he's gone, then ask around, see what people know. Until then, your half-pistole waits here." And he put it back in his pocket.

"I get it," said the lad, with that smirk unique to the gamins of Paris. "We'll wait, then."

They didn't have to wait long. Five minutes later, Bazin set off at a trot, slapping the withers of his horse with an umbrella. Bazin had always had the habit of using an umbrella as a riding crop. He'd scarcely turned the corner of the Rue de la Juiverie before the tavern boy was off like a bloodhound on his trail.

D'Artagnan sat back down at his table, certain that within ten minutes he'd know just what he wanted to know.

Indeed, the boy returned in even less time than that. "Well?" asked d'Artagnan.

"Well," the young lad said, "I found out a thing or two."

"So, where's he going?"

"I still get the half-pistole?"

"Oh, yes—but talk to me first."

"Let me see it again. I want to make sure it's the real thing."

"Here it is."

"Master host!" the boy said. "Monsieur here wants some change." The innkeeper took the half-pistole and gave the boy its change—which he put into his own pocket.

D'Artagnan watched this little game, chuckling, then said, "So where did he go?"

"He went to Noisy."[43]

"How do you know that?"

"Ah, pardieu, it didn't take long to figure that out. I recognized the horse as belonging to the butcher, who occasionally hires it out to Monsieur Bazin. I didn't think the butcher would hire out his horse without asking where Monsieur Bazin would be going with it—not that he'd be likely to go far."

"And he told you Monsieur Bazin . . ."

"Was going to Noisy. It's the usual thing, he goes there two or three times a week."

"And do you know Noisy?"

"I should, my nurse was from there."

"Is there a monastery in Noisy?"

"A famous one, a Jesuit monastery."

"Well, that's it, then," said d'Artagnan.

"So, you're satisfied?"

"Entirely. What do they call you?"

"Friquet."

D'Artagnan took out his notebook and wrote down the lad's name and the tavern's address. "So, Monsieur Officer," the tavern boy said, "might there be a way to earn more half-pistoles?"

"Could be," said d'Artagnan. And since he'd learned what he wanted to know, he paid for the hippocras, which he hadn't drunk yet, and marched on back to Rue Tiquetonne.

IX

In Which d'Artagnan, Seeking Aramis, Finds Him on Planchet's Crupper

Returning home, d'Artagnan found a man standing by the fireplace; it was Planchet, but a Planchet so different, thanks to the old clothes left behind by the vanished husband, that he hardly recognized him. Madeleine had just presented him to all the houseboys. Planchet then addressed d'Artagnan in some lovely Flemish, the officer replied in some made-up gabble, and the bargain was concluded: Madeleine's brother had entered d'Artagnan's service.

D'Artagnan's course was clear: he didn't want to arrive in Noisy during the day for fear of being recognized, but it was only three or four leagues from Paris, on the road to Meaux, so he had some time ahead of him. He spent the first part of it in taking a substantial lunch, which can be a liability for head work, but a useful precaution when one has work for the body. Then he changed his outfit, as he thought the uniform of a lieutenant of musketeers might inspire distrust. Finally, he got out the best and longest of his swords, one he'd relied upon back in the old days. About two o'clock he had a couple of horses saddled, and then, followed by Planchet, he rode toward the La Villette gate. The house next door to the Hôtel de La Chevrette was still undergoing an intensive search.

A league and a half outside Paris, d'Artagnan, seeing that in his impatience he'd still left too soon, stopped at an inn to breathe the horses. The bar was full of suspicious characters who gave them ugly looks and seemed to be organizing some sort of nocturnal expedition. A man wrapped in a cloak appeared at the door, but seeing a stranger within, he just gestured to two of the drinkers, who got up and went out to talk with him.

As for d'Artagnan, he approached the lady of the house, breezily praised her wine, some horrible swill from Montreuil, and plied her with questions about Noisy. He learned there were two buildings of note in the village, one belonging to the Archbishop of Paris, now in use by his niece, the Duchesse de Longueville,* the other a monastery managed by the worthy fathers of the Jesuits, and there was no way to mistake one for the other.

At four o'clock, d'Artagnan resumed his journey, marching on foot because he didn't want to arrive before nightfall. But walking while leading a horse, on a gray winter's day, across a featureless landscape, one has nothing better to do, as La Fontaine says of the hare in his hole, than to think. And so d'Artagnan thought. Planchet did too; but as we'll see, their thoughts were not the same.

A word from the inn's hostess had steered d'Artagnan's thoughts in a particular direction, and that word was the name of Madame de Longueville.

Indeed, Madame de Longueville was a lot to think about, as she was among the greatest ladies of the kingdom, and one of the reigning beauties of the Court. Wedded young in a loveless marriage to the old Duc de Longueville, she'd had an affair with Coligny,[44] who'd been killed on her account by the Duc de Guise in a duel on the Place Royale. Following that had been a spate of rumors that she was entirely too close to her brother, the Prince de Condé, talk that had scandalized the more timorous souls at Court, but their friendship had warped into a deep and abiding hatred. Now, it was said, she was involved in a political liaison with the Prince de Marcillac,* son of the old Duc de La Rochefoucauld, whom she was seducing into becoming an enemy of the Duc de Condé, her brother.

D'Artagnan thought about all of this. He thought of how, at the Louvre, he'd often seen the radiant and dazzling Madame de Longueville passing before him. He thought about Aramis, who with no more virtues than d'Artagnan, had formerly been the lover of Madame de Chevreuse, who'd been to the previous reign what Madame de Longueville was to this one. And he asked himself why there were people in the world who could get what they wanted, could satisfy political ambition or desire, while there were others who, by random chance, or some flaw in their natures, never got more than halfway to their hopes.

He was just facing up to the idea that, despite all his wits, finesse, and skill, he was probably one of these latter people, when Planchet caught up to him and said, "I'll bet, Monsieur, that you're thinking what I'm thinking."

"I doubt that, Planchet," said d'Artagnan, smiling. "But what are you thinking?"

"I'm thinking, Monsieur, about those ugly customers we saw drinking at the inn where we stopped."

"Planchet the ever prudent!"

"It's my instinct, Monsieur."

"Well, then! What do your instincts tell you in this situation?"

"Monsieur, my instincts told me those thugs were gathered at that inn for some sort of bad business. I was just thinking about that while I was back in a dark corner of the stable, and a man wrapped in a cloak came in, followed by two other men."

"Oh ho!" d'Artagnan said, as Planchet's story matched what he'd seen himself. "And then?"

"One of the men said, 'He's sure to be at Noisy, or be coming tonight, because I recognized his servant.' 'Are you sure?' said the man in the cloak. 'Yes, my Prince.'"

"*My Prince?*" d'Artagnan interrupted.

"Yes, 'my Prince.' But listen further: 'If he's really there, what should we do?' asked the other man. 'What should you do?' said the prince. 'Yes. He's a swordsman and won't be easily taken.' 'But you'll take him, just the same—and make sure you take him alive. Do you have rope to bind him and a gag for his mouth?' 'We have all that.' 'Pay close attention, because he'll probably be disguised as a cavalier.' 'Oh, yes, Monseigneur, never fear.' 'Besides, I'll be there to make certain.' 'And you assure us that the law . . .' 'I'll answer for everything,' the prince said. 'All right, we'll do our best.' And with that, they left the stable."

"Well," said d'Artagnan, "what's that matter to us? That nasty sort of affair happens every day."

"How do you know we're not the targets of it?"

"Us, the targets? Why?"

"*Dame!* Think of what they said: 'I recognized his servant,' which could apply to me."

"Do you think?"

"And the other one said, 'He's sure to be at Noisy, or be coming tonight.' That could apply to you."

"And so?"

"So, the prince said, 'Pay close attention, because he'll probably be disguised as a cavalier'—which is pretty clear, since you're dressed as a cavalier rather than an officer of musketeers. What do you think of that?"

"Alas, my dear Planchet!" sighed d'Artagnan. "It's been some time since princes wanted to have me murdered. But those days are gone! Rest assured, these people aren't after us."

"Monsieur is certain?"

"Quite certain."

"All right, then—I won't mention it again." Planchet resumed his place in d'Artagnan's wake, with that sublime confidence he'd always had in his master, and which fifteen years of separation had done nothing to diminish.

They rode on for another league before Planchet approached d'Artagnan again. "Monsieur," he said.

"Well?"

"Look, Monsieur, over that way," said Planchet. "I think I can see shadows passing by in the twilight. Listen, isn't that the sound of horses' hooves?"

"Not a chance," said d'Artagnan, "the ground is soaked from the rain. But now that you mention it, I *do* seem to see something." And he stopped to look and listen. "If their horses hear ours, they'll neigh."

And just as he said it, the neighing of a horse came to their ears.

"Those are our men, riding cross-country," he said. "But it's no business of ours; let's continue."

And they went on their way.

Half an hour later, around eight-thirty or nine o'clock, they reached the first houses of Noisy. As was usual in the country, everyone was already in bed, and not a light could be seen in the village. D'Artagnan and Planchet continued on their course.

Now to their right and left the sharp silhouettes of roofs stood out against the dark gray sky. Occasionally an awakened dog barked from behind a door, or a startled cat darted from the middle of the street to hide in a woodpile, out of which its frightened eyes glinted like carbuncles. These were the only living creatures that seemed to inhabit the village.

In the middle of the town, overlooking the main square, rose a dark mass between two streets, in front of which ancient lime trees spread their bony boughs. D'Artagnan carefully examined this building, which showed a light in only one window. "This," he said to Planchet, "must be the château of the archbishop, current home of *la belle* Madame de Longueville. But where is the monastery?"

"The monastery is at the far end of the village," Planchet said. "I know it."

"Well," d'Artagnan said, "trot over there, Planchet, while I tighten my horse's girth, and tell me if there are any lighted windows at the Jesuits' place."

Planchet obeyed, heading off into the darkness, while d'Artagnan dismounted to adjust his horse's tack.

After five minutes, Planchet returned. "Monsieur, there's only one lighted window, on the side that faces the fields."

"Hmm!" said d'Artagnan. "If I were a Frondeur, I'd knock here at the palace if I were looking for a night's lodging. If I were a monk, I'd knock over there to find myself a good dinner. But since we're us, I think we might be stuck between the château and the monastery and have to sleep on the hard ground, dying of thirst and hunger."

"Yes," said Planchet, "like Buridan's ass. But instead, let's pick one or the other."

"Hush!" d'Artagnan said. "The only window with a light in it just went out."

"Do you hear something, Monsieur?" said Planchet.

In fact, there was a sudden noise, like the sound of an approaching hurricane, and then two troops of riders, a dozen men apiece, came racing up the two streets that bordered the château, surrounding d'Artagnan and Planchet.

"*Ouais!*" said d'Artagnan, drawing his sword and stepping behind his horse, as Planchet did the same. "Were you right all the time? Is it really us they're after?"

"Here he is! We got him!" cried the horsemen closing in around d'Artagnan, waving their swords.

"Don't let him escape," a voice called loudly.

"Don't worry, Monseigneur!"

D'Artagnan thought it was high time for him to join the discussion. "*Holà*, Messieurs!" he said in his Gascon accent. "What are you doing? What do you want?"

"You'll find out!" cried the horsemen.

"Wait, stop!" shouted the one addressed as monseigneur. "Stop, or it's your heads! That's not his voice."

"*Ah çà*, Messieurs!" said d'Artagnan. "Has madness come to Noisy? Anyone who ventures too close had better watch out—my sword is long and will take you apart."

The leader approached. "What are you doing here?" he said, in a haughty voice accustomed to command.

"What about yourself?" said d'Artagnan.

"Mind your manners, or things won't go well. My name is my secret, but I still insist on the respect due to my rank."

"I'm sure if I was leading an ambush, I'd want to keep my name a secret, too," said d'Artagnan, "but I'm just traveling with my servant, so I've nothing to hide."

"Enough, enough! Who are you, then?"

"I'll tell you my name so you'll know how to find me, whether Monsieur or Monseigneur, gentleman or prince," said our Gascon, who didn't wish to appear to give in to a threat. "Have you heard of Monsieur d'Artagnan?"

"Lieutenant of the King's Musketeers?" said the voice.

"That's the one."

"Of course."

"Well!" the Gascon continued. "Have you heard he has a firm wrist and a sharp blade?"

"Are you Monsieur d'Artagnan?"

"That's me."

"So, are you here to defend . . . him?"

"Him? Who?"

"The one we seek."

"I thought I was in Noisy," d'Artagnan said, "not the Land of Mysteries."

"Answer me!" said the same haughty voice. "Whom do you await beneath these windows? Did you come to Noisy to defend him?"

"I'm not waiting for anyone," said d'Artagnan, losing his patience. "I'm not here to defend anyone but myself—but that, I'm warning you, I'm more than ready to do."

"All right," said the voice. "Be on your way, then."

"Be on *my* way!" said d'Artagnan, who wasn't about to leave. "I don't think so. I'm tired, and so is my horse. Unless you've got supper and a bed for us, we're not going anywhere."

"Varlet!"

"Monsieur!" said d'Artagnan. "Watch your language, if you please. Insult me again, and whether you're a marquis or a duke, a prince or a king, I'll spill your guts. Do you hear me?"

"Here now," said the leader. "That's a Gascon talking, and no doubt about it. He's not who we're after; we've missed it for tonight, so let's go. Master d'Artagnan," he said, raising his voice, "we'll meet again."

"That'll be bad luck for you," scoffed the Gascon, "because it will be daylight and you'll be alone."

"Fine, fine!" said the voice. "Let's go, Messieurs!" And the troop, muttering and growling, disappeared into the darkness toward Paris.

D'Artagnan and Planchet stayed on the defensive for a moment, but as the noise died away, they sheathed their swords. "You see, fool?" said d'Artagnan quietly to Planchet. "It wasn't us they wanted."

"But who, then?" asked Planchet.

"*Ma foi!* I don't know, and I don't care. I just want to get to that Jesuit monastery. Mount up, and let's go knock on their door. What the devil! They won't eat us." And d'Artagnan remounted.

Planchet did the same, but then an unexpected weight fell on his horse's withers. "Whoa, Monsieur!" Planchet cried. "There's a man on my crupper!"

D'Artagnan turned and saw two forms on Planchet's horse. "The Devil *is* after us!" he cried, drawing his sword and preparing to impale the newcomer.

"No, my dear d'Artagnan," said the latter. "It isn't the Devil—it's me, Aramis. To the gallop, Planchet, and when you reach the end of the village, bear left."

So Planchet galloped, carrying Aramis behind him, followed by d'Artagnan, who began to think he was trapped in a fantastic and ridiculous dream.

X

The Abbé d'Herblay

At the end of the village Planchet bore left, as Aramis ordered, and then stopped beneath the monastery's single lighted window. Aramis jumped down and clapped three times. At once the window opened and a rope ladder rolled down.

"My dear d'Artagnan," said Aramis, "if you'd care to climb up, I'd be delighted to receive you."

"*Ah çà*," said d'Artagnan. "So, this is how you get home?"

"Well, yes, after nine o'clock," said Aramis. "Pardieu, the monastery rules are quite strict."

"Pardon me, old friend," said d'Artagnan, "but did you swear pardieu?"

"Did I?" said Aramis, laughing. "It's possible. You can't imagine the bad habits one learns in these cursed monasteries. It's the wicked ways of these churchmen among whom I'm forced to live! Aren't you going to climb up?"

"Go ahead. I'm right behind you."

"All right, but in the words of the old cardinal to the late king, 'Only to show you the way, Sire.'" And Aramis went briskly up the ladder, arriving at the window in a moment.

D'Artagnan followed, but less quickly. Clearly this means of entrance was not as familiar to him as to his friend.

"I do beg your pardon," said Aramis, noting his careful climb. "This is good enough for me, but if I'd had the honor of knowing of your visit, I'd have brought out the gardener's ladder."

"Monsieur," said Planchet, as d'Artagnan neared the top, "that's fine for Monsieur Aramis, and even for you, and I might manage it as well—but our two horses can't climb a ladder."

"Take them under that shed, *mon ami*," said Aramis, pointing Planchet toward a sort of shack that stood on the edge of the fields. "You'll find straw and oats for them there."

"But what about me?"

"Come back under the window, clap three times, and we'll send down some food. Rest easy. *Morbleu*, it's not as if we'd let you die of hunger!" Then Aramis pulled up the ladder and shut the window.

D'Artagnan was looking around the room. Never had he seen a chamber so warlike, and yet so elegant. There were trophy stands in each corner displaying swords of all sorts, and four large paintings representing, armed and armored for battle, Cardinal Richelieu, Cardinal Lorraine, Cardinal La Valette, and the Archbishop of Bordeaux. Nor did the rest of the furnishings bespeak the abode of an abbot: the hangings were damask, the carpets from Alençon, and the bed especially seemed like that of a fine lady, with lace trim and counterpane. It was hardly the home of a man who'd sworn to gain heaven by abstinence and mortification.

"You're looking over my den," said Aramis. "Ah, *mon cher*, my apologies, but what would you have? They gave me a cell fit for a monk. What is it you're looking for?"

"I'm looking for whoever unrolled the ladder. I don't see anybody, but ladders don't unroll themselves."

"No, it was Bazin."

"Ah ha!" said d'Artagnan.

"But Monsieur Bazin," continued Aramis, "is well trained. When he saw I wasn't returning alone, he discreetly retired. Have a seat, *mon cher*, and let's talk." Aramis pushed a chair toward d'Artagnan, who dropped gratefully into it.

"You'll dine with me, I hope?" asked Aramis.

"Yes, of course," said d'Artagnan, "and with pleasure. I must admit, the ride has given me the devil of an appetite."

"Alas, my poor friend," said Aramis, "we can offer only meager fare, as we didn't expect you."

"Are you threatening me, as you did at Crèvecœur, with an omelet and *tetragons,* as I think you called the spinach?"

"Oh, no," said Aramis, "by the grace of God and Bazin, I hope we can find something better than that in the pantry of our worthy Jesuit fathers. Bazin, *mon ami*! Come here."

The door opened and Bazin appeared, but when he saw d'Artagnan he gave a gasp that sounded much like a cry of despair.

"My dear Bazin," said d'Artagnan, "I was delighted to see you tell a lie with such aplomb, especially in church."

"Monsieur," Bazin said, "I've learned from our worthy Jesuit fathers that it's permissible to state a falsehood when one's intentions are good."

"Fine, fine, Bazin, but d'Artagnan is dying of hunger," Aramis said. "Give us the best dinner you can find, and above all, the best wine."

Bazin bowed obediently, gave a great sigh, and left.

D'Artagnan turned his eyes from the bedchamber to its owner, from the fine furnishings to their owner's fine apparel, and said, "Now that we're alone, my dear Aramis, tell me: where the devil did you drop from when you landed behind Planchet?"

"Eh, *corbleu,*" said Aramis, "from heaven, of course!"

"From heaven?" said d'Artagnan, shaking his head. "You don't look like someone who came from there any more than you look like someone who's on his way there."

"*Mon cher,*" said Aramis, with an air of self-satisfaction d'Artagnan had never seen when he was a musketeer, "if I didn't come from Heaven, I came at least from Paradise, which is close enough."

"At last the great debate is settled," said d'Artagnan. "Up till now the sages had never been able to agree on the location of Paradise. Some said it was on Mount Ararat; others said somewhere between the Tigris and the Euphrates; but it seems it wasn't nearly so remote. Paradise is in Noisy-le-Sec, on the site of the château of the Archbishop of Paris, and one enters not by the door, but by the window. From it one descends not the marble steps of a peristyle, but the boughs of a lime tree, and the angel who guards it with a flaming sword isn't called Gabriel, but the far more earthly Prince de Marcillac."

Aramis laughed. "You were always such a jolly companion, *mon cher*," he said, "and your witty Gascon humor hasn't left you. Yes, there's something in what you say—so long as you don't think that means Madame de Longueville and I are lovers."

"Plague take me if I do!" said d'Artagnan. "After having been in love so long with Madame de Chevreuse, you'd hardly take up with her mortal enemy."

"Yes, quite so," said Aramis, with a casual air. "Alas, my poor duchess, I loved her well. To be fair, she did well by us, but what would you have? She was exiled from France. He was a hard man to dice against, that damned cardinal!" He glared at the portrait of the former minister. "He'd ordered her confined to the Château de Loches—though I swear he'd rather have had her head, as he did with Chalais, Montmorency, and Cinq-Mars. She escaped that place, fled disguised as a man, along with her maid, that poor Kitty. I even heard a story that, in some village or other, she asked a curate for hospitality, and he, taking her for a cavalier, offered to share the only bed he had with her. She had an amazing way of wearing men's garb and carrying it off, that dear Marie—I know only one other woman who wears it so well. They even wrote a verse about it: *Laboissière, please do tell* . . . do you know it?"

"I don't. Sing it, old friend."

Aramis began again, in his most cavalier tone:

> *Laboissière, please do tell*
> *Don't I seem like a man?*
> *My faith, you ride well*
> *Better even than we can*
> *Among the shining halberds*
> *Head held up, she rides out*
> *Past a regiment of guards*
> *Just like a cadet, no doubt.*

"Bravo!" said d'Artagnan. "You always did sing beautifully, my dear Aramis. I see that preaching the mass hasn't spoiled your voice."

"*Mon cher,*" said Aramis, "when I was a musketeer, I stood guard as little as possible—and now that I'm an abbot, I say as few masses as I can. But back to my poor duchess."

"Which one? The Duchesse de Chevreuse, or the Duchesse de Longueville?"

"*Mon cher,* I already told you there's nothing between me and the Duchesse de Longueville—a little flirtation, perhaps, but no more. No, I was speaking of the Duchesse de Chevreuse. Have you seen her since her return from Brussels, after the death of the old king?"

"Indeed I did, and she was still very beautiful."

"Yes," said Aramis. "I saw her then as well. I gave her excellent advice, to which she paid absolutely no attention. I did my best to persuade her that Mazarin was now the queen's lover, but she refused to believe it, saying she knew Anne of Austria, and the queen was too proud to fall for such a fop. She joined the Duc de Beaufort's cabal, and then the fop arrested Beaufort and exiled Madame de Chevreuse all over again."

"But you know she's since gotten permission to return," said d'Artagnan.

"Yes, she's back, and is bound to do something else foolish."

"But maybe this time she'll follow your advice."

"Oh, this time I haven't seen her," said Aramis. "She is much changed."

"Not like you, Aramis, for you never change. You still have your handsome black hair, that elegant figure, and those beautiful hands, like a lady's, really—hands well suited to a prelate."

"Yes," said Aramis, "I do what I can to take care of myself. But it's hard, *mon cher,* as I'm getting old—I'm nearly thirty-seven."

"Listen, '*mon cher,*'" said d'Artagnan with a smile, "since we're back together, let's agree on one thing: what age we shall be for the future."

"What do you mean?" said Aramis.

"I mean that I used to be younger than you by two or three years," d'Artagnan replied, "but unless I miscalculate, I'm now forty years old."

"Really!" said Aramis. "Then I must be the one who's miscalculated, *mon cher*, because you've always been an admirable mathematician. So, by your reckoning, I must be . . . forty-three! Double devils! Don't tell them at the Hôtel de Rambouillet, it would ruin me."

"Don't worry," said d'Artagnan, "I never go there."

"But damn me," cried Aramis, "where is that animal Bazin? Hey, Bazin, you clown! We're dying of hunger and thirst here."

Bazin entered at just that moment, both hands raised to heaven, each holding a bottle. "Finally!" said Aramis. "What took you so long?"

"I'm here, Monsieur," said Bazin. "It took me a while to climb all those stairs . . ."

"This is what comes of being a beadle," Aramis interrupted, "and wasting valuable time reading your breviary. I warn you that if you spend so much time polishing the relics in the chapel that you forget to polish my sword, I'll make a bonfire of all your breviaries and pictures of saints and roast you over it."

Bazin, shocked, made the sign of the cross with the bottle he held in his right hand. As for d'Artagnan, he was so surprised by the manner and tone of the Abbé d'Herblay compared to that of Aramis the Musketeer, he just stared.

Bazin quickly covered the table with a damask tablecloth, and then brought out such an array of sweetmeats, tasty morsels, and perfumed dainties that d'Artagnan was astonished. "So, this is what you have when you're not expecting anyone?"

"Oh," said Aramis, "we can always scare up a snack. But I'd heard you were looking for me."

"From who?"

"From Master Bazin, of course, who took you for the Devil, *mon cher*, and rushed to warn me of the peril to my soul if I risked the society of an officer of musketeers."

"Oh, Monsieur!" moaned Bazin, wringing his hands.

"Enough hypocrisy! You know I don't like it. You'd be better off opening the window and lowering down a loaf, a chicken, and a bottle to your friend Planchet, who's been clapping his hands down below for nearly an hour."

Planchet, having fed and watered the horses, was in fact waiting under the window, where he'd repeated the specified signal two or three times.

Bazin obeyed, tying the three designated items to a rope and lowering them to Planchet, who, quite satisfied, immediately retired to the shed.

"And now, let us eat," said Aramis.

The two friends sat down at the table, and Aramis began to slice up chicken, partridges, and ham with skill and dash. "Peste," said d'Artagnan, "you eat well here!"

"Yes, tolerably well. I have an exemption from Rome for fast-days that the coadjutor got me on account of my health, and I have Lafollone's former chef as cook. Remember Lafollone?[45] He was that crony of the old cardinal who was a famous gourmand, and always prayed after dinner, 'My God, grant me the grace to properly digest that which I've eaten so well.'"

"That didn't keep him from dying of indigestion," d'Artagnan laughed.

"What would you have?" Aramis shrugged. "No one can escape his destiny!"

D'Artagnan said, "I hope you won't mind the indelicate question I'm about to ask."

"Ask away—you know that between us, nothing is too delicate."

"So, are you rich, now?"

"Oh, *mon Dieu,* no! I make about twelve thousand livres a year, plus a small annuity of a thousand crowns granted me by the Prince de Condé."

"And how do you earn these twelve thousand livres?" said d'Artagnan. "From your poetry?"

"No, I gave up poetry, except for the occasional epigram, love sonnet, or drinking song. No, *mon cher,* I write sermons."

"You make money from sermons?"

"Ah, but they're excellent sermons, you see! Or so they tell me."

"And do you preach them?"

"No, I sell them."

"To whom?"

"To those of my fellow churchmen who wish to be known as great orators!"

"Really? And you haven't been tempted to find such glory for yourself?"

"I tried it, *mon cher,* but it's just not my forte. If I'm in the pulpit, and a pretty woman happens to look at me, I look back; and if she smiles, I smile too. And there goes the sermon! Instead of warning about the torments of hell, I speak of the joys of paradise. That exact thing happened to me one day in the Church of Saint-Louis in the Marais. A cavalier laughed and mocked me, and I interrupted my sermon to call him a fool. Some of the congregation went outside to gather rocks to stone me, but I spoke so persuasively to the rest that when the others returned, they ended up stoning the cavalier instead of me. Of course, he showed up at my house the next day with a challenge, thinking I was an abbot like other abbots."

"And what came of this challenge?" said d'Artagnan, holding his sides from laughing.

"What came of it was a rendezvous the following night in the Place Royale. Pardieu! I think you know something about that."

"Would that by any chance be the 'insolent dog' I helped you as second against?" d'Artagnan asked.

"Exactly. You saw how that turned out."

"Was he killed?"

"I don't know. But in any case, I gave him absolution *in articulo mortis.* It is sufficient to kill the body with slaying the soul."

Bazin made a gesture of despair that indicated that, while he might approve the theory, he deplored the tone of its expression.

"Bazin, *mon ami,* you overlook the fact that I can see you in the mirror, and that I forbade all such signs of approval or disapproval. So, you will do us the favor of serving us some Spanish wine, and then retire. Besides, my friend d'Artagnan has a secret he wishes to share with me. Isn't that so, d'Artagnan?"

D'Artagnan nodded, and Bazin withdrew, after placing some Spanish wine on the table.

The two friends, left alone, remained silent in each other's presence. Each of them, when he thought he wasn't observed, risked a glance at the other. Aramis pretended to savor his wine, while d'Artagnan considered how to begin.

It was Aramis who was first to break the silence.

XI

Pas de Deux[46]

"What are you thinking about, d'Artagnan," asked Aramis, "and why does that thought make you smile?"

"I was thinking that when you were a musketeer you were always acting the abbot, and now that you're an abbot, you behave like a musketeer."

"It's true," said Aramis, laughing. "Man is a strange animal, compounded of contrasts—as you know, *mon cher* d'Artagnan. Since becoming an abbot, I dream of nothing but battles."

"That's clear from your furnishings and decor. I've never seen so many different styles of rapiers. Do you still fence well?"

"As well as I used to—maybe even better. I do nothing else all day."

"And with whom do you spar?"

"Oh, we have an excellent master of arms."

"What, here?"

"Yes, here, in this very monastery, *mon cher*. A Jesuit monastery has everything."

"Then you would have killed Monsieur de Marcillac if he'd come after you alone, instead of with a troop of twenty?"

"Certainly," said Aramis, "and even with his troop of twenty, if I could have drawn steel before I was recognized."

"God help me," muttered d'Artagnan. "I think he's become more of a Gascon than I am." Then, aloud: "Well, then, Aramis, you were wondering why I was looking for you?"

"No, I didn't ask," said Aramis slyly, "but I expect you'll tell me anyway."

"Well, I've come to offer you a way to slay Monsieur de Marcillac, if that would please you, prince though he is."

"Well, well, well," said Aramis. "That's an idea, that is."

"And I invite you to take advantage of it. Let's see! With your abbacy worth a thousand crowns, and the twelve thousand livres you make selling sermons—are you rich? Be honest."

"Rich? I'm as poor as Job. Turn this place upside down if you like, but you won't find more than a hundred pistoles in it."

"Peste, a hundred pistoles?" d'Artagnan said to himself. "And he calls that being poor as Job? If I had that, I'd feel rich as Croesus." Then, aloud: "Are you ambitious?"

"As ambitious as Caesar."

"Well, then! I offer you the chance to be rich, powerful, and able to do whatever you like."

The shadow of a cloud passed over Aramis's brow as quick as that over the corn in August—but quick as it was, d'Artagnan saw it. "Go on," said Aramis.

"After one more question. Are you involved in politics?"

A light flashed in Aramis's eyes, quick as the shadow that had passed over his brow—but d'Artagnan saw that too. "No," said Aramis.

"Then you should be open to every side, since you have no master but God," said the Gascon, laughing.

"Possibly."

"Aramis, do you sometimes dream of those days of our youth, laughing, drinking, and fighting?"

"Yes, of course, and often missed them. It was a happy time, *delectabile tempus!*"

"Well, my friend, those happy times can come again. I've been given a mission to find my old companions, and I wanted to start with you, who was the heart and soul of our little band."

Aramis's bow was almost too courteous. "Me, go back into politics?" he sighed, and leaned loosely back in his chair. "But dear d'Artagnan, you see how comfortable and easy my life is now. In the past, we both suffered from the ingratitude of the great!"

"True enough," said d'Artagnan, "but perhaps the great repent of their ingratitude."

"If so," said Aramis, "that would be a change indeed. However, for every sin, a penance. But you're right about one thing: if one was of a mind to meddle in affairs of state, now would be the time to do it."

"And how would you know—you, who have nothing to do with politics?"

"*Mon Dieu!* How could I not? I live in a world devoted to it. When we talk of poetry or love, who is there but Monsieur Sarazin, the poetical friend of Monsieur de Conti? Or Monsieur Voiture,[47] who's allied with the coadjutor? Or Monsieur de Bois-Robert,[48] who, since he's no longer with Cardinal Richelieu, is with no one or everyone? You see, there's no escaping politics."

"No doubt about that," said d'Artagnan.

"And don't take what I say as the chatter of some little abbot who just repeats what he's heard," said Aramis. "I'm well aware that Cardinal Mazarin is worried about recent turns of events. It seems his decrees aren't regarded with the same respect as those of our old nemesis, the late cardinal, whose portrait you see here. Because despite all we said and did to thwart him, you must agree, *mon cher,* that he was a great man."

"No argument from me on that, friend Aramis. It was he who made me an officer."

"My instincts at first were entirely in favor of Cardinal Mazarin. Such a minister is rarely popular, but his brilliance was such that he seemed likely to triumph over his enemies, if only by fear, which, in my opinion, is often better than love."

D'Artagnan nodded to indicate his approval of this rather dubious maxim.

"That," Aramis continued, "was my first instinct—but since I know so little about such matters, I really couldn't trust my own opinion, so I humbly inquired further to ascertain the true situation. And, well, *mon cher ami . . .*"

"Well, what?" d'Artagnan asked.

"Well!" said Aramis. "Though it mortifies my pride, I had to admit I'd been wrong."

"Really?"

"Yes! I inquired further, as I said, and was told by people of all ranks, people who ought to know, that Mazarin was far from the brilliant man I'd taken him for."

"Bah!" said d'Artagnan.

"No. He is a man from nowhere, of no family, a mere servant of Cardinal Bentivoglio who got ahead by scheming. He's an upstart, a parvenu, who for France will never be more than a mere figurehead. Oh, he'll make himself a pile of gold, empty the king's treasury, pay to himself all the salaries Cardinal Richelieu shared out to everyone else—but he'll never put the law into the hands of the strongest, the noblest, or the most honorable. He appears, in manners and heart, to be less a gentleman than a sort of buffoon, a Pulcinello or Pantaloon. But you're the one who knows him, not me."

"Well," said d'Artagnan, "I admit there's some truth to what you say."

"Why, you fill me with pride, *mon cher.* To think that I, someone with just a touch of insight, could discern things as clearly as you, who are a man of the Court."

"But what you say applies to him personally, and not to his faction and its resources."

"That's true. He has the queen on his side."

"And that's something, I should think."

"But it's not like having . . . the king."

"Who's still a child!"

"A child who will be an adult in four years."

"But this is the present."

"Yes, it's not yet the future. But even in the present, Mazarin has neither the Parliament nor the people on his side—that is, the money—nor does he have the nobility and the princes—that is, the swords."

D'Artagnan scratched at his ear. He had to admit to himself that Aramis's summary was both thorough and undeniable.

"You see, my poor friend, that I still have my wits about me, as I used to. But maybe it's wrong for me to be so open and candid about the matter, since you seem to lean toward Mazarin."

"What, me?" cried d'Artagnan. "Not at all!"

"You were speaking of a mission."

"Did I say a mission? Sometimes I pick the wrong word. No, I think as you do: all is confusion. Well, then—let's throw the feather into the wind, follow where the wind takes it, and resume our life of adventures. We were four brave cavaliers, four hearts bound as one. Let's rejoin! It's not our hearts that have divided us, just time and fortune. This time, time is with us—and it's time to win something greater than a diamond."

"You're right, d'Artagnan—as always," said Aramis, "and the proof is that I've had the same idea. But you know me, ever anxious, imagining trouble. I was thinking that, the way things are today, we'd need allies. And then one came to me, speaking about our prowess in former days, and very persuasively too. I'll tell you frankly: I'm talking about the coadjutor."

"Monsieur de Gondy, the cardinal's enemy!" cried d'Artagnan.

"No—the king's friend," said Aramis. "The king's friend, do you hear? And I desire to serve the king—which is, after all, the duty of a gentleman."

"But . . . but the king is with Mazarin!"

"By fate, but not by his will; not by the urgings of his heart. The poor child is caught in the snare of his own enemies."

"*Ah çà!* But, my dear Aramis, what you propose leads to nothing less than civil war."

"War, indeed . . . war for the king."

"But the king will be at the head of Mazarin's army."

"But his heart will be with the army commanded by Monsieur de Beaufort."

"Monsieur de Beaufort? He's locked up in Vincennes."

"Did I say Monsieur de Beaufort?" said Aramis. "It could be anyone. Say Monsieur de Beaufort; say Monsieur le Prince de Condé."

"But Monsieur le Prince is committed to the army of the cardinal."

"Ah, er, yes!" said Aramis. "Of course! Though there have been certain

. . . discussions. However, if not Monsieur le Prince, say Monsieur de Gondy . . ."

"But Monsieur de Gondy wants to be a cardinal—he's asked for his red hat."

"And cardinals can't be generals?" said Aramis. "Look around you. Here are four cardinals who commanded armies just as well as Messieurs de Guébriant and de Gassion."

"Oh, but really, a humpbacked general?"

"When he's clad in armor, no one will notice his hump. Didn't Alexander have a limp, and wasn't Hannibal half blind?"

"And you see advantages to allying with this party?" asked d'Artagnan.

"I see the protection of powerful princes."

"Who are proscribed by the government."

"Balanced out by the Parliament and the rioters."

"But for this to work out . . . the king would have to be separated from his mother."

"Hmm. That could happen."

"Not likely!" said d'Artagnan, returning to his first conviction. "Think, Aramis, I appeal to you—you know Anne of Austria as well as I. Would she ever forget that her son is her safety and her anchor, that her life and fortunes are entirely bound up with his? If she broke with Mazarin she would have to follow her son and go over to the side of the princes—but you know there are . . . reasons . . . why she'll never abandon Mazarin."

"You're probably right," Aramis sighed, "but I just can't join him."

"With him, all right," said d'Artagnan, "but what about with me?"

"With nobody, I'm afraid. I'm a priest—what do I have to do with politics? I just read my breviary. I keep to my small circle of chatty abbots and witty women, and the more noise there is in public affairs, the less notice will be taken of my private life. I'm doing wonderfully well on my own, cher ami, and the less I meddle, the better off I'll be."

"Well, all right, then," said d'Artagnan. "I can't argue with your philosophy. I don't know what devil stung me and made me ambitious. After all, my position keeps me fed, and with the retirement of poor old Monsieur de Tréville, I may yet be made captain, which comes with a very pretty marshal's baton for a cadet from Gascony. If I'm in need of adventures, I can always accept Porthos's invitation and go hunt on his lands. Where are Porthos's lands, by the way?"

"You don't know? Well, I do. He has ten leagues of woods, hills, and dales—he's the Lord of Peaks and Plains and contends for his feudal rights with the Bishop of Noyon."

"Well," d'Artagnan said to himself, "at last we've got something I needed to know: Porthos is in Picardy." Then aloud: "And has he resumed his old name of du Vallon?"

"Yes, and he's added to it *de Bracieux*, which used to be a barony, by my faith!"

"So Porthos is finally a baron!"

"I don't doubt it. His 'Baroness Porthos' is particularly impressive!" And the two friends laughed.

"So," continued d'Artagnan, "you'll have nothing to do with Mazarin?"

"Nor you with the princes?"

"I'm afraid not. All right then, we'll keep to ourselves and remain friends, neither Cardinalists nor Frondeurs."

"Yes," said Aramis. "Just musketeers."

"Even with the priest's collar?" said d'Artagnan.

"Especially with the priest's collar," said Aramis. "That's what makes it so charming!"

"Very well, then—adieu," said d'Artagnan.

"I won't keep you, *mon cher*," said Aramis, "because I know where you'd have to sleep, and I can't see you spending the night in the shed with Planchet."

"Eh, I'm barely three leagues from Paris, the horses are rested, and in just over an hour I'll be home." And d'Artagnan poured out two last glasses of wine. "To our old days!" he said.

"Yes," said Aramis. "Sadly, those days are behind us. *Tempus fugit irreparabile . . .*"

"Bah!" said d'Artagnan. "They may yet return. If you want me, I'm in the Rue Tiquetonne, Hôtel de La Chevrette."

"And I'm in the Monastery of the Jesuits: by the door from six in the morning until eight at night, and by the window from eight at night until six in the morning."

"Goodbye, my friend."

"Oh, I'm not leaving you yet! Let me see you out." And he took up his sword and cloak.

"He wants to make sure I'm out of the way," said d'Artagnan to himself.

Aramis whistled for Bazin, but Bazin was sleeping in the antechamber over the remains of his supper, and Aramis had to shake him by the ear to wake him.

Bazin stretched out his arms, rubbed his eyes, and curled back up again. "Come, come, Master Sleeper," said Aramis, "rouse yourself."

"But Monsieur," said Bazin, yawning enough to break his jaw, "the ladder is still at the window."

"Get the gardener's ladder. Didn't you see the trouble d'Artagnan had getting up? He'll need help getting down."

D'Artagnan was about to assure Aramis that he could get down on his own, when he had an idea that silenced him.

Bazin sighed heavily and went to fetch the ladder. A few moments later, a good, solid wooden ladder was placed against the windowsill. "That's more like it," said d'Artagnan. "Why, even a woman could go up and down a ladder like that."

That brought a sharp look from Aramis, who seemed to wonder what he meant, but d'Artagnan gave him his most naïve smile.

And then he put his foot on the top rung of the ladder and climbed down.

A moment later he was on the ground. Bazin was still at the window. "One moment," said Aramis. "I'll join you."

Both down, the two walked toward the shed. At their approach Planchet came out, holding the horses by their bridles.

"Excellent!" said Aramis. "Here's a servant who's active and alert—not like that lazy Bazin, who's good for nothing since he became a beadle. Follow us, Planchet, until we reach the outskirts of the village."

And the two friends rode through the village, talking of this and that, until, at the last house: "On your way then, *cher ami*," said Aramis. "Follow your fate: Dame Fortune smiles on you, and don't let her escape, for she's a lady, and must be treated accordingly. As for me, I remain here, in humility and leisure. Adieu!"

"So, you're sure," said d'Artagnan, "that what I had to offer you is of no interest?"

"On the contrary, it would appeal to me strongly if I were anybody but who I am," said Aramis. "I'm a bundle of contradictions: what I hate one day, I love another, and vice versa. Unlike you, I can't settle on anything like a fixed plan."

"You are such a liar," d'Artagnan said to himself. "Of all of us, you're the one who knows best how to set a goal and stalk it by secret steps."

"Farewell, *mon cher*," Aramis continued. "Thank you for your good intentions toward me, and most of all for those happy memories that your visit has reawakened."

They embraced. Planchet was already mounted; d'Artagnan climbed into his own saddle, then shook Aramis's hand one last time. The riders spurred their horses and rode off toward Paris.

Aramis remained standing in the middle of the street until he'd lost sight of them at the curve of the road. But about two hundred paces beyond it, d'Artagnan stopped short, jumped down, and threw his bridle to Planchet. He took his pistols from their saddle holsters and thrust them through his belt. "What's wrong, Monsieur?" said Planchet, taken aback.

"What's wrong," said d'Artagnan, "is that no matter how sly he is, I won't be his dupe. Just don't move—wait right here by the side of the road until I come back."

With these words, d'Artagnan jumped the ditch by the side of the road and set off across the fields to circle around the village. He had noticed that the acreage between the house occupied by Madame de Longueville and the Jesuit monastery was mainly empty space enclosed by a thick hedge. An hour before he might have had a hard time finding this hedge, but since then the moon had risen, and though it was sometimes obscured by clouds, it still shone brightly enough for him to find his way.

D'Artagnan found the hedge and hunkered down behind it. As he'd passed the large château described earlier, he'd noticed that the same single window was once again lit. He smiled, convinced that Aramis had not yet returned home, and that when he did, it would not be alone.

Indeed, after a moment he heard footsteps approaching, and voices speaking low.

At the corner of the hedgerow, the footsteps stopped.

D'Artagnan dropped to one knee and did his best to merge with the hedge.

At that moment two figures came into view—two men, to d'Artagnan's astonishment. But his astonishment faded when one spoke in a soft and harmonious voice; for one of the two men was a woman garbed as a cavalier.

"Don't worry, dear René," said the soft voice. "That won't happen again. While waiting, I discovered a passage from the cellar that goes out under the street. You just have to raise a paving stone to find your way in."

"Oh!" said a second voice, which d'Artagnan recognized as that of Aramis. "I swear to you, Princess, that if our reputations didn't depend on these subterfuges, I'd rather risk my life . . ."

"Yes, yes, I know you're as brave and adventurous as any man in the world—but you don't belong just to me, you belong to our whole faction. So be careful."

"I shall always obey, Madame," said Aramis, "when commanded by a voice as sweet as yours." He kissed her hand tenderly.

"Ahh!" cried the sweet-voiced cavalier.

"What?" asked Aramis.

"Can't you see? The wind has blown off my hat!"

Aramis leapt after the fugitive felt. D'Artagnan took advantage of the confusion to find himself a less dense spot in the hedge from whence he could get a better look at the impostor cavalier. Just at that moment the moon, as inquisitive, perhaps, as our officer, came out from behind a cloud, and in the sudden clarity d'Artagnan recognized the blue eyes, golden hair, and noble features of the Duchesse de Longueville.

As the two went on their way toward the Jesuit monastery, d'Artagnan returned, laughing, to where he'd left Planchet. "Good!" said d'Artagnan, brushing off his knees. "Now, Aramis, I see you clearly: you're a Frondeur, and you're the lover of Madame de Longueville."

XII

Monsieur Porthos du Vallon de Bracieux
de Pierrefonds

Thanks to what he'd learned from Aramis, d'Artagnan, who already knew that Porthos's family name was *du Vallon*, of an uncertain domain, had learned that he was also called *de Bracieux*, and that from Bracieux he was suing the neighboring Bishop of Noyon. So, it was near Noyon that he needed to seek this estate, in other words, somewhere between the Île-de-France and Picardy.

His route was quickly decided upon: he would go to Dammartin, where the road forks, one branch toward Soissons, and the other to Compiègne. At the fork he would ask about Bracieux, and the answer would determine whether he went left or right.

Planchet, still worried about repercussions from his escapade in Paris, declared he would follow d'Artagnan to the end of the world, whether he went right or left. D'Artagnan thought maybe Planchet should notify his wife of his intentions, or at least tell her he still lived, but Planchet wisely replied that his wife wouldn't die of anxiety from not knowing his whereabouts, while he, wary of her sharp tongue, might die of anxiety if she did know them.

This made enough sense to d'Artagnan that he insisted no further, so at about eight the next evening, as the fog began to thicken in the streets, he left the Hôtel de La Chevrette and, followed by Planchet, went out of the capital by Porte Saint-Denis.

By midnight the two travelers were in Dammartin. It was too late to make inquiries: the host of the Cygne de la Croix inn had already gone to bed. D'Artagnan put off his questions till the following day.

The next morning, he sent for the host, but he was one of those sly Normans who never answer yes or no, unwilling to commit themselves by giving a straight answer. Eventually d'Artagnan divined from the host's equivocations that the road to the right was the one to follow, and he resumed his journey based on this doubtful information. By nine in the morning he'd reached Nanteuil, where he stopped for lunch.

This time the host was a frank and honest Picard who, recognizing Planchet as a compatriot, made no fuss about providing the information desired. The domain of Bracieux was just a few leagues from Villers-Cotterêts. D'Artagnan knew that town from three or four visits with the Court, because at that time Villers-Cotterêts was a royal château. So, he made his way there and went to the Golden Dolphin, the inn where he usually stayed.

There he learned what he wanted to know. The Bracieux estate was indeed about four leagues from the town, but he wouldn't find Porthos there. Porthos had been in a legal brawl with the Bishop of Noyon about the domain of Pierrefonds, which bordered his, and Porthos, tiring of a lawsuit that he didn't understand anyway, had settled it by simply buying the estate, thereby adding Pierrefonds to his list of noble titles. He now answered to the resounding name of du Vallon de Bracieux de Pierrefonds and had taken up residence in his newest home. Porthos was apparently collecting titles and wouldn't stop until he was Marquis de Carabas.[49]

D'Artagnan had to wait to continue until the following day, as the horses had just ridden ten leagues and were tired. He could have rented others, perhaps, but there was a great forest to pass through, and Planchet, it will be remembered, didn't like riding through woods at night.

Another thing Planchet didn't like was starting out in the morning with an empty stomach, so upon waking, d'Artagnan found his breakfast already prepared. He couldn't exactly complain about this delay, so he sat down to table, and Planchet, resuming his former humble position, felt no more shame eating d'Artagnan's scraps than Madame de Motteville[50] and Madame de Fargis[51] did eating the leftovers of Anne of Austria.

So d'Artagnan didn't take the road until after eight o'clock. There was no mistaking it: he had only to follow the road from Villers-Cotterêt toward Compiègne, and once through the woods, take the first right.

It was a beautiful spring morning, the birds singing in the tall trees, and broad sunbeams angling through the clearings like curtains of golden gauze. Elsewhere, the light scarcely penetrated the thick canopy of leaves, and the trunks of the old oaks grew so close together that the leaping squirrels dwelled in eternal shade. Dawn had released from the foliage the natural perfume of herbs, flowers, and leaves, which delighted the heart. D'Artagnan, sick of the stench of Paris, thought to himself that when one bore three names all stitched together, and owned such woods, it must be like living in Paradise. He shook his head and said, "If I were Porthos, and d'Artagnan came to me with a proposal such as the one I bear, I know what I'd tell d'Artagnan."

As for Planchet, he wasn't thinking; he was digesting.

As they emerged from the woods d'Artagnan saw the side road he'd been told of, and down the road the towers of an immense feudal castle. "Hmm," he murmured. "I think I recall that this castle belonged to an ancient branch of the Orléans family. Can Porthos have purchased it from the Duc de Longueville?"

"*Ma foi*, Monsieur," said Planchet, "here's a domain indeed. If all this belongs to Monsieur Porthos, my compliments to him."

"Plague take it," said d'Artagnan, "don't call him Porthos, or even du Vallon; address him as de Bracieux or de Pierrefonds, or you'll spoil my mission."

As they approached the castle that had first caught his eye, d'Artagnan realized that it couldn't be his friend's estate: the towers, though as solid as if built yesterday, were abandoned and emptied, as open to the sky as if some giant had split them with an ax.

Farther along, at the end of the road, d'Artagnan found himself gazing down into a beautiful valley, at the bottom of which slept a lovely lake. Houses were scattered along its shores, humble dwellings roofed with tile or thatch, all deferring as to a sovereign lord to an ornate château, built early in the reign of Henri IV and surmounted by stately weathervanes.

This time, d'Artagnan had no doubt but that he was gazing upon the home of Porthos.

The road led straight to this handsome château, which was to the feudal castle what a fop of the Duc d'Enghien's circle was to an armored knight of the reign of Charles VII. D'Artagnan put his horse into a trot and hastened down the road, followed by Planchet grimly matching his master's gait.

After a few minutes' ride, d'Artagnan found himself at the end of a carriageway lined with poplars that led to an iron gate with gilded points and crossbars. Halfway down this avenue was a sort of lord dressed in green, his clothes as gilded as the gate, and mounted on a sturdy hack. He was attended by a pair of liveried footmen and was receiving the respectful homage of a dozen or so peasants.

"Ah ha!" said d'Artagnan to himself. "Can that be the Seigneur du Vallon de Bracieux de Pierrefonds? If so, *mon Dieu*, he's shrunken since he gave up the name of Porthos!"

"That can't be him," said Planchet, who'd asked himself the same question. "Monsieur Porthos was well over six feet tall, and that man's no more than five and a half."

"Maybe," said d'Artagnan, "but look at the way they to bow to him." And with these words, d'Artagnan spurred his horse toward the hack and its respected rider.

As d'Artagnan approached, he began to realize who it was. "Jesus God, Monsieur!" said Planchet, who was coming to the same conclusion. "Is that who I think it is?"

At this exclamation, the mounted man turned with slow dignity and a lofty air, and the two travelers could see, displayed in all their splendor, the round eyes, ruddy complexion, and smug smile of Mousqueton.[52]

Indeed, it was Mousqueton—Mousqueton, grown gloriously portly—Mousqueton who, recognizing d'Artagnan, unlike that hypocrite Bazin, slipped off his steed and humbly approached the officer, hat in hand, so that the homage of the assembled crowd was transferred to this new sun that eclipsed the old.

"Monsieur d'Artagnan, Monsieur d'Artagnan," repeated Mousqueton, his enormous cheeks quivering with joy, "Monsieur d'Artagnan! Oh, what joy this will be to my lord and master du Vallon de Bracieux de Pierre-fonds!"

"My good Mousqueton! Is your master here, then?"

"You are within his domains."

"In which you are so splendid, so blooming, so enlarged!" continued d'Artagnan, listing the changes good fortune had wrought upon he who once had been always so hungry.

"Yes, Monsieur," said Mousqueton, "I'm doing pretty well, thank God!"

"But have you nothing to say to your friend Planchet?"

"My friend Planchet! Oh, Planchet, are you here, too?" cried Mousqueton, with open arms and tears in his eyes.

"In person," replied Planchet. "But I was wondering if you'd become too proud to notice me."

"Too proud to notice an old friend! Never, Planchet. If you wondered that, you don't know your Mousqueton."

"Then well met!" said Planchet, jumping down from his horse and throwing his arms around Mousqueton. "You're not like that wretch Bazin, who scarcely seemed to know me, and left me cooling my heels for two hours in a shed." And Planchet and Mousqueton embraced with such emotion, the onlookers assumed Planchet must be some lord in disguise, so well was he received by their hero Mousqueton.

"And now, Monsieur," said Mousqueton, when he'd pried himself away from Planchet, who'd tried to embrace him tightly enough to touch hands behind his back, but failed, "now let me take my leave of you, for I don't want my master to hear of your arrival from anyone but me. He would never forgive me for not warning him you were coming."

"So, your master, my old friend, hasn't forgotten me?" said d'Artagnan, careful not to call him by either his former name of Porthos or his cascade of new names.

"Forget! Him?" cried Mousqueton. "Hardly a day passes that we don't expect to hear that you've been made a marshal or promoted to replace Monsieur de Gassion or Monsieur de Bassompierre."

D'Artagnan allowed his lips to curve into one of those rare melancholy smiles that still rose from the depths of his heart despite the disappointment of years.

"And you, hayseeds," said Mousqueton to the locals, "stay near Monsieur le Comte d'Artagnan and escort him in honor, while I prepare monseigneur for his arrival."

Planchet, still nimble, leapt back on his horse, while Mousqueton, with the aid of two fawning peasants, remounted his own, then cantered off up the tree-lined avenue at a rate that said more about the strength of his mount's back than of its legs.

"Now that's more like it," said d'Artagnan. "No mystery, no cloaked figures, no politics here: just honest laughter and cries of joy. Everyone seems well-fed and happy, and even nature itself seems to celebrate, as if the trees, instead of growing leaves and flowers, had sprouted red and green ribbons."

"As for me," said Planchet, "I fancy I smell a delicious roast, and imagine the cooking staff lining up to bow as we pass. Ah, Monsieur—what a chef Monsieur de Pierrefonds must have, considering how he loved to eat when he was just Monsieur Porthos!"

"Stop that," said d'Artagnan, "you're frightening me. If the reality is as rich as the appearance, I'm done for. A man in Paradise will scarcely leave it, and I'll fail with him as I failed with Aramis."

XIII

In Which d'Artagnan Finds Porthos, and Learns That Money Can't Buy Happiness

D'Artagnan rode through the gate and found himself in front of the château. When he saw, on the porch, the silhouette of a giant, he immediately dismounted and hurried forward. Say what you will about d'Artagnan, his heart beat with joy at the sight of this tall and martial figure, the profile of a brave and good friend.

He ran to Porthos and rushed into his arms. All the servants, ranged in a circle at a respectful distance, looked on with humble curiosity. Mousqueton, in the front rank, dabbed at his eyes—the poor man hadn't stopped weeping for joy since he'd first recognized d'Artagnan and Planchet.

Porthos took his friend by the arm. "Ah, what joy to see you again, dear d'Artagnan!" he cried in a voice that had turned from baritone to bass. "So, you haven't forgotten me, then?"

"Forget you! Ah, my dear du Vallon, does one forget the finest days of his youth, his devoted friends and the perils they faced together? Seeing you brings every moment of our old friendship rushing back to me."

"Yes, yes," said Porthos, trying to give his mustache the rakish twist it had lost in his seclusion, "yes, we did a thing or two back in those days, when we gave the poor old cardinal such a hard time."

And he gave a great sigh—which d'Artagnan noted.

"In any case," continued Porthos, in a troubled tone, "welcome, dear friend. You'll help me regain my old high spirits. Tomorrow we'll hunt the hare across my fields, which are excellent, or chase the deer in my woods, which are also excellent. I have four hounds I believe are the quickest in the province, and a full pack nearly as good, the equal of any for twenty miles around."

And Porthos sighed a second time.

"Oh ho!" d'Artagnan muttered. "Is my brave gentleman less happy than he seems?" Then, aloud: "But first, present me to Madame du Vallon, because I remember that handsome letter of invitation you sent me, at the bottom of which she kindly added a few lines."

At this, a third sigh from Porthos. "I lost Madame du Vallon two years ago," he said, "and I'm still wounded by it. That's why I left my Château du Vallon near Corbeil to come and live on my estate of Bracieux, a change that led me to buy this domain of Pierrefonds. Poor Madame du Vallon," continued Porthos, with a grimace of regret, "she was a woman of many moods, but she eventually got used to me and my little ways."

"So, you're wealthy and unencumbered," said d'Artagnan.

"True, alas!" sighed Porthos. "I'm a widower with an income of forty thousand livres. Let's have breakfast, shall we?"

"The sooner the better," said d'Artagnan. "The morning air gave me an appetite."

"Yes," said Porthos, "I have excellent air."

They went into the château, which was gilded from top to bottom: the cornices were gilt, the moldings were gilt, even the wooden chairs shone with gold paint.

A table stood waiting, attended by servants. "You see?" said Porthos. "This is how I do things."

"Peste," said d'Artagnan, "my compliments to you. The king does no better."

"Yes," said Porthos, "I heard Monsieur de Mazarin doesn't feed him properly. Try this cutlet, d'Artagnan—it's mutton from my own sheep."

"I congratulate you," said d'Artagnan. "You have very tender sheep."

"Yes, they're fed in my meadows, which are excellent."

"I'll have a bit more."

"No, instead try some of this rabbit from a hare killed yesterday in my warrens."

"*Dame!* What is that rare flavor?" said d'Artagnan. "Do you feed them on wild thyme?"

"And tell me what you think of this wine," said Porthos. "Isn't it excellent?"

"It's quite charming."

"It's from my own vineyards."

"Really!"

"Yes, from that south-facing slope on that excellent hill. It gives me twenty hogsheads."

"That's a truly fine vintage, that is!"

And Porthos sighed for the fifth time—d'Artagnan had been counting them. "*Ah çà!*" he said. "Something's eating you, old friend. Are you suffering? Is it your health?"

"My health is quite excellent, better than ever. I could kill an ox with a single punch."

"Family troubles, perhaps . . ."

"Family! No, fortunately, I'm the only one of my clan left in this world."

"Then why these great sighs?"

"My friend," said Porthos, "no one is aware of this, but I'll tell it to you: I'm not happy."

"You, not happy, Porthos! You, who have a château, with meadows, hills, and woods, and an income of forty thousand livres—you aren't happy?"

"My friend, I have all this, it's true—but in the middle of it, I'm all alone."

"Oh, I see—you're surrounded by bumpkins and rabble who are beneath you."

Porthos paled slightly and emptied a great glass of the vintage from his vineyard. "No," he said, "on the contrary, I'm surrounded by gentry who trace their lines back to Pharamond, or Charlemagne, or at worst Hugues Capet.[53] At first, since I was the newcomer, I made advances to them, but as you know, my dear Madame du Vallon . . ." Porthos stopped, at a loss.

"Madame du Vallon," he continued, "had a dubious background—her first husband, as I'm sure you remember, d'Artagnan, was a mere attorney. They said she was . . . nauseating. Nauseating! At such a word, I might slay thirty thousand. As it happens, I killed only two, and though that silenced the rest, it didn't make me their friend. So, I'm an outcast; I live alone, I'm bored, and it eats at me."

D'Artagnan smiled—here was the chink in the armor, and he readied his blow. "But," he said, "now your wife is no longer a liability, and you're on your own."

"Yes, but you know, not being of the ancient nobility like the Coucy, who were content to be lords, or the Rohans, who disdained to be dukes, all these people hereabout, these viscounts and counts, they all have precedence over me—at church, at ceremonies, everywhere—and I have nothing to say about it. Ah, if only I were . . ."

"A baron?" said d'Artagnan, finishing his friend's sentence. "Is that it?"

"Ah!" cried Porthos, his face lighting up. "If only I were a baron!"

He's hooked, thought d'Artagnan. *Now to land him*. Then, aloud: "Well, old friend, that title is exactly what I've come here today to bring you."

Porthos jumped up in a bound that shook the room. Two or three bottles trembled, fell from the table and broke. Planchet started to clean up, as Mousqueton ran in. "Monseigneur needs something?" he asked. Porthos just waved him toward the broken bottles.

"I'm glad this brave fellow is still with you," said d'Artagnan.

"He is my steward," said Porthos. Then, raising his voice: "He's just an old rascal who's made good, as you can see, but," and he lowered his voice again, "he wouldn't leave me for the world."

And he calls you monseigneur, d'Artagnan thought, smiling to himself.

"You can go now, Mouston," said Porthos.

"You call him Mouston? You've abbreviated his name?"

"Yes," said Porthos, "his old name savored of the enlisted man a league off. But we were talking business, I think, when he came in."

"Quite so," said d'Artagnan, "and we can't be too careful. Your people might suspect something, and there could be spies even here in the country. You realize, Porthos, that these are serious matters."

"Peste!" said Porthos. "All right, let's take a walk in my park to aid our digestion."

"Gladly."

And as both had breakfasted well, they took a stroll into the gardens, down beautiful lanes of chestnuts and lime trees, thirty acres at least, among shrubbery and brushy thickets, where fat rabbits chased each other through the grass and between the bushes.

"My faith," said d'Artagnan, "your park is like everything else of yours. If there are as many fish in your ponds as there are rabbits in your warrens, you must be a happy man, Porthos—assuming you still have a taste for hunting and fishing."

"I leave the fishing to Mousqueton, as that's a pursuit for commoners. I do still hunt sometimes—that is to say, when I'm bored, I'll take Gredinet, my favorite dog, bring my gun, sit on one of my marble benches, and take shots at the rabbits."

"That sounds like fun!" said d'Artagnan.

"Yes," said Porthos. "What fun." And he sighed again, but d'Artagnan had quit counting.

"And good old Gredinet," Porthos added, "fetches the rabbits himself and carries them right to the cook in the kitchen."

"A fine animal indeed!" said d'Artagnan.

"But enough about Gredinet—you can have him if you want him, for I tire of hunting," said Porthos. "Let's get back to that business you mentioned."

"Certainly," said d'Artagnan, "but I warn you, old friend, it's the kind of business that means changing your life."

"What do you mean?"

"I mean getting back into harness, picking up your sword, and resuming your adventures, maybe taking some knocks along the way, like in the old days."

"The devil you say!" said Porthos.

"Oh, I know it would be a shock. You've been spoiled by the good life, old friend, and may not have the iron wrist and the dashing moves that once put fear into the Cardinal's Guards."

"Bah! My wrist is still solid," said Porthos, extending a hand like a shoulder of mutton.

"All the better."

"So, we're called to war?"

"We are, by God!"

"And against who?"

"Do you follow politics, old friend?"

"Me? Not in the least."

"Do you favor Mazarin or the princes?"

"I don't favor anybody."

"Which is to say you favor yourself. So much the better, Porthos, given the business that's ahead of us. Well, to be frank, I must say that I've come from the cardinal."

That title resonated with Porthos, as if it were still 1640 and they were speaking of the old cardinal. "Oh, ho!" he said. "So, His Eminence wants me?"

"His Eminence desires you to join his service."

"And who told him about me?"

"Rochefort. Remember him?"

"Pardieu, yes! He's the one who gave us so much trouble back when we were riding the roads, the one you stuck a sword into three times over. He had it coming too."

"But did you know he's now one of our friends?" said d'Artagnan.

"He is? I didn't know that. And he's forgiven us?"

"Say, rather, that I've forgiven him," said d'Artagnan.

Porthos couldn't quite comprehend this, but it will be remembered that comprehension wasn't his strong suit. "So you say," he continued, "it was the Comte de Rochefort who spoke of me to the cardinal?"

"Him, and the queen."

"The queen?"

"To inspire confidence, she even handed him that famous diamond you remember, the one I sold to Monsieur des Essarts but which, somehow, returned to her possession."

"But it seems to me she would have done better to give it to you," said Porthos. "That's just common sense."

"I'm with you," said d'Artagnan, "but you know how it is! Kings and queens have their caprices. In the end, since they're the ones with the power and honor, the ones who distribute titles and wealth, we devote ourselves to them."

"Yes, that's who we devote ourselves to!" said Porthos. "So right now, you're devoted to . . . ?"

"The king, the queen, and the cardinal—and I've answered to them for your loyalty."

"And you said you've obtained certain conditions for me?"

"Magnificent conditions, old friend, magnificent! You already have money, right? An income of forty thousand livres, you said?"

Porthos bridled. "Yes, but one can never have too much money. Madame du Vallon left my affairs in a tangle it would take a genius to sort out, and, well, I'm no genius. I barely get by from day to day."

He's afraid I'm here to borrow money from him, thought d'Artagnan. "Ah, old friend," he said aloud, "so much the better if you're hard up!"

"How so?" said Porthos.

"Because His Eminence is prepared to reward you with whatever you wish: land, money, and titles."

"Ah!" said Porthos, opening his eyes wide at that final word.

"Under the old cardinal," continued d'Artagnan, "we never found a way to make our fortunes, though the opportunity was there. Not that that matters much to you, who have forty thousand livres, and seem like the happiest man on earth."

Porthos sighed.

"However," d'Artagnan continued, "despite your forty thousand livres, or even because of them, it seems to me a little noble's coronet would look well on your carriage door. Eh?"

"It would," said Porthos.

"Then, old friend, reach for it—it's at the end of your sword! To each our own: your goal is a title, and mine is money. I need enough to rebuild the estate of Artagnan—which my ancestors, impoverished by the Crusades, let fall into ruin—and buy some thirty acres around it. That will do it for me; with that I'll retire."

"And I," said Porthos, "I want to be . . . a baron."

"And so you shall."

"Have you thought to propose this to our other friends?" asked Porthos.

"In fact, I've seen Aramis."

"And what does he want? To be a bishop?"

"Aramis, well," said d'Artagnan, who didn't want to disappoint Porthos, "Aramis, if you can imagine it, has become a monk and a Jesuit. He lives like a bear in a cave, renouncing the world and thinking only of salvation. I couldn't persuade him out of it."

"Too bad," said Porthos. "He had brains, that one. And Athos?"

"I haven't seen him yet, but I'll look him up after I leave you. Do you know where I can find him?"

"Near Blois, on a small estate he inherited, I'm not sure from who."

"What's it called?"

"Bragelonne. It's hard to understand—here's Athos, who was as noble as an emperor, yet all he inherits are mere counties. And what's he going to do with all these counties? The Comté de La Fère, and the Comté de Bragelonne? Eh?"

"It's a shame he has no children," said d'Artagnan.

"Hmm!" said Porthos. "I heard he'd adopted a young man who looks quite a bit like him."

"Athos, our Athos, who was as virtuous as Scipio? Have you seen this lad?"

"No."

"Well, perhaps I'll bring back news of him. But I fear the worst, for Athos's fondness for wine has probably ruined him."

"Yes," said Porthos, "it's true, he did drink a lot."

"And then, he was the eldest of us," said d'Artagnan.

"By just a few years," said Porthos. "It was his dark moods that made him seem old."

"Yes, that's so. Well, if Athos joins us, so much the better. If he doesn't, it'll be just us! We're as good as a dozen other men."

"Yes," said Porthos, smiling at the memory their former exploits, "but the four of us would have been as good as thirty-six! Especially if the business will be as dangerous as you say."

"Dangerous for recruits, maybe, but not for us."

"How long will it take?"

"*Dame!* Perhaps three or four years."

"Will there be much fighting?"

"I hope so."

"The more the better!" cried Porthos. "You have no idea, my friend, how creaky my old bones have become since I've been down here! Sometimes, on Sundays, coming home from mass, I ride through my neighbors' fields just to see if I can scare up a quarrel, but nothing doing. They've either learned to respect me or, more likely, learned to fear me. So they let me tramp down their clover with my dogs, nobody says *boo*, and I come home more bored than ever. At least, you say, they're getting up to some mischief in Paris?"

"Oh, it's charming, old friend—no more edicts against dueling, no Cardinal's Guards, no pesky Jussacs[54] or other bloodhounds meddling with us, by God! In the streets, in the taverns, everywhere, you just ask, 'Are you a Frondeur?' Then you draw your sword, and nothing more is said about it. Why, Monsieur de Guise killed Monsieur de Coligny right there in the Place Royale, and nothing came of it."

"That does sound good," said Porthos.

"And before long," continued d'Artagnan, "it'll be pitched battles, cannon fire, you name it!"

"I've decided then."

"You're committed?"

"Count me in. I'll cut and thrust for this Mazarin. But you swear . . ."

"What?"

"That I'll be made a baron."

"Pardieu!" said d'Artagnan. "It's as good as done. You'll have your barony. I'll answer for that."

And on that promise, Porthos, who never doubted his friend's word, walked back with him to his château.

XIV

In Which We Find That, If Porthos Was Unhappy with His Situation, Mousqueton Was Not

While returning to the château, as Porthos enjoyed his golden dreams of a barony, d'Artagnan reflected on the flaws in human nature, ever dissatisfied with what it had, always yearning for what it had not. In Porthos's place, d'Artagnan would have been the happiest man on earth, but Porthos was miserable because he was missing—what, exactly? Five little letters to place before all his names, and a coronet to paint on the doors of his carriage.

"Will I spend my whole life," d'Artagnan said to himself, "looking left, right, and center without ever seeing the face of a person who's completely happy?"

In the midst of these philosophical musings Providence saw fit to contradict him. Just after Porthos left him to go give orders to the cook, d'Artragnan saw Mousqueton approaching. The brave fellow's expression, but for the slightest shadow, like a passing summer cloud, seemed to be that of man who'd found perfect happiness.

"Now here's what I was looking for," said d'Artagnan. "It's a shame the poor boy doesn't know why I'm here."

Mousqueton hovered at a slight distance. D'Artagnan sat on a marble bench and beckoned him to approach. "Monsieur," said Mousqueton, taking advantage of the privilege, "I have a favor to ask you."

"Speak, my friend," said d'Artagnan.

"I'm afraid that if I do, you'll think prosperity has spoiled me."

"I certainly think it's made you happy."

"As happy as can be—but you could make me even happier."

"Just ask. If I can do it, I will."

"Oh, Monsieur, if only you would."

"So?"

"Monsieur, the favor I have to ask is that you call me not Mousqueton, but Mouston. Since I've had the honor to be monseigneur's steward, I've been known by the latter name, which is more dignified and commands respect from my subordinates. You know, Monsieur, how important it is for the servants to respect one."

D'Artagnan smiled; while Porthos added to his names, Mousqueton shortened his.

"Well, Monsieur?" said Mousqueton, trembling.

"Well, then: Mouston it is," said d'Artagnan. "And don't worry, I won't forget. In fact, if it makes you happy, I'll stop calling you *boy* as well."

"Oh!" cried Mousqueton, flushing with joy. "If you'll do me this honor, Monsieur, I'll be grateful all my life . . . if it's not asking too much?"

"*Hélas!*" said d'Artagnan to himself. "It's little enough to do for him, considering the unexpected trouble I'm about to bring this poor devil who's received me so well."

"Will Monsieur be staying with us long?" asked Mousqueton, whose face, restored to its former serenity, bloomed like a peony.

"I'm leaving tomorrow, my friend," said d'Artagnan.

"Ah, Monsieur!" said Mousqueton. "So, you only came to visit us in order to leave us with more regrets?"

"I'm afraid so," d'Artagnan said, but so low that Mousqueton, who was retiring behind a bower, didn't hear it. D'Artagnan's heart might have been like old leather, but at this it was touched with remorse. He didn't regret enticing Porthos onto a road that put his life and fortune at risk, because Porthos would willingly put everything on the line for the title of baron— but as for Mousqueton, who desired nothing more than to be addressed as Mouston, wasn't it cruel to snatch him away from his delicious life of abundance?

That idea was still gnawing at him when Porthos reappeared. "To dinner!" said Porthos.

"To dinner? Already?" said d'Artagnan. "What time is it?"

"Eh? Why, it's already past one o'clock."

"Porthos, your home is a paradise in which time is forgotten. I'll come, but I'm not hungry yet."

"Come, then—if you can't eat, you can always drink. That's one of the maxims of poor Athos that I remember when I'm bored."

D'Artagnan, whose brash Gascon nature needed little in the way of drink, didn't seem as committed to Athos's axiom as his friend, but nonetheless did what he could to keep up with his host.

However, while watching Porthos eating and drinking with such gusto, the thought of Mousqueton returned to his mind—all the more because Mousqueton, though he didn't wait at their table, which would have been beneath his new position, nonetheless appeared frequently at the door, and marked his gratitude to d'Artagnan by sending in wine of a superior age and vintage.

So, when they reached dessert, and at a sign from d'Artagnan, Porthos had dismissed his servants and they were alone, d'Artagnan said, "Porthos, who will accompany you on our campaign?"

"Why, Mouston, of course," replied Porthos.

That was a blow to d'Artagnan; already he imagined the benevolent smile of the steward twisted into a painful grimace. "Oh?" he said. "Mouston's no longer in the first blush of youth, you know. Plus, he's grown very . . . substantial. Perhaps he's lost the habit of active service."

"I'm aware of it," said Porthos. "But I'm used to him. And besides, he'd never leave me—he's too attached for that."

How blind is self-love! thought d'Artagnan.

"Besides, don't you still have your old lackey in your service?" asked Porthos. "That good, that honest, that intelligent . . . what do you call him?"

"Planchet. Yes, he's back with me, but he's no longer a lackey."

"What is he, then?"

"Well, with that sixteen hundred livres he earned at the siege of La Rochelle by carrying our letter to Lord de Winter—you remember that— he opened a small confectioner's shop in the Rue des Lombards."

"Oh, so he's a confectioner in the Rue des Lombards! . . .Then why is he with you?"

"He got involved in some escapades and is afraid of being found out." And the musketeer related to his friend how he had once again found Planchet.

"Well!" said Porthos. "If you'd told me that one day Planchet would save old Rochefort, and that you'd hide him as a result . . ."

"You never would have believed it. But what would you have? Things happen, and men change."

"That's true about everything," said Porthos, "except for wine, which never changes, except for the better. Taste some of this—it's a Spanish vintage called sherry that I learned about from our friend Athos."

Just then, the steward came in to consult his master on the matter of the next day's menu, and the planning for a hunt. "Tell me, Mouston," said Porthos, "are my weapons in good order?"

D'Artagnan began drumming his fingers on the table to hide his embarrassment.

"Your . . . weapons, Monseigneur?" asked Mousqueton. "What weapons?"

"Eh, pardieu! My equipment!"

"Which equipment?"

"My wartime equipment."

"Of course, Monseigneur. At least, I think so."

"Well, make sure of it, and do whatever's necessary. Which is my fastest horse in a sprint?"

"Vulcan."

"And for stamina?"

"Bayard."

"Which horse do you prefer?"

"I like Rustaud, Monseigneur—she's a good animal, and we get along well."

"She's strong, isn't she?"

"A Normand crossed with a Mecklenburg who can go all day and all night."

"That's settled, then. Get those three animals ready, tend to my arms, and see to your own—you'll need a brace of pistols and a hunting knife."

"Are we traveling then, Monseigneur?" asked Mousqueton anxiously.

D'Artagnan, who'd been drumming his fingers at random, began to beat out a quick march.

"Better than that, Mouston!" replied Porthos.

"We're going on an expedition, Monsieur?" said the steward, whose cheeks of rose paled into lilies.

"We're rejoining the service, Mouston!" replied Porthos, trying once more to give his mustache its old military curl.

These words were scarcely spoken before Mousqueton was stricken with a tremor that set his fat cheeks atremble. He looked at d'Artagnan with such an indescribable air of tender reproach the officer could hardly bear it. He reeled, and said, in a choked voice, "Rejoining the service? The service of the king?"

"More or less. We're going on campaign and can expect all kinds of adventures."

This last word struck Mousqueton like a thunderbolt. It was the terrible days of the past that made the days of the present so sweet. "Oh, *mon Dieu*! What's this I hear?" said Mousqueton, with a look of desperate appeal aimed at d'Artagnan.

"What would you have, Mouston?" said d'Artagnan. "A man's destiny . . ."

Despite the care d'Artagnan had taken to use the right name, for Mousqueton it was a blow to the heart, and he was so dismayed he fled from the room, forgetting to close the door.

"Ah, good Mousqueton, your joy is at an end," said Porthos, in the same tone that Don Quixote used when asking Sancho Panza to saddle his pony for one last campaign.

Left thus alone, the two friends talked about the future and built castles in the air. The fine wine Mousqueton had served them went to their heads, showing d'Artagnan a rosy prospect of doubloons and pistoles, and Porthos a ducal title and the *cordon bleu* of the Order of Saint-Esprit. When the servants came in to show them to bed, they were both asleep with their heads on the table.

Morning came, and Mousqueton was somewhat consoled to hear from d'Artagnan that their campaign would likely be on the battlefield of Paris, well within reach of the Château du Vallon, which was near Corbeil; of Bracieux, which was near Melun; and of Pierrefonds, which was between Compiègne and Villers-Cotterêts. "But it seems to me," Mousqueton said shyly, "in the old days . . ."

"Oh, nowadays we don't make war the old-fashioned way," said d'Artagnan. "Today it's all a political affair. Ask Planchet."

Mousqueton went to pump his old friend for information, who confirmed what d'Artagnan had told him—though he added that, in this war, those taken prisoner risked being hanged. "Plague take it," said Mousqueton. "I think I preferred the Siege of La Rochelle."

As to Porthos, after helping his guest hunt down a buck, visit his woods, hills, and ponds, admire his pack of greyhounds, the faithful Gredinet, and all else he possessed, and after three more sumptuous meals, he asked for final instructions from d'Artagnan, who had to be on his way.

"Let's see," said the musketeer, "I need four days to get from here to Blois, a day or so there, then three or four more to get back to Paris. You should gather your equipment and leave here a week from today; meet me in Rue Tiquetonne, at the Hôtel de la Chevrette, or wait there for me until I return."

"Excellent!" said Porthos.

"I'm off on my errand to see Athos," said d'Artagnan, "hopeless though it may be. I imagine he's pretty far gone by this time, but we must be loyal to our friends."

"It might distract me from my boredom if I went with you," said Porthos.

"It might," said d'Artagnan, "and you'd be welcome, but then you wouldn't have time to make your preparations."

"That's true," said Porthos. "Go, then, and good luck to you. As for me, I'm eager to get to it."

"Marvelous!" said d'Artagnan.

Porthos escorted him to the farthest limit of the domain of Pierrefonds, where they said goodbye. "Well," d'Artagnan said, as he took the road to Villers-Cotterêts, "at least I won't be alone. Porthos is as mighty as ever. If Athos joins us, well then! The three of us will laugh at Friar Aramis and his little dalliances."

At Villers-Cotterêts he wrote to the cardinal:

> *Monseigneur, I already have one recruit to offer to Your Eminence, and this one is worth twenty other men. I'm off to Blois to see the Comte de La Fère, at his estate of Bragelonne near that city.*

And with that, he took the road to Blois, chatting along the way with Planchet, who was a fine companion for a long journey.

XV

Angelic Youth

They had a long way to go, but d'Artagnan wasn't concerned: his horses were rested and well fed from their stay in the lavish stables of the Seigneur de Bracieux. He therefore set out with confidence on his four or five days' journey, accompanied by the faithful Planchet.

As we said, to ease the tedium of the journey, the two men rode side by side, talking away the miles. D'Artagnan had gradually lost the air of a master, and Planchet had long left that of a servant. He was a shrewd fellow, and since reinventing himself as a bourgeois, he'd missed the freedom of the highway as well as the conversation and company of gentlemen. He knew he had a measure of both courage and wit, and rubbing elbows all day with dull common folk didn't satisfy him.

Thus, with the man he still called master, he soon rose to the role of confidant. D'Artagnan hadn't opened his heart to anyone for years, and the two found that they got along very well indeed. For Planchet was no vulgar clod: he was a man of good judgment who, without looking for trouble, wasn't afraid of hard knocks, as d'Artagnan had had the opportunity to see for himself. He'd been a soldier, and a career under arms brings out the best in a man. Moreover, though d'Artagnan had helped Planchet, Planchet was more than a little useful to d'Artagnan. So they were on a friendly and nearly equal footing by the time they arrived in the region of Blois.

Along the way, d'Artagnan, shaking his head, repeatedly went back to the idea that obsessed him: "I know this errand to recruit Athos is useless, but I owe it to my old friend to try, for he once had the stuff in him to be the most generous and noble of men."

"Yes, Monsieur Athos was a true, proud gentleman!" said Planchet.

"Wasn't he, though?" replied d'Artagnan.

"Strewing coins as the sky rained hail," continued Planchet, "and handling his sword with a royal air. Do you remember, Monsieur, that duel with the English at the Luxembourg[55] paddock? Ah, how noble and magnificent Monsieur Athos was that day, when he told his opponent, 'You demanded I reveal my name to you, Monsieur—which is too bad for you, for now I must kill you!' I was nearby and I heard him. Those were his words, verbatim. And just as he said, Monsieur, he touched his opponent only once, and he fell dead without so much as a gasp. Yes, Monsieur, I repeat—there was a true gentleman."

"Yes," said d'Artagnan, "that's true as the gospel, but all those qualities were overshadowed by a single fault."

"Oh, I remember how well he liked to drink," said Planchet, "or rather, that he just drank. But he didn't drink like others do. His eyes revealed nothing as he brought the glass to his lips. Truly, never was silence so eloquent. To me, it seemed he was saying to himself, 'Come, liquor, and wash away my sorrows.' And how he could crack the stem of a glass or knock the neck off a bottle! No one could do it like he could."

"Well, that's the sad reality we're facing today," continued d'Artagnan. "That noble gentleman with the proud gaze, that handsome cavalier so brilliant under arms that one was amazed he bore a simple sword rather than a marshal's baton—ah! He'll have decayed into a bent old man with watering eyes and a red nose. We'll find him lying in the yard, watching us approach with dull eyes, maybe not even recognizing us. As God is my witness, Planchet, I'd turn tail rather than face such a sorry spectacle if I weren't bound to pay my respects to the shade of the glorious Comte de La Fère that was, whom we all loved so well."

Planchet hung his head and didn't say a word; it was plain to see he shared his master's fears.

"And then," resumed d'Artagnan, "to see him in infirmity, for Athos is old now, and in misery, because he's probably neglected what little property he had, and his wretched lackey Grimaud,[56] more mute and drunken even than his master . . . ah, Planchet, it rends my heart."

"I can almost see them before me, staggering and stammering," said Planchet in a piteous tone.

"I must confess, my greatest fear," said d'Artagnan, "is that Athos will accept my proposition in a moment of drunken belligerence. That would be bad luck for me and Porthos, and a real embarrassment—but the first time he goes on a drunken binge, we'll just leave him behind. When he comes around later, he'll understand."

"In any event, Monsieur," said Planchet, "we'll soon know the truth, because I think those high walls ahead, dyed red in the sunset, are the walls of Blois."[57]

"Probably," replied d'Artagnan, "and those crenellations and sharply turned turrets I see off to the left resemble what I've heard about Chambord."[58]

"Shall we go into the town?"

"Yes, to get information."

"Monsieur, as a confectioner, let me advise you that we must try some of those tasty little Blaisois *pots de crème* I've heard so much about, but have never been able to find in Paris."

"Then try them we shall, never fear!" said d'Artagnan.

Just then a heavy oxcart, laden with lumber from the nearby woods for the docks on the Loire, turned out of a rutted path onto the travelers' road. A drover walked alongside, waving a long pole with a nail in its end with which he spurred his slow team. "Hey, there, friend!" cried Planchet to the drover.

"What can I do for you, Messieurs?" said the peasant, in that pure accent of the lands of the Loire that would shame the proudest scholars of the Place de la Sorbonne or the Rue de l'Université.

"We're looking for the house of Monsieur le Comte de La Fère," said d'Artagnan. "Do you know anyone of that name among the local gentry?"

Upon hearing this name, the peasant removed his hat and replied, "Messieurs, this timber I'm carting is from his woods; I fell it in his grove and carry it to his château."

D'Artagnan asked no further questions of this man, reluctant to hear another confirm the fears he'd shared with Planchet.

"His *château*," he said to himself, "his *château*. Ah, I get it! Athos may be failing, but he's still proud, so like Porthos, he's forcing his peasants to title him *monseigneur*, and to call this shack 'the château.' Athos always had a heavy hand with the servants, especially when he was drunk."

The oxen were slow; d'Artagnan and Planchet, following the cart from behind, began to get impatient. "Does this path go anywhere else?" d'Artagnan asked the drover. "Can we follow it without taking a wrong turn?"

"*Mon Dieu*, yes, Monsieur! Don't tire yourself by following beasts as slow as mine. Go ahead half a league and you'll see a château on the right—you can't see it from here because of that row of poplars. But that's not Bragelonne, that's La Vallière. Go three musket-shots beyond and you'll see a large white house with slate roofs, built on a knoll and shaded by some big sycamores. That's the château of Monsieur le Comte de La Fère."

"And is this half-a-league very long?" asked d'Artagnan, as in our beautiful country of France, there are leagues and there are leagues.

"Ten minutes' ride and no longer, Monsieur, with a horse like yours."

D'Artagnan thanked the drover and spurred ahead, but then, still troubled by what he expected to find of the man he'd once so loved, who had contributed so much to his manhood by his advice and aristocratic example, he gradually dropped to a walk and rode onward slowly, head sunk on his chest.

Planchet was also giving some thought to their encounter with the peasant. Never, not in Normandy, nor in Franche-Comté, nor in Artois, nor in his own Picardy, had he ever encountered villagers with such self-possession, easy manners, and refined speech. He was tempted to take the drover for some gentleman in disguise, perhaps a rebel who for political reasons had disguised himself.

Soon they turned a corner and beheld the Château de La Vallière, just as the drover had told the travelers. A quarter mile beyond that they found the white house framed in sycamores, massive old trees that spring had frosted with a flurry of flowers.

At this sight, the usually unemotional d'Artagnan felt a strange lurch in the bottom of his heart, so strong are the currents that flow from the memories of youth. Planchet, not subject to the same feelings, was surprised to see his master so agitated, and glanced back and forth from d'Artagnan to the house.

The musketeer rode a few steps forward and then stopped before a gate, wrought in iron in the elegance that marked the restrained taste of the time. Beyond the gate were some neatly kept vegetable gardens, and a spacious courtyard where servants in various liveries stood holding several fine riding mounts, as well as two country horses hitched to a carriage.

"There must be some mistake, or that peasant misled us," said d'Artagnan. "This can't be where Athos lives. *Mon Dieu!* Has he died, and his property been inherited by what's-his-name? Dismount, Planchet, and go inquire; I confess I don't have the courage to do it myself."

Planchet got down. "You can add," said d'Artagnan, "that a passing gentleman wishes to have the honor of paying his respects to the Comte de La Fère—and if you're happy with their answer, you can say it's me."

Planchet, leading his horse by the bridle, approached the gate and rang the bell. Immediately a servant, white-haired but erect despite his age, came forward to receive Planchet.

"Is this the home of the Comte de La Fère?" asked Planchet.

"Yes, Monsieur, that it is," said the servant, who wore no livery.

"A nobleman retired from the service, right?"

"That's right."

"And who had a lackey named Grimaud?" asked Planchet, who, with his usual caution, didn't think one could have too much information.

"Monsieur Grimaud is away from the château at the moment," said the servant, suspiciously giving Planchet the once-over, as he wasn't used to such interrogation.

"Then," Planchet cried happily, "that's the same Comte de La Fère we're looking for. Please admit me so I can announce my master, one of his old friends, who has come to pay his respects to Monsieur le Comte."

"Why didn't you say so before?" said the servant, unlocking the gate. "But your master, where is he?"

"He's coming; he's right behind me."

The servant swung open the gate and led in Planchet, who beckoned to d'Artagnan. The musketeer, heart pounding harder than ever, rode into the courtyard.

As Planchet stepped onto the porch, he heard a voice from within the parlor that said, "Well, where is this gentleman, and why haven't you brought him in?"

This voice, when it reached d'Artagnan, awoke in his heart a thousand feelings, a thousand memories he'd forgotten. He jumped from his horse and ran to catch up with Planchet, who, smiling, advanced toward the master of the house.

"But I know this fellow," said Athos, appearing in the doorway.

"Yes, indeed, Monsieur le Comte, you know me, and I know you as well. It's Planchet, Monsieur, Planchet, you know . . ." But he choked up and could say no more.

"What! Planchet!" cried Athos. "Is Monsieur d'Artagnan with you?"

"I'm here, my friend!" said d'Artagnan, nearly overcome. "Athos—I'm here."

At these words a visible emotion flushed the handsome visage and calm features of Athos. He took two quick steps toward d'Artagnan, looked in his face with eyes filled with feeling, and then hugged him tenderly. D'Artagnan, all his fears banished, embraced him in his turn with tears in his eyes.

Athos then took him by the hand, pressed it between his own, and led him into the salon, where several people were gathered. Everyone stood.

"I have the honor to present," said Athos, "the Chevalier d'Artagnan, Lieutenant of the King's Musketeers, a very devoted friend, and one of the bravest and most congenial gentlemen I've ever known."

D'Artagnan, according to custom, received the compliments of those present, gave them his best in return, and then joined their circle. As the conversation was resumed, he began to examine Athos.

Strange thing! Athos had scarcely aged at all. His wondrous eyes, freed from redness and no longer buried in dark circles, seemed larger and more liquid than ever; his face, a trifle elongated, had gained in majesty what it had lost in feverish intensity; his hands, long, fine, and strong, were set like gemstones in lace cuffs, like hands by Titian or Van Dyck. He was less heavy than formerly, though his shoulders told of uncommon strength; his long black hair, just sprinkled with gray, fell elegantly to his shoulders in a natural wave. His voice was as strong and precise as it had been at twenty-five, and his beautiful teeth, white and sound, gave an inexpressible charm to his smile.

Meanwhile the count's guests, who had perceived by the faltering of the conversation that the two friends were eager to be left alone, began, with the courtly manners of a former time, to find excuses for their departure— taking one's leave being a matter to handle with grace and care, important to those graceful and careful enough to handle it properly. But then there came a great clamor of dogs barking in the courtyard, and several people said at the same time, "Ah, Raoul[59] has returned."

Athos, at the name of Raoul, glanced at d'Artagnan, as if to see if it inspired curiosity or attention in him. But d'Artagnan was still recovering from his astonishment and noticed nothing. So, it was without expectation that he turned to see a handsome young man of fifteen enter the room, dressed simply but in perfect taste, gracefully doffing a hat adorned with long red plumes.

But something about this newcomer struck him unexpectedly hard, and his mind awoke to a sudden flood of new ideas that, taking shape, began to provide an explanation for the changes in Athos that until then had seemed so inexplicable. For there was a strong resemblance between the young man and the noble count, a resemblance that might explain the mystery of his regeneration. Suddenly alert, d'Artagnan watched and listened.

"So, you've returned, Raoul?" said the count.

"Yes, Monsieur," replied the young man respectfully, "and the task you assigned me is completed."

"But what's wrong, Raoul?" said Athos, suddenly all solicitude. "You're pale—you're agitated."

"It's just that, Monsieur," the young man replied, "an accident has happened to our little neighbor."

"To Mademoiselle de La Vallière?"* Athos said quickly.

"What happened?" asked several voices.

"She was walking with Dame Marceline in the grove where the loggers were trimming their trees, and I was riding by and saw her and stopped. She saw me as well, from the top of a pile of logs, and jumped down to run to me, and—well—her foot came down wrong, and she fell and couldn't get up again. It looked to me like she sprained her ankle."

"God save her!" said Athos. "And her mother, Madame de Saint-Rémy, has she been told?"

"No, Monsieur, Madame de Saint-Rémy is in Blois with the Duchesse d'Orléans.⁶⁰ I'm afraid the first aid measures seemed rather clumsy, and ran to you to ask your advice."

"Send immediately to Blois, Raoul—or rather, mount up and go yourself."

Raoul bowed.

"But where is Louise now?" asked the count.

"I brought her here, Monsieur, and left her with Charlot's wife, who's bathing her ankle in ice water."

With this explanation, the guests needed no further excuses, and got up to take their leave of Athos—all but the old Duc de Barbé, who was an ancient friend of the house of La Vallière, and went to see Louise, who was crying but, upon seeing Raoul, immediately wiped her lovely eyes and smiled.

The duke offered to take little Louise to Blois in his carriage. "You are wise, Monsieur," said Athos, "that's the fastest way to get her to her mother. As for you, Raoul, I fear you've acted foolishly, and this is all your fault."

"Oh, no! No, Monsieur, I swear!" cried the girl, while the young man grew pale at the thought that he might be responsible for the accident.

"Oh, Monsieur, I assure you . . . ," Raoul said brokenly.

"You're going to Blois nonetheless," the count continued, more kindly. "Make your excuses, and mine, to Madame de Saint-Rémy, and then return."

The color returned to the young man's cheeks. After a glance at the count for approval, he lifted in his strong arms the little girl, who smiled and laid her head on his shoulder, and gently bore her to the carriage. Then, jumping onto his horse with the ease and elegance of a born horseman, after saluting Athos and d'Artagnan, he trotted quickly off next to the door of the carriage, looking constantly in through the window.

XVI

The Château de Bragelonne

Throughout this scene, d'Artagnan looked on with a bewildered expression, mouth almost gaping. Almost nothing here had accorded with his expectations, and he was mute with astonishment.

Athos took his arm and led him into the garden. "While they're preparing our dinner," he said, smiling, "I imagine you won't mind if I shed some light on all these perplexing mysteries?"

"True, Monsieur le Comte," said d'Artagnan, who was gradually falling back under the influence of Athos's commanding superiority.

Athos regarded him with a sweet smile. "Then first of all, my dear d'Artagnan," he said, "we'll have no more of this 'Monsieur le Comte.' If I called you Chevalier, it was only to introduce you to my guests, so they would know your quality. But for you, d'Artagnan, I hope I shall always be Athos, your old friend and companion. Or do you prefer the ceremonial because you love me less than formerly?"

"May God forbid!" said the Gascon, with one of those bursts of youthful loyalty found so rarely in those who've matured.

"Then it's back to our old habits—and for starters, let's be honest with each other. Any surprises here?"

"Plenty."

"But what astonishes you most," smiled Athos, "is me—confess it."

"I do confess it."

"I'm still youthful, aren't I? I still seem much the same, despite my forty-nine years?"

"On the contrary," said d'Artagnan, ready to be completely honest. "You're not much like your old self at all."

"Ah! I understand," said Athos, coloring slightly. "Everything comes to an end, d'Artagnan, including folly."

"And your fortunes have improved, it seems to me. You're admirably housed—this is your estate, I take it."

"Yes, a very modest domain—you remember, I told you I'd had a small inheritance when I left the service."

"You have a park, horses, servants . . ."

Athos smiled. "A park of about twenty acres," he said, "twenty acres that are mostly vegetable gardens and pasture. I have exactly two horses, not counting my valet's old nag. My servants consist mostly of four farm dogs, two greyhounds, and a retriever. Yet I don't keep this grand pack for myself," he smiled.

"Yes, I understand," said d'Artagnan. "It's for the young man—for Raoul." And d'Artagnan looked at Athos with a sudden smile.

"You have guessed it, my friend!" said Athos.

"And this young man is your adopted son—your relative, perhaps? Ah, but you've changed, Athos!"

"This young man, d'Artagnan," Athos replied calmly, "is an orphan abandoned by his mother with a poor country curate. I've fed and raised him."

"Then he must be quite attached to you?"

"I believe he . . . loves me like a father."

"But is grateful more than anything?"

"Oh, the gratitude is entirely reciprocated," said Athos. "I owe him quite as much as he owes me—even more, in fact, though I wouldn't tell him that."

"What do you mean?" asked the musketeer, astonished.

"I mean that, God be thanked, he is responsible for the changes you see in me. I was wasting away like a poor lonely tree on eroding ground; it took a deep affection to get me to take root in life once more. A mistress? I was too old. Friends? I no longer had you. Well! This child helped me find what I'd lost. If I didn't have the heart to live for myself, I found it in living for him. Lessons are fine for teaching a child, d'Artagnan, but a good example is better. I had to become his example. What vices I had, I corrected; what virtues I lacked, I pretended to have. I may be mistaken, but I think Raoul will become as complete a gentleman as one can in our degraded times."

D'Artagnan looked at Athos with increasing admiration. They walked along a cool, shady avenue, through which filtered the slanting rays of the setting sun. One of these golden beams caught Athos in profile, and his face seemed as radiant as the calm evening light that played upon it.

Unbidden, the idea of Milady[61] came into d'Artagnan's mind. "And so, you're happy?" he asked his friend.

The watchful eye of Athos seemed to penetrate d'Artagnan's heart and read his very thoughts. "As happy as a creature of God is permitted to be on this earth. But finish your thought, d'Artagnan, for I sense there is more."

"Athos, you're awful—no one can hide anything from you," d'Artagnan said. "And, yes . . . I wanted to ask if you're ever haunted by a feeling of horror, a feeling something like . . ."

"Like remorse?" Athos finished. "Yes—and no. Not remorse, because that woman, I believe, deserved the punishment she suffered. No remorse, because if we'd let her live, she would have undoubtedly continued on her path of destruction. But that doesn't mean, friend, that I'm convinced we had the right to do what we did. Perhaps all bloodshed requires expiation. She made hers; perhaps it is up to us to accomplish our own."

"I have sometimes had the same thought, Athos."

"That woman—she had a son, did she not?"

"Yes."

"Have you ever heard anything about him?"

"Never."

"He must be around twenty-three now," Athos mused. "I often think of that young man, d'Artagnan."

"How strange! I'd forgotten all about him."

Athos smiled sadly. "And Lord de Winter, have you had any news of him?"

"I'd heard he was greatly in favor with King Charles I."

"He's followed the royal fortune, which goes ill these days. See, d'Artagnan?" continued Athos. "It all comes back to what I was just speaking of. That king has spilled Strafford's blood,[62] and bloodshed calls for more. And the queen?"

"Which queen?"

"Madame Henriette of England, the daughter of Henri IV."

"She's lodged in the Louvre, as you know."

"Where she's given almost nothing, isn't she? During last winter's storms, her daughter was ill, it was said, and forced to shiver in bed for lack of firewood. Can you imagine that?" Athos huffed. "The daughter of Henri IV freezing for lack of a few sticks of wood! If only she'd asked one of us for hospitality when first she came, instead of Mazarin. She'd have wanted for nothing."

"Do you know her, then, Athos?"

"No, but my mother saw her as an infant. Have I ever mentioned that my mother was maid of honor to Marie de Médicis?"

"No. You never spoke of such things, Athos."

"Ah, *mon Dieu*—well, you see," said Athos, "the right opportunity never presented itself."

"Porthos never waited for the right opportunity," said d'Artagnan with a smile.

"Each to his nature, d'Artagnan. Porthos has excellent qualities, despite a touch of vanity. Have you seen him?"

"I left him five days ago," said d'Artagnan. He then recounted, with all the verve of his Gascon sense of humor, the magnificence of Porthos in his Château de Pierrefonds—and while lampooning his friend, he worked in two or three jests at the expense of Monsieur Mouston.

"I sometimes wonder," replied Athos, smiling with a gaiety that recalled their good old days, "how it was that we four random souls formed a friendship so loyal it still binds us after twenty years of separation. Friendship grows deep roots in honest hearts, d'Artagnan. It's only the wicked who deny the bonds of friendship, because they can't understand it. And Aramis?"

"I saw him, too," said d'Artagnan, "but he seemed . . . cold."

"So, you've seen Aramis as well," said Athos, giving d'Artagnan a penetrating look. "But this is practically a pilgrimage, friend—you're visiting the Stations of Friendship, as the poets would say."

"I guess so," said d'Artagnan, embarrassed.

"Aramis, you know, is naturally cold," continued Athos, "and is always caught up in the intrigues of the ladies."

"I believe he's involved in a very complicated one at the moment," said d'Artagnan.

Athos made no reply.

He's not even curious about it, thought d'Artagnan.

Athos suddenly changed the subject. "There, you see?" he said, pointing out to d'Artagnan that they were almost back at the château. "An hour's walk, and you've seen my entire domain."

"Everything is charming, and shows the touch of a real gentleman," replied d'Artagnan.

Just then came the sound of a horse's hooves. "That will be Raoul returning," said Athos. "We'll hear the news about that poor little girl."

Indeed, the young man appeared at the gate and rode into the courtyard, covered with dust. He leapt from his horse and handed the reins to a groom, then came and bowed to the count and d'Artagnan.

"Lad," Athos said, resting his hand on d'Artagnan's shoulder, "this is the Chevalier d'Artagnan, of whom you've often heard me speak, Raoul."

"Monsieur," said the young man, bowing to him even more deeply, "Monsieur le Comte mentions your name whenever he wants an example of a generous and intrepid gentleman."

This little compliment didn't fail to move d'Artagnan, who felt his heart gently stirred. He held out a hand to Raoul, saying, "My young friend, every virtue attributed to me really derives from the count, as he was my education in all things. It's not his fault if I took so little advantage of his lessons, but it looks to me like you won't miss a thing. I like your look, Raoul, and your words have touched me."

Athos was thoroughly delighted; he regarded d'Artagnan with real affection, and gave Raoul one of those rare, heartfelt smiles that children are so proud to receive, when they get them.

"Now," said d'Artagnan to himself, who'd missed nothing of this exchange, "now I'm certain of it."

"Well!" said Athos. "I hope that accident will have no ill results."

"We don't know anything yet, Monsieur—the doctor can't tell due to the swelling. But he's afraid there might be a damaged nerve."

"And you didn't think you ought to remain longer with Madame de Saint-Rémy?"

"I was afraid I wouldn't be back in time for your supper, Monsieur," said Raoul, "and you might be kept waiting."

At that moment a little boy, half peasant, half servant, appeared to announce that supper was served.

Athos led his guest into a simple dining room, but with doors that opened on one side out into the garden, and on the other into a greenhouse blooming with flowers.

D'Artagnan glanced at the table setting; the dishes were splendid, and he knew they must be family heirlooms. On the sideboard was a superb silver ewer, so fine that d'Artagnan stopped to look at it. "Ah, but this is divinely made!" he said.

"Yes," replied Athos. "It's a masterpiece by a great Florentine artist named Benvenuto Cellini."[63]

"And what battle is represented on it?"

"The Battle of Marignano.[64] It shows the moment when one of my ancestors gave his sword to King François I, who had just broken his. That was the occasion for which Enguerrand de La Fère, my grandfather, was made a Knight of Saint Michael. Fifteen years later, the king—who hadn't forgotten that he'd fought for three more hours with the unbreakable sword of his friend Enguerrand—made him a gift of this ewer, and another sword that you might have seen in my home, a nice example of the jeweler's art. That was a time of giants," said Athos. "We are dwarfs, these days, beside those men. Let's sit down, d'Artagnan, and dine. As to that," said Athos to the small servant who'd just served the soup, "please call for Charlot."

The child went out, and a moment later, the servant who had met the two travelers at the gate came in. "My dear Charlot," said Athos, "so long as he's here, I commend to your care Monsieur d'Artagnan's servant, the good Planchet. He is fond of good wine, and you have the key to the cellars. Moreover, as he's slept often on the hard ground, he'll appreciate a good bed. See to it, please."

Charlot bowed and left.

"Charlot is a good man," said the count, "who's served me for eighteen years."

"You think of everything," said d'Artagnan, "and I thank you on Planchet's behalf, friend Athos."

The young man blinked at this name, and looked carefully at the count to make sure it was he whom d'Artagnan addressed with it.

"A strange-sounding name, isn't it, Raoul?" said Athos, smiling. "It was my *nom de guerre* while Monsieur d'Artagnan, two brave friends, and I were fighting at the Siege of La Rochelle under the late cardinal and under Monsieur de Bassompierre, who has also passed on. Monsieur here still calls me that in the name of friendship, and every time I hear it, it gladdens my heart."

"It was a famous name indeed," said d'Artagnan, "and one day received triumphal honors."

"What do you mean, Monsieur?" asked Raoul, with youthful curiosity.

"I have no idea what he's talking about," said Athos.

"Have you forgotten the Saint-Gervais bastion, Athos, and the napkin that three bullet holes made a battle flag? My memory is better than yours—I recall every detail, and I'll tell you about it, young man."

And he told Raoul the story of the battle of the bastion, just as Athos had told him the tale of his grandfather.

Listening to this story, the young man thought he heard unfolding one of the exploits recounted by Tasso or Ariosto,[65] a tale of the glorious age of chivalry.

"But what d'Artagnan hasn't told you, Raoul," said Athos in his turn, "is that he was one of the finest swordsmen of his time: arm of iron, wrist of steel, with eyes of flame that missed nothing his opponent might try. He was but eighteen years old—three years older than you, Raoul—when I first saw him in action, and that against proven fighters."

"And Monsieur d'Artagnan was victorious?" asked the young man, whose shining eyes begged for more details.

"I might have killed one," said d'Artagnan, to Athos's inquiring look. "As to the other, I either disarmed or wounded him, I can't remember which."

"You wounded him. Oh, you were a tough customer."

"Eh, I haven't lost it," said d'Artagnan, with his smug Gascon laugh. "The other day, in fact . . ."

But a look from Athos silenced him.

"You know, Raoul," said Athos, "you may think yourself a fine swordsman, but such vanity can lead to a cruel disappointment. I want you to understand how dangerous a man is when he unites coolness and agility, and I can never offer you a more striking example than this. Tomorrow, if you ask Monsieur d'Artagnan very politely for a fencing lesson, and if he's not too tired, he might oblige you."

"Peste, Athos, you're a fine teacher yourself, especially regarding the qualities you attribute to me. Just today, Planchet mentioned that famous duel in the stable yard of the Luxembourg, versus Lord de Winter and his companions. Ah, young man," continued d'Artagnan, "somewhere around here must be the sword that I often called the finest blade in the realm."

"Bah! I've lost my touch while raising this child," said Athos.

"There are hands that never lose their touch," said d'Artagnan, "and just convey that touch to others."

The young man would have liked to draw out this conversation all evening long, but Athos told him their guest had traveled far and needed rest. D'Artagnan protested, but Athos insisted that Raoul show him to his room. Athos followed, to make sure the stories of their younger days didn't continue, and brought the pleasant evening to a close with a friendly hand shake and a wish that the musketeer should have a good night.

XVII

The Diplomacy of Athos

D'Artagnan went to bed, not so much to sleep as to be alone, and think about what he'd seen and heard that evening.

As he was good-natured and had had from first acquaintance with Athos an immediate liking that had ripened into sincere friendship, he was delighted to find him a strong man of acute intelligence rather than the drunken brute he'd expected to see, sleeping off some binge on a dung-hill. He accepted without resentment Athos's superior qualities where they exceeded his own, instead of feeling the jealousy and pique that would have tainted a less generous nature, and in short felt a sincere and loyal joy that gave him hope for the outcome of his plans and proposals.

However, it seemed to him that Athos had been less than frank and forthcoming with him on several points. Who was this young man who so resembled him, whom he claimed to have adopted? What was behind his return to the life of the world, and the exaggerated sobriety d'Artagnan had noticed at supper? And though it might seem insignificant, the absence of his servant Grimaud, whom Athos previously couldn't do without, had been left unexplained despite several opportunities, a lapse that worried d'Artagnan. It seemed he didn't have his friend's full confidence, or that Athos was bound by some secret obligation, and might even have been warned in advance about his visit.

He couldn't help thinking of Rochefort, and what he'd told him at Notre Dame. Could Rochefort have warned Athos that d'Artagnan was coming?

D'Artagnan had no time to waste on puzzling this all out. He resolved to find the answers to these questions on the following day.

However, he also thought that it's best to ride cautiously over unknown terrain, and he probably should take several days in scouting out this new

Athos to account for his changed ways and habits. If he could gain the confidence of the naïve young Raoul, perhaps by fencing or going hunting with him, he might be able to find out what he needed to know to connect the new Athos with the Athos of times past. It ought to be easy, if the trusting frankness of his teacher was reflected in the heart and mind of the student. But d'Artagnan was wary of overplaying his hand with the young man by making an awkward interrogation, as he knew that one false move would be enough to uncover his maneuvers to the eyes of Athos.

Further, it must be said that d'Artagnan, though ready to employ finesse against sly Aramis, or take advantage of Porthos's vanity, was unwilling to try deceit on the noble and forthright Athos. It seemed to him that, while he might be able to outfox Aramis and Porthos in matters of diplomacy, he had no such chance with Athos.

"Ah, why isn't silent old Grimaud here?" d'Artagnan mused. "His silence would have told me a lot, for never was anyone so eloquent in his silence as Grimaud!"

Meanwhile, the daytime activity of the estate gradually wound down: he heard doors and shutters being closed, movement ceased, and the sound of dogs barking to each other across the fields slowed and then stopped. Finally, around midnight a nightingale that had been singing in a nearby grove trailed off and fell asleep. The only noise remaining in the château was a monotonous pacing from the room below his own, which he supposed must be the bedchamber of Athos.

"He's walking and thinking," d'Artagnan thought, "but about what? It's impossible to know. All one can guess is that it must be important to him."

Eventually even this sound ceased, and he assumed Athos had gone to bed. In the silence, fatigue crept up on d'Artagnan; he closed his eyes in his turn, and almost immediately fell asleep.

D'Artagnan never needed much sleep. Dawn had scarcely gilded his curtains before he jumped out of bed and opened the windows. Through them he thought he saw someone prowling furtively and quietly across the stable yard. D'Artagnan had a habit of paying attention to everything that might be useful, so he silently watched the prowler until he recognized the garnet coat and dark hair of Raoul.

The young man, for it was indeed Raoul, opened the stable door and brought out the bay horse he'd ridden the day before, and saddled and bridled it with as much speed and skill as an expert groom. Then he led the beast down the path to the garden, opened a small side gate that let out onto a trail, drew the horse outside, closed the gate behind, and mounted and rode off. Over the top of the wall d'Artagnan saw him fly by like an arrow, bending down under the overhanging branches of the maples and flowering acacias.

D'Artagnan had noted the day before that that was the road to Blois. "Ah ha!" said the Gascon. "Here's a young gallant who doesn't share Athos's disdain for the fair sex. He's not going hunting, as he took neither arms nor dogs; he's not been sent with a message, because he's sneaking away. Is it me he's hiding from, or his father? . . . Because I'm sure the count must be his father. Parbleu! I'll learn the answer, because I'll bring it up with Athos himself."

The sun rose, and all the sounds d'Artagnan had heard grow silent the night before began successively to return, one after another: the birds in the branches, the dogs in the barn, the sheep in the field, even the boats on the Loire seemed to come alive, rocking at their moorings or bearing away with the current. To avoid disturbing anyone, d'Artagnan remained quietly at his window until he heard all the château's doors and shutters being thrown open. Then he combed back his hair, gave his mustache a final twist, brushed the edge of his hat against the sleeve of his coat, and went downstairs. He was on the last step of the bottom flight when he saw Athos outside in the garden, bent over the ground like a man looking for a lost coin.

"*Bonjour,*" said d'Artagnan.

"Bonjour, friend. Did you have a good night?"

"Very good, just like the supper that sent me there, and your reception before that. But what are you looking at with such care? Have you become a tulip fancier?"

"Don't mock, my friend. Living in the country, our tastes change, and we come to love all the beautiful things that God's gaze draws forth from the earth, and which we disdain in the cities. I was just looking at these irises planted by the pond, which are bent and broken. I have the clumsiest gardeners in the world—they bring the horses out to water them, and walk them across the flowerbed."

D'Artagnan smiled. "Really? Is that what you think?" And he led his friend along the path, where other plants were similarly crushed. "Looks like there are more this way, Athos."

"But yes! Also freshly broken?"

"Just as fresh." said d'Artagnan.

"Who went this way this morning?" Athos wondered anxiously. "Has a horse escaped the stable?"

"Unlikely," said d'Artagnan, "since the hoof-prints are equal and regular."

"Where's Raoul?" cried Athos. "Why haven't I seen him?"

"Easy, now!" said d'Artagnan, putting a finger to his smiling lips.

"What's he done?" asked Athos.

D'Artagnan related what he'd seen, while carefully watching his host's expression.

"Ah! I guess it all now," said Athos, with a slight shrug of his shoulders. "The poor boy has gone to Blois."

"To do what?"

"Eh, *mon Dieu*! To ask after the little girl, La Vallière. You recall, the child who sprained her ankle yesterday."

"You think so?" said d'Artagnan, incredulous.

"I not only think so, I'm sure of it," said Athos. "Haven't you noticed that Raoul is in love?"

"With whom? That seven-year-old child?"

"Friend, at Raoul's age, the heart is so full, it must overflow upon something, whether dream or reality. Well, his love for her is half of one and half the other."

"You're kidding me. That little girl?"

"Didn't you see her? She's the prettiest little thing in all the world: silver-blond hair, blue eyes adoring and mischievous at the same time."

"But what do you think of this feeling?"

"I don't oppose it, though I smile and gently make fun of Raoul. But a young heart's needs are so urgent, their feelings of yearning and melancholy so sweet and so sad, it often seems very much like true love. I remember when I was Raoul's age I fell in love with a Greek statue that good King Henri IV had given my father, and thought I'd go mad with grief when I was told that the story of Pygmalion was only a fable."

"A folly of idleness. You don't keep Raoul busy enough, so he fills the time in his own way."

"True enough. I've thought of moving away."

"Good idea."

"No doubt—but it would break his heart, and he'd suffer as much as if it were true love. For three or four years, since he himself was a child, he's admired and then adored this little doll, and if we stay here, it will ripen into true love. These youngsters share their dreams all day long and make plans as if they were lovers who were twenty years old. For a while, this made La Vallière's parents smile, but now I think they're beginning to frown."

"Childishness! Raoul just needs something to distract him. Get him away from here soon, or, morbleu, you'll never make a man of him!"

"I think," said Athos, "I'll send him to Paris."

"Ah!" said d'Artagnan. He thought this was his cue to begin his attack. "If you want," he said, "I think we could make a career for this young man."

"Ah!" said Athos in his turn.

"I want to consult you on a certain matter I've been thinking about."

"Say on."

"Do you think it might be time to rejoin the service?"

"But haven't you been in the service all along, d'Artagnan?"

"No, but listen: I mean active service. Aren't you tempted sometimes to return to our old life? I believe there are serious rewards to be gained, and you could relive the exploits of our youth along with me and Porthos."

"So, you're making me an actual proposition!" said Athos.

"Honest and true."

"To take the field again?"

"Yes."

"Who for and who against?" asked Athos, fixing his clear and benevolent gaze on the Gascon.

"The devil! You come right to the point."

"And I hit what I aim at. Listen carefully, d'Artagnan. There is only one person, or rather one cause, that a man like me can serve: that of the king."

"But of course," said the musketeer.

"Yes—but hear this," Athos said seriously. "If by the king's cause you mean that of Monsieur de Mazarin, we cease to understand each other."

"I didn't exactly say that," replied the Gascon, embarrassed.

"Come, d'Artagnan," said Athos, "no games. These little evasions tell me everything. Nobody likes to admit it when they're recruiting for Mazarin— they act sad and uncomfortable and won't look one in the eye."

"Oh, Athos!" said d'Artagnan.

"Oh, you know I don't mean you, who are a gem of courage and honesty," said Athos. "I'm talking about the cronies of this petty Italian intriguer who tries to wear a crown he stole off a pillow, this knave who calls his party the king's party, while daring to imprison royal princes—though he doesn't dare to execute them, as did our cardinal, the great cardinal. This skinflint, who weighs his golden crowns and pays only with the clipped coins, keeping the whole ones for himself. This buffoon, whom we hear mistreats the queen, and prepares for civil war just to protect his stolen sources of income. Is this the master you propose I should serve? No, thank you!"

"You're more fiery than you used to be, by God!" said d'Artagnan. "The years have warmed your blood instead of cooling it. So, you think this is the master I want you to serve?" And he thought: *Devil take me if I'll spill our secrets to someone so set against us.*

"If not that, friend," said Athos, "then what do you propose?"

"*Mon Dieu!* A simple alliance! You while away the time on your estate and seem happy in your golden daydream. Porthos has maybe fifty or sixty thousand livres of income, while Aramis has fifteen duchesses who vie for the attention of the prelate, as they once did for the musketeer, and lives like a spoiled child. But me—what am I in this world? I've worn my breastplate and buff coat for twenty years, clinging to my paltry rank, without advance, retreat, or risk. In short, I'm dead. Well! When I think the time has come to resurrect myself, you all tell me, 'Don't serve that man! He's a knave! A buffoon! A petty tyrant! An *Italian*!' And I agree with you, but so what? Find me a better master or show me where I can make a real living."

Athos reflected for a few seconds and understood d'Artagnan's position—he'd pressed too far too fast, and now tried to draw back to hide his hand. But he saw clearly that the musketeer's initial proposals were in earnest and would have been developed further if he'd lent them a sympathetic ear. "Very well, then," he said to himself, "d'Artagnan is for Mazarin."

From that moment, he conducted himself with extreme caution.

On his side, d'Artagnan played a closer game as well.

"But it seems to me you have a definite plan," Athos continued.

"Certainly. I wanted to take counsel of all three of you in order to find a common approach, since if we act on our own we'll always be incomplete."

"True enough. You spoke of Porthos—has he decided to seek for his fortune? It seems to me he has fortune enough."

"No doubt about it, but man is so constituted that whatever he has, he wants something more."

"And what does Porthos want?"

"To be a baron."

"Oh, right, I'd forgotten," said Athos, laughing.

You'd forgotten? thought d'Artagnan. *And when had you learned it? Are you in contact with Aramis? Ah, if I knew that, it would explain everything.*

The conversation ended there, for just then Raoul came in. Athos had intended to scold him, but the young man looked so stricken he didn't have the heart, and just asked him what had happened.

"Has your little neighbor grown worse?" d'Artagnan said.

"Ah, Monsieur!" said Raoul, almost choking with grief. "The fall was serious, and though there may be no deformity, the doctor fears she'll limp for the rest of her life."

"Oh! How terrible!" said Athos.

D'Artagnan had had a joke on the tip of his tongue, but seeing how hard Athos took this news, he swallowed it.

"Ah, Monsieur, I'm so wretched!" replied Raoul. "This terrible event is all my fault."

"Yours, Raoul? How?" asked Athos.

"But yes! Wasn't she coming to me when she jumped off the top of that woodpile?"

"There's only one recourse, Raoul: you'll have to marry her in expiation," said d'Artagnan.

"Oh, Monsieur, you're joking about genuine pain," said Raoul. "It isn't right." And Raoul, who wanted to be alone with his tears, returned to his room, where he remained until dinnertime.

The mutual admiration of the two friends wasn't injured in the least by the morning's skirmish, and they dined with good appetite, glancing from time to time at poor Raoul who, with moist eyes and a heavy heart, ate hardly anything.

As they were finishing their meal, two letters arrived, which Athos read with close attention, starting several times despite himself. D'Artagnan, who watched him reading these letters from across the table, and whose eyesight was keen, swore to himself that he recognized on one the compact handwriting of Aramis, and on the other the long, looping hand of a woman.

"Come," said d'Artagnan to Raoul, seeing that Athos wished to be alone to think about these letters or respond to them, "let's go spar a bit in the armory. It will distract you."

The young man looked at Athos, who replied with a nod of assent.

They went to the *salle* on the ground floor, where they found foils, masks, gloves, plastrons, and all the other accessories of fencing.

Fifteen minutes later Athos came in. "Well?" he said.

"He has your moves down already, Athos," said d'Artagnan. "If he only had your cool, I'd have nothing but praise for him . . ."

As for the young man, he was a trifle ashamed. He'd managed to touch d'Artagnan no more than a couple of times, on the arm and thigh, while the musketeer had buttoned him twenty times full on the body.

At that moment, Charlot came in bearing an urgent letter for d'Artagnan that had just come by messenger.

Now it was Athos's turn to watch from the corner of his eye as d'Artagnan read.

The musketeer read the letter with no visible sign of emotion, other than a curt nod when he reached the end. "See here, my friend," he said, "this is the service for you, and no wonder you've had enough of it. Monsieur de Tréville has fallen ill, and the company can't do without me, so my leave is at its end."

"You're returning to Paris?" asked Athos sharply.

"Yes, by God!" said d'Artagnan. "Why don't you come yourself?"

Athos colored slightly and replied, "If I come to town, it will please me to look you up."

"Holà, Planchet!" cried d'Artagnan from the door. "We leave in ten minutes; make sure the horses get oats." Then, turning to Athos: "My visit here just doesn't feel complete. It seems a shame to leave without once greeting good old Grimaud."

"Grimaud?" said Athos. "I'm surprised it took you this long to ask me about him. I lent him to a friend of mine."

"Someone who will understand his signs and gestures?" said d'Artagnan.

"I hope so," said Athos.

The two friends embraced warmly. D'Artagnan pressed Raoul's hand, and made Athos promise to visit him if he came to Paris and write to him if he didn't. He mounted his horse; Planchet, ever correct, was already in the saddle.

D'Artagnan smiled at Raoul. "Why don't you ride along with me? I'm going right past Blois."

Raoul glanced at Athos, who restrained him with a subtle gesture. "Sorry, Monsieur," the young man replied, "I'll stay here with Monsieur le Comte."

"In that case, farewell to both of you, my good friends," said d'Artagnan, pressing their hands one last time, "and God guard you! . . . As we used to say when we took our leave in the time of the late cardinal."

Athos waved his hand, Raoul bowed, and d'Artagnan and Planchet rode off. The count followed them with his eyes, his hand resting on the shoulder of the young man, whose height almost equaled his own. But as soon as they were out of sight, he turned to Raoul and said, "We leave this evening for Paris."

"What! Why?" said the young man, turning pale.

"You may go and tender my farewell, and yours, to Madame de Saint-Rémy. I'll expect you back by seven."

The young man bowed, his expression a mixture of grief and gratitude, and went off to go saddle his horse.

As for d'Artagnan, as soon as they were out of sight, he drew the letter from his pocket and reread it:

> *Return with all speed to Paris.*
> *—J.M.*

"This letter is rather curt," murmured d'Artagnan, "and if it didn't have a postscript, I might pretend I'd never received it—but fortunately it does have a postscript."

And he reread the postscript that made up for the letter's brevity:

> *P.S.: Call on the royal treasurer in Blois, tell him your name and show him this letter, and he will issue you two hundred pistoles.*

"That changes things," d'Artagnan said. "When the cardinal writes like that, then I like his style. Come, Planchet, we'll pay a visit to the royal treasurer, and then spur on."

"To Paris, Monsieur?"

"To Paris."

And they put their horses into a trot.

XVIII

Monsieur de Beaufort

Here are the events that had necessitated d'Artagnan's sudden return to Paris.

One evening when Mazarin, as usual, was on his way to the queen's suite after everyone else had retired, and was passing near the guardroom, one door of which opened onto his antechamber, he heard loud voices. Wishing to know what the soldiers were talking about, he approached in his usual stealthy manner, pushed the door open slightly, and peeked in.

The guards were having a heated discussion. "Well, I assure you," said one of them, "if Coysel predicted something, it's as good as already happened. I've heard it said that he's not just an astrologer, but an actual magician."

"If he's one of your friends, then watch what you're saying, plague take it! You'll do him an injury."

"What do you mean?"

"You're liable to get him arrested."

"Bah! Nobody burns witches anymore."

"No? It seems to me it hasn't been that long since the late cardinal burned Urbain Grandier.[66] I ought to know—I was on duty at the stake and saw him roasted."

"Oh, Grandier wasn't a sorcerer, he was a scholar, which is another thing entirely. He didn't predict the future, he studied the lessons of the past— which can be much worse, if you learn the wrong things."

Mazarin nodded in agreement—but he wanted to know what prediction they were talking about, so he continued to eavesdrop.

"I don't say Coysel isn't a wizard," the second guard replied, "but I do say that if you announce your prediction in advance, that's a sure way to see it thwarted."

"Why?"

"Listen, if we're fencing, and I tell you, 'I'm going to give you a straight thrust, then a thrust *en seconde*,' then naturally you'll parry. Well, if Coysel said loud enough for the cardinal to hear, 'Before a certain date, a certain prisoner will escape,' it's obvious the cardinal will then take precautions to make sure the prisoner does *not* escape."

"Eh? *Mon Dieu*," said a third guard, who'd appeared to be asleep on a bench, but who'd actually not missed a word of the conversation, "*mon Dieu*, do you think a man can escape his destiny? If it's written in the stars that the Duc de Beaufort will escape, then Beaufort will escape, and all the cardinal's precautions won't stop him."

Mazarin started. He was Italian—in other words, superstitious. He went in, and the guards, seeing him, halted their conversation. "What did you say, Messieurs?" he said in a silky voice. "You said Monsieur de Beaufort had escaped, I think?"

"Oh, no, Monseigneur!" said the second soldier, surprised. "He's still under guard. It's just said that he *will* escape."

"Who said that?"

"Come, repeat your story, Saint-Laurent," said the soldier, turning toward the tale-teller.

"Monseigneur," said the first guard, "I merely told these gentlemen what I've heard of the prediction of a man named Coysel[67] who claims that, no matter how well he's guarded, Monsieur de Beaufort will escape by Pentecost."

"And this Coysel, is he a dreamer, a fool?" asked the cardinal, still smiling.

"Not at all," said the guard, sticking to his story. "He's predicted many things that have come to pass, such as that the queen would give birth to a son, that Coligny would be killed in his duel with the Duc de Guise, and that the coadjutor will be made a cardinal. Well, Coligny *was* killed, and the queen not only had a son, but two years later she had another."

"Yes," said Mazarin, "but the coadjutor is not yet a cardinal."

"No, Monseigneur," said the guard, "but he will be."

Mazarin made a face that said, *He doesn't have that cardinal's hat yet.* Then he added, "So you think, *mon ami*, that Monsieur de Beaufort will escape?"

"No doubt about it, Monseigneur," said the soldier. "If Your Eminence offered to give me Monsieur de Chavigny's* job as warden of the Château de Vincennes,[68] I wouldn't take it. Now, the day after Pentecost, that would be another story."

There is nothing more convincing than conviction; it's persuasive even to skeptics, and far from being a skeptic, Mazarin, as we've said, was superstitious. He turned and went thoughtfully on his way.

"The tightwad!" said the guard on the bench. "He pretended not to believe in your magician, Saint-Laurent, so he wouldn't have to tip you for the warning. But as soon as he's back in his study he'll be profiting from your prediction."

In fact, instead of continuing on to the queen's chambers, Mazarin did return to his study, where, summoning Bernouin, he gave orders that on the morrow, at dawn, he should send for the officer in charge of Monsieur de Beaufort, and that Mazarin should be awakened as soon as the officer arrived.

Without knowing it, the guard had touched the cardinal in a sore spot. For five years Beaufort had been in prison, but not a day passed that the cardinal didn't think that he might escape. One couldn't expect to keep the grandson of Henri IV in prison all his life, especially when that grandson of Henri IV was scarcely thirty years old. But if he did escape, what hatred, forged in captivity, would he bear for his captor, the man who had taken the rich, brave, and splendid Beaufort—loved by women, feared by men—and stolen the best years of his life by clapping him in prison?

Already, Mazarin had doubled the watch around Beaufort—but he was like the miser in the fable who could sleep only with his treasure in sight. Often, he awoke in the night with a start, dreaming of Beaufort's escape. Then he would send to inquire after him, and each time was pained to hear that the prisoner still gamed, drank, and sang cheerfully—but while gaming, drinking, and singing, he would pause now and then to vow that Mazarin would pay dearly for all the pleasures he was forced to take in Vincennes instead of in freedom.

Such thoughts haunted the minister during his sleep that night, and when Bernouin entered his room to wake him at seven the next morning, his first words were, "Eh? What is it? Has Monsieur de Beaufort escaped from Vincennes?"

"I think not, Monseigneur," said Bernouin, whose professional calm never left him, "but in any case, we'll soon know all the latest, because the officer you sent for, La Ramée,* has arrived from Vincennes and is awaiting Your Eminence's orders."

"Bring him in," said Mazarin, arranging his pillows so as to receive him sitting in bed.

The officer entered. He was a large, portly man, good-looking, with an air of ease that worried Mazarin. "This buffoon seems less than clever," he murmured.

La Ramée stood silently in the doorway. "Come in, Monsieur!" said Mazarin.

The officer obeyed. "Do you know what they're saying here?" continued the cardinal.

"No, Your Eminence."

"Well! They're saying that Monsieur de Beaufort is going to escape from Vincennes—in fact, it's as good as done."

The officer gaped in surprise. He squinted and wrinkled his nose, as if trying to scent the joke in what His Eminence was telling him, then opened his eyes wide and burst out laughing, the flesh all over his large figure shaking with hilarity.

Mazarin was secretly delighted by this disrespectful display but maintained his grave expression. When La Ramée had had a good laugh and was wiping his eyes, the officer thought it was time to explain his inappropriate mirth. "Escape, Monseigneur!" he said. "Escape! Is Your Eminence not aware of Monsieur de Beaufort's situation?"

"I know he's in the dungeon at Vincennes."

"Yes, Monseigneur, in a room with walls seven feet thick, and iron cross-bars on the windows as thick as my arm."

"Monsieur," said Mazarin, "with patience one can bore through walls, and a watch spring can saw through a bar."

"But Monseigneur should know that he has eight guards at all times, four in the antechamber and four in his room, and these guards never leave him."

"But he leaves his room to go out and play tennis!"

"Well, yes, Monseigneur, for the prisoners must exercise. However, if Your Eminence commands, exercise will be forbidden."

"No need of that," said Mazarin, who didn't want to be too hard on the prisoner for fear of how vindictive he'd be if he ever did escape. "But I must ask with whom he plays tennis."

"Monsieur, he plays with the officer of the guards, or with me, or with the other prisoners."

"But doesn't that sometimes take him near the walls?"

"Has Your Eminence seen our walls? There's a sixty-foot drop from the parapet, and I doubt whether Monsieur de Beaufort is so weary of life that he's willing to risk breaking his neck by jumping down."

"Hmm!" said the cardinal, who began to be reassured. "So, you think, then, my dear Monsieur La Ramée . . . ?"

"I think that unless Monsieur de Beaufort finds a way to change into a bird, I can answer for him."

"Beware of overconfidence!" Mazarin replied. "Monsieur de Beaufort told the guards who escorted him to Vincennes that he'd often thought he might be imprisoned and had devised forty methods of escaping from it."

"Monseigneur, if even one of those forty methods had been any good, he'd have been gone a long time ago."

"Come now," muttered Mazarin, "he's not as stupid as I thought."

"Besides, Monseigneur forgets that Monsieur de Chavigny is the governor of Vincennes," continued La Ramée, "and Monsieur de Chavigny is no friend to the Duc de Beaufort."

"Yes, but Monsieur de Chavigny is away."

"He may be away, but I'm still there."

"And when you're away as well?"

"Oh, when I'm away, I have an assistant who hopes to become a royal officer, and who, I assure you, is a most vigilant guard. He's been with me for three weeks now, and my only complaint is that he's too hard on the prisoner."

"And who is this Cerberus?" asked the cardinal.

"A certain Monsieur Grimaud, Monseigneur."

"And what did he do before he came to Vincennes?"

"The one who recommended him said he was a country man who'd gotten into some kind of terrible trouble and hoped to find safety inside a royal uniform."

"And who recommended him?"

"The Duc de Grammont's steward."

"So, you think he's reliable?"

"As reliable as I am, Monseigneur."

"Is he a chatterer, this fellow?"

"Lord, no! At first, I thought he must be a mute, as he spoke and answered only with signs, but it seems that's just how his former master trained him."

"Well, then, my dear Monsieur La Ramée, tell him that if he makes a good and faithful guard, we'll overlook his problems in the provinces—we'll put a proper uniform on him, and put a few pistoles in its pockets so he can drink to the health of the king." Mazarin was big on promises—quite the opposite of Monsieur Grimaud, who spoke little but did much, as La Ramée had boasted.

The cardinal peppered La Ramée with a shower of further questions about the prisoner, how he was fed, lodged, and furnished, but the latter's answers were so satisfactory that by the time he was dismissed, the cardinal was almost reassured.

By then it was nine in the morning, so the cardinal got up, perfumed and dressed himself, and went to the queen to tell her what had kept him.

The queen, who feared Monsieur de Beaufort no less than the cardinal, and was nearly as superstitious as he was, made him repeat word for word all La Ramée's promises and the praise he'd heaped on his assistant. When he was finished, she said, "If only we had such a Grimaud shadowing every prince!"

"Patience," said Mazarin, with his Italian smile, "that may come in time. Meanwhile . . ."

"Meanwhile? What?"

"I'll take certain precautions."

And with that, he went off to write the order commanding d'Artagnan's return.

XIX

How the Duc de Beaufort Amused Himself
in the Dungeon of Vincennes

That prisoner so feared by the cardinal, whose potential escape preoccupied the entire Court, had no idea how often they thought about him at the Palais Royal.

He recognized the futility of trying to escape, so he kept himself busy by devising new ways to outrage or insult Mazarin. He had even tried writing satirical verses, but had soon given up, as heaven hadn't granted him the gift of poetry—in fact he had a great deal of difficulty expressing himself in simple prose. As Baron de Blot,[69] the great satirist of the age, had said about Beaufort:

> In a fight he shines, he thunders!
> A cannon on the loose!
> But when he thinks, he blunders
> And we take him for a goose
> Even Gaston, when he talks
> Can manage how to speak
> Beaufort's tongue just balks
> Much as Gaston's arm is weak!

So this prisoner confined himself to insults and curses.

The Duc de Beaufort was the grandson of Henri IV and his mistress Gabrielle d'Estrées—as strong, as brave, as proud, and above all, as Gascon as his grandfather, though far less literate. For a while, after the death of King Louis XIII, he'd been the queen's confidant, the leading favorite at Court—until he'd had to give way to Mazarin and found himself reduced to second place. He'd had the bad judgment to be angry at this demotion, and even worse to complain loudly about it, so the queen—and by the queen, we mean Mazarin—had had him arrested and taken to Vincennes by that same Guitaut we met at the beginning of our story, and whom we'll meet again later. Thereafter the queen and Mazarin were freed from his person and his pretensions, and he troubled them no more, popular prince though he was.

For five years he'd lived in a small chamber in the dungeon of the royal castle of Vincennes. This period of incarceration, which might have taught wisdom to someone other than Beaufort, had passed over his head without making any impression on him. It might have occurred to someone else that if he hadn't offended the cardinal, insulted the other princes, and made no effort to create a following, except, as the Cardinal de Retz said, for a few sad and sorry dreamers, he might have been at liberty for the last five years, or at least had some defenders. But such thoughts never even occurred to the duke, whose long imprisonment had only served to make him more petulant, and every report about him that reached His Eminence just reaffirmed the cardinal's decision to imprison him.

After failing at poetry, Beaufort decided to try painting. He made sketches of the cardinal with charcoal, but as his artistic talent was mediocre and the likenesses didn't much resemble their subject, to make it clear who they were supposed to represent, he titled them all, *"Ritratto dell'Illustrissimo Facchino Mazarini."* Chavigny, warned about this, visited the duke and begged him to take up another hobby, or at least to leave his portraits untitled. But Monsieur de Beaufort, like many prisoners, took great pleasure in juvenile acts of defiance, and the next day, the walls of Beaufort's room were covered in portraits with prominent titles.

Chavigny was informed about these additional portraits, which were all done in profile, as Beaufort wasn't good at full faces. One day, while Monsieur de Beaufort was playing tennis, Chavigny had the portraits sponged off and the walls whitewashed. Beaufort thanked Chavigny for giving him so much clean drawing space and made each wall a new gallery dedicated to some aspect of the life of Cardinal Mazarin.

The first gallery represented the Illustrious Scoundrel Mazarin being soundly thrashed by Cardinal Bentivoglio, in whose service he'd begun his career. In the second, the Illustrious Scoundrel was playing the part of the wounded Ignatius Loyola[70] in the tragedy of that name. The third showed the Scoundrel stealing the portfolio of prime minister from Chavigny, who'd thought he was going to have it. In the fourth, the Scoundrel was refusing to give clean sheets to La Porte, the valet of young Louis XIV, saying that clean sheets once per season was often enough for a King of France. These compositions, large and rather complicated, were beyond the prisoner's ability to depict in detail, so he contented himself with simply drawing their frames and lettering out their long titles.

But these frames and titles were enough to provoke Monsieur de Chavigny, who sent word to Beaufort that if he didn't give up these artistic projects, he would be denied their means of execution. Beaufort replied that since he'd been denied the opportunity to have a career in arms, and couldn't be a Bayard or a Trivulce,[71] then he would be a Michelangelo or a Raphael.

One day while Beaufort was taking a promenade in the prison yard, his fireplace was swept clean of coal and cinders, so that when he returned there was nothing he could use as a charcoal pencil. Beaufort swore, ranting and raving that they were trying to kill him with cold and damp, the way they'd killed Puylaurens, Marshal Ornano, and the younger Vendôme[72]—but Chavigny replied that Beaufort had only to give his word to make no more drawings, and he could have all the firewood he wanted. Monsieur de Beaufort refused to give his word and went without heat for the rest of the winter. Furthermore, on another day while the prisoner was out, upon returning he found the room once again whitewashed and without a trace of his frescos.

Monsieur de Beaufort then bought from one of his guards a dog named Pistachio. As there was no rule against a prisoner having a dog, Chavigny didn't oppose the creature's change of master. Beaufort then spent many quiet hours with this dog, and though it was suspected he was training Pistachio, no one knew what he was training it to do. One day, when

Pistachio's training was considered complete, Beaufort invited Chavigny and all the officers of Vincennes to a grand performance in his chamber. The guests arrived to find the room lit with every candle Beaufort could get. The performance then began.

The prisoner, with a piece of plaster pried from the wall, had drawn a long white line representing a rope on the floor down the middle of the room. Pistachio, at his master's command, placed himself on the line, stood up on his hind legs, and holding a stick used to beat clothes between his forepaws, began to follow the line, with all the balancing contortions of a tight-rope walker. After three times walking the length of the line back and forth, he gave the stick to Monsieur de Beaufort, then walked the line again without the stick for balance.

The intelligent animal was lauded with applause. The performance had three acts; the first completed, it moved on to the second: telling time. The audience was asked what time it was. Monsieur de Chavigny showed his watch to Pistachio; the time was half past six. Pistachio raised and lowered his paw six times; on the seventh, he left it in the air. It was as clear as could be and was better than a sundial—for as everyone knows, a sundial tells time only when the sun shines.

Next, the dog was asked to show who was the finest jailer in all the prisons of France. Pistachio went three times around in a circle, then laid down in the most respectful way at the feet of Chavigny. The governor pretended to enjoy the joke, laughing just enough to show his teeth. When he'd finished laughing, he gnawed his lip and began to frown.

Finally, Beaufort put this difficult question to Pistachio: Who was the world's greatest thief? Pistachio went all around the room but didn't stop at anyone, then went to the door, where he scratched at the panel and whined.

"See, Messieurs," said the prince, "this clever animal, not finding what I asked for, wants to look elsewhere. But don't worry, you'll get his answer. Pistachio, my friend, come here." The dog obeyed. "Is the world's greatest thief Le Camus, the king's secretary, who came to Paris with only twenty livres, and now has ten million?"

The dog shook his head *no*.

"Is it Superintendent d'Émery," continued the prince, "who gave his son Monsieur Thoré, upon his marriage, three hundred thousand livres and a mansion near the Tuileries compared to which the Louvre is a shack?"

The dog shook his head *no*.

"Not him, eh?" said the prince. "Now listen carefully: is it, by any chance, the Illustrious Scoundrel Mazarini of Piscina, then?"

The dog nodded wildly, raising and lowering his head nine or ten times.

"You see, Messieurs," said Beaufort to the officers, who this time didn't dare to laugh, "the Illustrious Scoundrel Mazarini is the world's greatest thief—at least, according to Pistachio."

And then it was time for the third and final act.

"Messieurs," said the Duc de Beaufort into the sudden silence, "you all remember how the Duc de Guise had all the dogs of Paris trained to jump for Mademoiselle de Pons when he declared her the fairest of the fair! Well, Messieurs, that was nothing, because the animals didn't know the dissidence"—he meant *difference*, but Monsieur de Beaufort often chose the wrong word—"between those they were to jump for, and those they weren't. Now Pistachio will show you how superior he is to his canine colleagues. Monsieur de Chavigny, be so kind as to lend me your cane."

Chavigny handed his walking stick to Beaufort, who held it horizontally one foot above the floor. "Pistachio, my friend," Beaufort said, "oblige me by jumping for Madame de Montbazon."[73]

Everyone laughed, because it was well known that Madame de Montbazon had been Beaufort's mistress at the time of his arrest.

Pistachio didn't hesitate and jumped happily over the cane.

"But," said Chavigny, "it seems to me Pistachio does no more than the other dogs did when they jumped for Mademoiselle de Pons."

"Wait for it," said the prince. He raised the cane by six inches. "Now, Pistachio, jump for the queen."

The dog jumped respectfully over the cane.

The duke raised the cane six more inches. "Now, Pistachio, jump for the king."

The dog was game, and despite the height of the cane, leapt lightly over it.

"And now, pay attention," said the duke, lowering the cane nearly to the floor. "Pistachio, my friend, jump for the Illustrious Scoundrel Mazarini of Piscina."

The dog turned his back on the cane.

"What's this, then?" said Monsieur de Beaufort, going around the animal from its back to its front. He presented the cane again. "Jump, Monsieur Pistachio."

But Pistachio again turned around and put his back to the cane.

Monsieur de Beaufort once more stepped in front of the dog and repeated his command—but this time Pistachio lost his patience, seized the cane with his teeth, snatched it from the prince, and chewed it to splinters.

Beaufort pried the cane's pieces from the dog's jaws, and then solemnly presented them to Chavigny with his sincerest regrets. He was sorry, but the performance was over—however, if they would return in three months for another session, Pistachio would regale them with a new set of tricks.

Three days later, Pistachio was found poisoned.

They searched for the poisoner, but as may be imagined, the culprit was never identified. Monsieur de Beaufort buried the dog, over which he placed this epitaph: "Here lies Pistachio, One of the Smartest Dogs Who Ever Lived."

This broke none of the prison rules, so Monsieur de Chavigny had nothing to complain about.

But then the duke spread the word that in poisoning his dog, they were just testing concoctions to try on him—and one day, after dinner, he went to bed crying out that he had cramps, and Mazarin had had him poisoned.

When news of this latest trick reached the cardinal, he was alarmed. The dungeon of Vincennes was notoriously unhealthy: Madame de Rambouillet had quipped that the chamber wherein Puylaurens, Marshal Ornano, and

Grand Prior Vendôme had died was worth its weight in arsenic, and the phrase had become a watchword. Mazarin ordered that the prisoner be served no food or wine that hadn't been tested. That's when La Ramée had been appointed to serve near the duke as his taster.

However, Chavigny wasn't satisfied with the death of the innocent Pistachio, and hadn't yet pardoned the duke's impertinence.

Monsieur de Chavigny was a creature of the late cardinal—some even said he was his son—and knew a few of the old tyrant's tricks. He deliberately began to provoke Monsieur de Beaufort: he removed what he had left of iron knives and silver forks, replacing them with silver knives and wooden forks; when Beaufort complained, Chavigny replied that as the cardinal had recently told Madame de Vendôme that her son was in prison for life, he was afraid this terrible news might result in a suicide attempt. Two weeks later, Beaufort found two rows of saplings newly planted along the path to the tennis court; when he asked about them, he was told they were intended to provide shade for him far into the future. Finally, one morning the gardener came to say that they were planting asparagus shoots for him, which everyone knows take years to mature—five back in those days, though in our time advances in gardening have gotten it down to four.

These provocations drove Beaufort into a fury. The duke thought it was time to start employing his forty methods of escape, starting with the simplest, an attempt to corrupt La Ramée. But as La Ramée had invested fifteen hundred crowns in purchasing his office, he stuck to his duty, and instead of succumbing to the attempted bribe, went and reported it to Chavigny. The governor immediately put eight men in the prince's rooms, doubled the guard, and tripled the sentries. From that moment, the prince went everywhere like one of those theatrical kings who's always followed by a chorus, four men before and four men behind, not counting the door-wardens who trailed the rest.

At first Beaufort laughed off this increased security, saying, "It amuses and diversifies me" (he meant *diverts*). "Besides," he added, "when I tire of these additional honors bestowed on me, I still have thirty-nine other methods." But living in a crowd began to wear upon him. He got through the first six months of it on sheer bluster, but eventually, seeing eight other men sit down whenever he sat, rise when he got up, and stop wherever he stopped, his mood darkened, and he began to count the days.

This new persecution provoked a resurgence of his hate for Mazarin. The prince began to swear from morning till night, vowing he'd make mince pie of Mazarin's ears. This was alarming; the cardinal, who heard everything that happened in Vincennes, pulled his biretta down over his ears.

One day Beaufort assembled all his guards and, despite his notorious speech issues, regaled them with this oratory, which had obviously been prepared in advance: "Messieurs, if you continue to tolerate the grandson of good King Henri IV being subjected to gross insults and ignobilities"— he meant *ignominies*—"then, *ventre-saint-gris,* as my grandfather used to swear! I was nearly the ruler of Paris—did you know that? Once I was charged with guarding the king and Monsieur for an entire day, and the queen flattered me and said I was the most honest man in the kingdom. Messieurs, I say to you now: take me outside! With you as my bodyguard, I'll go to the Louvre, twist Mazarin's neck for him, and appoint you all officers with fine pensions. *Ventre-saint-gris!* Forward, march!"

But, as moving as that was, the eloquence of the grandson of Henri IV failed to touch their stony hearts, and no one budged. Seeing this, Beaufort told them they were all blackguards, which made bitter enemies of the lot of them.

Sometimes when Monsieur de Chavigny came to see him, which he did two or three times a week, the duke took advantage of the visit to threaten him. "What will you do, Monsieur," he'd say, "when one day an army of Parisians appears, all armored and bristling with muskets, come to liberate me?"

"Monseigneur," answered Chavigny, bowing low, "as I have twenty artillery pieces on my ramparts, and thirty thousand rounds in my magazines, I'd do my best to cannonade them."

"Yes, but after you'd fired off your thirty thousand rounds, they would take the dungeon, and once the dungeon was taken I'd be forced to let them hang you—for which I'd be very sorry, I'm sure." And in his turn the prince bowed profoundly and politely to Chavigny.

"But I, Monseigneur," continued Chavigny, "when the first of the rabble burst in through my posterns, or clambered over my wall, would be forced, to my very great regret, to personally kill you with my own hands, as you have been placed in my particular care, not to be given up dead or alive." And once again he saluted His Highness.

"Yes," continued the duke, "but since those brave citizens won't have come here without first taking the time to hang Monsieur Guilio Mazarini, you would do well to keep your hands off of me, for fear of the Parisians tying you to four horses and quartering you in your own courtyard—which is even less pleasant than hanging, as those things go."

These exchanges of pleasantries could go on for ten, fifteen, or even twenty minutes, but they always ended the same way, with Chavigny turning toward the door and shouting, "Holà! La Ramée!"

La Ramée would come in. "La Ramée," Chavigny would say, "I commend Monsieur de Beaufort to your care. Treat him with the respect due to his name and rank, and don't let him out of your sight for a moment."

Then he would retire, saluting Beaufort with such ironical politeness that it threw the duke into a blue fury.

La Ramée had therefore become the prince's virtual twin, his eternal guardian and second shadow—but it must be said that La Ramée, that bon vivant, free liver, jolly drinking companion, fine tennis player, and all-around good fellow, had only one real fault as far as Beaufort was concerned, that of being incorruptible. Instead of being tiresome, he'd become for the prince a genuine diversion.

Unfortunately, La Ramée couldn't say the same about the prince, and though he valued the honor of being locked up with such an important prisoner, the pleasure of living cheek-by-jowl with the grandson of Henri IV didn't compensate for almost never seeing his family. He might have had the good fortune to be an officer of the king, but he was also a devoted father and husband. La Ramée adored his wife and children, and though he could see them occasionally from the top of the wall, when to give him some familial consolation they would take a walk along the other side of the moat, it was far too little for him. La Ramée felt that his jovial good humor, which he regarded as the basis of his good health—though in truth it was probably the reverse—was at risk of being lost to so rigorous a routine.

This belief only grew stronger when, the relationship between Beaufort and Chavigny having soured to hatred, Chavigny stopped visiting the prince. La Ramée then felt the burden of his responsibility weighing on him—so when, as mentioned earlier, he was in search of some relief, he found it in the recommendation of Marshal Grammont's steward that he take on an underling. He immediately brought up the idea with Monsieur de Chavigny, who said he had no objection provided the new subordinate suited him.

We'll spare our readers a detailed portrait of Grimaud, since if they remember him from the preceding works in this series, they'll recall his estimable character, which was unchanged except for being twenty years older. The years had made him only more taciturn and stoic—though, considering the role he was to enact, Athos had given him full permission to speak. But by then Grimaud had hardly said a word for a dozen years or more, and so prolonged a habit becomes second nature.

XX

Grimaud Assumes His Post

Grimaud brought all these fine qualities with him to his interview at the dungeon of Vincennes. Monsieur de Chavigny prided himself on having an infallible eye for character, which if true would have been an argument for him really being the son of Cardinal Richelieu, as the persistent story had it. So, he carefully examined the applicant, noting with approval his narrowed eyebrows, thin lips, hooked nose, and sharp cheekbones, all of which recommended him. He addressed Grimaud with twelve words; Grimaud replied with four.

"Here's an able lad, or I'm no judge of men," Chavigny said to himself. "Go report to Monsieur La Ramée, and if you satisfy him, you satisfy me."

Grimaud turned on his heel and went to subject himself to the more rigorous inspection of La Ramée, who was all the more meticulous because he knew Monsieur de Chavigny was relying on him, so he needed to be able to rely on Grimaud.

Grimaud had just the qualities one would look for in a subordinate officer, so, after a thousand questions that received monosyllabic answers, La Ramée, fascinated by the man's austere economy of words, rubbed his hands in satisfaction and signed Grimaud on.

"Orders?" asked Grimaud.

"They are these: never leave our sole prisoner alone, confiscate all sharp implements, and don't let him signal to outsiders or speak at length with his guards."

"That's all?" asked Grimaud.

"That will do for the moment," replied La Ramée. "New circumstances, if any, will bring new orders."

"Good," replied Grimaud. And he went in to join the Duc de Beaufort.

The duke was trying to comb out his hair and beard that he'd been growing out wild and untamed, to dismay Mazarin with reports of his general deterioration—but a few days earlier he thought he'd recognized, from the walls of the keep, the carriage of the lovely Madame de Montbazon, whose memory was so dear to him, and the thought of her carried more weight than thoughts of Mazarin. In hopes of seeing her again he'd decided to groom himself and had asked for a leaden comb, which had been granted him. Beaufort had asked for a leaden comb because, like all blonds, his beard was a bit red, and he darkened it by passing a lead comb through it.

Grimaud came in, saw the comb the prince had just set down on a table, bowed politely, and took it.

The duke looked at this strange intruder with astonishment as the newcomer put the comb into his pocket. "What the hell?" cried the duke. "What are you doing, you clown?"

For an answer, Grimaud just bowed a second time.

"Are you a mute?" the duke shouted. Grimaud shook his head. "What are you, then? Answer, I command you!"

"Guard," replied Grimaud.

"A guard!" cried the duke. "Great. The only thing my situation lacked was this sinister lout. Holà! La Ramée! Anyone!"

At this call, La Ramée came running—but unfortunately for the prince, La Ramée, counting on Grimaud to take his place, had been already halfway across the courtyard, and had to climb, wheezing, back up to the cell. "What is it, my Prince?" he asked.

"Who is this bandit who comes in, takes my comb, and puts it in his pocket?" Beaufort demanded.

"This is one of your guards, Monseigneur. He has many fine qualities that I'm sure you'll come to appreciate as much as Monsieur de Chavigny and I do."

"But why did he take my comb?"

"In fact," said La Ramée, "why *did* you take Monseigneur's comb?"

Grimaud took the comb from his pocket, pressed its teeth into his finger, showed the marks it made, and said a single word: "Sharp."

"That's . . . true," said La Ramée.

"What does this animal say?" demanded the duke.

"By royal order, Monseigneur may have no sharp implements."

"*Ah çà?*" said the duke. "Are you crazy, La Ramée? But you gave me this comb yourself."

"And I was wrong to do so, Monseigneur, because it was in contravention of my orders."

The duke glared furiously at Grimaud, who gave the comb to La Ramée. "I think I'm going to hate this clown," the prince murmured.

Indeed, there are no neutral feelings in prison: everything, people or practices, are loved or hated, sometimes with reason, but more often by instinct. Now, for the simple reason that Grimaud at first blush had pleased Chavigny and La Ramée, his virtues in the eyes of the governor and the officer had become vices to Beaufort, and hated by him.

On his side, Grimaud didn't want to drive the prisoner into a fury on the very first day—for his purposes he needed, not an outburst of temper, but a good, reliable, ongoing hatred. So, he withdrew when the four guards came in with the prince's dinner.

Meanwhile, the prince was eagerly contriving a new joke: he'd asked for crawfish for lunch the following day and had spent this day building a cute little gallows in the middle of his room upon which to hang them. The red color of the boiled crawfish would leave no doubt about the target of this allusion; he would thus have the pleasure of hanging the cardinal in effigy, while imagining he was hanging him in reality—and nobody could reasonably complain about the hanging of a crawfish.

The day was spent in happy preparation for the execution. One returns to childhood when imprisoned, and Beaufort had become more juvenile than ever. On his usual walk, he collected two or three small branches destined to play a role in his comedy, and after much searching, found a piece of broken glass, a discovery that pleased him no end. When he returned to his room, he began unraveling the threads of his handker-chief.

None of these details escaped the sharp eyes of Officer Grimaud.

The next morning the little gallows was complete, and set up in the middle of the room, where Monsieur de Beaufort finished trimming its wooden legs with his shard of glass. La Ramée watched with the curiosity of a father who's always on the lookout for a new toy for his children, while the four guards slumped idly nearby with the bored air that, then as now, is the principal hallmark of the professional soldier.

Grimaud came in just as the prince put down his shard of glass, inter-rupting his work of miniature carpentry to tie his handkerchief-threads into a noose. He gave Grimaud a dirty look that showed he hadn't forgiven him for the day before, but he was so preoccupied with his current project he paid him no further attention.

But when he'd finished tying a sailor's knot in one end of his string and a noose in the other, and examined the dish of crawfish in order to choose the most majestic, he turned back to pick up his piece of glass—and the shard of glass was gone.

"Who took my piece of glass?" huffed the prince.

Grimaud made a sign to show that he had.

"What? You again! And why did you take it?"

"Yes," asked La Ramée, "why did you take His Highness's piece of glass?"

Grimaud, who was holding the fragment of glass, passed his fingertip across its edge, and said, "Sharp."

"He's quite right, Monseigneur," said La Ramée. "The devil! This lad is as sharp as that glass."

"Monsieur Grimaud," said the prince, "I warn you, for your own good, keep well out of reach of my hands."

Grimaud bowed and withdrew to the far side of the room.

"Tut tut, Monseigneur, I'll do it," said La Ramée. "I'll finish trimming your little gallows with my knife."

"You?" said the duke, laughing.

"Yes, me. Don't you want it to be finished properly?"

"I do!" said the duke. "Go to it, my dear La Ramée. In fact, it will be even funnier if you do it."

La Ramée, though not quite sure what the duke meant by that remark, went to work with his knife, trimming the gallows's legs to a nicety. "There," said the duke. "Now, scoop out a little hole in the sand of the floor under it, while I fetch the victim."

La Ramée knelt and dug a shallow depression.

Meanwhile, the prince fitted the noose around his crawfish. Then, with a laugh, he set it swinging.

La Ramée also laughed heartily, without quite knowing why, and the guards joined in with the chorus.

Only Grimaud failed to laugh. He approached La Ramée, pointed to the crimson crawfish twisting on its thread, and said, "Cardinal!"

"Hanged by His Highness the Duc de Beaufort," declared the prince, laughing louder than ever, "with the aid and assistance of Master Jacques-Chrysostome La Ramée, Officer Royal!"

La Ramée cried out in terror, rushed to the gallows, smashed it to bits, and threw the pieces out the window. In a frenzy, he was about to do the same to the crawfish, when Grimaud snatched it from him. "Good food," he said, and put it in his pocket.

This so delighted the duke that he almost forgave Grimaud for the part he'd played in the scene. But over the course of the day, as he reflected on his new guard's behavior and the problems it had caused him, his hatred returned.

The story of the cardinal-crawfish hanging spread rapidly, to La Ramée's dismay—it was the talk of everyone within the dungeon, and even outside it. Chavigny, who in his heart hated the cardinal, shared the story with two or three of his closest friends, and they told it everywhere in town. Thus, Monsieur de Beaufort got two or three happy days out of the affair.

Meanwhile, the duke had noticed that one of his guards had an amiable demeanor, compared to which the dour Grimaud only displeased him all the more. One morning he took the man aside and was having a pleasant private conversation with him when Grimaud came in. He saw what was going on, and then, respectfully approaching the guard and the prince, he took the guard by the arm.

"What do you want now?" the duke asked sharply.

Grimaud walked the guard four paces away and showed him the door. "Let's go," he said.

The guard obeyed. "Agh!" cried the duke. "You're insufferable! You'll pay for this."

Grimaud bowed politely.

"I'll crack your bones, Monsieur Spy!" cried the exasperated prince.

Grimaud backed away, still bowing.

"I'll strangle you with my own hands!" continued the duke.

Grimaud retreated further, bowing again.

"And I'll do it," said the prince, "no later than now!"—thinking that if it was worth doing, it might as well be done quickly. So, he reached out for Grimaud, who merely pushed the guard outside and shut the door behind him.

He turned back around just as the prince's hands closed around his neck like two iron tongs. But instead of crying out or defending himself, he simply smiled, brought his index finger slowly to his lips, and said a single word: "Hush!"

It was so strange to see Grimaud gesture, smile, and speak, that His Highness stopped short, astonished.

Grimaud took advantage of the moment to reach into his vest and draw out a small envelope that wafted a charming perfume, which it retained despite its long residence in Grimaud's pocket, and which he presented to the duke without a word.

The duke, more and more astonished, let go of Grimaud, took the note, and seemed to recognize the handwriting. "From Madame de Montbazon?" he gasped.

Grimaud nodded yes.

The duke quickly tore open the envelope, gaping in amazement, and read the following:

My dear Duke,

You can rely entirely on the brave fellow who brings you this, as he's the servant of a gentleman who's on our side, as proven by twenty years of loyalty. This fellow agreed to enter the service of your warden and be locked up with you in Vincennes to help you get ready for your escape, which we're preparing now.

Your time of deliverance approaches! Have patience and fortitude, and remember that, no matter how much time has passed, your friends and allies still stand by you.

Ever yours, your affectionate,
MARIE DE MONTBAZON

P.S.: I sign my full name, because it would be the height of vanity to think that, after five years, you'd still recognize my initials.

The duke stood stunned for a moment. What he'd sought for in vain for five years—an aide and ally—had fallen suddenly from heaven when he least expected it. He looked at Grimaud in astonishment, and then returned to his letter and read it again.

"Oh! My dear Marie," he murmured, when he'd finished. "So that *was* her I saw passing in her carriage! And somehow, she still thinks of me after five years of separation! Morbleu! Who'd have thought to find in her the consistency of Astraea?"[74] Then, turning to Grimaud: "And you, my good fellow—so you've agreed to help us?"

Grimaud nodded.

"And that's why you're here?"

Grimaud nodded again.

"And to think I wanted to strangle you!" the duke cried.

Grimaud smiled reassuringly.

"But wait," said the duke. And he reached into his pocket. "No one shall say that such devotion to the grandson of Henri IV shall go unrewarded."

The Duc de Beaufort searched his pockets with the best of intentions—but one of the precautions taken at Vincennes was to leave the prisoners no money.

Grimaud, however, seeing the duke's disappointment, took from his own pocket a purse full of gold and presented it to him. "This is what you're looking for," he said.

The duke opened the purse and went to pour its contents into Grimaud's hands, but Grimaud shook his head. "Thank you, Monseigneur," he said, drawing back, "but I've been paid."

The duke was surprised yet again. He held out his hand; Grimaud leaned forward and kissed it respectfully. The courtly manners of Athos had rubbed off on Grimaud.

"And now," asked the duke, "what do we do next?"

"It's eleven in the morning," Grimaud replied. "Monseigneur will please arrange a game of tennis with La Ramée for two o'clock. During the game knock two or three balls over the parapet and off the walls."

"Well, what then?"

"Then, Monseigneur will approach the wall and call down to a man working in the dry-moat to return them."

"Understood," said the duke.

Grimaud's face showed relief and satisfaction; he spoke so infrequently that so much conversation was difficult for him. He began to take his leave.

"*Ah çà!*" said the duke. "Is there nothing I can give you?"

"Monseigneur can make me a promise."

"Whatever you ask."

"It's that, when we escape, allow me to always lead the way—first of all because if Monseigneur is caught, the worst that can happen is a return to prison, whereas if I'm caught, the best that can happen is I'll be hanged."

"That's only fair," said the duke. "I'll do just as you say—faith of a gentleman."

"Now," said Grimaud, "I have one more thing to ask of Monseigneur: that he shall continue to detest me as before."

"I'll try," said the duke.

There was a knock on the door.

The duke thrust the letter into his pocket and threw himself onto his bed. Everyone knew that was his retreat when lost in the depths of boredom. Grimaud went to open the door; it was La Ramée returning from having visited the cardinal, in the scene previously described.

La Ramée looked around inquiringly, but seeing only the expected antipathy between the prisoner and his guardian, he smiled in satisfaction. Then, turning to Grimaud, he said, "Good, *mon ami*—well done. I just put in a good word for you where it counts, and I hope that soon you'll be getting some good news."

Grimaud bowed in a grateful manner, and withdrew, as he usually did when his superior came in. "Well, Monseigneur!" La Ramée said with a jolly laugh. "Are you still sulking around that poor fellow?"

"Ah, it's you, La Ramée," said the duke. "My faith, it's about time you arrived. I'd thrown myself on the bed and turned my nose to the wall so as not to yield to the temptation to strangle that wretch Grimaud."

"I hardly think it was because he said something to offend Your Highness," chuckled La Ramée, trying to make a joke out of his subordinate's habitual silence.

"Pardieu, I should think not! He's like some mute Eastern monk. But I'm glad you're back, La Ramée, for I'm eager to see you."

"Monseigneur is too good," said La Ramée, flattered by the compliment.

"You see," continued the duke, "I'm feeling especially stiff and clumsy today, and thought you should have a chance to take advantage of it."

"Then perhaps a game of tennis?" said La Ramée, taking the hint.

"If you would be so good."

"I am Monseigneur's humble servant."

"My dear La Ramée," said the duke, "you're a most congenial fellow, and I'd almost stay here in Vincennes just for the pleasure of your company."

"Monseigneur," said La Ramée, "I think that wish would be fulfilled, if it were up to the cardinal."

"What do you mean? Have you seen him recently?"

"He sent for me this morning."

"Really! Did you talk about me?"

"What do you think I would talk to him about? You know, Monseigneur, you're his worst nightmare."

The duke smiled bitterly. "Ah, if only you'd accept my offers, La Ramée!"

"Monseigneur, we can talk all you like, but in the end I must disappoint you."

"La Ramée, I've told you, and I repeat it, that I can make your fortune."

"With what? The moment you escape from prison, all your property will be confiscated."

"The moment I escape from prison, I'll be the master of Paris."

"Hush, please! You know I can't listen to that kind of talk. That's a fine thing to say to an officer of the king! I can see I'm going to need another Grimaud."

"All right, then, we'll drop it. So, you had a talk with the cardinal! You know what, La Ramée? The next time he invites you for a visit, let me dress up in your clothes and go in your place. I'll strangle him, and then give up and meekly return to prison—faith of a gentleman!"

"Monseigneur, I can see that I must call for Grimaud."

"No, I'm done. So, what did he talk about, that liar?"

"I'll pretend I heard 'friar' and ignore that, Monseigneur," La Ramée said slyly. "What did he tell me? He told me to keep an eye on you."

"Keep an eye on me? Why?" asked the duke, anxiously.

"Because an astrologer has predicted that you'll escape."

"Really? An astrologer spoke of me?" Superstitious, the duke shuddered in spite of himself.

"*Mon Dieu*, yes! But these wretched magicians only say such things to disturb people, you know—word of honor."

"And what did you say about this to His Illustrious Eminence?"

"That if the astrologer in question was selling almanacs of his predictions, I wouldn't advise him to buy one."

"Why?"

"Because the only way you could escape would be to change into a finch or a wren and fly away."

"Isn't that the unfortunate truth. Let's go play a game of tennis, La Ramée."

"Monseigneur, I beg Your Highness's pardon, but I must ask for a half an hour's delay."

"Why's that?"

"Because, though his birth isn't nearly as good as Your Highness's, Monseigneur Mazarin is so proud that he didn't invite me to stay to lunch."

"Well, then! Would you like to join me for lunch?"

"Not this time, Monseigneur! I must tell you there's a baker named Père Marteau whose shop is just across from the castle . . ."

"So?"

"So last week he sold his bakery to a chef from Paris, one to whom the doctors, it seems, recommended he take country air."

"Well? What does that matter to me?"

"Listen, Monseigneur—this new baker had in front of his shop such delights as would make your mouth water."

"Oh, you glutton."

"Eh? *Mon Dieu*, Monseigneur," replied La Ramée, "one isn't a glutton just because one likes to eat well. It's the nature of Man to seek perfection in all things, including pies. Now, this beggar of a baker, when he saw me browsing his stall, came out all covered in flour and said, 'Monsieur La Ramée, you must help me find customers among the prisoners. I bought this establishment from my predecessor because he assured me that he supplied the château, but upon my honor, in the week since I've been here Monsieur de Chavigny hasn't purchased so much as a tartelette.'

"'Well,' I told him, 'probably Monsieur de Chavigny is afraid your pastry isn't any good.' 'My pastry, no good? Well, then, Monsieur La Ramée, you shall be the judge of that, and this very minute.' 'I can't,' I said to him, 'I have to get back to the dungeon.' 'Well, go on about your business,' he said, 'as you seem to be in a hurry, but come back in half an hour.' 'In half an hour?' 'Yes. Have you had lunch?' '*Ma foi,* no.' 'Well, there'll be a pie here waiting for you, along with a bottle of old Burgundy . . .'

"So, you see, Monseigneur, inasmuch as I'm starving, I would like, with Your Highness's permission . . ." La Ramée bowed.

"Go on, then, you animal," said the duke, "but take note that I, too, give you only half an hour."

"Can I promise your business to Père Marteau's successor, Monseigneur?"

"Yes, so long as he doesn't put mushrooms in his meat pies. For you know," added the prince, "the mushrooms of Vincennes forest are fatal to my family."[75]

La Ramée nodded, though he didn't understand the prince's allusion, and went out. Within five minutes the duty officer came in, on the pretext of paying his respects to the prince and keeping him company, but actually in accordance with the orders of the cardinal, who, as we've seen, had commanded that the prisoner be kept under close watch.

But during the five minutes he'd had alone, the duke had reread the letter from Madame de Montbazon, which assured him his friends had not forgotten him and were planning his escape. How? That he didn't know yet, but he promised himself he'd find out from Grimaud, despite his habitual silence. He admired him all the more now that he understood his conduct and realized that all the little persecutions he'd inflicted on the duke were to persuade the other guards of his hostility. This ruse had given the duke a high opinion of Grimaud's intellect, and he decided to trust in him completely.

XXI

What Was Hidden in the Pies of
Père Marteau's Successor

Half an hour later La Ramée returned, glowing with the good cheer of a man who's both eaten well and drunk well. He had found the pie delicious and the wine excellent.

The weather was perfect for a tennis party. The Vincennes tennis court was a "long palm" green, that is, open rather than enclosed, so it would be easy for the duke to do what Grimaud had proposed and send a few balls over the edge and down into the dry-moat.

However, as two o'clock—the designated time—had yet to strike, the duke wasn't too awkward at first. But he arranged to lose the first few games, which allowed him to get angry and behave as we do when that happens, making mistake after mistake.

Then, once two o'clock struck, the prince's balls began to go over the side and into the moat—to the delight of La Ramée, who scored fifteen points with each fault.

Soon enough balls had gone over that they had too few to continue. La Ramée proposed to send someone down to the moat to collect them, but the duke nonchalantly observed that that would be a waste of time, and approached the ramparts, which were, as the officer had noted, over fifty feet high. Looking down, he saw a man working in the little gardens kept by the peasants on the far side of the moat.

"Hey there, friend!" cried the duke.

The man looked up, and the duke suppressed a gasp of surprise. This peasant, this supposed gardener, was Rochefort, whom the prince thought was still in the Bastille.

"Hey, up there," the man called. "What can I do for you?"

"Be so kind as to throw back our tennis balls," said the duke.

The gardener nodded, scrambled down into the moat, and began to toss back the lost balls, which were picked up by La Ramée and the guards. One fell right at the feet of the duke, and as it was obviously intended for him, he put that one in his pocket. And then, giving the gardener a grateful wave, he returned to his game.

But the duke continued to have a bad day, and his balls went every which way, instead of confining themselves to the court; a few even went back into the moat, but as the gardener had gone, those weren't returned. The duke declared himself ashamed of his clumsiness and declined to continue.

La Ramée was delighted at having won such a victory over a prince of the blood. The prince returned to his cell and went to bed, which is what he did nearly every day since they'd taken away his books.

La Ramée gathered up the prince's discarded clothes, under the pretext that they were dusty and could use a good brushing, but actually to make sure the prince wouldn't go anywhere. He was a cautious man, that La Ramée.

Fortunately, the prince had had time to hide the tennis ball under his pillow. As soon as the door was closed, the duke tore open the ball's outer covering, using his teeth since they'd taken away every sharp implement, except for silver knives that bent rather than cut.

Under the skin of the ball was a letter that read as follows:

Monseigneur, your friends watch over you, and the time of your liberation draws near. Order a pie for the day after tomorrow from the new pastry chef who has purchased the bake shop, and who is none other than Noirmont, your steward. Be careful to open the pie only when you are alone. I think you'll be pleased with what it contains.

> *The ever-devoted servant of Your Highness,*
> *in the Bastille or out,*
> *Comte de ROCHEFORT*

P.S.: Your Highness can rely on Grimaud for everything—he's intelligent and utterly dedicated.

Beaufort, who'd been allowed to have a fire again since he'd given up painting, burned the letter—as he did, though more regretfully, with the letter from Madame de Montabazon. He was going to do the same to the ball when it occurred to him that it might be useful for sending Rochefort a reply.

He was alert, which was just as well, because all this activity drew the attention of La Ramée, who came into the cell. "Monseigneur needs something?" he asked.

"I felt a chill," replied the duke, "and lit a fire so I could warm up. The dungeons of Vincennes, you know, are renowned for their frigidity. We could keep ice in here, and even harvest saltpeter. As Madame de Rambouillet said, the cells where Puylaurens, Ornano, and my uncle the Grand Prior of Vendôme died are worth their weight in arsenic."

And the duke lay down again, covertly stuffing the ball under his pillow. La Ramée smiled sadly. He was a good man at heart, had become fond of his illustrious prisoner, and would have been sorry if anything unfortunate happened to him. And the terrible fates of the duke's three predecessors were incontestable. "Monseigneur," he said, "please don't indulge in such thoughts. Ideas like those are far more fatal than saltpeter."

"You, at least, are a charming fellow," said the duke. "If I could eat pies and drink Burgundy, like you do, at the shop of Père Marteau's successor, I'd be happier."

"In fact, Monseigneur," said La Ramée, "he stocks a proud wine, and his pastries should be famous."

"It certainly wouldn't be hard for his cellar and kitchen to be better than those of Monsieur de Chavigny," said the duke.

"Well, Monseigneur," said La Ramée, falling into the trap, "what prevents you from trying them? Besides, I promised you a sample."

"You're right," said the duke. "If I have to stay here forever, as Mazarin was kind enough to let me hear he intends, I'll need a distraction for my old age, and might as well become a gourmand."

"Monseigneur," said La Ramée, "take my advice, and don't wait for old age to begin."

"Good," Beaufort said to himself. "Every man, to tempt his heart and soul from heavenly grace, must be susceptible to one of the seven deadly sins—if not two. It seems that La Ramée's temptation is gluttony. We'll take advantage of that." Then, aloud: "Well, my dear La Ramée, shall we make a party of it then, the day after tomorrow?"

"Yes, Monseigneur—that's the day of Pentecost."

"Then will you read me a lesson on that day?"

"In what?"

"In gourmandizing!"

"Willingly, Monseigneur."

"But let's make it a private lesson. We'll send the guards to eat in Chavigny's mess hall while we dine here, at your direction."

"Hmm!" said La Ramée. It was an attractive prospect—but La Ramée, who was as canny as the cardinal had surmised, was an old hand at spotting prisoners' tricks. Beaufort had said he had forty ways to escape from prison—might not this tempting dinner be concealing one of them?

So, he thought about it for a moment, but considered that as he would be ordering the food and wine, no powder would taint the food, and no drug could be mixed in the wine. As to getting him drunk, the duke ought to know better than that. And then an idea occurred to him that settled the matter.

The duke had followed La Ramée's internal monologue by the worried expression on his guardian's face—but then that expression cleared. "Well," asked the duke, "shall we do it?"

"Yes, Monseigneur—on one condition."

"Which is?"

"That Grimaud shall serve at our table."

Nothing could suit the prince better, but he had enough self-control to frown and grimace. "To the devil with your Grimaud!" he cried. "He'll spoil all our fun."

"I'll order him to stand behind Your Highness and not say a word, so that, with a little imagination, it will seem like he's leagues away."

"I see very clearly how it is," said the duke. "You don't trust me."

"Monseigneur, the day after tomorrow is Pentecost."

"Well, what's that to me? Do you think the Holy Spirit is going to descend like a tongue of fire to blast open the doors of my prison?"

"No, Monseigneur—but I remember what that damned magician predicted."

"What did he predict?"

"That Your Highness would be free from Vincennes by the day of Pentecost."

"And you believe what such charlatans say? Folly!"

"Me, I care no more than this," said La Ramée, snapping his fingers. "It's Monseigneur Mazarin who cares—he's an Italian, and superstitious."

The duke shrugged. "Well," he said, pretending to a resigned good humor, "I can accept your Grimaud, for the sake of the thing, but nobody other than him. I put you in charge of everything: you order the entire dinner, but it must include one of those divine meat pies you mentioned. You can tell Père Marteau's successor that if he does well, he can depend on me as a customer for the rest of my stay in prison, and even after I'm released."

"You still think you're going to get out?" said La Ramée.

"*Dame*, yes!" replied the prince. "If only at the death of Mazarin, who's fifteen years older than I. Though it's true," he added with a smile, "that in Vincennes we age faster than those outside."

"Monseigneur," said La Ramée, "consider your dinner ordered."

"And do you think I'll be an apt pupil?"

"If you're willing to learn, Monseigneur," replied La Ramée.

"And if you have enough time to teach me," muttered the duke.

"What was that, Monseigneur?" asked La Ramée.

"Monseigneur says don't spare the cardinal's purse, since he seems determined to continue to board and lodge me."

On his way out, La Ramée paused at the door. "Who should Monseigneur like me to send in?"

"Anyone you like, except that Grimaud."

"The Officer of the Guard, then?"

"With his chessboard."

"Done." And La Ramée went out.

The Officer of the Guard came in, and five minutes later Beaufort seemed deeply engrossed in the sublime combinations that lead to checkmate.

What a singular thing is the mind, and what profound alterations a sign, a word, or a hope can cause in it! The duke had been five years in prison, but a look back made those five years, however slowly they'd passed, seem shorter than the forty-eight hours that now separated him from the time set for his escape.

It was the details that worried him. How would this escape be effected? What would be hidden in the mysterious pie? Which friends were waiting for him? How could he still have allies after five years in prison? It seemed he was a very privileged prince indeed.

To his astonishment, it seemed that his former friends—and most extraordinarily, his mistress—still remembered him. It's true she might not have been scrupulously faithful to him the entire time, but she hadn't forgotten him, and that was a lot.

This was more than enough for the duke to think about, and even distracted him on the tennis court, and as La Ramée had schooled him before, the next time he schooled him again. But at least these defeats kept him busy, and soon enough it was evening, with only three hours to go until bed. Then the night would come, and with it sleep.

Or so the duke thought. But sleep is a capricious deity that stays away just when it's most devoutly desired. The duke was awake well into the middle of the night, tossing and turning on his mattress like Saint Lawrence on his martyr's grille. Finally, he fell asleep.

And then, before the arrival of day, he had fantastic dreams: he grew wings, and naturally wanted to fly, and at first his wings fully supported him. But when he reached a certain height, this support suddenly failed, his wings were broken, and he plummeted toward a bottomless abyss. He awoke in a sweat, trembling as if he really had tumbled from the sky.

Then he fell asleep again to wander into a maze of dreams, each wilder than the last, and though his eyes were closed, his mind was turned toward a single goal: escape, always escape. He found an underground passage that would take him out of Vincennes, and followed it, Grimaud marching before him lantern in hand . . . but gradually the passage narrowed, and though the duke persevered, it finally became so narrow he could go no farther, no matter how he tried to squeeze through. The walls seemed to close in and press on him, yet he could still see in the distance Grimaud with his lantern, who continued to walk forward, and though he tried to call for help, he was gripped so tightly he couldn't utter a single word.

Then, from behind him, he could hear the footsteps of his pursuers, growing ever closer, and he knew that if they caught him, he would never escape. The enveloping walls seemed in league with his enemies, holding him when he needed to flee. He heard the voice of La Ramée, and then saw him, laughing, stretching out a hand to shake his shoulder, awakening him in the low, vaulted room where Marshal Ornano, and Puylaurens, and his uncle Vendôme had all perished. There, in the floor, were their three graves, with a fourth yawning open, awaiting his own corpse.

That woke him, and thereafter the duke tried as hard to stay awake as he had to fall asleep, so that when La Ramée entered in the morning, he found him so pale and tired that he asked if he were sick. "Indeed," said one of the guards who had stayed in the prince's room but had been unable to sleep due to a toothache, "Monseigneur had a restless night, and in his dreams called out for help two or three times."

"What's wrong, Monseigneur?" asked La Ramée.

"What's wrong, fool," said the duke, "is that all your silly talk about escape turned my brain, so that I dreamed about escaping, only in doing so I fell and broke my neck."

La Ramée laughed. "You see, Monseigneur," he said, "this is a warning from heaven, and I hope Monseigneur will never be so reckless as to act out his dream."

"You're right, my dear La Ramée," said the duke, wiping the sweat from his brow. "From now on, I'll dream of nothing but food and drink."

"Hush!" said La Ramée. He then sent the guards away, one by one, on various pretexts, until they were alone.

"Well?" asked the duke.

"Well!" said La Ramée. "Your dinner's been ordered."

"Ah!" said the prince. "And what will it consist of, Monsieur Major-domo?"

"Monseigneur promised to trust me on that."

"Will there be a pie?"

"As tall as a tower!"

"Baked by Père Marteau's successor?"

"It's all arranged."

"And you told him it was for me?"

"I told him."

"What did he say?"

"That he would do his best to please Your Highness."

"The time is coming!" said the duke, rubbing his hands.

"Peste, Monseigneur!" said La Ramée. "You *are* tending toward glut-tony! In five years, I haven't seen you look so cheerful as you do now."

The duke saw he'd been careless—but suddenly, as if he'd been listening at the door and realized it was time for a diversion, Grimaud came in and gestured to La Ramée that he had something to tell him.

La Ramée approached Grimaud, who spoke to him in a low voice. This gave the duke time to get hold of himself. "I have forbidden this man," he said, "to come in here without my permission."

"Monseigneur," said La Ramée, "you must forgive him, as I'm the one who summoned him."

"And why did you do that, since you know it displeases me?"

"Monseigneur should remember what we agreed about who will serve us this famous dinner," said La Ramée. "Did Monseigneur forget about the dinner?"

"No, but I'd forgotten about Monsieur Grimaud."

"Monseigneur knows that we can't have the dinner without him."

"Very well, do as you please."

"Come here, *garçon*," said La Ramée, "and listen to what I have to tell you." Grimaud approached, wearing his most sullen expression. La Ramée continued, "Monseigneur does me the honor of dining in private with him tomorrow."

Grimaud made a gesture to indicate he didn't see what that had to do with him.

"It does, in fact, have to do with you," said La Ramée, "as you will have the honor of serving us—and no matter how hungry and thirsty we may be, afterward there's bound to be something left in the dishes and bottles for you."

Grimaud bowed gratefully.

"And now, Monseigneur," said La Ramée, "I must beg Your Highness's pardon, but it seems Monsieur de Chavigny is going away for a few days, and before leaving he has some orders to give me."

The duke tried to catch Grimaud's eye, but Grimaud might as well have been blind. "Then go," the duke said to La Ramée, "but come back as soon as you can."

"Monseigneur wants to get revenge for yesterday's game of tennis?"

Grimaud gave a near-imperceptible nod.

"Yes," said the duke, "and beware, my dear La Ramée, for one day is not like another, and I've decided to play to win."

La Ramée went out; Grimaud watched him without so much as moving a muscle; then, when he saw the door was closed, he quickly drew a pencil and sheet of paper from his pocket. "Write, Monseigneur," he said.

"And what should I write?"

Grimaud pointed a finger and dictated: "'Everything is ready for tomorrow night. Be on watch from seven o'clock till nine and have two horses ready; we will come down from over the first window of the gallery.'"

"And what else?"

"What else, Monseigneur?" said Grimaud, surprised. "After that, sign it."

"And that's it?"

"What more needs to be said, Monseigneur?" said Grimaud, who was concise to the point of austerity.

The duke signed it. "Now," said Grimaud, "does Monseigneur still have the ball?"

"What ball?"

"The one that contained the letter."

"Ah, yes—I thought it might come in handy. Here it is." And the duke took the ball from under his pillow and gave it to Grimaud.

Grimaud smiled as pleasantly as he could. "Well?" asked the duke.

"Well, Monseigneur," said Grimaud, "I'll sew this letter up into the ball, and then, when playing tennis, you'll send the ball over into the dry-moat."

"But mightn't it be lost?"

"Rest assured, Monseigneur, someone will be there to pick it up."

"A gardener?" asked the duke.

Grimaud nodded.

"The same one as before?"

Grimaud nodded again.

"The Comte de Rochefort, then?"

Grimaud nodded a third time.

"But see here," said the duke, "give me at least some details on how we're going to escape."

"I'm not allowed to say," Grimaud replied, "before the time comes."

"Who will be waiting for me on the other side of the moat?"

"I don't know, Monseigneur."

"But at least tell me what's going to be in this famous pie, or I'm going to go mad."

"Monseigneur," said Grimaud, "it will contain two poniards,[76] a rope ladder, and a choke-pear."[77]

"Well . . . now I understand."

"Monseigneur will see that they've thought of everything."

"We will take the poniards and the rope," said the duke.

"And we'll feed the choke-pear to La Ramée," said Grimaud.

"My dear Grimaud," said the duke, "you don't speak often, but to be fair, when you do, you speak words of gold."

CATCL.   LESESTRE.

XXII

An Adventure of Marie Michon

Around the same time these escape plans were being hatched between the Duc de Beaufort and Grimaud, two men on horseback, followed by a pair of lackeys, entered Paris by the Rue du Faubourg Saint-Marcel. These two men were the Comte de La Fère and the Vicomte de Bragelonne.

It was the first time the young man had come to Paris. The capital was an old friend to Athos, but he wasn't showing it off to best advantage by bringing Raoul in by that route. Indeed, the ugliest village in the Touraine was better looking than Paris when entered from the direction of Blois. So, it must be said, to the shame of the great city, that it made a poor first impression on the young man.

Athos was nonchalant and serene, as always. Arriving in the Saint-Médard district, the count, who served as his companion's guide through the great maze, took the Rue des Postes to l'Estrapade, the Fossés Saint-Michel, and finally Vaugirard. At the corner of the Rue Férou, they turned down that short street. In the middle of the block, Athos looked up, smiling, and pointed out a common row house to the young man. "There, Raoul," he said, "is a house where I passed seven of the sweetest—and cruelest—years of my life."

The young man smiled back and gave the house a respectful salute. The admiration he had for his guardian showed itself in everything he did.

As for Athos, Raoul was not only the center of his life, but other than his memories of his old regiment, the single object of his affection, so deep and profound was the count's love for him.

The travelers stopped in the Rue du Vieux-Colombier at the sign of the Green Fox. Athos was an old customer of this inn, having gone there a hundred times with his friends, but twenty years had made many changes in the establishment, starting with the hosts.

The travelers turned their horses over to the stable boys, and as they were animals of a noble race, they ordered the steeds be treated with the greatest of care: fed with the finest straw and oats, after which their chests and legs were to be rubbed down with warm wine. After all, they'd ridden twenty leagues that day.

Having first attended to their mounts, as all true horsemen must, they then asked for two rooms for themselves. "Wash up, and dress to look your best, Raoul," said Athos. "I'm going to present you to someone."

"Today, Monsieur?" asked the young man.

"In half an hour."

The young man bowed. More tired than Athos, who seemed a man of iron, he might have preferred a dip in that River Seine of which he'd heard so much, though he was certain it couldn't compare to his Loire, followed by a fall into bed—but the Comte de La Fère had spoken, so his only thought was to obey.

"Be thorough, Raoul," added Athos. "I would like you to look hand-some."

"I hope, Monsieur," said the young man with a smile, "that you're not introducing me to a prospective bride. You know my commitments to Louise."

Athos smiled back. "No, don't worry," he said, "though I am presenting you to a lady."

"A lady?" asked Raoul.

"Yes, and I hope you'll like her."

The young man looked uneasily at the count, but seeing Athos's smile he was reassured. "And how old is she?" asked the Vicomte de Bragelonne.

"My dear Raoul, learn once and for all that that is a question you never ask," said Athos. "If you can tell a lady's age from her face, there's no point in asking, and if you can't, to ask is indiscreet."

"Is she beautiful?"

"Sixteen years ago, she was considered not only the prettiest but the most graceful woman in France."

This response completely reassured the viscount. Athos couldn't have any intentions for him toward a woman considered the prettiest and most graceful in France in the year before he was born.

He retired to his room, and with the vanity that comes with youth, applied himself to Athos's instructions to look as well as he could. With what nature had given him, this was no hard thing.

When he returned, Athos received him with that fatherly smile he used to bestow on d'Artagnan, but which was now reserved for Raoul with an even deeper tenderness. Athos inspected his feet, hands, and hair, those three signs of class. His black hair was parted and long, as was worn at the time, and fell in curls framing his tanned face. Gray suede gloves that matched his hat covered his fine and elegant hands, while his boots, which matched both hat and gloves, were tapered and as petite as those of a child of ten. "Well," he murmured, "if she's not proud of him, she's a hard woman to please."

It was three in the afternoon, a suitable time to pay a visit. The two travelers followed the Rue de Grenelle to the Rue des Rosiers, turned onto Rue Saint-Dominique, and stopped at a majestic mansion facing the Jacobins, its gate surmounted by the arms of de Luynes.

"This is it," said Athos. He entered the hôtel with the assurance that persuaded the Swiss Guard that he had the right to do so. He climbed the main staircase, and, addressing a footman in full livery, asked if the Duchesse de Chevreuse was receiving, and if so, would she receive the Comte de La Fère?

The servant returned a moment later and said that, though the Duchesse de Chevreuse did not have the honor of knowing the Comte de La Fère, she invited him to please come in.

Athos followed the footman, who led him through a long series of apartments to a parlor, where he stopped before a closed door. Athos gestured to the Vicomte de Bragelonne to wait where he was. The footman opened the door and announced the Comte de La Fère.

Madame de Chevreuse, so often mentioned in *The Three Musketeers* without actually having been brought on stage, was still a very beautiful woman. Indeed, though she was at this time forty-four or forty-five, she seemed still in the prime of her thirties, with lovely blond hair, and large, bright, intelligent eyes that had so often been opened in intrigue and closed in love. She retained her nymph-like figure, and from behind still seemed to be the young woman of 1623 who had jumped the moat of the Tuileries with Anne of Austria, a folly that had deprived the crown of an heir.[78] In most ways, she was still the same wild creature who'd thrown herself into love affairs with such passion and originality that it became a hallmark of her descendants.

She was in a little boudoir with a window overlooking a garden. This room, decorated in the mode made fashionable by Madame de Rambouillet in her famous hôtel, was hung in blue damask with pink flowers and golden trim. It was daring for a lady of the duchess's age to receive visitors in such a boudoir, especially in her current posture, stretched out on a chaise longue with her head against the tapestry. She was holding a book half-open, her arm resting on a cushion. At the footman's announcement, she rose on one arm and cocked her head curiously.

Athos appeared. He was dressed in dark purple velvet with similar trim, embellished with silver aiguillettes. His simple cloak bore no gold trim, and a single violet feather adorned his black felt hat. He wore tall boots of black leather, and at his belt hung that sword with a magnificent hilt so often admired by Porthos when Athos lived in Rue Férou, but which he'd never consented to lend to him. Splendid white lace erupted from the collar of his shirt and bedecked the tops of his boots.

There was in this man, though completely unknown to Madame de Chevreuse, such an air of high nobility, that she half rose and graciously beckoned him to take a seat beside her.

Athos bowed and obeyed. The footman was about to withdraw, but Athos made a gesture that restrained him. "Madame," he said to the duchess, "I had the audacity to present myself at your hôtel without having been introduced to you—successfully, since you deigned to receive me. I now ask the favor of a half hour's interview."

"Granted, Monsieur," said the duchess, with her most gracious smile.

"But that's not all, Madame. It's presumptuous, I know, but I further request that our interview be a private one, as I keenly desire not to be interrupted."

"I am at home to no one," the duchess told the footman. "You may go."

The footman went out.

There was a moment of silence, during which these two embodiments of the nobility sized each other up, without embarrassment on either side. The duchess was the first to break the silence. "Well, Monsieur," she said with a smile, "can't you see I await you with impatience?"

"While I, Madame," replied Athos, "regard you with admiration."

"Monsieur," said the duchess, "you must excuse me, but I long to learn with whom I'm speaking. You have the undeniable air of a courtier, yet I've never seen you at Court. Have you been in the Bastille, and just been released?"

"No, Madame," Athos replied with a smile, "though I may be on my way there."

"Ah! In that case, introduce yourself quickly, and then go away," the duchess said playfully, in a charming tone. "I am already quite compromised enough without you making it worse."

"Who am I, Madame? They announced my name: the Comte de La Fère, a name unknown to you. I once bore another that you might have heard, though you've certainly forgotten it by now."

"Tell me, Monsieur."

"In former times," said the Comte de La Fère, "I was known as Athos."

The duchess's eyes widened in astonishment. It was obvious that name still meant something to her, though it wasn't clear what. "Athos?" she said. "Wait, wait . . . !" She pressed both hands to her forehead as if to marshal in her memories a colorful crowd of people and events.

"Shall I give you a hint, Madame?" smiled Athos.

"But yes," said the duchess, head in a whirl, "please do."

"This Athos was affiliated with three young King's Musketeers who went by the names of d'Artagnan, Porthos, and . . ." Athos paused.

"And Aramis," gasped the duchess.

"And Aramis, that's it," said Athos. "So, you haven't quite forgotten his name?"

"No," she said, "no, my poor Aramis! Such a lovely gentleman—elegant, discreet, a writer of pretty verses. I think he turned out badly," she added.

"Very badly: he became an abbot."

"Ah! What a shame!" said the duchess, flipping her fan carelessly. "My thanks, Monsieur, truly."

"For what, Madame?"

"For reviving that memory, a pleasant recollection of my youth."

"Will you permit me, then," said Athos, "to revive another one?"

"Is it connected with the former?"

"Yes . . . and no."

"Well, *ma foi*," said Madame de Chevreuse, "for a man like you I'd risk anything."

Athos bowed. "Aramis," he continued, "was connected with a young seamstress of Tours."

"A young seamstress of Tours?"

"Yes, a sort of cousin of his, called Marie Michon."

"Ah, I recall her," said the duchess. "During the Siege of La Rochelle, she was the one who wrote to try to foil that plot against poor Buckingham."

"Exactly," said Athos. "Will you allow me to speak of her?"

Madame de Chevreuse gave Athos a long look. "Yes," she said, "so long as you don't speak ill of her."

"That would make me an ingrate," said Athos, "and I regard ingratitude not as a fault or a crime, but as a sin, which is far worse."

"You, ungrateful to Marie Michon, Monsieur?" said the duchess, trying to read Athos's eyes. "But how could that be? You never knew her personally."

"Eh, Madame! Who knows?" said Athos. "There's a proverb that says it's only mountains that never meet, and proverbs are often based in truth."

"Then go on, Monsieur, go on!" the duchess said brightly. "You can't imagine how diverting this all is."

"Since you encourage me," said Athos, "I will continue. This cousin of Aramis, this Marie Michon, despite her modest rank, had knowledge of the highest degree, and called the grandest ladies of the Court her friends. Even the queen, proud though she is, in her dual capacity of Austrian and Spaniard—even she called her sister."

"Hélas," said Madame de Chevreuse, with a tiny sigh and a twitch of her eyebrows, "things are much changed since that time."

"But at that time the queen was in the right," continued Athos, "for this seamstress was devoted to her, so much so that she served as an intermediary with the queen's brother, the King of Spain."

"An act that nowadays," said the duchess, "is considered treason."

"And so," continued Athos, "the cardinal—the true cardinal—resolved one morning to arrest poor Marie Michon and confine her in the Château de Loches. Fortunately, such an act could not be prepared entirely in secrecy, and in any event, Marie Michon was ready: if she was ever menaced with real danger, the queen was to send her a prayer-book bound in green velvet."

"Quite so, Monsieur! You are well informed."

"One morning that green-bound book was brought to her by the Prince de Marcillac. There was no time to lose. Fortunately, Marie Michon and a servant of hers, named Kitty,[79] looked extremely well when dressed in men's clothes. The prince brought Marie Michon a cavalier's ensemble, and a lackey's outfit for Kitty, as well as two excellent horses. Quickly, the two fugitives left Tours, headed for Spain—traveling by back roads to avoid the highways, starting at every sound, and begging for hospitality wherever they couldn't find an inn."

"In truth, that's just how it happened!" cried the duchess, clapping her hands together. "But it's very curious . . ." She paused.

"I need not follow the fugitives to the end of their journey," said Athos. "No, Madame, for my tale I need take them only as far as a town in Limousin between Tulle and Angoulême, a little village called Roche-l'Abeille."

Madame de Chevreuse gasped in surprise and looked at Athos with an expression of such astonishment that it made the old musketeer smile. "Hear me, Madame," he continued, "for what I have yet to say is even stranger than what has gone before."

"Monsieur," said the duchess, "I think you must be a sorcerer. I'll listen, but in truth . . . never mind. Go on."

"The ride that day had been long and tiring; it was October eleventh, getting cold, the village had neither inn nor château, and the peasants' houses looked poor and dirty. Marie Michon had the tastes of the highborn, she was accustomed to fine linen and clean lodging, so she decided to ask for hospitality from the village priest." Athos paused.

"Oh, continue!" said the duchess. "I warn you that now I expect to hear everything."

"The travelers knocked at the door; it was late; the priest, already in bed, called out for them to enter. They found the door unlocked and opened it—they don't lock their doors out in the villages. A lamp was burning in the priest's house. Marie Michon, the most charming cavalier in the world, opened the door, put in her head, and requested hospitality for the night. 'Willingly, my young cavalier,' said the priest. 'You can have half the bedchamber and whatever's left of my supper.' The two travelers consulted for a moment; the priest heard them laugh, and then the master—or rather the mistress—replied, 'Thank you, Monsieur Curate, we accept.' 'Then come in,' he said, 'eat up, and make as little noise as you can, because I also traveled all day and won't be sorry to get a good night's sleep.'"

Madame de Chevreuse went from surprise to astonishment and on to stupefaction, gaping at Athos, who wore an expression impossible to describe; she seemed to want to say something, but held her tongue, for fear of missing a single word. Finally, she said, "And . . . after?"

"After?" said Athos. "Ah! That's the hardest part to tell."

"Tell it! Tell it! I'm the kind of person you can say anything to. Besides, it's not about me, it's about this Mademoiselle Michon."

"Ah! Just so," said Athos. "Well! Marie Michon had supper with her servant, and afterward, in accordance with the permission she'd been granted, she went into her host's bedroom, while Kitty made herself comfortable on a chair in the room where they'd eaten."

"Really, Monsieur," said Madame de Chevreuse, "unless you're the Devil himself, I don't know how you can know all these details."

"She was a charming woman, Marie Michon," said Athos, "one of those wild creatures that recognizes no limits, a being born to damn those of us who do. It occurred to her that, since her host was a priest, it would be amusing to give him a happy memory to cherish in his old age—and on her part, she would have the droll recollection of having tempted a curate to perdition."

"Count," said the duchess, "on my word of honor, you give me chills."

"Alas for the chastity of the poor curate, he was no St. Ambrose," said Athos, "and as I said, Marie Michon was an adorable creature."

"Monsieur," cried the duchess, seizing Athos's hands, "tell me immediately how you come to know all these details, or I will call for a monk from the Augustinian convent and have you exorcised!"

Athos laughed. "It's easily explained, Madame. A cavalier, himself charged with an important mission, had stopped at the rectory just an hour earlier to beg hospitality of the priest, who had just been called away to attend to a dying congregant, leaving his house and village overnight. The man of God, who trusted his guest, as he was clearly a gentleman, had left him his house, dinner, and bed. So, it was this guest of the curate whom Marie Michon had asked for hospitality."

"And this cavalier, this guest, this gentleman who came before was . . . ?"

"Myself, the Comte de La Fère," said Athos, rising and bowing respectfully to the duchess.

The duchess was stunned for a moment, and then burst into laughter. "Oh, my faith!" she said. "That's hilarious! For once, little Marie Michon got more than she expected. Sit down, dear Count, and finish your story."

"Now I become the villain of the piece, Madame. As I told you, I was traveling on an important mission; early the next morning I silently left the bedroom, leaving my charming companion asleep. In the front room her servant rested her head in an armchair, still slumbering like her mistress. I was struck by her pretty face; I approached and recognized her as that little Kitty whom our friend Aramis had found a place for. Then I realized the charming cavalier must be . . ."

"Marie Michon!" the duchess quickly interrupted.

". . . Marie Michon," said Athos. "So, I left the house and went to the barn, where I found my horse saddled and my lackey ready, and we rode away."

"And you never returned to this village?" asked Madame de Chevreuse pointedly.

"I did, Madame—a year later."

"Well?"

"Well! I stopped to visit that good curate. I found him very concerned about something that greatly mystified him. A week before he'd been left a small cradle bearing a charming little boy three months old, along with a purse of gold and a note that said only: *11 October 1633.*"[80]

"That was the date of this strange adventure," said Madame de Chevreuse.

"Yes, but that told the curate nothing, other than reminding him he'd spent that night with a dying congregant, for Marie Michon had left the rectory before he returned."

"You should know, Monsieur, that when Marie Michon returned to France in 1643, she sought news of this child, which, as a fugitive, she hadn't been able to keep—but which, finally having returned to Paris, she wanted to raise as her own."

"And what did the curate say?" asked Athos.

"That a nobleman he didn't know had volunteered to raise the child, had guaranteed his future, and taken him when he went."

"And that was true."

"Ah, I understand now! You were that nobleman—you are his father!"

"Hush! Not so loud, Madame—he's waiting outside."

"He's here!" cried Madame de Chevreuse, jumping up eagerly. "He's here, my son—I mean the son of Marie Michon—here! I must see him this instant!"

"Take care, Madame," Athos interrupted. "He knows the identity of neither his father nor his mother."

"You kept the secret, and then you brought him to me, thinking how happy I'd be. Oh! Thank you, Monsieur! Thank you!" cried the duchess, seizing his hand and carrying it to her lips. "Thank you! You have a noble heart."

"I brought him to you," said Athos, gently withdrawing his hand, "so that you in your turn can do something for him, Madame. So far, I've watched over his education, and I think I've made a proper gentleman of him—but the time has come when I'm forced to take up arms again and resume the dangerous career of partisan. Tomorrow I join an adventurous exploit in which I may be killed—and then he will no longer be able to depend on me to see that he finds his proper place in the world."

"Rest easy as to that!" said the duchess. "Unfortunately, I don't have much political leverage at the moment, but what I have is at his disposal. As to his title and fortune . . ."

"I have provided for that, Madame, never fear; I've given him the domain of Bragelonne as inheritance, which grants him the title of viscount and an income of ten thousand livres."

"Upon my soul, Monsieur," said the duchess, "you are a true gentleman! But I'm eager to see our young viscount. Where is he?"

"Outside, in the parlor; I'll bring him in, if you wish."

Athos started toward the door, but Madame de Chevreuse stopped him. "Is he handsome?" she asked.

Athos smiled. "He resembles his mother," he said. Then he opened the door and beckoned to the young man, who appeared in the doorway.

Madame de Chevreuse couldn't contain her cry of joy at the sight of such a charming young cavalier, who exceeded all the expectations even her pride had conceived.

"Come in, Viscount," said Athos. "Madame la Duchesse de Chevreuse permits you to kiss her hand."

The young man approached with uncovered head and a shy smile, dropped to one knee, and kissed the hand of the duchess. "Monsieur le

Comte," he said, turning to Athos, "were you hoping not to unnerve me by telling me madame was a duchess? Surely this is the queen!"

"No, Viscount," said Madame de Chevreuse, taking his hand in turn and making him sit beside her, and then looking at him with eyes sparkling with joy. "No, unfortunately, I'm not the queen—for if I were, I'd be able to give you what you deserve right away. But never mind, such as I am, I'll do what I can. Now," she added, scarcely able to keep from embracing him, "what career do you hope to pursue?"

Athos, still standing, regarded them both with an expression of unspeakable happiness.

"Well, Madame," said the young man, in a voice both sweet and resonant, "it seems to me the only career for a gentleman is that of arms. Monsieur le Comte raised me, I believe, with the intention that I'd be a soldier, and allowed me to hope that in Paris he would introduce me to someone who could give me a recommendation, perhaps even to the Prince de Condé."

"Yes, I understand, and it would become a young soldier like you to serve under a general like him, but I don't stand very well with the prince, thanks to the way my stepmother, Madame de Montbazon, has quarreled with his sister Madame de Longueville . . . but maybe the Prince de Marcillac—yes! See here, Count, that's it! The Prince de Marcillac is an old friend of mine; he will recommend our young soldier to Madame de Longueville, who will give him a letter for her brother Condé. He loves her too tenderly not to grant everything she asks for."

"Excellent! That would be marvelous," said the count. "Only dare I request it be done with dispatch? I have reasons for wishing the viscount gone from Paris by tomorrow night."

"Do you wish it known this is done at your behest, Count?"

"It might be best for the time being if his name were not connected with mine."

"Oh, Monsieur!" cried the young man.

"You know, Bragelonne," said the count, "that I never do anything without a reason."

"Yes, Monsieur," replied the young man. "I know how wise you are, and I'll obey you as I always do."

"Well, then, Count, allow me," said the duchess. "I'll send for the Prince de Marcillac, who fortunately is in Paris right now, and I won't give up until the matter is accomplished."

"Very good, Madame la Duchesse—a thousand thanks. I myself have several errands to run today, and upon my return at about, say, six o'clock, I'll expect to meet the viscount at our lodgings."

"What are your plans for the evening?"

"We go to visit the Abbé Scarron,* for whom I have a letter, and where I expect to meet a friend of mine."

"Very well," said the duchess. "This will take only a moment, so don't leave my parlor until I return."

Athos bowed to Madame de Chevreuse and prepared to leave the room.

"Really, Monsieur le Comte?" laughed the duchess. "Are we so formal in leaving our old friends?"

"Ah!" murmured Athos, kissing her hand. "If I'd only known sooner that Marie Michon was such a charming creature . . . !"

And he withdrew with a sigh.

XXIII

The Abbé Scarron

There was, in the Rue des Tournelles, an address known to all the coachmen and sedan-chair porters of Paris—and yet that address was the home of neither a nobleman nor a banker. No one went there to dine, to play cards, or to dance.

Nonetheless, it was a magnet for all the high society of Paris. This was the house of little Abbé Scarron.

There, at the house of this witty abbot, everyone went to laugh and to talk. There, everyone heard the latest news, and that news was instantly recounted, dissected, analyzed, and turned into epigrams or satirical verse. Everyone wanted to spend an evening's hour with little Scarron, to hear what was being said, and what he had to say about it. Everyone longed to get in a word or two of their own—and if those words were clever, they were welcome.

This little Abbé Scarron—who was an abbot because he possessed an abbacy, not because he'd actually taken orders—had once been one of the most fashionable clerics of Le Mans, where he'd resided. One day during Carnival, he'd wanted to bless his city with a jest they'd always remember, so he'd had his valet coat him in honey, and then, having torn open his feather bed, he'd rolled in it, becoming hilariously grotesque. He then went from door to door, visiting all his friends in this bizarre attire; the citizens were first amazed, and then offended; people insulted him, children threw stones, and he was forced to flee to escape the attacks. As soon as he fled, everyone pursued; reviled, harried, and hunted on all sides, Scarron had had no recourse but to jump into the river to escape. He swam like a fish, but the water was icy cold, and when he finally pulled himself out of it, his limbs were crippled for life.

Every known means had been tried to restore the use of his limbs, but he suffered so much pain from the treatments he'd dismissed his doctors, saying he preferred the malady. He relocated to Paris, where his reputation for wit was already established. There he had made an elaborate wheelchair of his own invention—and one day, in that chair, he visited Queen Anne of Austria, and the regent, charmed by his wit and wisdom, asked if she could grant him a title.

"Yes, Your Majesty," Scarron had replied, "in that regard I have a singular ambition."

"And what is that?" asked Anne of Austria.

"To be known as your patient," replied the abbé.

And thereafter Scarron had been appointed "The Queen's Patient," with an annual income of fifteen hundred livres.

From that moment Scarron, with no fears for the future, had led a joyous life on his carefully spent salary.

One day, however, an emissary from Cardinal Mazarin had called to tell him that it was a mistake for him to receive the coadjutor, Monsieur de Gondy, at his salon.

"And why is that?" Scarron had asked. "Isn't he a man of good birth?"

"Indeed, pardieu!"

"Congenial?"

"Undoubtedly."

"Spiritual?"

"He might, unfortunately, show a bit too much spirit."

"Even so," said Scarron, "why do you want me to stop receiving such a man?"

"Because he has improper ideas."

"Really? And who says so?"

"The cardinal."

"What?" said Scarron. "I should continue to receive Monsieur Gilles Despréaux, who doesn't like me, but I should stop receiving Monsieur le Coadjuteur because someone else doesn't like him? Impossible!"

The conversation ended there, and Scarron, a contrarian at heart, had invited Monsieur de Gondy to visit as often as he liked.

On the morning of the day at which we've arrived, which was the first day of the new trimester, Scarron, according to his custom, had sent his servant with his invoice to collect his salary for the quarter—but his servant had been told, "The State has no more money for Monsieur l'Abbé Scarron."

When the servant brought this reply to Scarron, he was being visited by the Duc de Longueville, who offered to give him twice the salary that Mazarin had denied him, but Scarron was too clever to accept it. Instead he made sure that, by four o'clock that afternoon, the entire city knew of the cardinal's refusal. As it was Thursday, the day the abbot received everyone, crowds of well-wishers came from across the city, all reviling the name of the cardinal.

In the Rue Saint-Honoré Athos encountered two gentlemen he didn't know, on horseback and followed by lackeys just as he was, and headed in the same direction. One of them took his hat in his hand and said, "Can you believe, Monsieur, this cowardly Mazarin has cut off poor Scarron's pension?"

"That is absurd," said Athos, bowing to both cavaliers.

"We see you are an honest man, Monsieur," replied the gentleman who had spoken to Athos, "while this Mazarin is a living plague."

"Alas, Monsieur," replied Athos, "take care whom you say that to." And they bowed and separated.

"This event is well-timed for our visit this evening," Athos said to the viscount. "We will pay our compliments to this poor fellow."

"But who is this Monsieur Scarron who puts all Paris in an uproar?" asked Raoul. "Is he some disgraced minister?"

"*Mon Dieu*, no, Viscount," replied Athos, "he's just a petty gentleman of wit and spirit who's made an enemy of the cardinal by writing some verses about him."

"Do gentlemen write verses?" Raoul asked naïvely. "I thought that was beneath them."

"It is, my dear Viscount," Athos replied, laughing, "when they write bad ones—but when they're good, it enhances them. Look at Monsieur Rotrou.[81] However," continued Athos, in the tone of one who gives good advice, "on the whole I think it's better not to do it."

"But then," asked Raoul, "is this Monsieur Scarron a poet?"

"He is, Viscount, so beware what you say in his house—or better yet, confine yourself to nods, or just listen."

"Yes, Monsieur," Raoul replied.

"You'll see me talking quite a bit with a gentleman who's a friend of mine, the Abbé d'Herblay, about whom you've heard me speak."

"I remember, Monsieur."

"Approach us sometimes as if to speak to us, but say nothing—and likewise, do not listen. This ruse will keep intruders from bothering us."

"Very well, Monsieur, I'll obey you to the letter."

Athos made two stops in Paris, then at seven turned them toward the Rue des Tournelles. The street was crowded with porters, horses, and footmen. Athos made his way through the press to the house that was his goal and entered, followed by the young man. Upon gaining the interior, the first person he noticed was Aramis, loitering near a unique wheelchair, wide and covered with a tapestry canopy, under which, fidgeting and wrapped in an embroidered blanket, was a small figure: a person young and cheerful, yet pale and weak, but whose active eyes were lively, clever, and gracious. This was the Abbé Scarron, ever laughing, joking, complimenting, wincing with pain, and massaging his limbs with a little rod.

Around this sort of rolling pavilion clustered a crowd of gentlemen and ladies. The room was well and simply furnished; fine curtains of silk embroidered with flowers, their bright colors now somewhat faded, framed the windows; the wall hangings were modest but tasteful. Two polite and well-dressed footmen served the distinguished guests.

Seeing Athos, Aramis approached him, took him by the arm, and presented him to Scarron, who received him with both pleasure and respect, and gave a very pretty compliment to the viscount. Raoul was speechless, unready for this level of discourse, so he bowed with what grace he could muster. Athos received the compliments of several nobles to whom Aramis presented him, and then, the flurry of his entrance passed, the general conversation resumed.

After four or five minutes, which Raoul used to recover his self-possession and begin to size up the assembled company, the main door opened and a servant announced Mademoiselle Paulet.[82]

Athos tapped the viscount's shoulder. "Take note of this lady, Raoul," he said, "she's a historical figure—it was to visit her that King Henri IV was going when he was assassinated."

Raoul started; it seemed that every moment, these days, brought him face-to-face with history. Here was a lady, still young and beautiful, who had known Henri IV and had spoken to him.

Everyone hastened to greet the newcomer, for she was never out of fashion. She was a tall and graceful figure, crowned by a head of glorious golden hair, such as Raphael loved to paint and Titian gave to all his Magdalenes. This tawny hair, or perhaps the ascendancy she'd won over other women, was why she was known as the Lioness. Our *belles dames* of today who aspire to this title should know that it comes to them, not from England, as they might think, but from their august compatriot Mademoiselle Paulet.

Amid the murmur that her arrival evoked on all sides, Mademoiselle Paulet went right up to Scarron. "Well then, my dear Abbé," she said in her serene voice, "are you now in poverty? We heard all about it this afternoon, at Madame de Rambouillet's, from Monsieur de Grasse."

"Yes, but we enrich the State thereby," said Scarron. "We must, after all, make sacrifices for our country."

"Monsieur le Cardinal will spend that fifteen hundred *livres* on more pomades and perfumes," said Monsieur Ménage, a Frondeur whom Athos recognized as the gentlemen he'd met in Rue Saint-Honoré.

"But what will the Muse say?" replied Aramis in his voice of honey. "That Muse, who requires a golden mediocrity? After all, *Si Virgilio puer aut tolerabile desit Hospitum, caderent omnes crinibus Hydri.*"[83]

"Well said!" said Scarron, extending his hand to Mademoiselle Paulet. "But if I no longer have my Hydra, at least I have my Lioness."

Every word Scarron said that night seemed exquisite. Such is the privilege of persecution. Monsieur Ménage couldn't contain his praise.

Mademoiselle Paulet went to assume her accustomed place—but before taking her seat, she stood in her grandeur and surveyed all those assembled, her eyes finally resting on Raoul.

Athos smiled. "You have been noticed by Mademoiselle Paulet, Viscount; go and greet her. Presume to be nothing more than what you are, a French provincial—and don't dare to speak to her of Henri IV."

Blushing, the viscount approached the Lioness, and joined the other nobles who clustered around her throne.

The gathering now divided into two distinct groups: those who surrounded Monsieur Ménage, and those paying court to Mademoiselle Paulet. Scarron rolled from one to the other, maneuvering his wheelchair in the press with as much skill as an experienced pilot steering a boat in a crowded harbor.

"When shall we talk?" said Athos to Aramis.

"Shortly," came the reply. "The crowd isn't thick enough yet; we'd be noticed."

At that moment the door opened and the footman announced the coadjutor.

At this title, everyone turned, for it belonged to one who was already on his way to becoming famous.

Athos turned with the others. He knew the Abbé de Gondy only by name. He saw a small, dark man come in, awkward and short-sighted, clumsy in everything except drawing his sword or pistol; though he stumbled against a table and nearly knocked it over, there was nonetheless something fierce and proud in his expression.

Mademoiselle Paulet offered him her hand, and Scarron rolled up to greet him from his chair. "Well!" said the coadjutor, upon seeing Scarron. "I hear you're in disgrace, Monsieur l'Abbé?"

It was the greeting of the hour and had already been said a hundred times that evening, so Scarron had to find a hundredth witty rejoinder, but he replied without effort, "Cardinal Mazarin has been kind enough to think of me."

"Brilliant!" cried Ménage.

"But how will you continue to be able to receive us?" continued the coadjutor. "If your income dwindles to naught, I'll have to appoint you a canon of Notre Dame."

"Oh, no!" said Scarron. "I'd bring you into disgrace as well."

"Do you have any resources we're unaware of?"

"I'll just borrow from the queen."

"But Her Majesty has no income of her own," said Aramis. "Doesn't she live on the conjugal funds?"

The coadjutor turned with a smile and acknowledged Aramis with a friendly gesture. "Pardon me, my dear Abbé d'Herblay," he said, "but I see you're behind the times, and I must give you something to bring you up to date."

"What's that?" said Aramis.

"A hatband."

Everyone turned toward the coadjutor, who drew from his pocket a silk ribbon tied in a distinctive shape. "Ah!" said Scarron. "It's tied into a sling—a *fronde*!"

"Exactly," said the coadjutor. "Everything now must be done *à la fronde*. Mademoiselle Paulet, I have for you a fan à la fronde. I'll give you the name of my glover, d'Herblay—he makes gloves à la fronde. And for you, Scarron, my baker, who bakes excellent loaves à la fronde."

Aramis took the ribbon and tied it around his hat. Just then the door opened, and the footman announced, "Madame la Duchesse de Chevreuse!"

At this name, everyone rose. Scarron turned his chair toward the door. Raoul blushed. Athos gestured to Aramis, who withdrew into a window embrasure.

Amidst the respectful compliments that greeted her entrance, the duchess seemed to be looking for something—or someone. Finally, her gaze lighted on Raoul, and her eyes sparkled. She saw Athos and looked thoughtful; and she saw Aramis by the window and started slightly behind her fan. "What's the latest?" she asked, as if to conceal the thoughts crossing her mind. "How is poor Voiture? Do you know, Scarron?"

"What? Is Voiture ill?" asked Ménage. "What ails him?"

"He played cards overlong without reminding his servant to bring him a change of shirts," said the coadjutor, "caught a terrible cold, and is dying."

"Where is he?"

"*Mon Dieu!* At my place, where else? Think of it—he'd made a solemn vow to give up gambling, but after three days he couldn't stand it anymore. He came to the archbishop's house to ask me to relieve him of his oath, but I was out on business visiting our good Councilor Broussel. However, in my rooms Voiture found the Marquis de Luynes at a card table, shuffling and looking for an opponent. The marquis called him over, but Voiture said he couldn't play until he'd been relieved of his sacred vow. Luynes engaged in my name to take the sin upon himself, so Voiture sat down at the table, played until he lost four hundred crowns, then took a chill and lay down, to rise no more."

"Is he in danger, our dear Voiture?" asked Aramis, half hidden by the window curtain.

"Hélas! The great man," said Monsieur Ménage. "Perhaps this time we will lose him, *deseret orbem*."

"You pity him?" said Mademoiselle Paulet wryly. "On his deathbed he's surrounded by sultanas, like a Grand Turk! Madame de Saintot comes running with soothing soups, La Renaudot warms his sheets, and Madame de Rambouillet sends herbal tisanes."

"You wouldn't miss him, my dear Parthénie?" said Scarron, laughing.

"How unjust you are! Of course, I would. I'd happily say masses for the repose of his soul."

"It's not for nothing you're called the Lioness," said Madame de Chevreuse. "Your bite is as sharp as ever."

"But . . . you speak ill of a poetic giant, Madame," said Raoul, hesitantly.

"He, a giant? Clearly, Viscount, as you said, you *have* just arrived from the provinces, and have never seen him. A giant? Why, he's scarcely five feet tall."

"*Brava!* Hear, hear!" said a tall man, dark and gaunt, with a bristling mustache and a long rapier at his side. "Brava, lovely Paulet! It's past time someone put that little Voiture in his place. I think I know more than a little about poetry, and I've always found his detestable."

"Who is that swashbuckler, Monsieur?" Raoul asked Athos.

"Monsieur de Scudéry."

"The author of *Clélie* and *The Grand Cyrus*?"

"Coauthor, an honor he shares with his sister, Mademoiselle de Scudéry,[84] that imposing woman over there next to Monsieur Scarron."

Raoul turned and saw two figures who had just entered: an older lady, prim, stiff, and arid, who held herself near like a duenna or chaperone, next to a lovely young woman, frail and sad of demeanor, with luxurious black hair and thoughtful, violet eyes.

Raoul vowed to himself not to leave the salon before he'd had a chance to speak to the beautiful young lady with violet eyes, who, to his mind, though she had no resemblance to her, recalled to him poor little Louise whom he'd left suffering at Château de La Vallière, and whom his encounters with high society had made him forget for a moment.

Meanwhile, Aramis had approached the coadjutor, who without ceasing to smile had whispered a few words in his ear. Aramis, despite himself, started slightly in surprise. "Laugh with me," said Monsieur de Gondy. "We're being watched." And he moved away toward Madame de Chevreuse, who had a lively circle gathered around her.

Aramis pretended to laugh to throw off any curious listeners, then seeing that Athos had gone into the embrasure he'd left a minute before, tossed a few words left and right before moving to join him.

There at the window they finally had their conversation, a quiet one but accented with many gestures. Raoul approached them, as Athos had requested. "Monsieur l'Abbé has been repeating one of Monsieur

Voiture's rondeaus that I'd never heard," Athos said loudly. "It's quite charming."

Raoul stood near them awhile, pretending to listen, then went to join the group around the duchess, which included Mademoiselle Paulet on one side and Mademoiselle de Scudéry on the other.

"Well, as to me," the coadjutor was saying, "I don't share Monsieur de Scudéry's opinion. I think Monsieur Voiture is indeed a poet, but solely of poetical ideas, without a touch of politics to them."

Meanwhile: "And so?" asked Athos.

"It's tomorrow," Aramis said quickly.

"At what time?"

"Six o'clock."

"And where?"

"At Saint-Mandé."

"Who told you this?"

"The Comte de Rochefort." A guest drew near. "Political ideas?" said Aramis aloud. "Our poor Voiture hasn't a one—on this I agree with Monsieur le Coadjuteur. He's purely a poet."

"Oh, certainly—a prodigious poet," said Ménage. "And yet posterity, while admiring him, will surely reproach him for having too little regard for the laws of poetry. He simply murders the rules."

"Murders them, that's the word for it," said Monsieur de Scudéry.

"But admit that his letters are literary masterworks," said Madame de Chevreuse.

"Oh, in that regard," said Mademoiselle de Scudéry, "his fame is assured."

"True enough," replied Mademoiselle Paulet, "so long as he's being humorous; but as a serious epistolary writer he's pitiful, his words blunt, unadorned, and put quite badly—as you must agree."

"So long as *you* agree that at humor, he's inimitable."

"Inimitable? Certainly," said Monsieur de Scudéry, twisting his mustache, "for who would imitate comedy that's forced and jokes that are overfamiliar? For example, his 'Letter from a Carp to a Sturgeon.'"

"And you know," said Ménage, "he gets all his best ideas eavesdropping at the Hôtel Rambouillet. Look at his *Zélide* and *Alcidalis*."

"As for me," said Aramis, approaching the circle and bowing respectfully to Madame de Chevreuse, "as for me, I find him too careless in his regard for those of high rank. He's frequently disrespectful of Madame la Princesse, the Maréchal d'Albret, Monsieur de Schomberg,[85] and the queen herself."

"What, even the queen?" demanded Monsieur de Scudéry, advancing his right leg and assuming a belligerent pose. "Morbleu! That I hadn't heard. And how has he disrespected Her Majesty?"

"You haven't heard his piece, 'I Thought'?"

"No," said Madame de Chevreuse.

"No," said Mademoiselle de Scudéry.

"No," said Mademoiselle Paulet.

"Ah! In fact, I think the queen has shared it with only a few—but I have it from a reliable source."

"And you know it?"

"I *could* bring it to mind, I think."

"Let's have it! Let's have it!" said every voice.

"Here's how it came about," said Aramis. "Monsieur Voiture was in the queen's carriage, riding with her through the forest of Fontainebleau; he put on a look of deep thought, which never fails to incite the queen to ask him what he's thinking about. And so, 'Of what are you thinking, Monsieur Voiture?' Her Majesty asked.

"Voiture smiled, pretended to ponder for about five seconds so he would appear to be improvising, and replied:

> "*'I thought—that Destiny,*
> *After so much unearned misfortune,*
> *Had finally crowned you*
> *With glory, splendor, and fortune*

"'But before, when you suffered,
I think you were happier . . .
I'll not say more beloved
Though that's what the rhyme calls for.'"

Monsieur Ménage and Mesdemoiselles de Scudéry and Paulet shrugged, unimpressed.

"Wait for it, wait for it," said Aramis. "There are two strophes."

"Oh, say rather two couplets," said Mademoiselle de Scudéry, "as this is at best a song."

"'I thought—that poor Love,
Who always lent you his arms,
Is banished from your Court,
Without looks, bow, or charms—

"'And for me, what's the use
Of thinking about you,
If you only abuse
Those who've served you so well?'"

"Well, as to that last trait," said Madame de Chevreuse, "it might murder the laws of poetry, but it's certainly the truth—as Madame de Hautefort and Madame de Sennecey would surely attest, not to mention Monsieur de Beaufort."

"Go on, go on," said Scarron, "that no longer concerns me, since as of this morning I'm no longer 'her patient.'"

"And the final couplet?" said Mademoiselle de Scudéry. "Let's have the final couplet."

"Here it is," said Aramis. "This one goes to the trouble of naming names, so no one has to guess:

"'I thought—we who are poets,
Ideas tumbling in torment,
What, given your mood,
You would do in this moment,

"'If you saw enter, in this place
The Duke of Buckingham,
Who would you sooner disgrace,
The duke or Père Vincent?'"[86]

At this final verse, there was a general cry of outrage at Voiture's impertinence.

"Speaking for myself," said the girl with violet eyes, quietly, "I'm afraid I find these verses quite charming."

Raoul thought so as well; blushing, he approached Scarron and said, "Monsieur Scarron, do me the honor, if you please, to tell me who is this young lady whose opinion stands against that of this entire illustrious assembly."

"Oh ho, my young Viscount!" said Scarron. "I gather you wish to propose an alliance both offensive and defensive?"

Raoul blushed again. "I admit," he said, "I thought the verses very pretty."

"And so they are," said Scarron, "but hush! Between poets, we don't say such things."

"But I don't have the honor to be a poet," said Raoul, "so I ask you . . ."

"That's right—you wanted to know who the young lady is, no? She's the girl known as the *Beautiful Indian.*"

"Excuse me, Monsieur," said Raoul, coloring, "but that doesn't tell me anything. Alas! I'm such a provincial."

"Which just means you're not infected yet with the wild nonsense we spew here from every mouth. All the better, young man, all the better!

Don't try to understand it all, it's a waste of time—but when you grasp a bit more of it, we'll speak again."

"But forgive me, Monsieur," said Raoul, "and do please tell me who is this person you call the Beautiful Indian?"

"Oh, of course, she's one of the nicest people you could hope to meet: Mademoiselle Françoise d'Aubigné."[87]

"D'Aubigné? Is she of the family of the famous 'Agrippa,' the friend of King Henri IV?"

"She's his granddaughter. She came here from Martinique, which is why she's called the Beautiful Indian."

Raoul's eyes widened, and met the violet gaze of the young lady, who smiled.

Everyone was still talking about Voiture. "Monsieur," Mademoiselle d'Aubigné said to Scarron, inserting herself into his conversation with the young viscount, "don't you admire these friends of poor Voiture? Listen to how they prick him even as they praise him. One denies him the possession of common sense, the next all talent for poetry, then any originality, or sense of humor, or independence, or . . . why, good God! What has he left but celebrity?"

Scarron laughed, and Raoul joined in. The Beautiful Indian, astonished by the effect she'd achieved, looked down and resumed her air of innocence. Raoul said to himself, "This is a person of refined spirit."

Athos, still in the window embrasure, surveyed the entire scene with a disdainful smile on his lips. "Call over the Comte de La Fère," Madame de Chevreuse said to the coadjutor. "I need to speak with him."

"Whereas I," said the coadjutor, "need it to be thought that I *don't* speak with him. I like and admire him, as I know at least something of his former adventures—but I shouldn't seem to know him until after tomorrow morning."

"Why after tomorrow morning?" asked Madame de Chevreuse.

"You'll know that tomorrow night!" said the coadjutor, laughing.

"Faith, my dear Gondy," said the duchess, "you always talk like it's the

Apocalypse. Monsieur d'Herblay," she added, turning toward Aramis, "will you be my servant this evening?"

"Tonight, tomorrow, and forever, Duchess," said Aramis. "Command me."

"Well, then, fetch me the Comte de La Fère. I want to talk to him."

Aramis went and brought back Athos.

"Monsieur le Comte," said the duchess, giving Athos a letter, "here is that which I promised you. Our protégé will be well received."

"Madame," said Athos, "he is happy to be in your debt."

"You have nothing to envy him in that regard, for without you, I would never have known him," replied the wayward lady, with an impish smile that recalled Marie Michon to both Aramis and Athos.

And with that, she rose and called for her carriage. Mademoiselle Paulet had already gone, and Mademoiselle de Scudéry was leaving.

"Viscount," said Athos to Raoul, "follow Madame la Duchesse, and beg the favor of escorting her out—and as you do, be sure to thank her."

Meanwhile, the Beautiful Indian approached Scarron to take her leave of him. "What? Leaving already?" he said.

"But one of the last to go, as you see. If you hear news of Monsieur Voiture, and if it's good, please do me the favor of letting me know tomorrow."

"Oh, but you know," said Scarron, "he may die."

"Do you mean it?" said the girl with violet eyes.

"Certainly, now that his panegyric is complete."

And they parted, laughing, the girl turning to give the poor paralytic a fond look, while the poor paralytic followed her out with a look of love.

Gradually the groups broke up. Scarron pretended not to notice that some of his guests had had mysterious discussions, that letters had arrived for others, and that his party seemed to have an undercurrent that had nothing to do with literature, despite all the noise devoted thereto. But what did that matter to Scarron? He was already out of favor—as he'd said, as of that morning he was no longer "The Queen's Patient."

As to Raoul, he had indeed escorted the duchess to her carriage, where she gave him her hand to kiss—and then, in one of those wild caprices that made her so adorable, and so dangerous, she suddenly took him by his ears and kissed him on the forehead, intoning, "Viscount, by this kiss, and by my wishes, may you find happiness!"

Then she pushed him away and ordered the coachman to take her to the Hôtel de Luynes. The duchess favored the young man with a final wave, the carriage rolled away, and Raoul went back inside, dazed.

Athos understood what had happened and smiled. "Come, Viscount," he said, "it's time we retired. You leave tomorrow for the army of Monsieur le Prince, so sleep well on your last night in the city."

"I'm going to be a soldier?" said the young man. "Oh, Monsieur! I thank you with all my heart!"

"Adieu, Count," said the Abbé d'Herblay. "I must return to my monastery."

"Adieu, Abbot," said the coadjutor. "I preach tomorrow, and still have twenty texts to consult this evening."

"Adieu, Messieurs," said the count. "I'm so tired, I'm sure I'll spend the next twenty-four hours asleep."

The three men bowed, after exchanging a final look.

Scarron watched them from the corner of his eye as they went out the doors of his salon. "And not a one of them will do what he said," he whispered with his simian smile. "But there they go, the brave gentlemen! And who knows? Perhaps they'll find a way to restore my pension . . . ! At least they can move their limbs, and that's more than enough. As for me, I have only language—but I'll try to show the world yet that that's something. Holà! Champenois! It's striking eleven already; come and roll me to my bed. . . . Ah, but in truth, that Demoiselle d'Aubigné is quite charming . . . !"

And with that, the poor paralytic disappeared into his bedroom, the door closed behind him, and the lights went out one by one in the salon on the Rue des Tournelles.

XXIV

Saint-Denis

Day had barely broken when Athos arose and dressed; it was easy to see, from the pale traces insomnia had left on his face, that he'd gone most of the night without sleep. No matter how firm and decisive he usually was, this morning there was something slow and irresolute about him.

As a way of gaining time, he occupied himself with preparations for Raoul's departure. First, he inspected a sword that he drew from its oiled leather sheath and checked the grip to make sure it was well wrapped and the blade's tang was fixed firmly in the hilt.

Then he threw into the bottom of the young man's luggage a small bag full of *louis d'or*, called Olivain, the lackey who'd come with him from Blois, placed the portmanteau before him, and made sure that it held everything a young man needs on campaign.

Finally, after expending nearly an hour on these preparations, he opened the door to the viscount's room and quietly entered.

The sun, already high, shone in through the wide-framed windows, because Raoul, returning late the night before, had neglected to close the curtains. He was still asleep, head resting gracefully on his arm, his long black hair half-covering his charming face, bedewed in the warmth with pearls of moisture that rolled down the dreaming youth's cheeks.

Athos approached and, bent in an attitude of tender melancholy, watched for a time the sleeping young man with his smiling mouth and half-closed eyes, whose dreams should be sweet and his slumbers light, given the silent guardian angel who watched over him with care and affection. Gradually, in the presence of youth so rich and so pure, Athos was drawn into a reverie of his own youth, of half-formed memories that were more phantasms than thoughts. Between that past and this present stretched an abyss. But imagination is an angel's flight that darts back over the dark seas where our illusions were shipwrecked, past the rocks that shattered our happiness. He recalled how the first part of his own life had been destroyed by a woman; and thought with dread what an influence love can have over even the finest and strongest.

Recalling all that he'd suffered, he foresaw all that Raoul might yet suffer, and the deep and tender compassion in his heart distilled itself into a single tear that dropped upon the young man.

At that moment Raoul awoke from his cloudless dreams, showing none of the sadness or grief that afflicts some of those of sensitive spirit. His eyes rose to meet those of Athos, and he felt some of what was passing in the heart of this man who awaited his awakening, much as a lover awaits the awakening of his mistress, with a gaze expressing an infinite love.

"You've been here, Monsieur?" he said with respect.

"Yes, Raoul, right here," said the count.

"And you didn't wake me?"

"I wanted to let you enjoy your last moments of sound sleep, *mon ami;* you must be still weary from yesterday, which extended so far into the night."

"Ah, Monsieur, you're so good to me!" said Raoul.

Athos smiled. "How do you feel?" he asked.

"Fine, Monsieur—fully recovered and refreshed."

"You're still growing," continued Athos, with a fatherly interest charming in such a mature man, "and at your age fatigue is doubly felt."

"Oh, please, Monsieur," said Raoul, shy at receiving so much attention. "Just give me a moment and I'll get dressed."

Athos called Olivain to assist, and in only ten minutes, with the military punctuality that Athos had passed on to his pupil, the young man was ready.

"Now," the youth said to the servant, "let's prepare my luggage."

"Your luggage is already prepared," said Athos. "It was packed under my supervision and should lack for nothing. If the lackeys have followed my orders, your bags should already be placed on the horses."

"Everything has been done as Monsieur le Comte desired," said Olivain, "and the horses are ready."

"And I slept on," cried Raoul, "while you, Monsieur, attended to all these details! Oh, truly, you overwhelm me with kindness."

"So, you love me just a little? I hope so, at least," Athos replied in an almost tender tone.

"Oh, Monsieur!" cried Raoul, struggling to keep control of his emotions. "As God is my witness, I love and revere you."

"Make sure you don't forget anything," said Athos, pretending to look around to conceal his feelings.

"Of course, Monsieur," said Raoul.

The lackey approached Athos hesitantly, and whispered, "The viscount lacks a sword, as Monsieur le Comte had me take away the one he wore last night."

"It's all right," said Athos. "That's my business."

Raoul didn't seem to notice this exchange. He went toward the front door, glancing at the count every few seconds to see if the moment of parting had come, but Athos seemed unmoved.

Arriving on the steps, Raoul saw three horses. "Oh, Monsieur!" he cried, radiant. "You're going with me?"

"I'll ride with you part of the way," said Athos.

Joy shone in Raoul's eyes, and he sprang lightly onto his horse.

Athos mounted more slowly, after whispering a few words to the lackey, who, instead of following immediately, went back into the house. Raoul, delighted to be in the count's company, noticed, or pretended to notice, nothing.

The two gentlemen rode across the Pont Neuf, and then went along the quays, around what was then called Pepin's Pond, then past the walls of the Grand Châtelet.[88] The lackey caught up to them as they turned onto Rue Saint-Denis.

They rode in companionable silence. Raoul felt that the time of separation was approaching; the night before the count had given certain orders respecting the events of the day. He looked at the youth with undisguised tenderness, and from time to time let slip an affectionate remark, or some thoughtful and caring advice.

After passing through the Saint-Denis gate, and climbing the heights past the monastery of the Récollets, Athos looked at the viscount's mount. "Take care, Raoul," he said. "Look! Your horse is already tired and foaming, while mine seems like it's just out of the stable. I've told you this often, as it's a common failure of horsemen: the way you tug on her mouth will harden her jaws, and if you do that too much, she won't respond as quickly as you might need her to. A rider's safety depends on his mount's prompt obedience. Remember, in a week you'll be riding, not around a track, but on a battlefield."

Then quickly, to take the sting out of the observation, Athos continued, "Look there, Raoul—what a fine meadow for hunting partridge."

The young man appreciated the lesson, and even more the delicate way in which it was given.

"I also noticed the other day," said Athos, "that when aiming a pistol, you extend your arm too far. The extra tension can interfere with your aim, so that out of a dozen shots you might miss three times."

"Whereas out of twelve shots you, Monsieur, would hit twelve times," replied Raoul, smiling.

"Because I bend my arm and rest my elbow on my other hand. Do you understand what I'm saying, Raoul?"

"Yes, Monsieur; I tried it myself after the last time you advised me, and it was a complete success."

"And then," said Athos, "when fencing, you charge your adversary too often. It's because you're young, I'm well aware—but the angle of the body when charging takes your sword out of line, and a level-headed opponent will stop you at the first step with a simple disengage, or even a stop-thrust."

"Yes, Monsieur, as you've done to me often enough—but not everyone has your courage and *sangfroid*."

"Now there's a cool breeze!" said Athos. "A reminder that winter is on its way. By the way, I must say, if you're going to shoot—and you will, as you're being sent to a young general who likes the smell of gunpowder— keep in mind that in an engagement, especially against other cavaliers, remember not to be the one who fires first. The first to fire rarely hits his man, and then he's disarmed himself in the face of an armed adversary. As your opponent fires, make your horse rear up—that maneuver has saved my life two or three times."

"If I can remember to do that, I will."

"What?" said Athos. "Are those poachers being placed under arrest over there? It seems so . . . Another important thing, Raoul: if you're wounded during a charge, and fall from your horse, if you have the strength for it, try to get out of your regiment's line of advance—for if they fall back, you could get trampled. In any case, if you are injured, write me right away, or get someone to write for you. We veterans know how to deal with wounds," added Athos, smiling.

"Thank you, Monsieur," the young man answered with some emotion.

"Ah! And here we are at Saint-Denis," murmured Athos.

They had just arrived at the town gate, where two sentries stood on guard. One said to the other, "Here's another young gentleman on his way to join the army."

Athos turned toward them; everything that concerned Raoul, even indirectly, was important to him. "How do you know that?" he asked.

"By his martial air, Monsieur," said the sentry. "And he's the right age. This is the second one today."

"A young man like me has already passed this morning?" asked Raoul.

"Yes, *ma foi,* with a haughty look and some fancy equipment—clearly the son of a family of rank."

"That sounds to me like he could be a companion for the road," said Raoul, as they continued on their way. "It's a shame that I missed him."

"You may yet join up with him, Raoul, after I have a talk with you here. What I have to say won't take long, and then perhaps you can catch up to your young gentleman."

"As you wish, Monsieur."

As they spoke they made their way through streets crowded for the coming festival of Pentecost, and stopped in front of the old basilica,[89] within which first mass was being said. "Let's dismount here, Raoul," said Athos. "Olivain, give me that sword, and stay here to hold the horses."

Athos took the sword the lackey held out to him, and the two gentlemen went into the church. Athos offered some holy water to Raoul. In the hearts of some fathers is a tenderness like that for a lover. The young man touched Athos's hand, genuflected, and crossed himself. Athos spoke a word to one of the guards, who bowed and marched away toward the crypts. "Come, Raoul," said Athos, "let's follow this man."

The guard opened the iron gate to the royal tombs and stood on the top step while Athos and Raoul descended into the crypts. In a sepulcher at the bottom of the stairs burned a silver lamp, and below this lamp rested a catafalque supported by an oaken stand, covered by a large cloak of purple velvet adorned with golden lilies.

The sadness that seemed to pervade this majestic church had prepared the young man for this scene, and he descended, step by solemn step, to the sepulcher, where he uncovered his head and stood before the mortal remains of the last king,[90] who would be buried with his ancestors only when his successor came to take his place, and who until then remained here, seemingly to say to human pride, so easily exalted when upon a throne: "Dust of the earth, I await you!"

They stood a moment in silence. Then Athos raised his hand, and pointing at the coffin, he said, "This is the catafalque of a man who was weak and lacked grandeur, and yet whose reign was full of important events. This king was guided by the ever-watchful mind of another man, who enlightened his liege the way this lamp illuminates his coffin. That man was the real king, Raoul; the other was a phantom into which he poured his soul. And yet, so powerful is the majesty of monarchy, that wise man doesn't have the honor to be buried at the feet of he for whose glory he expended his life. Remember, Raoul, that though that wise man served a little king, he by his devotion made his monarchy great. For there are two things within the palace of the Louvre: a king, who dies—and royalty, which does not.

"That reign is passed, Raoul; that minister, so dreaded, so feared, so hated by his master, has gone to his grave, drawing after himself the king who didn't dare to survive alone, lest he should destroy his own great work—for a king only builds when he has God, or the spirit of God, near to him. Back then everyone regarded the death of the cardinal as a deliverance—just as I myself, as blind as my contemporaries, sometimes opposed the designs of that great man who held France in his hands, and who, clenching or opening them, choked it or gave it air as he willed. If I wasn't crushed, me and my friends, by his terrible wrath, then I was probably spared so I could tell you this today: Raoul, do not confuse the king with the monarchy. The king is only a man, but the monarchy is the divine rule of God; if you are ever in doubt about which to serve, abandon the material incarnation in favor of the invisible principle—for the invisible principle is everything. Only God could make this principle tangible by incarnating it in a man.

"Raoul, I feel I can see your future, as if through a cloud. It's better than ours was, I think. Unlike us, who had a minister without a real king, you will have a king without a minister. You can serve, love, and respect such a king. If this king becomes a tyrant—for omnipotence is dizzying and can drive one to tyranny—then serve, love, and respect the monarchy, the infallible spirit of God upon earth, the celestial spark that makes this dust here so great and so holy that we, gentlemen of high rank as we are, are as nothing before this body at the foot of the staircase, just as this body itself is nothing before the throne of the Lord."

"As I love God, Monsieur," said Raoul, "I will respect the monarchy. I will serve the king, and I will try, even unto death, to live for the king, the monarchy, and God. Have I understood you correctly?"

Athos smiled. "You have a noble nature," he said. "Take, now, your sword."

Raoul went down on one knee.

"This sword was borne by my father, a gentleman loyal to the crown. I bore it in my turn, and did honor to him sometimes when the hilt was in my hand and the scabbard hung at my side. If your hand is not yet strong enough to wield it,[91] Raoul, so much the better, as you will have more time to learn what to do when the time comes to draw it."

"Monsieur," said Raoul, receiving the sword from the hands of the count, "I owe everything to you—but this sword is the most precious gift you have given me. I shall bear it, I swear, as a grateful man."

And he put his lips to the hilt and kissed it respectfully.

"It is well," said Athos. "Rise, Viscount, and embrace me."

Raoul rose and fell with emotion into the arms of Athos.

"Adieu," murmured the count, his heart melting. "Adieu, and think sometimes of me."

"Oh, forever and always!" cried the young man. "I swear to you, Monsieur, that at my end, your name will be the last name I speak, and my final thought will be the memory of you."

To hide his feelings, Athos climbed quickly back up the stairs, gave a gold coin to the tomb guardian, bowed before the altar, and went back out the entrance of the church, where he found Olivain waiting with the horses.

"Olivain," he said, pointing to Raoul's baldric, "tighten that belt's buckle, as the sword is hanging a bit low on it. Good. Now, you will accompany Monsieur le Vicomte until Grimaud joins you, at which time you'll leave the viscount. Do you hear, Raoul? Grimaud is a wise old servant full of courage and prudence; Grimaud will do well for you."

"Yes, Monsieur," said Raoul.

"Now to horse! I want to see how you ride."

Raoul obeyed.

"Goodbye, Raoul!" said the count. "And fare you well, my dear child."

"Goodbye, Monsieur," said Raoul, "and farewell, my beloved protector!"

Athos waved his hand, because he dared not speak, and Raoul rode away, his head uncovered in respect.

Athos stood, motionless, watching him go until he disappeared around the corner of the street. Then the count tossed his horse's bridle to a peasant, slowly went back up the stairs, entered the church, knelt down in the darkest corner, and prayed.

XXV

One of the Duc de Beaufort's Forty Methods of Escape

The same time passed for the prisoner as for those working on his escape—but for the prisoner, it passed far more slowly. Unlike those men who eagerly commit to a dangerous enterprise and grow cooler and calmer as the time for action approaches, the Duc de Beaufort, whose fiery courage was proverbial, but who had been chained up for five years, now seemed to want to hurry the very hours themselves toward the designated time to break out. There was nothing for him now but the escape, other than those projects he planned for afterward—projects, it must be admitted, that in comparison had grown vague and uncertain, though the desire for revenge still choked his heart. Beaufort's escape would be a terrible blow to Monsieur de Chavigny, whom he hated due to the petty persecutions he'd suffered at his hands, and an even worse disaster for Mazarin, whom he loathed for the unforgivable insult of his imprisonment. (We note that Monsieur de Beaufort maintained a due proportion in his hatred of the governor and the minister, placing the master over his subordinate.)

Seething in his prison, Beaufort, who knew so well the court of the Palais Royal, and the relationship between queen and cardinal, imagined to himself the dramatic reaction to the news, the cries that would echo from the minister's office to Anne of Austria's chambers: *Beaufort has escaped!* Repeating this to himself, Beaufort smiled softly, as though already out and breathing the open air of fields and forests, with a powerful horse galloping beneath him as he shouted aloud, "I'm free!"

But when he came out of his reverie he was still between four walls, no more than ten paces from where La Ramée sat twiddling his thumbs, while outside in the antechamber the guards drank and laughed.

The only thing that made this odious tableau bearable, so strange is the human mind, was the sullen face of Grimaud, whose features he had so hated at first, but which now embodied all his hopes. To him, Grimaud was as handsome as Antinous.[92]

Needless to say, this was all a fancy of the prisoner's feverish imagination. Grimaud was the same as he'd always been. That was how he maintained the confidence of his superior, La Ramée, who now relied on him more than he did on himself, since, as we've said, La Ramée felt at heart a certain sympathy for Monsieur de Beaufort.

Also, the good La Ramée was looking forward to his private supper party with the prisoner. La Ramée had only one fault: he was a gourmand who loved a good pastry and adored an excellent wine. And the successor to Père Marteau had promised him a pie of pheasant instead of chicken, and Chambertin instead of the usual Macon vintage. All this, plus the company of this excellent prince of whom he'd grown fond, who played such clever tricks on Chavigny and made such droll jests about Mazarin, all this made Pentecost for La Ramée the most anticipated festival of the year.

So, La Ramée awaited the hour of six o'clock with nearly as much impatience as the duke.

In the morning he had occupied himself by double-checking the details, and, trusting only himself, had made a personal visit to Père Marteau's successor. His expectations were surpassed: he was shown a true colossus of a pie, its upper crust adorned with the Beaufort coat of arms—and though it was as yet empty, nearby were a prime pheasant and two partridges, neatly larded and perforated like pincushions. Then La Ramée's mouth had begun to water, and he returned to the duke's cell rubbing his hands together.

To crown it all, as we said, Chavigny, trusting in La Ramée, had taken a little trip, leaving that morning after appointing La Ramée Deputy Governor of Vincennes Château.

As for Grimaud, he just seemed more sullen than ever.

In the morning, Beaufort had challenged La Ramée to a game of tennis, and at a sign from Grimaud recognized that he needed to pay close attention to everything that followed.

Grimaud, leading the way, traced the path they were to follow that evening. The tennis court was in what was called the small courtyard of the château. It was usually deserted, only guarded by sentries when Beaufort was playing there, though given the height of the drop over the outside walls this seemed unnecessary.

There were three doors to open before reaching the small courtyard. Each opened with a different key.

Once they were in the small courtyard, Grimaud marched stiffly over to sit in a crenellation, his legs dangling outside the wall. It was clear that this was where he intended to tie the rope ladder.

All of this pantomime, though quite clear to the Duc de Beaufort, was of course unintelligible to La Ramée.

The contest began. This time, Beaufort was on his game, and it seemed as if he could put the ball wherever he wanted. La Ramée was completely routed.

Four of Beaufort's guards assisted in collecting the balls. When the game was over, Beaufort, after lightly mocking La Ramée for his clumsiness, offered the guards two *louis d'or* to go and drink his health with their other comrades.

The guards asked permission of La Ramée, and he granted it, but only for the evening. Till then La Ramée had important details to take care of, and he wanted to make sure the prisoner didn't disappear while he ran his errands. Monsieur de Beaufort could hardly have arranged matters better if he'd done it himself.

Finally, the clock struck six, and though seven was the hour set for dinner, the food was prepared and served. There on a sideboard stood the colossal pie bearing the arms of the duke, seemingly cooked to perfection, if one could judge by the golden color of its flaky crust. The rest of the dinner matched its quality in every way.

Everyone was impatient: the guards to go and drink, La Ramée to sit down and dine, and Monsieur de Beaufort to escape.

Only Grimaud was unmoved; Athos had trained him well for this. There were moments when, looking at him, the Duc de Beaufort wondered if he were not in a dream, if this marble figure was actually in his service, and would animate when the time came.

La Ramée sent away the guards, commending them to drink the prince's health; then, when they were gone, he closed the doors, put the keys in his pocket, and beckoned the prince to the table with a look that said: *Whenever Monseigneur desires.*

The prince looked at Grimaud, and Grimaud looked at the clock; it was barely a quarter after six, and the escape was fixed for seven, so there were still three-quarters of an hour to pass.

The prince, to gain fifteen minutes, pretended to be engrossed in reading, and asked to finish his chapter. La Ramée approached and looked over his shoulder to see what book so engaged the prince that he would delay sitting down to table when dinner was ready. It was *Caesar's Commentaries,* which he himself, contrary to Chavigny's orders, had provided to the duke three days earlier.

La Ramée promised himself not to contravene the dungeon's regulations again. Meanwhile, he uncorked the bottles, and surreptitiously sniffed the pie.

At half past six, the duke rose and solemnly declared, "No doubt about it, Caesar was the greatest man of antiquity."

"You think so, Monseigneur?" said La Ramée.

"Yes."

"Well! As for me," said La Ramée, "I prefer Hannibal."

"Why's that, La Ramée?" asked the duke.

"Because he left behind no *Commentaries,*" said La Ramée with his big smile.

The duke took the hint and sat down, gesturing for La Ramée to take the place opposite him. The officer didn't wait to be asked twice.

Nothing is so expressive as the figure of a true gourmand sitting down to a fine dinner. As he received his bowl of soup from the hands of Grimaud,

La Ramée's face beamed with an expression of perfect bliss. The duke looked at him with a smile. "*Ventre-saint-gris,* La Ramée!" he cried. "If you told me that somewhere in France, at this moment, there was a happier man, I wouldn't believe it!"

"And you would be right, Monseigneur," said La Ramée. "As for me, I confess that when I'm hungry, I know of no more pleasant sight than that of a well-laid table. And if on top of that he who presides over the table is the grandson of Henri the Great, then you'll understand, Monseigneur, that the honor one receives doubles the pleasure one takes."

The prince bowed in acknowledgment, while a nearly imperceptible smile touched the face of Grimaud where he stood behind La Ramée. "My dear La Ramée," said the duke, "truly, you know how to turn a compliment."

"No, no, Monseigneur," said La Ramée, sincere and earnest, "no, truly, I say just what I think—there's no flattery in it."

"So, you really do like me?" asked the prince.

"So much so," said La Ramée, "that I'll be inconsolable on the day Your Highness leaves Vincennes."

"Saying that is a strange way of showing your affliction." (The prince meant *affection.*)

"Ah, but Monseigneur, what would you do on the outside?" said La Ramée. "Some exploit that would embroil you with the Court and get you locked up in the Bastille instead of Vincennes. Chavigny is not very friendly, I admit," continued La Ramée, sipping a glass of Madeira, "but Monsieur du Tremblay is much worse."

"True enough!" said the duke, amused at the turn the conversation was taking, and glancing at the clock, whose hands moved painfully slowly.

"What do you expect from the brother of a Capuchin who studied in the school of Cardinal Richelieu? Ah, Monseigneur, believe me, it's a good thing that the queen, who's always favored you, or so I'm told, had the good idea of sending you here instead, where you can promenade, play tennis in the fresh air, and eat well."

"Truly," said the duke, "to hear you, La Ramée, I'd have to be some sort of an ingrate to want to leave here."

"In fact, Monseigneur, to leave *would* be the height of ingratitude," said La Ramée. "But surely Your Highness isn't speaking seriously."

"Alas, I must confess," said the duke, "perhaps it's sheer folly, but I still dream of escape."

"By one of your famous forty methods, Monseigneur?"

"But yes!" replied the duke.

"Monseigneur," said La Ramée, "so long as we're baring our souls, tell me of one of these forty methods Your Highness has concocted."

"With pleasure," said the duke. "Grimaud, bring me the pie."

"I'm listening," said La Ramée, leaning back in his chair, holding up his glass, and squinting at it through one eye, in order to see the sun through its ruby liquid.

The duke glanced at the clock. In ten more minutes, it would strike seven.

Grimaud brought the pie and placed it before the prince, who lifted his slim silver knife to slice it open, but La Ramée, who feared the flimsy blade would mar the beautiful pastry, handed the duke his own knife, which had a sturdy blade of iron. "Thanks, La Ramée," said the duke, taking the utensil.

"Well, Monseigneur," said the officer, "what is this famous method?"

"Should I tell you," replied the duke, "of the one I think the best of all, the one I've decided would actually work?"

"Yes, that one," said La Ramée.

"Very well!" said the duke, holding the pie plate with one hand while carving a circle in the pastry with the knife he held in the other. "First of all, I would have to have as a guardian a brave fellow like you, Monsieur La Ramée."

"Good!" said La Ramée. "As you see, you have him. What next, Monseigneur?"

"I would give him my regards."

La Ramée bowed.

"I said to myself," continued the prince, "that once I had watching me a good fellow like La Ramée, I would have a friend of mine, whom he doesn't know is my friend, advise him to hire as a subordinate a man who is secretly devoted to me, and will help prepare for my escape."

"Go on!" said La Ramée. "That's not bad."

"It isn't, is it?" said the prince. "For example, the servant of some brave gentleman who is opposed to Mazarin—as all true gentlemen must be."

"Hush, Monseigneur!" said La Ramée. "Don't bring politics into this."

"Once I have this servant near me," continued the duke, "assuming he's skillful enough to get and keep my guardian's confidence—then with his aid, I'll be able to get news from outside."

"Ah, yes!" said La Ramée. "But how would you get this news from outside?"

"Oh, nothing could be easier," said the Duc de Beaufort. "For example, I could get it by playing tennis."

"By playing tennis?" asked La Ramée, beginning to pay closer attention to the duke's story.

"Yes, like this: I send a ball into the dry-moat, where a man collects it. The ball contains a letter; from the ramparts I request the man return it, but in place of my ball he throws me a different one—one that, also, contains a letter. So, we've exchanged ideas, and no one's the wiser."

"The devil you say!" La Ramée replied, scratching his ear. "I'm glad you warned me of this—I'll keep a close eye on your ball collector."

The duke smiled.

"But," said La Ramée, "that's really no more than a means of correspondence."

"That's not nothing, it seems to me."

"It's not enough, though."

"Ah, but how about this: suppose I tell my friends, 'Do you think that, at a given hour on a given day, you could be on the other side of the moat with two spare horses?'"

"What use is that?" said La Ramée, with some anxiety. "Unless those horses have wings to fly to the top of the wall to pick you up."

"Eh, *mon Dieu*," the prince casually said, "the horses don't need to fly to the top of the wall so long as I have a way to get down."

"Such as what?"

"Such as a rope ladder."

"Yes, but," La Ramée said, trying to laugh, "a rope ladder can't come up in a tennis ball."

"No, it has to enter inside something else."

"Inside something else! Such as . . . ?"

"Oh, perhaps . . . in a pie."

"In a pie?" cried La Ramée.

"Sure. Suppose, for a moment, that my faithful butler, Noirmont, spent enough money to purchase the bakery of Père Marteau . . ."

"Well, what then?" asked La Ramée, trembling.

"What then? My La Ramée, a confirmed gourmand, sees his lovely pies, which look so much better than their predecessors, and offers to get me a sample. I accept, provided that La Ramée shares this sample with me. For comfort and privacy, La Ramée dismisses the guards, keeping only Grimaud to serve us. Grimaud, naturally, is the servant recommended by my friend, secretly devoted to me and ready to assist in everything. The time of my escape is fixed for seven o'clock. And, well! As you can see, it's very nearly seven . . ."

"And when it's seven . . . ?" continued La Ramée, sweat beading his forehead.

"When it's seven," replied the duke, suiting his actions to his words, "I cut the crust off the top of this giant pie. Within it I find two poniards, a rope ladder, and a choke-pear. I place the point of one poniard to La Ramée's chest and I say, '*Mon ami*, I'm very sorry, but if you make a move or cry out, you're a dead man!'"

As we said, the duke's words reflected his actions. The duke ended standing beside La Ramée, pressing the point of a poniard into his chest with such resolve that his threat couldn't be doubted.

Meanwhile Grimaud, still silent, drew out of the pie the second poniard, the rope ladder, and the choke-pear.

La Ramée's eyes followed the appearance of each of these objects with increasing terror. "Oh, Monseigneur!" he cried, with such an expression of stupefaction that at any other time the prince would have laughed. "You wouldn't have the heart to kill me!"

"No—unless you try to thwart my escape."

"But, Monseigneur, if I let you escape, I'm a ruined man."

"I'll make sure you're repaid the full value of your position."

"Are you really determined to leave the dungeon?"

"Pardieu!"

"And nothing I can say will make you change your mind?"

"This evening, I shall be free."

"And if I defend myself? If I cry out?"

"Faith of a gentleman: I'll kill you."

At that moment the clock struck seven.

"Seven o'clock," said Grimaud, who until then hadn't said a word.

"Seven o'clock," said the duke. "You see, I mustn't be late."

La Ramée, driven by conscience, made a small movement. The duke frowned, and the officer felt the point of the dagger penetrate his clothes and prick his flesh. "Enough, Monseigneur!" he said. "Enough. I'll hold still."

"We must hurry," said the duke.

"Monseigneur, one final favor."

"What? Speak quickly."

"Tie me up, Monseigneur."

"Tie you up? Why?"

"So no one will think I was your accomplice."

"Tie his hands!" said Grimaud. "Not in front, but behind."

"But with what?" said the duke.

"With your belt, Monseigneur," said La Ramée.

The duke unbuckled his belt and gave it to Grimaud, who bound La Ramée's hands tightly behind him.

"Now his feet," said Grimaud. La Ramée stretched out his legs; Grimaud tore a strip from the tablecloth and tied him with it.

"Now my sword," said La Ramée. "Tie its hilt onto the sheath."

The duke took a lacing from his breeches and bound the sword to its owner's satisfaction.

"Now," said poor La Ramée, "the choke-pear—I insist upon it. Otherwise they'll put me on trial because I didn't scream for help. And tightly, Monseigneur—tightly."

Grimaud prepared to fulfill the officer's request, but the man signaled that he had something more to say. "Speak," said the duke.

"Please, Monseigneur," said La Ramée, "don't forget, if I get in trouble because of you, that I have a wife and four children."

"Don't worry. . . . Tightly, Grimaud."

In a moment La Ramée was gagged and laid on the ground, and then two or three chairs were overturned to indicate there'd been a struggle. Grimaud collected all the officer's keys from his pockets; the first opened the door of the cell they were in, then locked it behind them after they left. They went quickly along the gallery that led to the small courtyard. The three doors along the way were speedily unlocked and opened by Grimaud in an impressive display of dexterity.

Finally, they arrived at the tennis court; it was completely deserted, unlit and unguarded. The duke ran to the wall and saw, across the moat, three cavaliers holding two spare horses. The duke, excited to see them, exchanged waves with them.

Meanwhile, Grimaud attached the rope ladder—or rather, what passed for one, a ball of silk cord with a rung at each end. One rung was lodged in the embrasure, the other the climber was to place behind his legs as he unwound the cord in descending.

"Go," said the duke.

"Me first, Monseigneur?" asked Grimaud.

"Quite so," said the duke. "If they catch me, I go back into prison; if they catch you, you hang."

"Fair enough," said Grimaud. And immediately, setting himself astride the lower rung, he began his perilous descent. The duke watched him with eyes wide in helpless terror, as three-quarters of the way down the wall, the cord suddenly broke, and Grimaud fell heavily into the dry-moat.

Though the duke cried out, Grimaud didn't even groan—but he had to be badly injured, as he remained lying where he'd fallen. At once one of the waiting men dropped down into the moat and untangled Grimaud from the cord, after which the other two helped him up and out. "Come down, Monseigneur," called the first man. "The drop at the end is only fifteen feet, and the grass here is soft."

The duke was already on his way. His task was more difficult without the lower rung for support—he had to descend fully fifty feet solely by the strength of his arms and wrists. But the duke, as we've said, was nimble, athletic, and cool in the face of danger; in less than five minutes, he was at the end of the cord, which as the waiting gentleman had told him was only fifteen feet from the ground. He took a breath, closed his eyes, and dropped, landing harmlessly on his feet.[93]

Immediately he turned and began to climb out of the moat, at the top of which he met the Comte de Rochefort. The other two gentlemen were unknown to him. Grimaud, knocked out, was tied to his horse.

"Messieurs," said the prince, "I will thank you later, but right now there's not a moment to lose. Let's ride! And if you love me, ride hard!"

And he sprang onto his horse and put it into a gallop, drawing the fresh air deep into his chest, and shouting, with a joy impossible to describe, "Free! *Free! FREE!*"

XXVI

A Timely Arrival and a Hasty Departure

At Blois, d'Artagnan collected the sum that Mazarin, to speed his return, had authorized to cover his immediate needs.

It took an ordinary rider four days to travel from Blois to Paris. D'Artagnan arrived at the Saint-Denis gate at about four in the afternoon of the third day. Once he would have done it in two. We've already seen that Athos, who set out three hours after him, had arrived twenty-four hours ahead of him. But Planchet had lost the habit of these wild, forced rides, and d'Artagnan chided him for his softness.

"What do you mean, Monsieur? We did forty leagues in three days! I think that's pretty good for a confectioner."

"Have you really become just a grocer, Planchet—and now that we're reunited, are you seriously thinking of returning to vegetate in your grocery?"

"Hmph," said Planchet. "You're the only one still pursuing such an overactive life. Look at Monsieur Athos, now—does he spend his time seeking out strenuous adventures? No, he lives like a gentleman farmer, a true country seigneur. The tranquil life, Monsieur, is the only life."

"Hypocrite!" said d'Artagnan. "We're almost back to Paris, where there's a rope and a scaffold waiting for you and your 'tranquil life'!"

Indeed, as they were speaking the travelers rode up to the barrier at the gate. As they were entering a neighborhood where he thought he might be recognized, Planchet pulled down the brim of his hat. D'Artagnan twisted his mustache and remembered that Porthos should be awaiting him in Rue Tiquetonne. He'd been considering how to tempt him away from his green domain of Bracieux and the heroic kitchens of Pierrefonds.

Turning the corner of the Rue Montmartre, he saw, in one of the windows of the Hôtel de la Chevrette, Porthos dressed in a sky-blue doublet edged with silver embroidery, and yawning so as to nearly dislocate his jaw, while passersby gazed with respectful admiration upon such a gentleman, so handsome, so wealthy, and so bored with his own wealth and grandeur.

D'Artagnan and Planchet had scarcely turned the corner when Porthos spotted them. "Hey, d'Artagnan!" he called. "God be praised! It's you at last."

"And good afternoon to you, too, old comrade!" d'Artagnan replied.

A small crowd of idle onlookers gathered around the riders as the house grooms took their horses by the bridle, but at a frown from d'Artagnan and a gesture from Planchet the busybodies dispersed, since they weren't quite sure why they'd gathered in the first place.

Meanwhile Porthos had come down to the doorstep. "Ah, my dear friend," he said, "I see my horses have been hard put to it."

"So true!" said d'Artagnan. "My heart breaks for these noble creatures."

"I feel the same—they need a proper stable," said Porthos. "If it wasn't for the hostess here, who looks fine and knows a joke when she hears it," he said, smugly preening, "I'd have sought lodging elsewhere."

The fair Madeleine, who'd appeared behind him, stopped when she heard this and turned pale as death, for she thought it would be the scene with the Swiss Guard all over again—but to her amazement d'Artagnan didn't frown, and instead of getting angry, he said to Porthos with a laugh, "Yes, dear friend, I understand that the air of the Rue Tiquetonne can't compare to that of the valley of Pierrefonds, but don't worry—I've got better prospects ahead."

"Really? When?"

"Very soon, I hope."

"Ah! All the better!"

Porthos's exclamation was followed by a deep groan that came from beyond the angle of the door. D'Artagnan, dismounting, saw the silhouette of the bulging belly of Mousqueton, whose sad mouth was the source of the complaint. "So, you, too, my poor Monsieur Mouston, have moved into this boarding house?" d'Artagnan asked in a tone equal parts compassion and mockery.

"Yes—and he finds the cooking terrible," said Porthos.

"Well, then, why not do it himself, as he did at Chantilly?" said d'Artagnan.

"Ah, Monsieur, I don't have here, as we did there, the ponds of Monsieur le Prince, filled with lovely fish, or the forests of His Highness, where one could take such fine partridges. As for the cellar here, I've inspected it in detail, and it's deeply disappointing."

"Truly, Monsieur Mouston," said d'Artagnan, "I would pity you, if I didn't have more pressing business to attend to."

Then, taking Porthos aside: "My dear du Vallon," he said, "your outfit is splendid, which is appropriate, as I'm about to present you to the cardinal."

"Bah! Are you really?" said Porthos, his eyes widening.

"Yes, my friend."

"An official presentation?"

"Does that worry you?"

"No, but I admit I'm anxious."

"Oh, don't worry! It's not like you have to deal with the old cardinal—this one won't overwhelm you with his majesty."

"All the same, d'Artagnan—it's the Court, you know!"

"Oh, *mon ami*, there's no real Court these days."

"But—the queen!"

"And as I was about to add, there is no queen. Anyway, we certainly won't see her."

"You say, then, that we're going from here to the Palais Royal?"

"Right away. Only, so we won't be late, I'm going to have to borrow one of your horses."

"As you like. There are four of them in your stables, all at your disposal."

"Oh, one will be good enough for the moment."

"Should we bring our servants?"

"Yes, it wouldn't hurt to bring Mousqueton with us. As for Planchet, he has reasons for not appearing at Court."

"Like what?"

"He did some deeds that put him at odds with His Eminence."

"Mouston," said Porthos, "saddle Vulcan and Bayard."

"And for myself, Monsieur, shall I take Rustaud?"

"No, we're going on a ceremonial visit, so take a more stylish horse, like Phoebus or Superb."

"Ah!" breathed Mousqueton with relief. "So, we're just paying a visit?"

"*Mon Dieu*, yes, Mouston, no more than that. Only—just in case—put your pistols in your saddle holsters. I have mine, already loaded."

Mouston sighed; he knew all about the kind of ceremonial visits one made while armed to the teeth.

"In fact, d'Artagnan," said Porthos, complacently surveying his old lackey, "you're right, Mouston will do nicely—he looks quite magnificent."

D'Artagnan smiled. "And you," said Porthos, "aren't you going to change into a fresh outfit?"

"No, I'm fine as I am."

"But you're filthy with sweat and dust, and your boots are quite muddy!"

"All of which testifies to how eagerly I obey the cardinal's orders."

Mousqueton came back with three horses, fully equipped. D'Artagnan remounted as if he'd just had a week's rest. "Oh, Planchet!" he said. "I'll need the long rapier . . ."

"As for me," said Porthos, displaying a small dress sword with a golden hilt, "I have my court sword."

"Take your rapier, old friend."

"Why's that?"

"I'm not sure—just trust me and take it."

"My rapier, Mouston," commanded Porthos.

"But that's combat equipment, Monsieur!" replied Mouston. "Are we going on campaign? If so, tell me now, so I can take appropriate precautions."

"You know how it is, Mouston," said d'Artagnan. "With us, it's always appropriate to take precautions. Or has your memory grown so dim, you've forgotten that we don't usually spend our evenings at balls and serenades?"

"You're right—I should have known better," said Mousqueton, quickly arming himself from head to foot. ". . . Alas!"

They rode off at a trot and arrived at the Palais Royal at a quarter past seven. The streets were crowded, as it was the day of Pentecost, and as they rode by the citizens looked with surprise at these two cavaliers, one so shiny and fresh he might have come right out of a box, and the other so dusty he seemed to have come from a battlefield. Mousqueton also attracted the attention of the onlookers, who said, as the novel *Don Quixote*[94] was then in vogue, that he looked like Sancho who, having lost one master, had found two others.

Arriving in the palace antechamber, d'Artagnan found himself in familiar territory, as the musketeers of his own company were on guard duty. He called over the audiencer and showed him the cardinal's letter, which ordered him to return without losing a second. The audiencer bowed and went in to announce him to His Eminence.

D'Artagnan turned toward Porthos, who seemed agitated and was ever so slightly trembling. He smiled, leaned up toward Porthos's ear, and said, "Take courage, my brave friend! We no longer brave the eye of an eagle, we're just dealing with a vulture. Stand as straight as you did at the Saint-Gervais bastion, and don't bow too deeply to this Italian; it will give him the wrong impression of your worth."

"Well, all right," said Porthos.

The audiencer returned. "Enter, Messieurs," he said. "His Eminence awaits you."

In fact, Mazarin was seated in his study, poring over a list of names of those receiving pensions and benefits to see who he might safely strike off. He watched d'Artagnan and Porthos enter from the corner of his eye, and though that eye had sparkled with satisfaction at the audiencer's announcement, he now pretended not to notice them.

"Ah, is that you, Monsieur Lieutenant?" he said, looking up. "You've shown great diligence, and your arrival is welcome."

"Thank you, Monseigneur. I've come at Your Eminence's orders, and brought with me one of my old friends, Monsieur du Vallon, who once disguised his nobility under the name of Porthos."

Porthos bowed to the cardinal.

"A magnificent cavalier indeed," said Mazarin.

Porthos shook his head slightly, and gave his giant shoulders a modest shrug.

"He's the mightiest sword in the realm, Monseigneur," said d'Artagnan, "though many who know it won't inform you of it—or can't."

Porthos saluted d'Artagnan.

Mazarin loved handsomely turned-out soldiers almost as much as Frederick of Prussia would in a later era. He took a moment to admire Porthos's sinewy hands, broad shoulders, and steady eye. It seemed to him that he had before him the means of salvation of his ministry and the kingdom, carved from muscle and bone. He remembered that there had once been four such impressive musketeers. "And your other two friends?" he asked.

Porthos opened his mouth, thinking it was time to get a word in, but d'Artagnan quelled him with a twitch of his eye. "Our other friends are engaged at present but will join us later."

Mazarin coughed lightly. "And Monsieur here, freer than they, has volunteered to rejoin the service?"

"Yes, Monseigneur, and out of sheer devotion, for Monsieur de Bracieux is quite wealthy."

"Wealthy?" said Mazarin, repeating the single word that always got his attention.

"An annual income of fifty thousand livres," said Porthos, speaking for the first time.

"Out of sheer devotion," continued Mazarin, with his cunning smile. "Sheer devotion, eh?"

"Perhaps Monseigneur no longer believes in such a thing?" d'Artagnan asked.

"Do you, Monsieur Gascon?" said Mazarin, resting his elbows on his desk and his chin on his hands.

"Me?" said d'Artagnan. "I think 'Devotion' makes a fine baptismal name, so long as it's followed by something more earthly. Everyone starts out more or less devoted, but devotion eventually needs a reward."

"So, your friend—for example. What would he like to have as a reward for his devotion?"

"Well, Monseigneur! My friend has three magnificent estates: Vallon at Corbeil, Bracieux near Soissons, and Pierrefonds in the Valois. And what he would like is to have one of these estates elevated to a barony."

"Is that all?" said Mazarin, eyes sparkling at the happy idea that he could reward Porthos's devotion without opening his purse. "Is that all? Well, the thing can be arranged."

"Me, a baron!" cried Porthos, taking a step forward.

"I told you so," said d'Artagnan, stopping him with a movement of his hand, "and Monseigneur confirms it."

"And you, Monsieur d'Artagnan—what do you want?"

"Monseigneur," said d'Artagnan, "in September it will be twenty years since Cardinal Richelieu made me a lieutenant."

"Indeed—and you'd like Cardinal Mazarin to make you a captain."

D'Artagnan bowed.

"Well, that's not an impossibility! We'll see, Messieurs, we'll see. Now, Monsieur du Vallon," said Mazarin, "which do you prefer: to serve in the city, or go out on campaign?"

Porthos opened his mouth to answer.

"Monseigneur," said d'Artagnan, "like me, Monsieur du Vallon prefers extraordinary services, that is to say, those missions that others consider insane or impossible."

This little gasconade did not displease Mazarin, and it started him thinking. "Maybe, but I must confess I summoned you here for a more sedentary task. I'm anxious about . . . Here, now! What's that noise?"

A great clamor came from the antechamber, the office door opened suddenly, and a man covered in dust rushed in, shouting, "Monsieur le Cardinal? Where's His Eminence?"

Mazarin recoiled, thinking it was an assassin, and took shelter behind his chair. D'Artagnan and Porthos moved to put themselves between the cardinal and the newcomer.

"Eh, Monsieur!" said Mazarin. "What are you doing, bursting in here and shouting like some crier in the markets?"

"Monseigneur," said the officer so reproached, "I must tell you what I have to report quickly and in confidence. I'm Poins, Officer of the Guards at the dungeon of Vincennes."

The officer was so pale and distraught that Mazarin, convinced he brought news of importance, waved d'Artagnan and Porthos aside to make way for the messenger. The two cavaliers withdrew into a corner of the office.

"Speak, Monsieur, and quickly," said Mazarin. "What is it, then?"

"Just this, Monseigneur," said the messenger. "Monsieur de Beaufort has escaped from the Château de Vincennes."

Mazarin uttered a cry and turned even paler than the messenger. He fell back into his chair in a near-faint. "Escaped!" he gasped. "Beaufort—escaped?"

"From the parapet, Monseigneur, I saw him riding away."

"And you didn't shoot him?"

"He was out of range."

"But Chavigny, what was he doing?"

"He was away."

"And La Ramée?"

"He was found tied and gagged in the prisoner's cell, near a fallen poniard."

"But what about his assistant?"

"He was the duke's accomplice and escaped with him."

Mazarin groaned.

"Monseigneur," said d'Artagnan, taking a step toward the cardinal.

"What?" said Mazarin.

"It seems to me Your Eminence is losing precious time."

"What do you mean?"

"If Your Eminence will order the prisoner pursued, he might still be caught. France is large, and it's sixty leagues to the closest border."

"And who would go after him?" cried Mazarin.

"Pardieu! Me!"

"You would arrest him?"

"Why not?"

"You would take the Duc de Beaufort from amidst his armed allies?"

"If Monseigneur ordered it, I'd arrest the Devil himself. I'd grab him by the horns and haul him in."

"Me, too," said Porthos.

"You too?" said Mazarin, astonished. "But the duke won't give up without a fierce fight."

"Well!" said d'Artagnan, his eyes afire. "A fight! It's been a while since we had a good fight, isn't it, Porthos?"

"To battle!" said Porthos.

"And you think you can catch him?"

"Yes, if we're better mounted than he is."

"Then take whatever troops you want with you and go."

"At your orders, Monseigneur."

"At my orders," said Mazarin, taking a sheet of paper and writing a few lines.

"Add, Monseigneur, that we may confiscate any horses we need along the way."

"Yes, yes," said Mazarin. "On the king's service! Take whatever you need and go!"

"Very good, Monseigneur."

"Monsieur du Vallon," said Mazarin, "you'll find your barony just beyond the Duc de Beaufort—all you have to do is catch him. As for you, Monsieur d'Artagnan, I make no promises, but if you bring him back, dead or alive, you may ask for what you will."

"To horse, Porthos!" said d'Artagnan, taking his friend by the arm.

"I'm with you," replied Porthos, with his serene composure.

And they ran down the grand staircase, gathering up guards as they passed, shouting, "To horse! To horse!"

Ten men were quickly assembled. D'Artagnan and Porthos mounted up, the former on Vulcan and the latter on Bayard, while Mousqueton straddled Phoebus.

"Follow me!" shouted d'Artagnan.

"Let's ride," said Porthos.

And they dug their spurs into the flanks of their noble steeds and galloped up Rue Saint-Honoré like a raging storm.

"Well, now, Monsieur le Baron!" called d'Artagnan. "I promised you some exercise, didn't I?"

"You did, Monsieur le Capitaine!" replied Porthos.

They glanced behind: Mousqueton, sweating even more than his horse, was right behind them, followed at a gallop by the ten troopers.

The citizens gazed in amazement from their doorsteps as their excited dogs barked and nipped at the cavaliers' heels.

At the corner of the Saint-Jean cemetery, d'Artagnan's horse knocked down a pedestrian, but their business was too pressing to stop. The galloping troop continued on its way as if the horses had wings. But alas! Every action, however small, has its consequences, and we'll see how this one nearly led to the fall of the monarchy.

XXVII

The King's Highway

Headed toward Vincennes, they galloped through the Faubourg Saint-Antoine and soon found themselves outside the city, riding through a wood and then into a village. The horses seemed to stretch out more with every step, their red nostrils roaring like blazing furnaces. D'Artagnan, working the spurs, led Porthos by no more than two feet. Mousqueton followed by two lengths. The troopers trailed in a scattering behind, depending on the virtues of their horses.

Coming over a crest d'Artagnan saw a group of people clustered along the moat where the Château de Vincennes faces Saint-Maur. He realized that must be from whence the prisoner had fled, and that was where he'd find more information. He reached the group within five minutes, followed successively by his troopers.

The folk who made up the group were completely engrossed. They stared at the cord that still hung from the parapet and ended, broken, twenty feet from the ground. They estimated the height of the drop and shared theories of the escape. Nervous sentries passed along the top of the wall, peering down anxiously.

A squad of soldiers, commanded by a sergeant, arrived to drive the idlers away from where the duke had taken to horseback. D'Artagnan went straight up to the sergeant. "*Mon Officier,*" said the sergeant, "you can't linger here."

"Your orders don't apply to me," said d'Artagnan. "Has anyone gone after the fugitives?"

"Yes, Officer, but unfortunately the escapees were well mounted."

"How many were there?"

"Four healthy, and one injured, whom they took with them."

"Four!" said d'Artagnan, looking at Porthos. "Did you hear that, Baron? Only four!"

A happy smile lit Porthos's face.

"And how much of a lead do they have?" asked d'Artagnan.

"Two hours and a quarter, Officer."

"Two hours and a quarter, that's nothing. We're well mounted, aren't we, Porthos?"

Porthos sighed at the thought of what was ahead for his poor horses.

"Very well," said d'Artagnan. "Now, which direction did they go?"

"As to that, Officer, I'm not supposed to say."

D'Artagnan drew a paper from his pocket. "The king's orders," he said.

"Speak to the governor, then."

"And where is the governor?"

"He's away."

Anger colored d'Artagnan's face; his brow furrowed, his temples flushed. "You wretch!" he said to the sergeant. "Do you think you can toy with me? Just wait."

He unfolded the paper and held it up in front of the sergeant with one hand, while with the other he drew a pistol and cocked it. "The king's orders, I said. Look at this and answer me, or I'll blow out your brains! Which way did they go?"

The sergeant saw that d'Artagnan was serious. "The road to Vendôme!" he said.

"By what gate did they leave?"

"The Saint-Maur gate."

"If you're lying to me, dog, you hang tomorrow," said d'Artagnan.

"And if you catch up to them, you'll never return to hang me," muttered the sergeant.

D'Artagnan shrugged, beckoned to his troop, and spurred on. "This way, Messieurs, this way!" he cried, pointing toward the gate that gave onto Saint-Maur.

But now that the duke had escaped, the gatekeeper thought it prudent to lock the gate. He had to be persuaded in the same way as the sergeant, which cost them ten more minutes.

That final obstacle passed, the troop resumed its ride with the same haste. But the horses couldn't maintain that pace, and after an hour's gallop, three balked and halted; one fell. D'Artagnan didn't pause, or even turn his head. In his calm voice, Porthos reported the loss to him.

"So long as the two of us get there," said d'Artagnan. "Against four, we're plenty."

"True," said Porthos. And he put the spurs to his horse.

After two hours, the horses had gone twelve leagues without a pause; their legs began to tremble, the foam blown from their muzzles speckled their riders' doublets, and their sweat soaked the riders' breeches.

"Let's rest a few minutes to let these poor creatures breathe," said Porthos.

"No—we ride them to death, if we must," d'Artagnan said. "Look! Fresh tracks. They're no more than a quarter of an hour ahead of us."

And in fact, by the last rays of the setting sun, they could see the road was freshly furrowed by horses' hooves.

They rode on—but two leagues later Mousqueton's horse staggered and fell.

"Oh, great!" said Porthos. "There's Phoebus burned out."

"The cardinal will pay you ten thousand pistoles."

"Right you are!" said Porthos. "I'm over it."

"Resume the pursuit, at the gallop!"

"We will, if we can."

But in fact, d'Artagnan's horse refused to take another step; his breathing shuddered to a halt, and a final touch of the spur, instead of reviving him, made him fall.

"The devil!" said Porthos. "That's the end of Vulcan."

"*Mordieu!*" cried d'Artagnan, pulling out his hair by the handful. "Have I hit a wall? Porthos—give me your horse. But wait, what the devil are you doing?"

"Pardieu! I'm falling," said Porthos, "or rather, it's Bayard who falls."

D'Artagnan assisting, Porthos tried to spur the horse back up, but suddenly blood gushed from its nostrils. "Three down!" said Porthos. "It's all over."

At that moment a neighing was heard. "Hush!" said d'Artagnan.

"What is it?"

"I heard a horse."

"It's just our companions rejoining us."

"No," said d'Artagnan, "it's ahead of us."

"Oh? Well that's something else entirely," said Porthos.

And he listened in his turn, focusing on the direction d'Artagnan had indicated.

"Monsieur," said Mousqueton, who, having abandoned his horse on the highway, had just walked up to rejoin his maser, "Monsieur, Phoebus couldn't handle another . . ."

"Hush there!" said Porthos.

And just then a second neigh was borne to them on the night breeze.

"They're about five hundred paces ahead of us," said d'Artagnan.

"True, Monsieur," said Mousqueton, "and five hundred paces ahead of us there happens to be a small hunting lodge."

"Mousqueton, your pistols," said d'Artagnan.

"They're ready, Monsieur."

"Porthos, do you have yours?"

"I have them."

"Well," d'Artagnan said, drawing his own, "do you get it, Porthos?"

"Not so much."

"We're riding in the king's service."

"So?"

"So, in the king's service, we require those horses."

"Right," said Porthos.

"No more talk, then. Let's do it!"

All three advanced through the dark, silent as ghosts. At a bend in the road, they saw a light shining through the trees.

"There's the house," said d'Artagnan quietly. "I'll go first—follow my lead, Porthos."

They glided from tree to tree and moved to within twenty paces of the house unnoticed. From that distance, thanks to a lantern hanging from a shed, they could see four horses of the finest quality. A groom was tending to them; nearby were saddles and bridles.

D'Artagnan made a sign to his companions to stay a few steps behind him, and then moved quickly forward. "I'm buying these horses," he said to the groom.

The man turned around, surprised, but made no reply.

"Didn't you hear what I said, dolt?" snapped d'Artagnan.

"I heard it," said the groom.

"Why didn't you answer me?"

"Because these horses aren't for sale."

"Nonetheless, I'm buying them," said d'Artagnan. And he reached out for the closest horse. His two companions came up and did the same.

"But, Messieurs!" cried the groom. "They just traveled six leagues and have been unsaddled barely half an hour."

"Then they're already warmed up," said d'Artagnan. "Half an hour's rest is plenty."

The groom called for help. A steward came out just as d'Artagnan and his companions were getting the saddles on the horses. The steward began to object loudly.

"My dear fellow," said d'Artagnan, "say one more word and I'll blow your brains out." And he showed him the barrel of a pistol that he immediately tucked back under his arm so he could continue his work.

"But, Monsieur," said the steward, "don't you realize these horses belong to Monsieur de Montbazon?"

"All the better," said d'Artagnan. "That explains their quality."

"Monsieur," said the steward, backing away toward the door of the house, "I warn you, I'll call for my people."

"And I'll call for mine," said d'Artagnan. "I'm a lieutenant of the King's

Musketeers, with ten troopers coming up behind me. Can't you hear them? Then we'll see."

No one heard anything, but the steward went quietly back inside.

"Are you ready, Porthos?" said d'Artagnan.

"I've finished."

"And you, Mouston?"

"Me too."

"Then into the saddle, and ride."

The three sprang onto their horses, just as the steward reappeared. "There they are!" he shouted. "Quick! The pistols and carbines!"

"Off we go, before there's musketry!" said d'Artagnan. And they spurred off like the wind.

"Help!" bellowed the steward, as the groom appeared from another building with some armed men.

"Careful! They'll kill your horses!" cried d'Artagnan, laughing.

"Fire!" replied the steward.

Sudden lightning lit the road, followed by a detonation, then the sound of bullets whistling past the riders. "They shoot like peasants," said Porthos. "Marksmanship isn't what it was in Monsieur de Richelieu's time. Do you remember the road to Crèvecœur, Mousqueton?"

"Ah, Monsieur, my right buttock sure remembers it!"

"Are you certain we're on the right track, d'Artagnan?" asked Porthos.

"Pardieu! Didn't you hear what he said?"

"What?"

"That these horses belong to Monsieur de Montbazon."

"What of it?"

"What of it? Monsieur de Montbazon is the husband of Madame de Montbazon . . ."

"He must be, no?"

"And Madame de Montbazon is the mistress of Monsieur de Beaufort."

"Ah, I get it," said Porthos. "She provided the relays."

"Exactly."

"And now we're chasing the duke on the horses he just left behind."

"My dear Porthos, you really do possess a rare intelligence," said d'Artagnan, half serious and half jesting.

"Bah!" said Porthos. "You must take me as I am."

They ran the horses for an hour, until they were white with foam and blood streamed from their flanks. "Hey! What's that I see ahead?" said d'Artagnan.

"You're lucky you can see anything on a night like this," said Porthos.

"Sparks!"

"Yes!" said Mousqueton. "I saw them too."

"Ah ha!" said Porthos. "Have we caught up to them?"

"Here we go—a dead horse," said d'Artagnan, reining in his own horse as it shied. "It seems they're also reaching the end of their breath."

"I think I hear a troop of riders ahead," said Porthos, bending forward over his horse's mane.

"A troop? Impossible."

"No, there are a lot of them."

"All right, if you say so."

"Here's another horse!" said Porthos.

"Dead?"

"No, dying."

"Saddled or unsaddled?"

"Saddled."

"That's them, then."

"Courage! We have them."

"But if they're so many," said Mousqueton, "we don't have them, they have us."

"Bah!" said d'Artagnan. "They'll think they're outnumbered, since they're caught up—they'll be afraid and scatter."

"Right," said Porthos.

"Ah! Look there," cried d'Artagnan.

"Yes, more sparks—this time I saw them, too," said Porthos.

"Forward, forward!" d'Artagnan shouted. "Five minutes from now we'll be laughing."

And they hurtled ahead. The horses, furious from pain and fatigue, flew up the dark highway, and ahead they began to see a dark mass moving against the horizon.

XXVIII

Encounter

They continued the chase for ten more minutes. Suddenly, two black blots detached themselves from the dark mass ahead, approached, grew, and assumed the silhouettes of two riders.

"Uh-oh," said d'Artagnan. "They're coming to us."

"Too bad for them," said Porthos.

"Who's that?" cried a hoarse voice.

The three riders dashed ahead without pause or reply, though from the approaching phantoms they heard the sound of swords being drawn and of pistols being cocked.

"Reins in your teeth!" said d'Artagnan. Porthos understood, and then he and d'Artagnan each drew a pistol left-handed and cocked it.

"Who's that?" the voice cried a second time. "Not one more step or you're dead!"

"Bah!" replied Porthos, nearly choking on dust and chewing the reins as his horse was chewing his bit. "We've heard that before."

At these words the two shadows reined up and barred the way, and starlight glinted from the barrels as they aimed their pistols.

"Back off!" cried d'Artagnan. "Or it's you who'll be dead."

Two pistol shots replied to this threat, and the shooters followed their shots so closely that they were upon their opponents a moment later. A third pistol cracked, fired at close range by d'Artagnan, and an enemy fell. As for Porthos, he struck his opponent with his sword so hard that, though the blade was turned, he sent the man tumbling ten paces from his horse.

"Finish him, Mousqueton!" said Porthos. And he spurred forward to catch up to his friend, who had already resumed the pursuit. "Well?" said Porthos.

"Head shot," shrugged d'Artagnan. "And you?"

"Just knocked him out of the saddle—but wait . . ."

They heard the crack of a carbine: it was Mousqueton, following his master's orders as he passed.

"Two down!" said d'Artagnan. "First trick to us."

"Yes," said Porthos, "but here come some more players."

In fact, two more horsemen appeared to have detached from the main group and were hastening back to bar the road once more.

This time d'Artagnan didn't even wait for them to address him. "Make way!" he cried first. "Make way!"

"What are you after?" said a voice.

"The duke!" shouted Porthos and d'Artagnan with one voice.

The response was a burst of laughter, but it ended in a whimper, as d'Artagnan ran the man through with his sword.

At the same time two pistols boomed as Porthos and his adversary fired at each other.

D'Artagnan turned and saw Porthos right behind him. "Bravo, Porthos!" he said to him. "Do you think you killed him?"

"I think I killed his horse," said Porthos.

"Well, what would you have? You can't hit the bull's-eye every time—so long as you're on the target, we can't complain. . . . Hey! Parbleu! What's wrong with my horse?"

"Your horse is done in," said Porthos, reining in his own.

Indeed, d'Artagnan's horse stumbled, fell to its knees, then groaned and lay down. It had been struck in the chest by his first opponent's bullet. D'Artagnan's curses were sharp enough to crack the sky.

"Does Monsieur need a horse?" said Mousqueton.

"By God! I'll say," cried d'Artagnan.

"Take this one," said Mousqueton.

"How the devil do you have two horses?" said d'Artagnan, jumping on the second one.

"Their masters were dead, and I thought they might come in handy, so I took them."

Meanwhile Porthos was reloading his pistols.

"Heads up!" said d'Artagnan. "Here come two more."

"They keep coming like there's no tomorrow," said Porthos.

Indeed, two more riders were rapidly approaching. "Watch out, Monsieur!" said Mousqueton. "The one you unhorsed has gotten up."

"Why didn't you treat him like the first one?"

"I was busy rounding up the horses."

A shot rang out, and Mousqueton screamed in pain. "Ah, no, Monsieur! Not the other one! It's like the road to Amiens all over again!"

Porthos turned and leapt like a lion on the dismounted rider, who tried to draw his sword, but before it was out of its scabbard Porthos had cracked his head with such a blow from his pommel that he dropped like an ox under the butcher's axe.

Mousqueton, groaning, slid down from his horse, as his wound wouldn't let him stay in the saddle.

Watching the approaching riders, d'Artagnan had paused to reload his pistol, and discovered that his new horse had a carbine in a long saddle holster.

"I'm back!" said Porthos. "Do we wait for them, or charge?"

"We charge," said d'Artagnan.

"We charge!" said Porthos.

They dug their spurs into their horses. The oncoming riders were no more than twenty paces from them. "In the king's name!" cried d'Artagnan. "Let us pass."

"There's no king here," replied a dark, resonant voice that seemed to come from a cloud, as the rider came wreathed in a mist of dust.

"And I say the king is everywhere," said d'Artagnan.

"We'll see," said the same voice. Two shots rang out simultaneously, one from d'Artagnan, the other from Porthos's adversary. D'Artagnan's ball shot off his enemy's hat, while the bullet from Porthos's opponent tore out the throat of his horse, which collapsed with a groan.

"For the last time, where do you think you're going?" said the same dark voice.

"To the Devil!" d'Artagnan replied.

"Fine! I'll send you to him." D'Artagnan saw him bring up the barrel of a musket; there was no time to reach for his holsters, but he remembered some advice Athos had once given him and made his horse rear.

The musket ball struck his mount in the belly. D'Artagnan felt his horse going down, and with marvelous agility he leapt off, landing safely.

"What's this?" said the same vibrant and mocking voice. "We're not here to slaughter horses, but men! Draw your sword, Monsieur! Draw your sword!" And the man leapt down from his horse.

"Let it be swords, then," said d'Artagnan, "because the sword is my business."

In two bounds d'Artagnan was within reach of his opponent and felt his steel on his enemy's. D'Artagnan, cool as ever, engaged him in *tierce*, his favorite guard.

Meanwhile Porthos knelt, a pistol in each hand, behind his dying horse, which writhed in convulsions of agony.

But the mêlée was on between d'Artagnan and his opponent. D'Artagnan launched his usual fierce attack—but this time he met a strength and skill that gave him pause. He attacked twice in *quarte*, then stepped back, but his adversary didn't advance into the trap; d'Artagnan resumed his attack in *tierce*. Each lunged and parried twice, but flying sparks were the only result.

Finally, d'Artagnan thought he saw the opportunity to unleash his favorite feint; he lunged with finesse, drew his opponent's point out of line, then remised like lightning, sure that he had him.

The remise was parried.

"*Mordioux!*" he swore in his Gascon accent.

At this exclamation, his opponent sprang back and cocked his head, as if trying to see through the gloom. Meanwhile d'Artagnan, fearing a feint, fell into a defensive guard.

"Take care," said Porthos to his opponent. "I still have two loaded pistols."

"Then I give you leave to shoot first," his adversary replied.

Porthos fired, the flash lighting up the battlefield.

At this sudden light, both fencers cried out.

"Athos!" said d'Artagnan.

"D'Artagnan!" said Athos.

Athos raised his sword's point; d'Artagnan lowered his. "Aramis!" called Athos. "Don't shoot."

"Oh ho, is that you, Aramis?" said Porthos. And he tossed away his second pistol.

Aramis holstered his own pistol and sheathed his sword.

"My son!" said Athos, extending his hand to d'Artagnan. It was what he used to call d'Artagnan in the old days.

"Athos," said d'Artagnan, wringing his hands, "so you're defending the duke? And here I am, having sworn to take him dead or alive. Agh! I'm dishonored."

"Kill me, then," said Athos, lowering his guard, "if your honor requires my death."

"Oh! Devil take me!" cried d'Artagnan. "There was only one man in the world who could stop me, and fate put him in my path. Gah! What am I going to tell the cardinal?"

"You will tell him, Monsieur," said a voice that rang out over the battlefield, "that he sent against me the only two men who could beat four other cavaliers, fight the Comte de La Fère and the Chevalier d'Herblay to a standstill, and then yield to fifty more."

"The prince!" said Athos and Aramis, stepping aside to make way for the Duc de Beaufort, while d'Artagnan and Porthos took a step back.

"Fifty more!" muttered Porthos and d'Artagnan.

"Look around you, Messieurs, if you doubt me," said the duke.

D'Artagnan and Porthos did look around and saw that they were surrounded by horsemen.

"By the sound of the encounter," said the duke, "I thought you must be twenty men. Fed up with fleeing, and ready for a little sword work, I turned back with my entire troop, to find you were only two."

"Yes, Monseigneur," said Athos, "but you were not in error, for these two are worth twenty."

"Come, Messieurs—surrender your swords," said the duke.

"Our swords!" said d'Artagnan, raising his head and regaining his self-possession. "Our swords! Never!"

"Never!" said Porthos.

The riders began to close in.

"One moment, Monseigneur," said Athos. "A few words."

He approached the prince, who leaned toward him and listened as he whispered. "Whatever you say, Count," said the prince. "I'm too much in your debt to refuse your first request. Fall back, Gentlemen," he said to his escort. "Messieurs d'Artagnan and du Vallon, you're free to go."

The order was followed immediately, and d'Artagnan and Porthos found themselves at the center of a widening circle.

"Dismount now, d'Herblay," said Athos, "and come with me."

Aramis got down and approached Porthos, as Athos came up to d'Artagnan. The Four were thus reunited.

"Friends," said Athos, "are you still sorry you didn't shed our blood?"

"No," said d'Artagnan. "My only regret is to see us pitted against each other, when before we'd always been together. Alas! We'll never succeed at anything again."

"Never, *mon Dieu*. It's over," said Porthos.

"Well, then! Why don't you join us?" said Aramis.

"Silence, d'Herblay," said Athos. "Don't make such a proposal to gentlemen such as these. If they've joined Mazarin's faction, their honor is engaged, just as ours is to the side of the princes."

"But meanwhile, we're enemies," said Porthos. "*Sangbleu!* Who would have thought it?"

D'Artagnan said nothing, just sighed.

Athos looked at them, then took up their hands in his. "Messieurs," he said, "the matter is serious, and my heart suffers as if you'd pierced it through. Yes, it's the sad truth that we are on opposite sides—but we haven't declared war on each other. Perhaps we can come to an understanding. I believe a private conference is called for."

"As for me, I agree," said Aramis.

"Then I agree, as well," d'Artagnan said proudly.

Porthos nodded in assent.

"Let's set a place of rendezvous," continued Athos, "somewhere convenient to all, where we can state our positions and decide how we shall conduct ourselves vis-à-vis each other."

"Fine!" said the other three.

"So, we're agreed?"

"Entirely!"

"Well, then! Where shall it be?"

"How about the Place Royale?" asked d'Artagnan.

"In Paris?"

"Yes."

Athos looked at Aramis, who nodded. "The Place Royale, then!" said Athos.

"And when?"

"Tomorrow night, if that suits you."

"You'll be there?"

"Yes."

"What time?"

"Would ten o'clock at night be convenient?"

"Perfectly so."

"Then," said Athos, "whether we settle on peace or war, friends, our personal honor, at least, will be satisfied."

"Maybe so," murmured d'Artagnan, "but our honor as soldiers is lost to us."

"D'Artagnan," said Athos gravely, "what wounds me more deeply is that circumstances have caused us to cross swords with each other. Yes," he continued, shaking his head sorrowfully, "yes, as you said, evil times are upon us. Come, Aramis."

"While we, Porthos," said d'Artagnan, "must go back and confess our shame to the cardinal."

"But be sure you mention," shouted a voice that d'Artagnan recognized as the voice of Rochefort, "that I'm not yet too old to be a man of action!"

"Is there anything I can do for you, Messieurs?" asked the prince.

"Bear witness that we did all we could, Monseigneur."

"Rest easy, I'll see to that. Adieu, Messieurs—I hope to meet you again sometime, perhaps in Paris, and then you may have your revenge." With these words, the duke waved to them in salute, put his horse into a gallop, and rode off, followed by his escort, who disappeared into the night, the sound of their hoofbeats dwindling until it was lost.

D'Artagnan and Porthos found themselves alone on the king's highway, except for a man holding the bridles of two spare horses. They thought it was Mousqueton and approached him. "But who's this?" cried d'Artagnan. "Is that you, Grimaud?"

"Grimaud!" said Porthos.

Grimaud just nodded to tell the two friends that they weren't mistaken.

"And whose horses are these?" asked d'Artagnan.

"Where do they come from?" asked Porthos.

"Monsieur le Comte de La Fère."

"Athos, Athos," murmured d'Artagnan. "The consummate gentleman! You really do think of everything."

"And just in time!" said Porthos. "I was afraid we were going to have to walk." He climbed into the saddle.

D'Artagnan did the same. "Well, now! So where are you off to, Grimaud? Are you leaving your master?"

"Yes," said Grimaud. "I go to join the Vicomte de Bragelonne with the army in Flanders."

For a while they rode together in silence down the road back to Paris, until they suddenly heard groans that seemed to rise out of a ditch.

"What's that?" asked d'Artagnan.

"That," said Porthos, "is Mousqueton."

"Oh, yes, Monsieur, it's me," said a sad voice, from a shadow by the side of the road.

Porthos rushed to his steward, to whom he was really quite attached. "Were you badly wounded, my dear Mouston?" he said.

"Mouston!" said Grimaud, eyes wide.

"No, Monsieur, I don't think so—but I'm injured in an embarrassing way."

"So, you can't ride a horse?"

"No, Monsieur—and what am I to do?"

"Can you walk?"

"I'll try, at least as far as the first house we come to."

"What are we going to do?" said d'Artagnan. "We have to get back to Paris."

"I'll take care of Mousqueton," said Grimaud.

"Thanks, that's good of you, Grimaud!" said Porthos.

Grimaud dismounted and went to lend a hand to his old friend, who greeted him tearfully, though Grimaud wasn't sure whether the tears were due to their reunion or his injury.

As for d'Artagnan and Porthos, they rode silently back to Paris.

Three hours later they were passed by a dusty courier, a messenger sent by the duke with a letter for the cardinal in which, as the prince had promised, he bore witness to the deeds of Porthos and d'Artagnan.

Mazarin had already passed a miserable night before this letter arrived, in which the prince announced that he was free and ready to undertake a war to the death.

The cardinal read it two or three times, then folded it, put it into his pocket, and said, "Though d'Artagnan has failed, what consoles me at least is that on his way he trampled Broussel. That Gascon is a valuable man and serves me even in his clumsiness."

The cardinal was referring to the man whom d'Artagnan had knocked over in Paris at the corner of Saint-Jean, who was none other than the worthy Councilor Broussel.

XXIX

Good Councilor Broussel

But unfortunately for Cardinal Mazarin, and despite his malicious hopes, the worthy Councilor Broussel had not been exterminated.

It was true, he had been quietly crossing Rue Saint-Honoré when d'Artagnan's speeding steed had struck him in the shoulder and knocked him into the mud. As we said, at the time d'Artagnan hadn't paid any attention to the event, not realizing its significance. Besides, d'Artagnan shared the deep disdain that the nobility of that period, and especially the nobility of the sword, felt for the bourgeoisie. He paid no mind to the small man dressed in black, though he was the cause of the man's misfortune. No one even heard him cry out until after the storm of armed cavaliers had thundered past; only then was the injury noticed.

Passersby ran up to the moaning man and asked him his name, title, and address; and when told that his name was Broussel, he was a councilor of parliament, and he lived in Rue Saint-Landry, an angry cry went up from the gathering crowd, a cry so terrible and threatening that the wounded man feared another hurricane was about to pass over him.

"Broussel!" they cried. "Broussel, our dear father! He who defended our rights against Mazarin! Broussel, the friend of the people—trampled, nearly killed by those Cardinalist scoundrels! To arms! To arms!"

Within moments the crowd became an immense mob. They commandeered a passing carriage to convey the little councilor home, but an outraged citizen said that, in the wounded man's state, the movement of the coach would make him worse. The zealot proposed that the crowd carry him by hand, a proposal that was enthusiastically and unanimously accepted. No sooner said than done: the people lifted him, with gentle menace, and bore him away, the crowd like a grumbling giant in a fable lumbering along while cradling a dwarf in its arms.

Broussel must have had some idea how attached the Parisians had become to him—after all, he hadn't spent three years sowing the seeds of opposition to the cardinal without hoping to someday reap rewards in popularity. So, this demonstration made him pleased and proud, but though it showed the extent of his power, the triumph was shadowed by anxiety. Already suffering from wounds and bruises, he feared at every corner to see the crowd confronted by a troop of guards or musketeers, who might charge his mob—and who then would be triumphant?

He couldn't help recalling that whirlwind of cavaliers, that iron-hooved hurricane that had thrown him down so pitilessly. And so, he kept repeating, in a voice growing ever fainter, "Hurry, my children, make haste, for truly I am suffering." But at each of these complaints, the cries and curses of those who bore him redoubled.

They finally brought him, though not without further bumps and bruises, to Broussel's own house. Those who had surged on ahead already filled the street, and his neighbors thronged their windows and doorways. At the window of his own house, above a narrow door, could be seen an old servant woman who cried out in dismay, beside another woman, also elderly, who wept copiously. These two, clearly upset, kept asking the crowd what had happened, but received only confused and contradictory responses.

But when the councilor, carried between eight men, was brought pale and apparently dying to the steps of his house, his lady, Goodwife Broussel, and her maid disappeared from the window to reappear at the door. There the maid, raising her arms to the sky, rushed down the stairs to her master, crying out, "Oh, *mon Dieu! Mon Dieu!* If Friquet is here, send him for a surgeon!"

And Friquet, of course, was there. What gamin of Paris wouldn't be?

Friquet had naturally taken advantage of the Pentecost holiday to ask his innkeeper for the day off, a request that couldn't be refused, as it had been a condition of his employment that he needn't work during the year's four chief holidays.

So Friquet was already at the head of the mob. It had occurred to him that probably he ought to fetch a surgeon, but he found it more amusing to shout his head off, crying, "They've killed Monsieur Broussel! Broussel, the father of the people! *Vive* Monsieur Broussel!" This was much more fun than scouring the streets for a doctor just so he could say, "Come, Monsieur Surgeon, good Councilor Broussel needs you."

Unfortunately for Friquet, who'd assumed a leading role in the procession, he had the imprudence to jump on the sill of the house's ground floor window to exhort the crowd to greater outrage—and there his mother saw him and sent him to find a doctor.

Then she took the councilor in her arms and tried to carry him inside, but at the bottom of the stairs Broussel stood up and said he felt strong enough to make it on his own. He also asked Gervaise, which was the name of his maid, to try to dismiss the crowd, but Gervaise wasn't listening. "Oh, my poor master!" she cried. "My dear master!"

"Yes, yes, Gervaise," said Broussel, trying to calm her. "It's nothing, really."

"Nothing, when you are crushed, annihilated, destroyed!"

"No, no, really, it's nothing," said Broussel, "or almost nothing, anyway."

"Nothing, and you covered in mud! Nothing, and you with blood in your hair! Ah, my God, my God, my poor master!"

"Hush, now!" said Broussel. "Hush!"

"But the blood, my God, the blood!" cried Gervaise. "A doctor! A doctor!"

"A doctor!" the crowd howled. "A surgeon! Councilor Broussel is dying! Mazarin has killed him!"

"Oh my God!" cried Broussel. "This is awful! This mob is going to burn down the house!"

"Then go up to the window to show them you're all right, master!"

"A plague on that!" said Broussel. "That's what kings do. Tell them I'm getting better, Gervaise—tell them I'm going to go, not to the window, but to bed, and to please go away!"

"But why should they go away? They're here to honor you!"

"Oh, can't you see?" said Broussel, desperate. "They'll honor me by getting me hanged! Now come on! My wife's fainting dead away."

"Broussel! Broussel!" cried the crowd. "*Vive* Broussel! A surgeon for Broussel!"

They made such a clamor that what Broussel feared came to pass: a platoon of guards appeared and began to clear the crowd from the street with their musket butts. At the first cry of "The guard! The guard!" Broussel, trembling for fear they'd take him for the instigator of the riot, sought refuge by hiding under his bed.

At the guards' assault, the crowd crying for Broussel was forced to fall back, and old Gervaise was finally able to shut the front door. But the door was scarcely shut, with Gervaise on her way up to find her master, when it began to resound with knocking. Madame Broussel, ahead of Gervaise, found her husband by his shoes sticking out from under their bed, where he was shaking like a leaf.

"Go see who's knocking, Gervaise," called Broussel, "and don't open the door unless you have to."

Gervaise took a look. "It's Monsieur Blancmesnil, the president of parliament," she said.

"Oh, no problem, then," said Broussel. "Open up."

"Well!" said the president, coming in. "What have they done to you, my dear Broussel? I hear you were nearly assassinated!"

"In fact, it seems likely they were trying to kill me," said Broussel, so firmly it almost seemed stoic.

"My poor friend! Yes, though they started with you, they have to destroy all of us, and since they can't defeat us *en masse*, they'll try to take us one by one."

"If I survive," said Broussel, "I shall crush them, all of them, under the weight of my words!"

"You'll recover," said Blancmesnil, "and I don't doubt you'll make them pay dearly for this attack."

Meanwhile Madame Broussel was crying, and Gervaise was in despair. "What's this?" cried a handsome and burly young man as he rushed into the room. "My father, wounded?"

"He's a victim of tyranny," said Blancmesnil, "and yet a true Spartan."

"Oh!" cried the young man, turning toward the door. "They'll pay, whoever dared to touch you!"

"Jacques," said the councilor, getting up, "for now, just go get a doctor."

"I hear more cries from the people," said the old woman. "Friquet has probably found one—no, wait, it's a carriage."

Blancmesnil looked out the window. "It's the coadjutor!" he said.

"The coadjutor!" repeated Broussel. "My God! I must go down to meet him!" And the councilor, forgetting his wounds, started to rush downstairs to meet Monsieur de Gondy, but Blancmesnil stopped him.

"Well, my dear Broussel," said the coadjutor, coming in, "what's this we hear? Tales of ambushes and assassinations! My doctor's house was on the way, so I brought him with me. Ah, bonjour, Monsieur Blancmesnil!"

"Oh, Monsieur," said Broussel, "what thanks I owe you! It's true, I was cruelly knocked down and trampled by the King's Musketeers."

"Say, rather, the musketeers of Cardinal Mazarin," said the coadjutor. "But we'll make him pay for this, never fear. Won't we, Monsieur de Blancmesnil?"

Blancmesnil was still bowing when the door was thrust open by the hands of a porter. He was followed by a footman in full livery, who loudly announced, "Monsieur le Duc de Longueville!"[95]

"What?" cried Broussel. "The duke, here? What an honor for me! Ah, Monseigneur!"

"I come to decry the terrible fate suffered by our brave defender," said the duke. "Are you wounded, my dear Councilor?"

"If I were, your visit would heal me, Monseigneur."

"But you suffer, though?"

"A great deal," said Broussel.

"I brought along my personal doctor," said the duke. "May he come in?"

"How's that?" said Broussel.

The duke motioned to his footman, who ushered in a man in black. "We both had the same idea, Monseigneur," the coadjutor said.

The two doctors looked each other over. "Ah, is that you, Monsieur le Coadjuteur?" said the duke. "The friends of the people all share the same goal."

"I was alarmed by the clamor and came running—but I think the most important thing is for our doctors tend to our brave councilor."

"What, in front of everyone?" said Broussel, intimidated.

"Why not? You're a victim of tyranny, and in the name of justice, we must bear witness to your injuries."

"Dear God, is that more shouting?" cried Madame Broussel.

"No, it's applause," said Blancmesnil, dashing to the window.

"What?" cried Broussel, pale as death. "What is it now?"

"It's the livery of the Prince de Conti!"* cried Blancmesnil. "The Prince de Conti himself!"

The coadjutor and the Duc de Longueville shared a look and tried not to laugh. The doctors had started to unbutton Broussel's clothes, but the councilor stopped them. At that moment the Prince de Conti came in.

"Ah, Messieurs!" the prince said, seeing the duke and the coadjutor. "You have anticipated me! But don't blame me for being late, my dear Monsieur Broussel. When I heard about your accident, I thought you might need a doctor, so I went to get mine. How are you, and what's the story of this assassination everyone's talking about?"

Broussel tried to talk, but words failed him; he was crushed by the weight of the honor done to him. "Come in, then, Doctor, and take a look," said the Prince de Conti to a man in black who entered after him.

"Messieurs," said one of the first two doctors, "This isn't an examination, it's a consultation."

"If you like," said the prince. "Just reassure us about the condition of our dear councilor."

The three doctors approached the bed, into which Broussel had retreated and pulled up the covers, but despite his best efforts he was stripped and examined.

They found no wounds but a bruise on the arm, and another on the thigh.

The three doctors shared a significant look—never had three of the most learned physicians of the faculty of Paris been convened over such a trifle.

"Well?" said the coadjutor.

"Well?" said the duke.

"Well?" said the prince.

"We hope that monsieur will never suffer an actual accident," said one of the doctors. "We'll be in the next room until you need us."

"Broussel! How is Broussel?" shouted the people. "What's the news about Broussel?"

The coadjutor stepped to the window. At the sight of him, the people fell silent.

"My friends," he said, "have no fear: Monsieur Broussel is out of danger. However, his wounds are serious, and rest is required."

Shouts of "Long live Broussel! Long live the coadjutor!" echoed down the street.

Monsieur de Longueville was jealous and went to show himself at the window next. "Long live Monsieur de Longueville!" someone obligingly cried.

"My friends," said the duke, waving, "go home in peace, and don't give our enemies the pleasure of suppressing a riot."

"Well said, Monsieur le Duc!" said Broussel from his bed. "Now that was good, plain speaking."

"Friends and gentlemen of Paris!" said the Prince de Conti, taking his turn at the window to get his share of applause. "Monsieur Broussel has heard you! But he is in need of rest, and the clamor disturbs him."

"Long live the Prince de Conti!" shouted the crowd, as the prince saluted them.

The three lords then took leave of the councilor, and the crowd that had gathered on Broussel's behalf became their escort. They all moved off toward the docks, still calling Broussel's name.

The old maid, stupefied, regarded her master with admiration. The councilor had grown at least a foot in her eyes.

"That's what it's like when a man serves his country with good conscience," said Broussel with satisfaction.

After an hour of deliberation, the doctors came out and bathed his bruises with salt and water.

Meanwhile, the procession of carriages of the important and self-important kept coming. All day long the luminaries of the Fronde came to call on Broussel.

"What a great triumph, Father!" said the young son, who didn't quite grasp the real motive all these churchmen, lords, and princes had for visiting his injured parent.

"Alas, my dear Jacques!" said Broussel. "I fear this will be an expensive triumph, and unless I'm wrong, even now Monsieur Mazarin is figuring out how to make us pay for it."

Friquet finally returned at midnight, never having found a doctor.

XXX

Four Old Friends Prepare for a Council

"Well!" said Porthos, sitting in the courtyard of the Hôtel de La Chevrette, as d'Artagnan returned from the Palais Royal with a grim expression. "So, he took it badly, my brave friend?"

"*Ma foi,* yes! Really, what an ugly beast that man can be. What are you eating there, Porthos?"

"As you see, I'm soaking a biscuit in a glass of Spanish wine. Give it a try."

"I will. Gimblou! A glass!"

The lad who enjoyed this euphonious name brought the requested glass, and d'Artagnan sat down next to his friend.

"How did it go?"

"*Dame!* Well, of course, there are two ways to report a failure. I walked in, he looked at me sideways, I shrugged my shoulders and said, 'Monseigneur, we were outnumbered.' 'Yes,' he said, 'so I've heard—however, give me the details.' But you know, Porthos, I couldn't give him the details without naming our friends, which would be a disaster."

"Pardieu!"

"'Monseigneur,' I said, 'they were fifty, and we were two.' 'Indeed,' he said, 'but nonetheless I hear there was an exchange of pistol shots.' 'In fact, both sides burned some powder,' I said. 'And your swords saw the light of day?' 'Say, rather, the starlight, Monseigneur,' I replied.

"'*Ah çà!*' continued the cardinal. 'And I thought you were a Gascon.' 'I'm always a Gascon—when I succeed, Monseigneur.' That answer pleased him, and he laughed. 'That will teach me, to give my guards better horses,' he said, 'for if they'd been able to keep up with you, and had done as well as you and your friend, you would have kept your promise to bring the duke back dead or alive.'"

"Well, that's not so bad," said Porthos.

"Eh, well, not so bad, maybe, but not so good," said d'Artagnan. "My, how these biscuits soak up the wine! They're like sponges! Gimblou, another bottle."

The bottle came with a speed that showed what esteem d'Artagnan was held in the establishment. He continued, "I began to retire, but he called me back. 'You had three horses killed from under you?' he asked me. 'Yes, Monseigneur,' I said. 'How much were they worth?'"

"A fine question, it speaks well of him," said Porthos.

"'A thousand pistoles,' I said."

"A thousand pistoles!" said Porthos. "That's rather high! If he knows horseflesh, he'd have to haggle."

"I could tell he wanted to, the weasel, because he winced and gave me a look. But then he nodded, reached into a drawer, and pulled out some bearer bonds drawn on the Bank of Lyon."

"For a thousand pistoles?"

"Exactly, and not a *sou* more, the miser."

"And you have them?"

"Here they are."

"My faith! That seems quite proper," said Porthos.

"Proper! Is 'proper' good enough when lives were at risk, and when I've done him a huge favor?"

"A huge favor? What was that?"

"By our Lady! It seems I ran over a troublesome councilor of parliament."

"Really! Would that be the little man in black at the corner of the Saint-Jean cemetery?"

"That's the one. A troublemaker. Unfortunately, I merely knocked him down, and he'll recover to bedevil us again."

"And to think that I swerved to avoid him when I could have squashed him flat," said Porthos. "Now there's a lesson for next time."

"I should have had a bonus for that!"

"Well, to be fair, he wasn't totally crushed."

"Bah! Richelieu would have said, 'Here's five hundred crowns for running down that councilor!' But enough about that. What were your horses really worth, Porthos?"

"Ah, my friend, if poor Mousqueton were here, he could tell you, to the livre, *denier*, and sou."

"Whatever! So long as I was close."

"Well, Vulcan and Bayard cost me around two hundred pistoles apiece, while Phoebus was nearly a hundred and fifty, as I recall."

"So, we're four hundred and fifty pistoles to the good," said d'Artagnan, pleased.

"Yes," said Porthos, "but there's still the saddles and tack."

"Pardieu, that's true. How much was the tack?"

"Say, a hundred pistoles for all three . . ."

"All right, a hundred pistoles," said d'Artagnan. "That still leaves three hundred fifty more."

Porthos nodded in agreement.

"Let's give fifty pistoles to our hostess for our expenses, and divide the remaining three hundred," said d'Artagnan.

"Split it up," said Porthos.

"A paltry payout," murmured d'Artagnan, putting the bills in two piles.

"As usual!" said Porthos. "Did he say anything else?"

"What about?"

"Oh, well . . . about me?"

"Ah, right!" said d'Artagnan, afraid of discouraging his friend by telling him the cardinal hadn't mentioned him. "Right! Uh, he said . . ."

"He said?" replied Porthos.

"Wait, I want to remember his exact words: he said, 'As to your friend, tell him he can sleep soundly.'"

"Good," said Porthos. "That tells me clear as day that he still intends to make me a baron."

At that moment nine o'clock sounded from the nearby church. D'Artagnan started.

"Oh!" said Porthos. "There's nine striking now, and at ten, you remember, we have that rendezvous at the Place Royale."[96]

"Bah! Don't mention it, Porthos!" snapped d'Artagnan, with an impatient gesture. "Don't remind me—that's what I've been sulking about since yesterday. I won't go."

"Not go? But why?" asked Porthos.

"Because it's too painful to meet with the two men who foiled our mission."

"Foiled? It was a draw," replied Porthos. "Neither side had the advantage— I still had a loaded pistol, and you two were facing each other, sword in hand."

"Yes," said d'Artagnan. "But if there's a hidden scheme behind this rendezvous . . ."

"Oh, d'Artagnan, you don't believe that," Porthos said.

It was true—d'Artagnan didn't believe Athos was capable of anything underhanded, but he was looking for an excuse not to go to the rendezvous.

"We must go, or they'll think we're afraid," stated the superb Seigneur de Bracieux. "Really, *cher ami,* we faced fifty enemies on the king's highway—I think we can face two good friends in the Place Royale."

"Yes, yes, I know," said d'Artagnan, "but they took the side of the princes without warning us, and Athos and Aramis have toyed with me in an alarming manner. Last night we found out the truth; what's the point of going tonight to learn the same thing over again?"

"Do you really distrust them?" said Porthos.

"As to Aramis, ever since he became an abbot: yes. You can't imagine how changed he is. He sees us as obstacles on the road to his bishopric and could shove us aside without being any too sorry about it."

"Oh, well, Aramis, sure," said Porthos. "That wouldn't surprise me."

"Or Monsieur de Beaufort might lay a trap to take us."

"Bah! He had us and let us go. But we'll be on our guard; we can arm ourselves and take Planchet with his carbine."

"Ha! Planchet's a Frondeur," said d'Artagnan.

"Damn all civil wars!" said Porthos. "We can't count on our friends, or even our lackeys. Ah, if only poor Mousqueton was here! There's one who will never abandon me."

"Yes, so long as you're still rich! But you know, old friend, it's not the civil wars that separate us, it's the fact that we're all twenty years older. The happy loyalty of youth has given way to the voice of self-interest, the spur of ambition, and the conceit of pride." He sighed. "Yes, you're right, we have to go, Porthos—but let's go well armed. If we don't go, it's true, they'll say we're afraid. Holà! Planchet!"

Planchet appeared.

"Saddle the horses and bring your carbine."

"But, Monsieur, who are we going up against?"

"We're not going up against anyone," said d'Artagnan. "It's just a simple precaution in case we're attacked."

"Do you know, Monsieur, that today they tried to assassinate good Councilor Broussel, the father of the people?"

"Is that so?" said d'Artagnan.

"Yes, but the attempt was rebuffed, for he was borne home in the people's arms. Since yesterday his house is never empty. He was visited by Coadjutor de Gondy, by Monsieur de Longueville, and by the Prince de Conti. Madame de Chevreuse and Madame de Vendôme have signed his visitors' book, and whenever he gives the word . . ."

"Well? What happens when he 'gives the word'?"

Planchet began to sing:

> *The Fronde wind blows*
> *So, let her in*
> *I think it goes*
> *Against Mazarin*
> *If the Fronde wind blows*
> *We'll let her in!*

"Now I understand," d'Artagnan said quietly to Porthos, "why Mazarin would have preferred it if I'd annihilated that councilor."

"So, you see, Monsieur," said Planchet, "that if it was for some mission like the one that injured Monsieur Broussel that you wanted me to bring my carbine . . ."

"No, nothing like that, don't worry. But where did you hear all these details?"

"Oh, from a good source, Monsieur—from Friquet."

"From Friquet?" said d'Artagnan. "I know that name."

"He's the son of Monsieur Broussel's maid, and one who, in a riot, I wouldn't mind having at my side."

"Isn't he also a choirboy at Notre Dame?" asked d'Artagnan.

"Yes, that's right—he's a protégé of Bazin."

"Of course," said d'Artagnan. "And he's pot boy at a tavern in Rue de la Calandre?"

"That's him. What business could you have with a street urchin?"

"He's already given me good information," said d'Artagnan, "and may give me better yet."

"What, to someone who nearly crushed his master?" said Porthos, in what was for him a low voice.

"And who will tell him that?"

"Good point."

At that very moment, Athos and Aramis were entering Paris through the Faubourg Saint-Antoine. They had rested on the road and were hurrying so as not to miss the rendezvous. Bazin was their only follower, since Grimaud, as may be recalled, had stayed behind to care for Mousqueton, and was then supposed to leave to rejoin the young Vicomte de Bragelonne with the army in Flanders.

"Now," said Athos, "we need to find an inn where we can change into our city clothes, store our pistols and rapiers, and disarm our lackey."

"Disarm? By no means, my dear Count—in this, you must allow me not only to disagree with you, but to try to persuade you to my opinion."

"Why should I do that?"

"Because we're going to a rendezvous of war."

"What do you mean, Aramis?"

"I mean that the meeting in the Place Royale is nothing but the sequel to the encounter on the king's highway."

"What? But our friends . . ."

"Have become our most dangerous enemies, Athos. Believe me, they can't be trusted—especially by you."

"Oh, but my dear d'Herblay . . . !"

"How do you know d'Artagnan hasn't blamed his defeat on us, and warned the cardinal? How do you know the cardinal won't take advantage of this rendezvous to arrest us?"

"Oh, really, Aramis! Do you think d'Artagnan and Porthos would lend their hands to such treachery?"

"You're right, *mon cher* Athos—between friends. But between enemies, it's a legitimate ruse."

Athos crossed his arms and bowed his handsome head on his chest.

"What do you expect, Athos?" said Aramis. "Men are like that, and they can't stay twenty years old forever. We've wounded d'Aragnan in the pride that spurs him on—you know it's true. He was defeated. Didn't you hear his despair on the highway? As for Porthos, his barony probably depended on the outcome of this affair. Well, he ran into us along the way, and won't be a baron anytime soon—unless his barony depends on what happens at tonight's meeting. We must take proper precautions, Athos."

"But what if they show up unarmed? How that will shame us, Aramis!"

"Oh, rest easy, *mon cher,* that's not going to happen. Besides, we have an excuse: we had to travel, and we're outlawed rebels!"

"Us, to need an excuse! An excuse with d'Artagnan! An excuse with Porthos! Oh, Aramis, Aramis," said Athos, shaking his head sadly, "upon my soul, you make me the most wretched of men. You are disenchanting a heart that was not yet dead to friendship. I'd almost prefer you just wrench it from my chest. You do as you please, Aramis. As to me, I'll go unarmed."

"You'll do no such thing, because I won't let you. It's not just one man, not even Athos, not even the Comte de La Fère you betray by such weakness—it's an entire faction to which you belong, and that relies on you."

"Have it your way, then," replied Athos sadly.

And so, it was settled.

They had scarcely reached Rue du Pas-de-la-Mule, at the gates of the deserted square, when they saw three horsemen under the Place Royale's outer arcade at the entrance of Rue Sainte-Catherine. In front were d'Artagnan and Porthos, wrapped in cloaks bulged out by their swords. Behind them came Planchet, carbine at his knee.

Seeing d'Artagnan and Porthos, Athos and Aramis dismounted. D'Artagnan and Porthos did the same. D'Artagnan saw that Bazin, instead of holding the others' three horses, had tied them to rings on the arcades. He ordered Planchet to do the same.

Then they advanced, two against two, followed by their lackeys, and met with polite bows.

"Where shall we have our discussion, Messieurs?" asked Athos, who saw that several people had stopped to look at them, as if expecting one of those famous duels still remembered by the people of Paris, and especially those living on the Place Royale.

"The gates are shut," said Aramis, "but if you gentlemen don't mind waiting a moment here under these trees, I'll get the keys to go in through the Hôtel de Rohan, which should suit us perfectly."

D'Artagnan peered into the shadows of the Place, while Porthos considered the mansion's gates, and what might be behind them. "If you prefer somewhere else, Messieurs," said Athos, in his refined and persuasive voice, "just name it."

"This place, if Monsieur d'Herblay can get the key, will do just fine, I think."

Aramis went off, after warning Athos to stay out of range of d'Artagnan and Porthos, but Athos only smiled disdainfully and moved closer to his old friends, who remained where they were.

Meanwhile Aramis was knocking at the Hôtel de Rohan, and talking with a footman who said, "You swear it's no duel, Monsieur?"

"Upon this," said Aramis, offering him a *louis d'or.*

"So, you won't swear, good Gentleman?" said the footman, shaking his head.

"Oh, who can be sure of anything?" said Aramis. "I tell you only that, at the moment, these gentlemen are our friends."

"He's right," intoned Athos, d'Artagnan, and Porthos.

D'Artagnan had overheard the entire conversation. "You see?" he whispered to Porthos.

"See what?"

"He wouldn't swear."

"Swear about what?"

"That man wanted Aramis to swear that we hadn't come to the Place Royale to fight."

"And Aramis wouldn't swear?"

"No."

"Then be on your guard."

Athos observed this whispered exchange. Aramis opened the gate and stepped back so d'Artagnan and Porthos could enter. The hilt of d'Artagnan's sword caught on the gate and pulled back his cloak, exposing his brace of pistols, which gleamed in the moonlight.

"You see?" said Aramis, touching Athos's shoulder with one hand and pointing with the other at the arsenal in d'Artagnan's belt.

"Alas, yes!" said Athos, with a deep sigh.

He went in third. Aramis entered last and closed the gate behind him. The two lackeys remained outside, but they were suspicious of each other, and kept their distance.

XXXI

The Place Royale

They walked silently toward the center of the square, but as they did the moon emerged from the clouds; this made them feel exposed, so they went under the lime trees, where the shade concealed them.

Benches were placed here and there, and the four stopped before one of them. Athos gestured, and d'Artagnan and Porthos sat. Athos and Aramis remained standing.

After a silent moment, during which they all began to feel embarrassed, Athos decided to begin the discussion. "Messieurs," he said, "our presence at this rendezvous is proof of the power of our old friendship. No one is missing, so no one needs reproach himself."

"Listen, Count," said d'Artagnan, "instead of paying compliments we may or may not deserve, let's be open and forthright."

"I ask nothing better," said Athos. "I will be candid, so you may speak with all honesty. Do you have any issue to take with myself or the Abbé d'Herblay?"

"Yes," said d'Artagnan. "When I had the honor to speak with you at the Château de Bragelonne, I made proposals to you that you couldn't fail to understand—but instead of answering me as a friend, you treated me like a child. This friendship you boast about wasn't broken yesterday by our clash of swords, but by your dissembling at your château."

"D'Artagnan!" said Athos, in a tone of gentle reproach.

"You asked me to be frank," said d'Artagnan, "so there it is. Whenever you want to know what I think, I tell you. And I have the same complaint to make of you, Monsieur l'Abbé d'Herblay, as you abused me in the same fashion."

"Really, Monsieur, this is beyond strange," said Aramis. "You say you came to me to make proposals, but did you? No, you sounded me out, that's all. And what did I tell you? That Mazarin was a buffoon, and that I wouldn't serve him. But that's all. Did I say I wouldn't serve someone else? On the contrary, I gave you to understand, it seems to me, that I favored the party of the princes. We even joked, if I'm not mistaken, that the cardinal might very well send you to arrest me. Were you a man of his party? No doubt about it. Then why couldn't we be men of a different party? If you could have your secrets, then we could have ours—and if we kept quiet, all the better. It just proves we know how to keep a secret."

"I don't blame you for it, Monsieur," said d'Artagnan. "It's only because the Comte de La Fère speaks of friendship that I consider your conduct."

"And what do you find?" asked Aramis, haughtily.

The blood immediately went to d'Artagnan's head, and he stood and barked, "I find it worthy of a student of the Jesuits."

Seeing d'Artagnan stand, Porthos got up as well. All four now stood in threatening postures. Leaning toward d'Artagnan, Aramis dropped his hand toward his sword.

Athos stopped him. "D'Artagnan," he said, "you come here tonight still furious about yesterday's encounter. I thought you had enough heart that a friendship of twenty years' standing would overcome a quarter-hour's injury to your pride. Come, tell me truly—do you have something to blame me for? If I'm at fault, d'Artagnan, I'll own that fault and confess it."

The soothing and sonorous voice of Athos had its old effect on d'Artagnan, calming him where the voice of Aramis, which became sharp and shrill when angry, provoked him. He said to Athos, "I think, Count, that you had a confidence to share with me at the Château de Bragelonne, as monsieur here," he continued, pointing at Aramis, "had in his monastery. I hadn't yet committed to anything that might pit me against you. But just because I was discreet didn't mean you should take me for a fool. If I'd wanted to expose the difference between those Monsieur d'Herblay receives by rope and those who come by ladder, I could have."

"Where are you going with this?" cried Aramis, pale with anger at the thought that d'Artagnan might have spied him with Madame de Longueville.

"I go only where my own business takes me. I don't concern myself with things I shouldn't see—but I do hate hypocrites, and in that category I put musketeers who play at being abbots, and abbots who play at being musketeers. And monsieur here," he added, turning to Porthos, "agrees with me."

Porthos, who hadn't uttered a word up to this point, just said, "Yes," and drew his sword. Aramis leapt back and drew his own. D'Artagnan leaned forward, ready to attack or defend.

But Athos stopped them, extending his hand with that supreme gesture of command that belonged only to him. He slowly drew his own sword with the other hand, and then broke it over his knee and threw the pieces down in front of him.

Then he turned to Aramis and said, "Aramis, break your sword."

Aramis hesitated.

"Do it," Athos said. Then, in a softer tone: "I wish it."

Aramis grew pale, but overcome by the gesture, overwhelmed by the voice, he bent and broke his sword, and then crossed his arms and stood, quivering with rage.

At this, d'Artagnan and Porthos stepped back. D'Artagnan kept his hand away from his sword, and Porthos returned his to its sheath.

"Never," said Athos, slowly raising his right hand toward heaven, "never, I swear before God who sees and hears us in the solemnity of this night: never will my sword strike yours; never will my eye look upon you in anger; never will my heart beat toward you with hate. We have lived together, hated and loved together, poured out our blood together—and moreover, we are bound by what is perhaps a stronger bond than that of friendship, the bond of a shared crime. For together the four of us judged, condemned, and executed a human being that perhaps we had no right to send from this world, even if the world she seemed to belong to was Hell.

"D'Artagnan, I have always loved you like a son. Porthos, we slept side by side for ten years; Aramis is your brother as he is mine, for Aramis has loved you as I love you still and will always love you. What can Cardinal Mazarin be to us, who have defied the heart and the hand of a man like Richelieu? Who is this prince or that to us, who have steadied the crown on the head of a queen? D'Artagnan, I ask your pardon for having crossed swords with you yesterday, and Aramis does the same for Porthos. So now, hate me if you must, but I assure you that despite your hatred, I will have nothing but friendship and esteem for you. Now repeat my words, Aramis—and afterward, if it's what they want, and what you want, part from our old friends forever."

For a moment there was a heavy silence, which was broken by Aramis. "I swear," he said, with a calm brow and steady look, but in a voice that trembled with emotion, "I swear I have no hatred against those who were my friends. Porthos, I regret having crossed swords with you. I swear for good and all that my blade will never threaten you again, and moreover, that even deep in my secret thoughts, I will bear you no hostility. Now come, Athos."

Athos made a move as if to withdraw. "Oh, no you don't! You're not going anywhere!" cried d'Artagnan, led by one of those irresistible impulses that betrayed the warmth of his heart and the honesty of his soul. "You're going nowhere, because I, too, have an oath to swear. I swear I would give the last drop of my blood, the last beat of my heart to keep the esteem of a man like you, Athos, and the friendship of a man like you, Aramis."

And he leapt into the embrace of Athos. "My son!" said Athos, pressing him to his heart.

"And I," said Porthos, "I swear nothing, because I'm choking. *Sacre bleu!* If I had to fight you, I think I'd let you stab me through and through, because I never loved anyone so much in this world!" And honest Porthos, bursting into tears, threw himself into Aramis's arms.

"My friends," said Athos, "that's what I was hoping for, that's what I was expecting from two hearts like yours. I've said it and I repeat, our destinies are inextricably twined, even when we go by different routes. I respect your judgment, d'Artagnan; I respect your conviction, Porthos; but though we fight for opposing sides, we must remain friends. Ministers, princes, even kings may pass by like storms, and civil war may drown everything in flames, but will we withstand all that? I believe we will."

"Yes," said d'Artagnan, "we're fellow musketeers to the end, our single flag that famous bullet-riddled napkin of the Saint-Gervais bastion, which the great cardinal had embroidered with three *fleur-de-lys.*"

"Yes," said Aramis, "Cardinalist or Frondeur means nothing! In duels we are each other's seconds, in dangerous affairs we're devoted friends, and in revelry we're joyous companions!"

"And every time we meet in the fray," said Athos, "recall these words: the Place Royale! Then let us shift our swords to our left hands and reach out with our right, even in the midst of slaughter!"

"I just love the way you talk," said Porthos.

"You are the greatest of men," said d'Artagnan. "Next to us, you are a true giant."

Athos smiled with ineffable joy. "Then it is settled," he said. "Come, Messieurs, your hands. Do you consider yourself Christians?"

"Pardieu!" said d'Artagnan.

"We will be so, at least on this occasion, to remain faithful to our oath," said Aramis.

"Ah, I'll swear by whatever you like," said Porthos, "even Mahomet! Devil take me if I've ever been as happy as I am now." And the good Porthos wiped his still-moist eyes.

"Does anyone have a cross?" asked Athos.

Porthos and d'Artagnan winced and shook their heads, like men embarrassed by the amount of a tavern bill. But Aramis smiled and drew from his breast a cross glittering with diamonds, hanging from his neck by a string of pearls. "I've got one," he said.

"Good!" said Athos. "Now swear on this cross, which, bejeweled though it is, is still a cross—swear we shall be united, forever and always. And may this oath bind not just ourselves, but even our descendants. Does this oath suit you?"

"Yes!" they said with one voice.

"You dog!" d'Artagnan whispered to Aramis. "You've made us swear on the crucifix of a lady Frondeur!"

XXXII

The Oise Ferry

We hope that the reader has not forgotten the young traveler we left on the road to Flanders.

As Raoul, looking behind him, finally lost sight of his guardian, whom he'd left in front of the royal basilica, he spurred his horse onward to escape his sad thoughts, and to hide from Olivain their traces on his face.

An hour's brisk ride soon dissipated the dark clouds that shadowed the young man's imagination. For Raoul, the unwonted pleasures of freedom—pleasures so sweet, even to those who have never known constraint—turned to gold heaven, earth, and especially that far horizon of life called the future.

However, after several attempts at conversation with Olivain, he realized that days passed in that manner would be sadly long and dull, and he missed talking with the count. That voice, so mild, so engaging and persuasive, came back to him as he passed through towns that were new to him, places that would have come alive with the fascinating, and useful, information that would have been conveyed by Athos, that wisest and most amusing of guides.

A different memory saddened Raoul when they reached the town of Louvres and he saw, half-hidden behind a screen of poplars, a small château that strongly reminded him of La Vallière. He stopped to gaze at it for almost ten minutes, and then resumed his journey with a sigh, not even answering Olivain's respectful question as to what had attracted his attention. The appearance of some objects plucks at the strings of memory, striking a chord can sometimes evoke a thread that, like Ariadne's, leads through a labyrinth of thoughts where we go astray, following shadows of the past. The sight of that château had sent Raoul fifty leagues to the west, back to the moment when he'd taken his leave of little Louise, and every landmark—a copse of oaks, a wind vane atop a slate roof—reminded him that instead of returning to his childhood friends, each step took him further from them, and that perhaps he had left them forever.

Head hanging, heart heavy, he ordered Olivain to lead the horses to a little inn he saw about a musket-shot up the road. There he alighted, sat at a table under a beautiful stand of flowering chestnuts murmuring with a multitude of bees, and told Olivain to go to the host and get stationery, pen, and ink.

Olivain went on his way, while Raoul sat, elbows on the table, gazing sightlessly across a charming landscape of green fields dotted with stands of trees, his hair slowly frosting as blossoms fluttered down to land unnoticed on his head.

Raoul sat for several minutes, lost in his reveries, before he noticed a ruddy figure had entered his field of vision, white cap on his head, apron around his waist, towel on his arm, while offering him a pen and paper. "Ah ha!" said the apparition. "It's clear that all young gentlemen think alike, as it isn't a quarter of an hour since a young lord, well mounted like you, good looking and about your age, stopped before this grove and made me bring out this table and chair. He had dinner here with an older gent I took to be his tutor, and they ate a fine loaf of paté without leaving behind a morsel, and drained a bottle of old Mâcon wine without leaving a drop—but fortunately we have more loaves and more bottles, and if Monsieur would like to order something . . ."

"No, my friend," said Raoul, smiling, "I thank you, but right now all I need are the things I asked for—but if the ink is black and the pen good, I'm happy to pay the price of a bottle for the pen, and a loaf for the ink."

"Well, Monsieur, in that case," said the host, "I'll give the loaf and bottle to your servant and throw the pen and ink into the bargain."

"Do as you like," said Raoul, who was unfamiliar with this ornament of society, the brand of innkeeper who, when there were robbers on the highway, served them as guests, and when there were none, did their best to take their place. The host, satisfied with this response, put paper, ink, and pen on the table. As it happened, the pen was passable, and Raoul began to write.

The host lingered for a moment, struck with involuntary admiration by that charming young face, at once so sweet and so serious. Beauty has power over everyone.

"He's not like that guest who just left," the host said to Olivain, who'd come to see if Raoul needed anything. "Your young master has no appetite."

"Monsieur had appetite enough three days ago, but what can you do? He lost it the day before yesterday." Olivain and the host walked toward the inn, with Olivain, as usual with servants who are happy in their service, regaling the innkeeper with all his young master's virtues.

Meanwhile, Raoul wrote:

Monsieur,

After four hours on the march, I pause to write you because I miss you at every moment—I keep turning my head to speak to you, as if you were still there. I was so dazed when I left, so distracted by the sadness of our separation, that I only feebly expressed all the gratitude and affection I feel for you. Please pardon me, Monsieur, for your heart is so generous, I'm sure you understood all that was happening in mine. Write to me, Monsieur, I beg you, as your advice is food and drink to me—and I admit, if I may, that I'm anxious, as it seemed to me you were preparing yourself for some sort of dangerous venture, something I didn't dare ask about, since you said nothing about it to me. Now that you're no longer near I'm afraid every minute of going wrong somehow. You have always been my guide and support, Monsieur, and today, I swear, I feel very alone.

If you receive news from Blois, Monsieur, would you be so kind as to pass along anything about my little friend Mademoiselle de La Vallière, whose health, you'll remember, gave me some anxiety?

Please understand, my dear Guardian, how precious to me are the memories of the time I spent with you. I hope you'll also think of me sometimes, and if you miss me and regret my absence, it will fill me with joy to know you appreciate the tiniest part of how I feel about you.

Having finished his missive, Raoul felt better; he checked to make sure neither the host nor Olivain was looking, and then kissed the paper: a mute and touching gesture he hoped Athos would instinctively feel when he opened the letter.

Meanwhile, Olivain emptied his bottle and ate his paté, while the horses were also fed and watered. Raoul waved to the host, threw a crown on the table, mounted his horse, and at Senlis, dropped his letter in the mail.

This brief rest enabled the riders and their horses to continue their journey without stopping. At Verberie, Raoul directed Olivain to ask about the young gentleman who preceded them; he was said to have passed not three-quarters of an hour earlier, but he was well mounted, as the innkeeper had said, and was keeping a good pace.

"Let's try to catch up to this gentleman," Raoul said to Olivain. "If he's going to the army like us, it'll be pleasant to have company."

It was four in the afternoon when Raoul arrived at Compiègne; he dined heartily, and again asked about the young gentleman who preceded him. He had also paused there at the Bell and Bottle Inn, the best in Compiègne, but had continued on his way, saying he intended to sleep at Noyon. "Then we'll sleep in Noyon as well," said Raoul.

"Monsieur," said Olivain respectfully, "allow me to point out that we've already tired out our horses today. It would be better, I think, to spend the night here, and leave early in the morning tomorrow. Eighteen leagues are enough for a first day's ride."

"The Comte de La Fère wants me to make haste and reach Monsieur le Prince by the morning of the fourth day," Raoul replied. "If we push on to Noyon, that will be no longer a ride than those we made going from Blois to Paris. We'll arrive by eight, the horses will have all night to rest, and we'll be on the road again by five tomorrow morning."

Olivain didn't dare to oppose such determination, but as he followed, he muttered through his teeth, "Go ahead, burn yourself out on the first day; tomorrow, instead of making twenty leagues, you'll do only ten, and then five the day after that, and you'll spend the fourth day in bed. These young folk are all such show-offs."

We can see that Olivain was not quite of the caliber of Planchet or Grimaud.

Raoul was tired, in fact, but he wished to test his strength, and raised on the principles of Athos, whom he was sure had spoken a thousand times of riding in twenty-five-league stages, he wanted to try to match his model. D'Artagnan as well, that man of iron who seemed made of nothing but nerve and muscle, had fired him with admiration.

So, he kept pushing his horse's pace, despite Olivain's muttered commentary, following a charming little road that led to a ferry, which he'd been assured would cut a league-long loop out of his route. Topping a crest, he saw before him the Oise River. A small troop of horsemen stood on the bank, preparing to embark on the ferry. Raoul had no doubt this was the gentleman and his escort; he uttered a cry but was too far away to be heard. Then, despite his horse's fatigue, he put it into a gallop, but a dip in the terrain caused him to lose sight of the travelers, and when he reached the next crest, the ferry had already left the near bank and was crossing to the other side.

Raoul, seeing he had no chance to catch the travelers in time, paused to wait for Olivain. Just then a cry seemed to come from the direction of the river; Raoul turned back toward it and, shading his eyes from the setting sun with his hand, called out, "Olivain! What's going on over there?"

A second cry came, more piercing than the first.

"Oh, Monsieur!" Olivain said. "The ferry rope broke, and the boat is drifting. But is someone in the water? I can't tell."

"No doubt about it!" cried Raoul, squinting at the river against the glare from the sun. "A horse and its rider."

"They're sinking!" cried Olivain.

It was true: Raoul was certain an accident had occurred, and a man was drowning before his eyes. He slapped his horse on the withers, dug in his spurs, and the animal, inspired to move, galloped to the dock, leapt over the guardrail and plunged into the river, splashing waves of foam.

"Monsieur!" cried Olivain. "Good God! What are you doing?"

Raoul guided his swimming horse toward the man in danger. It was a familiar exercise for the mount; raised on the banks of the Loire, it was at home in the water, and had crossed that river a thousand times. Athos, foreseeing the time when the viscount would be a soldier, had trained him in every eventuality.

"*Mon Dieu!*" sputtered Olivain desperately. "What would the count say if he saw you?"

"The count would do just as I'm doing," Raoul replied, pressing his horse forward.

"But, but, what about me?" called Olivain, pacing back and forth along the bank. "How am I supposed to get across?"

"Jump in, faint-heart!" cried Raoul, still swimming. Then, addressing the traveler, who was struggling not twenty paces from him, he called, "Courage, Monsieur, courage! We're coming to help."

Olivain went forward, then back, made his horse rear, turned it away, and finally, stabbed to the heart by shame, rushed it into the river as Raoul had done, while repeating, "I'm lost, I'm dead, I'm lost, I'm dead!"

Meanwhile the ferry boat drifted away, borne downstream by the current, and shouts were heard from the passengers. A gray-haired man had leapt into the river and was swimming strongly toward the drowning person, but he made slow progress as he was swimming upstream.

Raoul continued his efforts and was visibly gaining ground, but the horse and rider were sinking right before his eyes; the horse had only his nostrils above water, and the rider, who'd dropped the reins, was extending his arms as he slipped deeper. Another moment and he would be gone.

"Courage," cried Raoul, "courage!"

"Too late," murmured the young man. "Too . . . late."

The water closed over his head and his voice was silenced.

Raoul stood and jumped from his horse, which he left to save itself, and in three or four strokes was near the gentleman. He immediately got hold of the horse's bridle and lifted its head from the water; the animal breathed more freely, and as if it understood that help had arrived, it redoubled its efforts. Raoul meanwhile grabbed one of the young man's hands and carried it to the horse's mane, which the man clung to with the tenacity of the drowning. Sure that the cavalier wouldn't let go, Raoul turned his attention to the horse, which he guided to the opposite bank by swimming alongside and talking to it in an encouraging tone.

At last the animal stumbled into the shoals and set firm foot on the sand.

"Saved!" cried the gray-haired man, as he arrived on the horse's other side.

"Saved," the young gentleman murmured weakly, releasing the mane and slipping from the horse into Raoul's arms.

Raoul was only a few steps from shore; he carried the unconscious cavalier, laid him on the grass, loosened his collar, and undid the buttons of his doublet. A moment later, the gray-haired man joined him.

Olivain finally managed to reach shore as well, after making the sign of the cross over and over again. The folks on the ferry were headed back upstream as best they could, poling their boat along the shallows.

Gradually, thanks to the care of Raoul and the cavalier's elder companion, the bloom returned to the victim's pale cheeks. He opened his eyes and looked around wildly, but soon focused on the one who'd saved him. "Ah, Monsieur, there you are!" he cried. "If not for you, I'd be dead twice over."

"But you're recovering, Monsieur, as you see," said Raoul, "and now we can both forego our next bath."

"Oh, Monsieur, how much we owe you!" cried the gray-haired man.

"Ah, there you are, good d'Arminges! I gave you a scare, didn't I? But it's your own fault: as my tutor, why didn't you teach me how to swim?"

"Oh, Monsieur le Comte," said the older man. "If you had a mischance, how could I ever face your father the marshal?"

"But how did the thing happen?" asked Raoul.

"Eh, Monsieur, that's easy to tell," said he who'd been addressed as *count*. "We were a third of the way across when the ferry rope broke. The boatmen shouted and grabbed for it, and my horse took fright and jumped into the water. I swim badly and didn't dare to let go; I froze, and instead of helping my horse I was hindering it. I was drowning as bravely as I could, when you arrived just in time to pull me from the water. And now, since you saved my life, we must be friends till death."

"Your servant, Monsieur, I assure you," said Raoul, bowing.

"I'm called the Comte de Guiche,"* continued the cavalier. "My father is the Maréchal de Grammont.* And now that you know my name, will you do me the honor to tell me yours?"

"I'm the Vicomte de Bragelonne," said Raoul, blushing because he was unable to name his father, as the Comte de Guiche had.

"Viscount, your look, your kindness, and your courage all appeal to me—and you have my gratitude. Let's embrace and be friends."

"Monsieur," said Raoul, hugging the count, "I love you with all my heart already, so I beg you to consider me your devoted friend."

"So, where are you off to, Viscount?" asked de Guiche.

"To the army of Monsieur le Prince, Count."

"Why, so am I!" laughed the young man. "All the better! We'll share our first action under fire together."

"Indeed, you should be friends," said the tutor. "You're both young, and the same star doubtless shines on you both—you were fated to meet."

The two young men smiled with the confidence of youth.

"And now," said the tutor, "you must change your clothes. Your lackey, whom I gave orders to when he came off the ferry, has gone ahead to the inn. Dry linen and warmed wine await us there—let's go."

The young men had no objections to this plan—in fact, they found it excellent. So, they immediately mounted, and then paused to admire each other; for a fact, they were both elegant cavaliers, lithe and slender, with broad brows above noble faces, looks gentle but proud, smiles sincere and loyal. De Guiche had to be about eighteen, but he was scarcely taller than Raoul, who was only fifteen.

They reached out spontaneously and shook hands, and then, spurring their horses, rode along the river path to the nearby inn, one laughing and enjoying the life he'd almost lost, while the other thanked God that he'd lived long enough to do a deed that would make his guardian proud.

As for Olivain, he was the only one his master's exploit had left entirely dissatisfied. As he rode along, wringing out his sleeves and cuffs, he was thinking that if they'd stopped in Compiègne, he would have been spared an accident he'd barely survived, as well as the influenza and rheumatism that was bound to follow.

XXXIII

Skirmish

Their stay at Noyon was short, though everyone got a good night's sleep. Raoul had asked to be awakened if Grimaud arrived, but Grimaud never came.

The horses, for their part, doubtless appreciated the abundant hay and eight hours of complete rest they got. The Comte de Guiche was awakened at five in the morning by Raoul, who came in to wish him good day. They ate a quick breakfast, and by six o'clock had already ridden two leagues.

Raoul found the young count's conversation fascinating, so he mainly listened as de Guiche talked. He'd been raised in Paris, which Raoul had only seen once, and largely at Court, which Raoul had never seen. His youthful follies as a page, and two duels he'd managed to have despite the royal edicts and the injunctions of his tutor, excited Raoul's admiration. Bragelonne had paid only the one visit to Monsieur Scarron, and he named to de Guiche the people he'd seen there. De Guiche knew everybody: Madame de Neuillan, Mademoiselle d'Aubigné, Mademoiselle de Scudéry, Madamoiselle Paulet, even Madame de Chevreuse. And he made fun of everyone—Raoul trembled, afraid he was going to joke about Madame de Chevreuse, for whom he felt a deep sympathy—but either instinctively or from affection for the duchess, de Guiche spoke only good of her. This made Raoul feel even more friendly toward the count.

Next, they turned to the subject of love and gallantry—and here again, Bragelonne had more to hear than to say. So, he listened, and it seemed to him that despite the count's tales of three or four thinly veiled amorous adventures that de Guiche, like himself, was hiding a secret in his heart.

De Guiche, as we've said, had been brought up at Court, and the intrigues of the royal courtiers were all open secrets to him. It was the same French

Court of which Raoul had heard so much from the Comte de La Fère—
only it had changed quite a bit since the days when Athos had frequented
it. The Comte de Guiche's stories were thus entirely new to his traveling
companion. With comments witty and irreverent, the young noble passed
everyone in review: he recounted the former affairs of Madame de Longueville with Coligny, and of the latter's fatal duel over them at the Place Royale,
which madame watched secretly from behind window blinds; of her new
affair with the Prince de Marcillac, a jealous man who wanted to kill his
rivals, even the Abbé d'Herblay, her confessor; and the romance of the Prince
of Wales with Prince Gaston's daughter, "La Grande Mademoiselle,"[97] notorious at a later time for her secret marriage with Lauzun. Not even the queen
was spared, and Cardinal Mazarin came in for his share of mockery as well.

The entire day passed as if it were no more than an hour. The count's
tutor, a gentleman, bon vivant, and "a scholar to his teeth," as the saying
has it, often reminded Raoul of the erudition, wit, and soaring disdain
of Athos—but without his grace, delicacy, and innate nobility. In those
regards, no one compared to the Comte de La Fère.

The horses, managed more carefully than the day before, brought them
by four o'clock to Arras. They were now approaching the theater of war,
and decided to spend the night in the town, as the Spaniards sometimes
took advantage of darkness to mount raids to the very outskirts of Arras.

The French army held a line from Pont-à-Marcq to Valenciennes, cen-
tering on Douai. It was said Monsieur le Prince himself was at Béthune.

The enemy's line extended from Cassel to Courtray, and as there was no
sort of rapine and pillage they wouldn't commit, the poor folk of the border
counties had left their rural homes and taken refuge in the nearby walled
cities. Arras was teeming with refugees.

There was talk that a decisive battle was imminent, the prince having
only maneuvered till then while waiting for reinforcements, which had
finally arrived. The young men congratulated themselves on coming at the
right time.

They supped together, and then shared a room. They were at the age of sudden friendships, and it seemed to them that they'd known each other since birth and would never find it possible to part.

The evening was spent talking about war; the lackeys polished their weapons, while the young men loaded their pistols in case of a skirmish on the morrow. They awoke feeling apprehensive, both having dreamed they'd arrived at the army too late to take part in the battle.

In the morning the rumor spread that the Prince de Condé had evacuated Béthune to fall back upon Carvin, while leaving a garrison in the former town. But this news couldn't be confirmed, so the young men decided to continue making their way toward Béthune, leaving the road, if necessary, to veer right toward Carvin.

De Guiche's tutor was familiar with the area and proposed that they take a byway that crossed the country midway between the road to Lens and the road to Béthune. At Ablain they stopped to make inquiries and leave directions for Grimaud. They set off again at about seven o'clock.

De Guiche, who was young and hot-blooded, said to Raoul, "Here we are then, three masters and three servants. Our valets are well armed, and your lackey seems stubborn enough."

"I've never seen him in a fight," said Raoul, "but he is a Breton, and that's something."

"Yes, indeed," de Guiche replied. "I'm sure he's fired a musket or two in his time. As for me, I have two reliable men who've been to war with my father, so we're six fighters in total. If we encounter a small troop of the enemy equal in number to ourselves, Raoul, or even superior—don't you think we should charge them?"

"By all means," the viscount replied.

"Whoa, young gentlemen! Hold on, there!" said the tutor, joining the conversation. "*Vertudieu!* And what of my instructions, Monsieur le Comte? Do you forget that I have orders to conduct you safely to Monsieur le Prince? Once you reach the army, go get killed all you like—but I'm warning you that until then, in my capacity as superior officer, I'll order a retreat at the first sight of an enemy's plume."

De Guiche and Raoul glanced at each other from the corners of their eyes and smiled.

The country became more wooded, and from time to time they met small fleeing groups of farmers, driving their cattle before them and carrying their most valuable goods on their backs or behind them in carts.

They arrived at Ablain without any trouble. There they made inquiries and learned that Monsieur le Prince had, in fact, left Béthune and was now between Cambrin and La Venthie. After leaving word for Grimaud, they continued on their way, taking a side road that led the little band after half an hour to the banks of a small stream that flowed into the Lys.

It was lovely country, crossed by small wooded valleys as green as emeralds. Occasionally the trail they were following led through small woodlands; as they approached each wood, in case of ambush, the tutor sent the count's two servants ahead as a vanguard. The tutor and the two young men formed the corps of the army, with Olivain, alert and with his carbine on his knee, as the rear guard.

Eventually, they found before them the thickest wood yet; a hundred paces from its verge, Monsieur d'Arminges took his usual precautions, sending the count's servants ahead as scouts. The lackeys had just disappeared under the eaves of the trees, the young men and the tutor laughing and chatting as they followed a hundred paces behind, when suddenly five or six musket shots rang out. The tutor called a halt, and the young men obeyed, reining in their horses. Just then they saw the two lackeys galloping back.

The two young men, eager to hear about the musketry, spurred toward the lackeys. The tutor followed, lagging behind. "Were you stopped and chased?" shouted the young men.

"No," replied one of the lackeys. "We probably weren't even seen. The gunfire broke out a hundred paces ahead of us, in pretty much the thickest part of the wood, so we came back to ask for advice."

"My advice," said Monsieur d'Arminges, "and my orders, if necessary, are that we retreat. This could conceal an ambush."

The other lackey said, "I thought I saw some horsemen in yellow outfits sneaking along the banks of the creek."

"That's it," said the tutor. "We've run afoul of a party of Spaniards. Fall back, Messieurs, fall back!"

The young men looked at each other inquisitively—and at that moment they heard a pistol shot, followed by two or three cries for help.

The two young men reassured each other with a nod, and as the tutor turned his horse away, they both spurred forward. Raoul cried, "With me, Olivain!"

Meanwhile the Comte de Guiche shouted, "Urbain and Blanchet! *À moi!*" And before the tutor could recover from his surprise, the little troop was already disappearing into the forest.

As they spurred their horses forward, both young men drew their pistols. Within moments, they arrived near where the sounds had seemed to come from. They slowed their horses and advanced cautiously. "Hush!" said de Guiche. "Horsemen."

"Yes, I see three on horseback, and three who've dismounted."

"What are they doing? Can you see?"

"They seem to be searching a dead or wounded man."

"It's some cowardly assassination!" said de Guiche.

"They're soldiers, though," said Bragelonne.

"Yes, but irregulars—in other words, highway robbers."

"Let's get them!" said Raoul.

"Let's get them!" repeated de Guiche.

"Messieurs!" cried the poor tutor. "Messieurs, in the name of heaven . . ."

But young men don't listen to such talk. They took off, each vying to get ahead of the other, and the only effect of the tutor's cries was to alert the Spaniards.

Immediately the three mounted soldiers charged to meet the young men, while the other three finished looting the travelers—for the young men could now see there were two victims on the ground.

At ten paces away, de Guiche fired first, and missed his man. The Spaniard charging Raoul fired in his turn, and Raoul felt a sting in his left arm like the stroke of a whip. When they closed to four paces, he fired, and the Spaniard, struck in the center of his chest, threw out his arms and fell backward off his horse, which turned and fled.

At that moment Raoul saw through the powder smoke the barrel of a musket leveled at him. Athos's advice came to his mind, and quick as a flash he pulled his mount and reared it back, just as the gun went off. His horse jumped sideways, lost its footing, and fell, trapping Raoul's leg beneath it. The Spaniard leapt down, grabbing his musket by the barrel to crack Raoul's skull with its butt.

Unfortunately, trapped as he was, Raoul could neither draw his sword from its sheath nor reach his other holster. He saw the heavy musket rise above his head and started to shut his eyes, when with a bound de Guiche arrived next to the Spaniard and put a pistol to his head. "Give up!" he said. "Or you're dead!"

The musket fell from the soldier's hands, which he raised in surrender.

De Guiche called over one of his lackeys, ordered him to guard the prisoner, and blow his brains out if he tried to escape, then leapt from his horse and approached Raoul. "My faith, Monsieur!" said Raoul, laughing, although his pallor betrayed the inevitable reaction to a first combat. "You pay your debts quickly, and no mistake! Without you," he added, repeating the count's own words, "I'd have been dead twice over."

"My opponent fled," said de Guiche, "so I was free to come to your aid. But are you seriously hurt? There's blood all over you."

"I think a bullet scratched me on the arm," said Raoul. "Help me get out from under my horse, and then nothing, I hope, will prevent us from continuing on our way."

Monsieur d'Arminges and Olivain had already dismounted, and together they worked to lift the horse, which was struggling in agony. Raoul managed to get his foot out of the stirrup and his leg from under the horse, and a moment later he was standing, free.

"Nothing broken?" asked de Guiche.

"*Ma foi,* no, thank heaven," replied Raoul. "But what happened to the poor victims waylaid by those wretches?"

"We arrived too late—they killed them, I think, and got away with their loot. My lackeys are guarding the bodies."

"Let's see if they still live, and need our help," said Raoul. "Olivain, we've inherited two horses, but I've lost mine; give me yours, and take the best of the new ones."

And they went to where the victims were lying.

XXXIV

The Monk

Two men were lying there. One was facedown, pierced by three bullets and drowned in a pool of his own blood, quite dead. The other, leaned up against a tree by the lackeys, had his eyes shut and his hands clasped in fervent prayer. A bullet had broken his thigh.

The young men looked first at the corpse, and started, astonished. "He's a priest," said Bragelonne. "See his tonsure? Oh, those dogs! Raising their hands against a minister of God!"

"Come here, Monsieur," said Urbain, an aging veteran who'd soldiered under Cardinal Richelieu. "Over here. There's nothing you can do for the priest, but maybe we can still save this one."

The wounded man smiled sadly. "Save me?" he said. "No—but you can help me to die."

"Are you also a priest?"

"No, Monsieur."

"Your unfortunate companion seemed to be a man of the Church," said Raoul.

"He was the Curate of Béthune, Monsieur; he was carrying his church's treasury and sacred vessels to safety, because Monsieur le Prince abandoned our town yesterday, and the Spanish might occupy it tomorrow. He knew enemy troops were prowling the countryside, and the trip was perilous, so when no one else dared to accompany him, I offered to go."

"And those miserable dogs attacked you—those wretches shot a priest!"

"Messieurs," said the wounded man, looking around him, "I'm in terrible pain, but I wish you could get me to a house."

"Where you could recover?"

"No, where I can be confessed."

"Maybe you're not hurt as badly as you think," said Raoul.

"Trust me, Monsieur, there's no time to lose," said the wounded man. "The ball broke my thigh-bone and has lodged in my bowels."

"Are you a doctor?" asked de Guiche.

"No," said the dying man, "but I know something about wounds—and mine is mortal. So, try to get me somewhere I can find a priest, or get one and bring him here, and God will reward such a holy deed. Help save my soul, for my body is lost."

"You were undertaking a holy task. God won't abandon you."

"Messieurs, in the name of heaven!" said the wounded man, gathering all his strength to try to get up. "Don't waste time in useless talk. Help me to get to the next village, or swear to me as you hope for salvation that you'll send me the first monk, curate, or priest you encounter. But what if no one dares do it, because they know the Spaniards are coming, and I die without absolution?" he added, in a tone of despair. "My God!" cried the wounded man with a terror that made the young men shudder. "You wouldn't allow that, would you? It would be too cruel!"

"Easy, Monsieur, easy," said de Guiche. "I swear we'll find you the consolation you need. Just point us toward a house where we can ask for help, or a village from which we can fetch a priest."

"Thank you, and may God reward you! There's an inn half a league along this road, and a league beyond that you'll find the village of Greney. Look for the curate, but if he's not home, go to the Augustinian monastery on the far side of the town. Bring me a friar, a monk, or a curate—whoever, so long as he's received from Holy Church the power of absolution *in articulo mortis.*"

"Monsieur d'Arminges," said de Guiche, "stay here with this poor man, and prepare to move him as gently as possible. Make a stretcher of our coats and some tree branches; two of our lackeys can carry him, with the third ready to switch out when one gets tired. The viscount and I will ride ahead to find a priest."

"Go, Monsieur le Comte," said the tutor, "but in heaven's name, don't take any risks!"

"Never fear. Besides, we're done for one day. You know the saying: *Non bis in idem.*"[98]

"Don't lose heart, Monsieur," said Raoul to the wounded man. "We'll find what you need."

"God bless you, Messieurs!" replied the dying man, in a tone of gratitude deep and profound.

And the two young men galloped off in the direction indicated, while the count's tutor oversaw the construction of a stretcher.

Within ten minutes the young men found the inn. Raoul, without dismounting, called for the innkeeper, warned him a wounded man was being brought there, and asked him to prepare everything needed to treat him, including a bed, bandages, and lint. He also asked if there was a nearby doctor or surgeon who could be summoned, adding that he was willing to pay for a messenger.

The innkeeper, addressed by two richly appointed young lords, promised to do everything they asked. Once they saw preparations were begun, the two cavaliers went on their way, spurring their horses toward Greney.

They had ridden nearly a league, and had just sighted the village's first houses, whose red-tiled roofs stood out distinctly against the green of the surrounding trees, when they saw coming toward them, mounted on a mule, a poor monk wearing a broad hat and a gray woolen robe. They took him for an Augustinian friar; it seemed chance had sent them just what they needed.

They cantered toward the monk. He was a man of twenty-two or twenty-three, but ascetic habits seemed to have added years to his appearance. He was fair-skinned, with an unhealthy pallor tinged a bilious yellow. His short hair, which extended from under his hat in a line across his forehead, was pale blond, and his eyes, though of a clear blue, seemed devoid of life.

"Monsieur," said Raoul, with his usual politeness, "are you an ecclesiastic?"

"Why do you ask?" said the stranger, coldly impassive.

"To get an answer," said the Comte de Guiche haughtily.

The stranger touched his heel to his mule and continued on his way.

De Guiche turned his horse and blocked him. "Answer, Monsieur!" he said. "You were asked politely, and every question deserves an answer."

"I'm free, I think, to speak or not to speak to random people who decide to interrogate me on a whim."

De Guiche, with some difficulty, suppressed the urge to give the monk an immediate thrashing. "First of all," he said, making an effort to speak calmly, "we are not 'random people'—my friend here is the Vicomte de Bragelonne, and I am the Comte de Guiche. More importantly, we don't question you on a whim, but because a man is dying nearby who needs the aid of the Church. If you're a priest, I demand, in the name of humanity, that you follow me to aid this man. If you're not—well, that's something else. But I warn you, in the cause of common courtesy which you seem to prefer to ignore, that further insolence will be punished."

The monk's face went from pale to livid, and he smiled so strangely that Raoul, who was watching him closely, felt something tighten around his heart. "He's some kind of Spanish or Flemish spy," he said, putting his hand on his pistol.

The monk's reply was a brief but menacing glare. "*Eh bien*, Monsieur!" said de Guiche. "What do you have to say?"

"I am a priest, Messieurs," said the young man. And his face resumed its former passivity.

"Then, *mon Père*," said Raoul, leaving his pistol in its holster, and speaking with a respect he didn't feel in his heart, "if you're a priest, we offer you, as my friend said, an opportunity to fulfill your vows—there's a badly wounded man ahead in the next inn calling for the aid of a minister of the Lord. Our men are waiting there with him."

"I will go," said the monk. And he dug his heels into his mule.

"You'd better go, Monsieur," said de Guiche, "because our horses can catch your mule if you go anywhere else, and then, I swear to you, your trial will be a short one, and your execution quick, because we have rope and there are trees everywhere."

The monk's eyes flashed again, but that was all; he just repeated, "I will go," and left.

"Let's follow him to make sure," said de Guiche.

"That's just what I was going to propose," said Bragelonne.

And the two young men rode slowly, matching their pace to the monk's and following about a pistol-shot behind.

After five minutes the monk turned to see whether he was followed.

"See that?" said Raoul. "We did the right thing."

"What a horrible face that monk has!" said the Comte de Guiche.

"Appalling!" Raoul agreed. "That yellow hair, his dead eyes, and especially his expression, with those thin lips that disappear whenever he speaks."

"Yes," said de Guiche, who hadn't been as observant of these details as Raoul, who'd been looking while de Guiche was talking. "A strange face indeed—but these monks have such degrading habits. Their fasting makes them pale, they beat themselves, the hypocrites, and their eyes sink and grow dull from weeping for life's lost joys."

"At least the poor dying man will have his priest," Raoul said. "Though God knows, the penitent looks like he has a clearer conscience than the confessor. As for me, I confess I'm not used to seeing priests who look like this one."

"You aren't?" said de Guiche. "This is one of those wandering friars who go begging down the highway in hopes a benefice will fall from heaven. They're mostly foreigners: Scots, Irish, Danes—I've seen their like before."

"As hideous as this one?"

"No, but pretty ugly, mostly."

"I feel bad for the dying man, having to receive consolation at the hands of such a friar!"

"Bah!" said de Guiche. "Absolution comes not from the confessor, but from God. Nonetheless, I must say I'd rather die impenitent than have to spend my final minutes with the likes of him. You agree with me, don't you, Viscount? I saw you gripping the pommel of your pistol as if you wanted to crack it over his head."

"Yes, Count—it's a strange thing, and might surprise you, but at the sight of that man I felt struck by a horror that's hard to describe. Have you ever been walking and almost stepped on a snake?"

"Never," said de Guiche.

"Well, that happened to me in the woods near Blois, and I can't forget the way it looked at me, its eyes dull as it reared back its head, tongue flickering. I stood stunned, frozen and fascinated, until the Comte de La Fère . . ."

"Your father?" asked de Guiche.

"No, my guardian," replied Raoul, blushing.

"All right."

"Until the Comte de La Fère said, 'Come, Bragelonne—draw your blade.' Then I drew, stepped toward the reptile, and cut it in two, just as it reared up, hissing, to strike at me. Well! I swear I felt exactly the same sensation at the sight of this fellow when he said, 'Why do you ask?' and glared at me."

"So, you're sorry you didn't cut him in half, as you did with your snake?"

"I almost wish I had," said Raoul.

At that moment they came in sight of the little inn, where they could see the procession bearing the wounded man just arriving. The tutor led the two lackeys who carried the dying man, while the third brought the horses.

The young men spurred forward. "As you see, here comes the wounded man," said de Guiche as he passed the Augustinian friar. "Be so kind as to pick up your pace, Monsieur Monk." Raoul, meanwhile, rode past, giving the friar as wide a berth as he could, looking aside in disgust.

Thus, the young men arrived ahead of the confessor, rather than behind him. They went to meet the dying man to give him the good news. He rose slightly to look where they pointed, saw the monk approaching at the trot on his mule, and fell back again on his litter, his face glowing with joy.

"Now," said the young count, "we did what we promised you, and are eager to get on to join the army of Monsieur le Prince—so if we continue on our way, you'll excuse us, won't you, Monsieur? They say they're preparing for battle, and we'd hate to arrive a day late."

"Go, my young Seigneurs," said the wounded man, "and may you be blessed for your piety. You have indeed done all you can do; I can only say once more, God bless you and those you hold dear!"

"Monsieur," de Guiche said to his tutor, "we're going to ride on ahead. You can catch up to us on the road to Cambrin."

The innkeeper was at the door; he'd prepared everything, bed, bandages, and lint, and had sent a groom to fetch a doctor from Lens, the nearest large town. "We'll do just as you asked," said the host, "but you, Monsieur," he continued, addressing Bragelonne, "won't you stop to have your wound tended to?"

"What, this wound? It's nothing," said the viscount. "It's time we got on to our next bivouac. But if a rider should stop and ask if you've seen a young man on a chestnut horse followed by a lackey, be so kind as to tell him that you've seen me, and that I plan to dine at Mazingarbe and sleep at Cambrin. That rider is my servant."

"Wouldn't it be better and more certain if I ask him his name and tell him yours?" replied the host.

"No harm in that," said Raoul. "My name is the Vicomte de Bragelonne, and his is Grimaud."

At this moment the wounded man arrived from one direction, and the monk from the other; the two young men drew back to give room for the stretcher, while the monk got down from his mule, and ordered that it be taken to the stables without having its saddle removed.

"Monsieur Monk," said de Guiche, "give that brave man a proper confession, and don't worry about your expenses or those of your mule—everything is covered."

"Thanks, Monsieur," said the monk, with one of those false smiles that made Bragelonne shiver.

"Come, Count," said Raoul, repelled by the Augustinian. "Let's go. I feel a chill here."

"Thank you again, my fine young Seigneurs," said the wounded man, "and remember me in your prayers."

"Rest easy!" said de Guiche, spurring along to catch up to Bragelonne, who was already twenty paces ahead.

The stretcher, carried by the two lackeys, was borne into the inn. The host and his wife, who had joined him, watched from the staircase. The wounded man seemed to be in terrible pain, but he seemed most concerned about whether the monk was following after him.

At the sight of the pale and bloody man, the woman grasped her husband's arm. "What's the matter?" he asked her. "Are you ill?"

"No, but look!" said the hostess.

"*Dame!*" said the innkeeper. "He's in bad shape."

"That's not what I mean," said the woman, trembling. "Don't you recognize him?"

"The wounded man? Wait a moment . . ."

"Ah! I see you do recognize him," the woman said, "because now you're as pale as I am."

"It's true!" cried the host. "Bad luck has come to our house—it's the old executioner of Béthune."

"The executioner of Béthune!" murmured the young monk, stopping short, his expression betraying the repugnance he felt for his penitent.

Monsieur d'Arminges, standing on the threshold, saw this hesitation. "Monsieur Monk," he said, "this man may have been an executioner, but he is no less a man, so give him the final services he requires. It will make your labors all the more meritorious."

The monk didn't reply, just silently followed the two lackeys into the rear chamber, where they placed the dying man on a bed. Seeing the man of God approach the bedside, the lackeys went out, closing the door on the monk and the penitent. D'Arminges and Olivain were waiting for them outside; they mounted their horses, and all four trotted off after Raoul and his companion.

They were just disappearing around a bend in the road when a new traveler arrived at the threshold of the inn.

"What can I do for you, Monsieur?" asked the innkeeper, still pale and trembling from his fearful discovery.

The traveler made the gesture of a man drinking, and then dismounted, pointed to his horse, and pantomimed giving it a rubdown.

"The devil!" the host said to himself. "It seems the man's a mute." He asked, "And where would you like to drink?"

"Here," said the traveler, pointing to a table.

"I was wrong," said the host to himself. "He's not a mute." So, he bowed and went to get a bottle of wine and some biscuits, which he placed before his taciturn guest. "Would Monsieur like anything else?" he asked.

"I would," said the traveler.

"What does Monsieur wish?"

"To know if you've seen a young gentleman of fifteen riding a chestnut horse and followed by a lackey."

"The Vicomte de Bragelonne?" said the host.

"Exactly."

"So, you're the one he called Monsieur Grimaud?"

The traveler nodded.

"Well!" said the host. "You missed your young master by no more than a quarter of an hour. He plans to dine at Mazingarbe and sleep tonight at Cambrin."

"How far is Mazingarbe?"

"Two and a half leagues."

"Thank you."

Grimaud, certain now of rejoining his young master by the end of the day, relaxed, mopped his brow, and poured himself a glass of wine, which he sipped silently.

He had just set down his glass and was preparing to refill it when a terrible scream came from the back room where the monk and the dying man had gone.

Grimaud leapt to his feet. "What was that?" he said. "Where was that scream from?"

"From the wounded man's room," said the host.

"What wounded man?" asked Grimaud.

"The old executioner of Béthune, who was ambushed by some Spaniards, then brought here to be confessed by an Augustinian friar. He must be suffering terribly."

"The old executioner of Béthune?" Grimaud muttered, calling up his memories. "A man of fifty-five to sixty, tall, strong, with a dark complexion, black hair and beard?"

"That's him, except his beard is gray and his hair is white. Do you know him?" asked the host.

"I met him once," said Grimaud, his expression darkening at the memory it recalled.

The hostess rushed up, trembling. "Did you hear that?" she asked her husband.

"Yes," the host replied, looking anxiously toward the door at the rear. Just then there came a second cry, less loud than the first, but followed by a long, extended groan.

The three listeners shuddered. "We have to find out what's going on," said Grimaud.

"That sounded like a man being murdered," whispered the host.

"*Jésus!*" said the woman, crossing herself.

Though Grimaud spoke slowly, he could act quickly. He rushed to the door of the back room and shook it by the knob, but it was locked from within.

"Open up!" cried the host. "Open up this instant, Monsieur Monk!"

No one answered.

"Open up, or I'll break down the door!" said Grimaud.

Silence.

Grimaud looked around and spotted a crowbar in a corner of the common room. He went and grabbed it, and before the host could object, pried the door open.

The back room was spattered with blood, a stream of which flowed from the mattress. The wounded man said nothing, for he was on the brink of death.

The Augustinian friar had disappeared. "The monk!" cried the host. "Where's the monk?"

Grimaud rushed to the window, which opened onto the courtyard. "He got out this way," he said.

"You think so?" said the host, thoroughly frightened. "Groom! See if the monk's mule is still in the stable!"

"The mule's gone!" the groom shouted back.

Grimaud frowned, while the host wrung his hands and looked around in dismay. His wife, terrified, didn't even dare to enter the room, and stood at the door.

Grimaud approached the dying man, recognizing his blunt, scarred features, which brought back a terrible memory. Finally, after a moment of sad and silent contemplation, he said, "There's no doubt about it: it's him."

"Is he still alive?" asked the host.

Grimaud didn't reply, just opened the man's doublet to feel his heart, as the host came around to the other side. Suddenly both started back, the host uttering a cry of terror, while Grimaud turned pale.

The blade of a dagger was buried to the hilt in the left side of the executioner's chest.

"Run for help," said Grimaud. "I'll stay here with him."

The host left the room in a hurry; as for his wife, she'd fled when she heard her husband cry out.

XXXV

The Absolution

Here's what had happened within the room.

We've seen that it was not by his own will, but rather against it that the monk attended the wounded man whose need had been forced upon him. Perhaps he'd thought to escape, if he got the chance—but he'd been prevented by the threats of the two gentlemen, and of their retainers, who'd apparently been given strict orders, as well as by the monk's own need to play the part of confessor convincingly. So, once he entered the room, he approached the wounded man's bedside.

The executioner quickly looked the monk over, with the efficient glance of those who know they are dying and therefore have no time to lose. As he took in the figure of the one who was to give him consolation, he started in surprise and said, "You're very young, Father."

"Those who wear these robes are of no age," the monk replied drily.

"Please speak gently to me, Father," said the wounded man. "I need a friend in these final moments."

"Do you suffer much?" asked the monk.

"Yes—but in soul even more than in body."

"We shall save your soul," said the young man. "But tell me, were you really the executioner of Béthune, as these people say?"

"In a manner of speaking," the man replied quickly, doubtless fearing that the title of *executioner* would drive away the final blessing he needed. "At one time I was, but I haven't been for fifteen years, since I sold the office. I still attend the executions, but I don't strike the blow—not me!"

"But you feel horror at once having done so?"

The executioner gave a deep sigh. "As long as I swung the blade in the name of law and justice I could sleep soundly, as the responsibility was that of justice and the law—but since one terrible night when I served as an instrument of vengeance and raised my sword with hatred over one of God's creatures . . ."

The executioner stopped, shaking his head in despair. "Speak," said the monk, who took a seat next to the bed, showing interest in the wounded man's strange story.

"Ahh!" cried the dying man, with the remorse of a long-buried grief that finally found expression. "After that, I renounced the savagery of the slayer's work, and tried to assuage my guilt by twenty years of good works. I've risked my life to aid those in peril and saved many lives to balance those I took. And that's not all: the money I made in the exercise of my vocation, I've given to the poor, to the Church, and to refugees fleeing persecution. All have pardoned me—some have even become my friends—but I believe that God has *not* pardoned me, because the memory of that execution pursues me when I sleep, and every night I see rising before me the specter of that woman."

"A woman! So, it was a woman you murdered?" cried the monk.

"Now you say it, too!" cried the executioner. "You use the word that echoes in my ears: *murder!* I didn't execute her, I murdered her! I'm not an instrument of justice, I'm a murderer!" And he closed his eyes with a groan.

The monk must have feared the man would die before continuing, for he quickly said, "Go on, go on, I know nothing about it. When you've finished your story, then God—and I—will judge."

"Oh! *Mon Père*," continued the executioner without opening his eyes, as if he feared by opening them to see some frightful object, "especially when it's nighttime, and I'm crossing a river, this terror I can't resist overwhelms me. My hands hang so heavy I can barely lift them, as if weighted by my heavy sword; the water turns the color of blood, and all the voices of nature, the rustling of trees, the murmur of the wind, the lapping of the waves, all share a single voice, despairing and terrible, crying out to me, 'Let God's justice be done!'"

"Delirium!" muttered the monk, shaking his head.

The executioner opened his eyes, twisted toward the young man, and seized his arm. "Delirium?" he repeated. "Delirium, you say? No, not at all. Because it was in the night—because I threw her body in the river—because the words my remorse always repeats, those very words, it was *I* in my pride who spoke them. After having been an instrument of human justice, I believed I embodied God's justice."

"But, look here, how did it happen? Speak," said the monk.

"It was at night; a nobleman came to me; he showed me an order, and I followed him. Four other seigneurs awaited us. They blindfolded me and took me with them. I had always reserved the right to refuse a job if what I was asked to do seemed unjust. We rode for five or six leagues, somber, silent, almost without saying a word. Finally, we reached a small cottage, where through the window I could see a woman leaning on a table, and they said, 'This is who you must execute.'"

"Horrid!" said the monk. "And you obeyed?"

"But *mon Père,* this woman was a monster, they said, who had poisoned her second husband, and then tried to murder his brother, who was among the men who'd brought me. She had just poisoned to death a young woman who was her rival, and they said that before leaving England she had conspired at the assassination of the king's favorite."

"Buckingham?" cried the monk.

"Yes, Buckingham—that's the name."

"So, this woman was English?"

"No, she was French, but she'd married in England."

The monk paled, wiped his forehead, got up, and locked the door from the inside. The executioner thought he was being abandoned and fell back moaning on the bed.

"No, no, here I am," said the monk, returning quickly. "Continue—who were these men?"

"One was a foreigner—English, I think. The other four were French and wore the uniform of the King's Musketeers."

"Who were they?"

"I didn't know them. But the French seigneurs called the Englishman *milord.*"

"And this woman . . . was she beautiful?"

"Young and beautiful! Oh, yes! I can still see her, kneeling at my feet as she prayed, her beautiful head thrown back. I've never been able to understand how I could have taken such a head, so beautiful, so pale."

The monk seemed agitated by a strange emotion. He trembled as if he wanted to ask a question but didn't dare. Finally, after a violent effort to control himself, he asked, "And the name of this woman?"

"I don't know. As I told you, they said she was twice married, once in France and once in England."

"And she was young, you say?"

"Twenty-five."

"Beautiful?"

"Ravishing."

"Blond hair?"

"Yes."

"She had full, flowing hair, didn't she? That fell to her shoulders?"

"Yes."

"Eyes large and expressive?"

"When she wanted them to be. Oh, yes, that was her."

"A voice of strange sweetness?"

"How . . . how do you know?"

The executioner raised himself on his arm and stared, terrified, at the monk, who flushed. "And you killed her!" said the monk. "You served as the tool of those cowards who didn't dare to kill her themselves! Had you no pity for her youth, her beauty, her helplessness? You killed her?"

"Alas!" said the executioner. "I told you, Father, that beneath her heavenly trappings this woman hid an infernal spirit, and when I saw her, when I remembered the evil she'd done to me . . ."

"To you? What could she have done to you? Tell me."

"She had seduced and run off with my brother, who was a priest; she had escaped with him from her convent."

"With your brother?"

"Yes—my brother was her first lover. She was the cause of my brother's death. Oh, Father, Father! Don't look at me like that! Am I guilty? Will I not be forgiven?"

The monk composed his face. "All right, all right, I will forgive you—if you tell me everything!"

"Yes!" cried the executioner. "Everything! Everything!"

"Then answer me: if she seduced your brother . . . you said she seduced him, didn't you?"

"Yes."

"If she caused his death . . . you said she caused his death?"

"Yes," repeated the executioner.

"Then, you must know her maiden name."

"Ah! My God, my God!" said the executioner. "I feel I'm dying. Absolution, Father! Absolution!"

"Say the name!" cried the monk. "Say the name, and I will give it."

"Her name . . . ah, God pity me!" the executioner murmured. And he fell back on the bed, pale, shivering, almost convulsing.

"Her name!" repeated the monk, bending over the dying man as if to draw it out of him. "Her name! Speak, or no absolution!"

The dying man seemed to gather all his remaining strength. The monk's eyes glistened. "Anne de Breuil," the dying man murmured.

"Anne de Breuil!" cried the monk, straightening and raising his hands to heaven. "Anne de Breuil! That was the name, wasn't it?"

"Yes, that was her name—and now absolve me, for I'm dying."

"I, absolve you?" cried the priest, with a laugh that made the hair stand on the dying man's head. "I, absolve you? I am no priest!"

"You're not a priest!" cried the executioner. "But . . . but what are you, then?"

"I shall tell you, wretch!"

"Oh, Lord—oh, my God!"

"I am John Francis de Winter!"

"I don't know you!" cried the executioner.

"Patience, patience, because you shall know me. I am John Francis de Winter," he repeated, "and that woman . . ."

"That woman?"

"Was my mother!"

The executioner gave a great and horrible scream, the first cry that was heard outside. Then he gibbered, "Oh, forgive me, forgive me, if not in the name of God, then in your own name—if not as a priest, then as her son."

"Forgive you!" cried the false monk. "Forgive you! God may do so, but as for me—never!"

"Pity me," said the executioner, holding his hands out to him.

"No pity for those who had no pity. Die without confession—die in despair—die and be damned!"

And drawing a dagger from his robes, he plunged it into the man's chest. "There!" he said. "That is my absolution!"

It was then that those outside heard the second, quieter cry, followed by a prolonged groan.

The executioner, who had half risen, fell back across the bed. As for the false monk, leaving the dagger in his victim, he ran to the window, opened it, jumped out onto the flowerbed, slipped into the stable, and took his mule out the back door. He led it to the nearest copse of trees, threw off his monk's robe, pulled a full cavalier's outfit from his saddle bags, donned it, and rode to the nearest posting-house. There he hired a horse and galloped off at full speed toward Paris.

XXXVI

Grimaud Speaks

The innkeeper had gone for help, his wife was outside praying, and Grimaud was left alone with the executioner.

After a moment, the wounded man opened his eyes. "Save me!" he murmured. "Save me! O, my God, is there no friend in the world who'll help me live—or die?" With an effort, he lifted his hand to his chest, and felt the hilt of the dagger. "Oh," he said, like one who suddenly remembers.

And he dropped his arm back on the bed.

"Take courage," said Grimaud. "We've sent for help."

"Who are you?" asked the wounded man, eyes widening as he looked at Grimaud.

"An old friend," said Grimaud.

"You?" The man tried to remember him, to recognize the features of the one speaking to him. "When did we meet? What happened then?"

"It was one night twenty years ago. My master brought you from Béthune to Armentières."

"Yes, I remember you," said the executioner. "You were one of the four lackeys."

"That's right."

"How is it you're here?"

"I was passing on the road and stopped at this inn to rest my horse. They'd just informed me the old executioner of Béthune was here when we heard your cries. We tried to rush to your aid but had to break down the door."

"And the monk?" said the executioner. "Have you seen the monk?"

"What monk?"

"The monk who was locked in with me?"

336

"No, he's gone; it looks like he fled out the window. Is he the one who stabbed you?"

"Yes," said the executioner.

Grimaud turned as if to leave. "What are you going to do?" asked the wounded man.

"We have to go after him."

"If you do—take care!"

"Why?"

"This was his revenge upon me, and so this is my expiation. Now I hope God will forgive me."

"Explain," Grimaud said.

"That woman that you and your masters had me kill . . ."

"Milady?"

"Yes, Milady, that's what you called her."

"What did this monk have to do with Milady?"

"She was his mother."

Grimaud staggered and gazed at the dying man as if stunned. "His . . . mother?" he repeated.

"Yes, his mother."

"So, he knows the secret of her death?"

"I took him for a monk and told him everything in confession."

"Woe!" cried Grimaud, sweat breaking out on his brow at the thought of the consequences of such a revelation. "You . . . you gave him no names, I hope?"

"No names, because I didn't know any, except the maiden name of his mother, which he recognized—but he knows that his uncle was one of the judges." And with that, the executioner fell back, exhausted.

Grimaud wanted to help him and reached out for the hilt of the dagger. "Don't touch it," said the executioner. "If you pull out the dagger, I'll die."

Grimaud froze, hand outstretched, then balled it into a fist and struck his forehead. "Ah! But if that man learns who the others were, my master is lost."

"Hurry, then! Go to him!" cried the executioner. "Warn your master, if he's still alive—and warn his friends. Believe me, my death won't be the end of his terrible vengeance."

"Where was he going?" asked Grimaud.

"To Paris."

"Where in Paris?"

"To track back two young gentlemen who passed on their way to the army, one of them—I heard his companion say his name—called the Vicomte de Bragelonne."

"Was that the young man who brought the monk to you?"

"Yes."

Grimaud raised his eyes to heaven. "Then it's the will of God," he said.

"It must be," said the wounded man.

"This is terrifying," muttered Grimaud. "And yet that woman deserved her fate," he said aloud. "Don't you think so?"

"When one is dying," said the executioner, "the crimes of others seem tiny compared to one's own." And he fell back, eyes closed in exhaustion.

Grimaud was torn between a pity that forbade him to leave the man before help came, and the fear that commanded him to leave at once to bring this news to the Comte de La Fère. He heard a noise in the corridor and saw the host returning with the surgeon, who had finally been found. They were followed by several busybodies, drawn by curiosity; news of the strange event had started to spread.

The surgeon approached the dying man, who seemed unconscious. Shaking his head doubtfully, he said, "First we must draw the blade from his chest." Grimaud remembered what the wounded man had said and looked away. The surgeon opened the man's doublet, tore a hole in his shirt, and laid his chest bare. The blade, as we said, was buried to its hilt.

The surgeon took hold of the pommel and pulled; as he did so the wounded man opened his eyes in a startled stare. When the blade was pulled out, a bloody froth foamed from the executioner's mouth, and when he breathed, blood spurted from his wound. The dying man fixed his eyes on Grimaud with a strange expression, uttered a muffled groan, and died in an instant.

Grimaud picked up the bloody dagger from where the surgeon had dropped it on the bedroom floor, horrifying everyone, and gestured for the host to follow him. He paid all the host's expenses with a generosity worthy of his master, and then mounted his horse.

At first Grimaud had thought he should return immediately to Paris, but then he remembered that his prolonged absence would make Raoul anxious—Raoul, who was only two leagues ahead of him, and could be caught in a quarter of an hour. He would explain everything to Raoul, then head back to Paris. He put his horse into a gallop, and fifteen minutes later he pulled up at the Crowned Mule, the only inn at Mazingarbe.

After a few words with the host, he knew he was in the right place. Raoul was dining with the Comte de Guiche and his tutor, but the grim adventure of the morning had left the young men in a somber mood. This didn't dampen the cheer of Monsieur d'Arminges, whose greater experience made him more philosophical about such events.

Suddenly the door opened and Grimaud appeared before them, pale, dusty, and still spattered with the dying man's blood. "Grimaud, my good Grimaud," cried Raoul. "Here you are at last! Excuse me, Messieurs—he's not a servant, he's a friend." And rising and racing to him, he continued, "How is Monsieur le Comte? Have you seen him since we parted? Please tell me—but I also have much to tell you. In the last three days we've had many adventures . . . but what's wrong? You're so pale. And blood! What's this blood?"

"You're right, he's all bloody," said de Guiche, rising. "Are you hurt, *mon ami*?"

"No, Monsieur," said Grimaud, "the blood is not mine."

"Whose, then?" asked Raoul.

"It's the blood of that luckless man you left at the inn, and who died in my arms."

"That man died—in your arms! But do you know who he was?"

"Yes," said Grimaud.

"He was the old executioner of Béthune."

"I know it."

"How did you know?"

"I knew him . . . before."

"And he's dead?"

"Yes."

The two young men gaped at each other.

"What would you have, Messieurs?" said d'Arminges. "Death is the universal law, and not even an executioner is exempt. From the moment I saw his wound, I figured he would die—and you know, that was his opinion too, which was why he asked for a monk."

At the word *monk*, Grimaud paled.

"Come, sit down, eat!" said d'Arminges, who like all men of that period, and especially those of his maturity, didn't allow sentiment to get in the way of a good meal.

"Yes, Monsieur, you're right," said Raoul. "Come, Grimaud, call for what you need, get served, and after you've rested, we'll talk."

"No, Monsieur, no," said Grimaud. "I can't stop for a moment—I need to get back to Paris."

"What, you, go back to Paris? You're mistaken, it's Olivain who's going back—you're staying with me."

"On the contrary, it's Olivain who's staying, and I who am leaving. I came expressly to tell you that."

"But what's the reason for this change?"

"I can't tell you."

"Explain yourself."

"I can't explain."

"Come, is this some kind of joke?"

"Monsieur le Vicomte knows I never joke."

"Yes, but I also know that the Comte de La Fère said you would stay with me while Olivain went back to Paris. We will follow the orders of Monsieur le Comte."

"Not in this circumstance, Monsieur."

"Are you disobeying me, by any chance?"

"Yes, Monsieur—because I must."

"You persist, then?"

"Yes, because I must. I'm going. Good luck, Monsieur le Vicomte." Grimaud bowed and turned toward the door to leave.

Raoul, angry and anxious at the same time, followed and grabbed him by the arm. "Grimaud!" Raoul cried. "I said you're staying!"

Grimaud faced him. "To do that would mean the death of Monsieur le Comte." And again, he bowed and turned to leave.

"Grimaud, my friend," said the viscount, "you can't go this way, leaving me dying of worry. Grimaud, speak, speak, in heaven's name!"

And Raoul, staggering, fell into a chair.

"I can tell you only one thing, Monsieur, for the secret you demand isn't mine to share. You met a monk, didn't you?"

The two young men exchanged fearful glances. "Yes."

"You led him back to the wounded man?"

"Yes."

"Did you get a good look at him?"

"Yes."

"Enough that you'd recognize him if you met him again?"

"Yes, I swear it," said Raoul.

"And I, as well," said de Guiche.

"Well, if you ever meet him again," said Grimaud, "whether on the highway, on the street, in church, wherever—put your boot on him and crush him without pity or mercy, as you would a viper, a serpent, or a cobra. Crush him, and don't stop until you're sure he's dead; the lives of five men are in jeopardy so long as he lives."

And without adding another word, Grimaud took advantage of his audience's shock and terror to leave the premises.

"Well, Count!" said Raoul, turning to de Guiche. "Didn't I tell you that monk reminded me of a snake?"

A moment later they heard a horse gallop past in the street. Raoul ran to the window; it was Grimaud, returning down the road to Paris. He saluted the viscount, waved his hat, and disappeared around the corner.

As he galloped Grimaud had two thoughts. The first was that, at the rate he was going, his horse wouldn't last ten leagues. The second was that he was out of money. But Grimaud's wits had been sharpened by his habitual silence: at the first relay he sold his horse and used the money to hire post-horses for the rest of the journey.

XXXVII

The Eve of Battle

Raoul was roused from these somber reflections by the innkeeper, who rushed into the common room shouting, "The Spaniards! The Spaniards!"

If true, this was serious enough to drive all other thoughts from their minds. The young men asked for confirmation and were told that the enemy was advancing by way of Houdin and Béthune.

While Monsieur d'Arminges called for the horses, which were feeding in preparation for departure, the young cavaliers went up to the inn's highest windows, from which they could see a full corps of infantry and cavalry on the horizon toward Hersin and Lens. This wasn't just a band of irregulars, this was a whole army. It seemed like a good idea to obey the wisdom of Monsieur d'Arminges this time and retreat.

The young men ran back downstairs. Monsieur d'Arminges was already mounted, Olivain held the young men's horses, while the Comte de Guiche's lackeys guarded the Spanish prisoner between them, mounted on a nag they'd bought to bear him. As an added precaution, his hands had been tied.

The little troop left at a trot on the road to Cambrin, where they expected to find the prince. But he'd moved the evening before, drawing back toward La Bassée in response to a false report that the enemy was crossing the Lys at Estaires. In fact, misled by this information, the prince had withdrawn his troops from Béthune and concentrated all his forces between Vieille-Chapelle and La Venthie, while he himself, after a reconnaissance ride along the line with the Maréchal de Grammont, had just returned to his headquarters, where he interrogated the officers of his commands as to their situations. But no one had any positive news: for forty-eight hours there had been no contact with the enemy, who seemed to have vanished.

Never does an enemy army seem so near and therefore so threatening as when it disappears completely. So, the prince's mood, unlike his usual habit, was sullen and anxious, when a duty officer entered and announced to the Maréchal de Grammont that someone wanted to speak to him. The Duc de Grammont glanced at the prince, who nodded, and the marshal went out. The prince followed him with his eyes, his gaze fixed on the door, and no one dared to speak for fear of interrupting his thoughts.

Suddenly a distant thud trembled the air. The prince leapt up, extending his hand in the direction whence the sound came. He knew quite well what it was: cannon fire.

Everyone else had risen as well. At that moment the door opened: "Monseigneur," said the Maréchal de Grammont, radiant, "if Your Highness will permit, my son, the Comte de Guiche, and his traveling companion, the Vicomte de Bragelonne, can give him news of the enemy—for they've seen them."

"How's that?" the prince said eagerly. "If I'll permit it? I don't just permit it, I require it! Have them enter."

The marshal pushed in the two young men, who found themselves in front of the prince. "Speak, Messieurs," said the prince, saluting them. "Talk first, and we'll exchange the usual compliments later. The most urgent thing now is to know where the enemy is and what he's doing."

It fell naturally to the Comte de Guiche to do the talking—not only was he the older of the two youths, but he'd already been presented to the prince by his father. Raoul had never seen the prince before, but de Guiche had known him quite a while, so he was the one who told the prince what they'd observed from the inn at Mazingarbe.

Meanwhile, Raoul was studying this young general, already so famous from the battles of Rocroi, Fribourg, and Nördlingen. Since the death of his father, Henri de Bourbon,[99] Louis de Bourbon was Prince de Condé, and was nicknamed, according to the custom of the time, "Monsieur le Prince." He was a young man aged twenty-six or twenty-seven, eagle-eyed and hook-nosed—an *agl' occhi grifani,*[100] as Dante put it. He was of middle height, with long, flowing hair, and had all the qualities of a great general, being decisive, courageous, and quick-witted. This didn't prevent him from being at the same time a gentleman of elegance and spirit, so that besides the revolution he brought to warfare due to the new ideas that he embodied, he also led a social revolution in Paris among the young nobles of the Court, of whom he was the natural leader. These young courtiers were called the *petit-maîtres* by the aging social lions of the previous reign, for whom Bassompierre, Bellegarde, and the Duc d'Angoulême had been the models.

A few words from the Comte de Guiche, along with the sound of the guns, enabled the prince to grasp the situation. The enemy had crossed the Lys at Saint-Venant was marching on Lens, doubtless intending to take the city and cut off the French army from France. They could hear closer cannon fire now, louder thumps drowning out the farther thunder, as French heavy guns began to reply to the Spanish and Lorrainer artillery.

But how strong was this attack? Was it just a corps intended to create a diversion, or was it the entire army? That was the prince's next question, to which de Guiche was unable to give a definitive response. It was the critical issue, the one for which the prince needed an exact and positive answer.

By this time Raoul had gotten over his initial timidity, and approached the prince to say, "If Monseigneur will allow me to hazard a few words on the subject, I might be able to help."

The prince turned, looked the young man over, and seemed to size him up at a glance. Seeing the youth was no more than fifteen, he smiled reassuringly. "Of course, Monsieur—speak," he said, softening his commanding voice, as if addressing a woman.

Raoul said, blushing, "Monseigneur might want to interrogate our Spanish prisoner."

"You took a Spanish prisoner?" the prince cried.

"Yes, Monseigneur."

"Why, so we did," added de Guiche. "I'd quite forgotten."

"Don't be so modest—you're the one who took him," Raoul said, smiling.

The old marshal turned toward the viscount, grateful for this praise of his son, while the prince called out, "This young man is right—bring in the prisoner."

While they were marching him in, the prince took de Guiche aside and asked him how the prisoner had been taken, and who this young man was.

The prince, returning to Raoul, said, "Monsieur, I know you have a letter of recommendation from my sister, Madame de Longueville, but I see you prefer to recommend yourself by giving such good advice."

"Monseigneur," said Raoul, blushing, "I didn't wish to interrupt Your Highness's important conversations with my small affairs—but here's the letter."

"Very well," said the prince. "You can give it to me later. Here comes the prisoner, and right now that's the urgent thing."

They brought in the Spanish irregular. He was a *condottiere*, one of those mercenaries who at that time were still selling themselves to anyone who could pay and give them free reign to pillage. Since his capture he hadn't said a word, so that even his captors didn't know his nationality.

The prince regarded him with an air of disgust. "What country do you come from?" he asked.

The prisoner replied with a few words in a foreign language.

"Hmm. Apparently, he's Spanish," said the prince. "Do you speak Spanish, Grammont?"

"Not much, Monseigneur."

"And I, not at all," said the prince, laughing. "Messieurs," he said to his gathered staff, "does anyone speak Spanish who can act as an interpreter?"

"I do, Monseigneur," said Raoul.

"Ah! So, you speak Spanish?"

"Well enough, I think, to serve Your Highness's purpose in this matter."

All the while, the prisoner stood impassively, as if he had no idea what was being said.

"Monseigneur desires to know your nationality," Raoul said in the purest Castilian.

"*Ich bin ein Deutscher,*" replied the prisoner.

"What the devil did he say?" asked the prince. "What fresh gibberish is this?"

"He says he's a German, Monseigneur," said Raoul. "But I don't believe it, because his accent is bad, and his pronunciation is terrible."

"So, you speak German, too?" asked the prince.

"Yes, Monseigneur," Raoul said.

"Well enough to interrogate him in that language?"

"Yes, Monseigneur."

"Question him, then."

Raoul began the interrogation, and the results supported his first opinion. The prisoner couldn't or wouldn't understand what Raoul was saying, and Raoul, in return, only poorly understood his responses, which came in a mix of Flemish and Alsatian. But despite the prisoner's efforts to avoid being understood, Raoul identified the man's native accent.

"*Non siete Spagnuolo, non siete Tedesco, siete Italiano,*" Raoul said. "You're neither Spanish nor German, you're Italian."

The prisoner started and bit his lip.

"Ah! I understood that perfectly," said the Prince de Condé, "and since he's Italian, I'll continue the interrogation. Thank you, Viscount," continued the prince, laughing. "I appoint you from this moment to be my interpreter."

But the prisoner was no more disposed to answer in Italian than in any other language; what he wanted was to evade giving answers. Thus, he knew nothing—not the number of the enemy, nor who commanded them, nor the direction of their movements.

"Very well," said the prince, who understood what was behind this pretended ignorance. "This man was caught plundering and murdering, and could have purchased his life by answering—but since he won't talk, take him out and shoot him."

The prisoner turned pale, and the two soldiers who'd brought him each took an arm and led him to the door, while the prince, turning to the

Maréchal de Grammont, seemed already to have dismissed the matter from his mind.

At the door, the prisoner tried to stop the soldiers, who, following their orders, tried to force him to continue. "Hold on," said the prisoner in French. "I'm ready to talk, Monseigneur."

"Oh ho!" said the prince, laughing. "I thought you might. I have a secret method for loosening tongues; young men, profit by my example for when your time comes to command."

"But only on condition," continued the prisoner, "that Your Highness swears to let me live."

"By my faith as a gentleman," said the prince.

"In that case, ask away, Monseigneur."

"Where is the army crossing the Lys?"

"Between Saint-Venant and Aire."

"Who is in command?"

"Count Fuensaldagna, General Beck, and the archduke[101] in person."

"How many men do they have?"

"Eighteen thousand men and thirty-six guns."

"And their goal?"

"They march on Lens."

"You see, Messieurs!" said the prince, turning in triumph toward the Maréchal de Grammont and the other officers.

"Yes, Monseigneur," said the marshal. "You've gained all that human intelligence could learn."

"Call back Le Plessis-Bellièvre, Villequier, and d'Erlac," said the prince. "Recall all the troops that are south of the Lys, and prepare them to march tonight; tomorrow, in all probability, we attack the enemy."

"But, Monseigneur," said the Maréchal de Grammont, "consider that even with all the troops we have available, it's no more than thirteen thousand men."

"Monsieur le Maréchal," said the prince, with that noble look that belonged only to him, "it's with small armies that we win the greatest battles." Then, turning to the prisoner: "Take this man out and guard him carefully. His life depends on the information he's given us: if it's wrong, he's to be shot."

The prisoner was led away.

"Comte de Guiche," said the prince, "it's been too long since you saw your father; stay close to him. Monsieur," he continued, addressing Raoul, "if you're not too fatigued, follow me."

"To the end of the world, Monseigneur!" cried Raoul, feeling for this young general, who seemed to live up to his reputation, a genuine admiration.

The prince smiled; he despised flatterers but enjoyed being admired. "Well, Monsieur," he said, "you're a good advisor—you've already proven that. Tomorrow we'll see how you behave in action."

"And I, Monseigneur," said the marshal, "what shall I do?"

"Stay here to receive the troops. I'll either come back to take command myself, or I'll send a courier to have them led to me. Twenty guards, well mounted, is all I'll need as escort."

"That's not very many," said the marshal.

"It's enough," said the prince. "Have you a good horse, Monsieur de Bragelonne?"

"Mine was killed this morning, Monseigneur, and for the time being I'm mounted on my lackey's."

"Go to my stables and choose for yourself the horse that best suits you. No false modesty, take the horse that seems best to you. You may need it tonight, and you're sure to need it tomorrow."

Raoul didn't wait to be told twice; he knew that with superiors, and especially when superiors were princes, the height of etiquette is to obey without question or delay. He went to the stables and chose an Andalusian dun, and then put on its saddle and bridle himself—for Athos had warned him that, in times of danger, he should never entrust that important task to anyone else. He then rejoined the prince, who had just that moment mounted his own horse. "Now, Monsieur," he said to Raoul, "would you show me that letter of recommendation?"

Raoul handed the letter to the prince. "Stay with me, Monsieur," the prince said to him.

The prince spurred on, wrapped the reins around his saddle's pommel, as he usually did when he wanted his hands free, unsealed Madame de Longueville's letter, and galloped up the road to Lens, accompanied by Raoul and followed by his small escort. Meanwhile, the messengers who were to recall the troops were riding off at full speed in all directions.

The prince read the letter as he rode. "Monsieur," he said after a moment, "you are described in the best possible terms. The only thing I have to say is, from what little I've already seen and heard, I think even better of you than they do." Raoul bowed.

However, at every step the little troop took toward Lens, the cannon fire seemed closer. The prince's gaze turned toward the thunder with the fierce concentration of a bird of prey. It was as if his eyes had the power to see through the barrier of trees that stretched before him toward the horizon. From time to time his nostrils dilated, as if seeking the scent of gun smoke, and he blew like a horse.

Finally, they heard a gun thump so close that it was obvious they were less than a league from the fighting. As they rounded a bend, they saw ahead the little village of Aunay.

The peasants were in a panic. The rumors of Spanish cruelty had everyone terrified; the women had already fled, retreating toward Vitry, leaving but few men behind. They ran at the sight of the prince, until one of them recognized him. "Ah, Monseigneur," he said, "have you come to chase off those wretched Spaniards and thieving Lorrainers?"

"Yes," said the prince, "if you'd be willing to serve as my guide."

"Willingly, Monseigneur. Where would Your Highness like to go?"

"To some elevated spot where I can see Lens and its environs."

"In that case, I'm your man."

"I can trust you? You're a good Frenchman?"

"I was a soldier at Rocroi, Monseigneur."

"Here," said the prince, giving him his purse. "That's for Rocroi. Now, do you want a horse, or would you rather walk?"

"On foot, Monseigneur, on foot—I always served in the infantry. Besides, I intend to lead Your Highness by paths we'll have to pursue afoot."

"Let's go," said the prince, "there's no time to lose."

The veteran set off, running ahead of the prince's horse. A hundred paces outside the village, he took a small path that wound along the bottom of a pretty glen. For half a league they rode through the woods, with cannon fire so close that it seemed after each shot they could hear the whistling of the ball. Finally, they found a path that left the valley to climb the hillside. The peasant turned up this path, inviting the prince to follow him. The latter dismounted, ordered Raoul and one of his aides to do the same, told the others to stay behind but remain on the alert, and began to climb the path.

After a few minutes they reached the ruins of an old château whose tumbled walls crowned a hilltop with a view of the surrounding region. A quarter-league away they could see Lens, and in front of Lens, the entire enemy army.

At a single glance the prince surveyed the ground from Lens to Vimy. In an instant, the complete plan of the battle that was to save France the next day formed in his mind. He took a pencil, tore a page from his tablet, and wrote:

> *My dear Marshal,*
>   *In an hour Lens will be in the hands of the enemy. Come to me and bring the whole army with you. Meet me at Vendin, where I'll have orders for the troops' disposition. By tomorrow night we'll have retaken Lens and beaten the enemy.*

Then, turning toward Raoul, he said, "Go, Monsieur, at full speed to deliver this letter to Monsieur de Grammont."

Raoul bowed, took the paper, ran back down the slope, jumped on his horse, and galloped off. Fifteen minutes later he reached the marshal.

Some of the summoned troops had already arrived, and the rest were coming in from moment to moment. The Maréchal de Grammont placed himself at the head of all the available infantry and cavalry and took the road to Vendin, leaving the Duc de Châtillon to assemble and bring up the rest. All the artillery had arrived and was added to the march.

It was seven in the evening when the marshal arrived at the rendezvous. The prince was there and waiting; as he'd foreseen, Lens had fallen into the enemy's hands shortly after Raoul's departure. The ending of the cannonade as good as announced this event.

They waited for nightfall. As the darkness increased, the rest of the troops summoned by the prince gradually arrived. All had been ordered to march without beating drums or sounding trumpets.

By nine o'clock full night had fallen, though a dim twilight still lit the plain. The French marched forward silently, the prince leading the column. Once they passed Aunay, the army could see Lens ahead: two or three houses were in flames, and distant shouts, denoting the agony of a town taken by assault, reached the soldiers' ears.

The prince ordered the units into position. The Maréchal de Grammont was to hold the far left, anchored on Méricourt; the Duc de Châtillon commanded the center; while the prince, commanding the right wing, formed his troops in front of Aunay. The next day's order of battle was to be based on the positions occupied during the night. Each unit would awaken on the ground from whence it would maneuver.

The movements were executed in the most profound silence and with the greatest precision. By ten o'clock everyone was in position, and at half past ten the prince inspected the posts and gave the orders for the next day.

Three instructions in particular were given to each commander, with orders that the troops were to obey them scrupulously. First, each unit in line should stay in contact with the units to its right and left, while maintaining a proper distance. Second, they were to advance at no faster than a walk. And third, they were to let the enemy fire first.

The prince sent the Comte de Guiche to join his father, keeping Bragelonne for himself—but the two young men asked to spend the night before the battle together, and their request was granted.

A tent was raised for them near that of the marshal. Though the day had been long and tiring, neither was ready for sleep. The eve of battle is a somber and serious time, even for old soldiers, let alone for two young men who would be seeing the terrible spectacle for the first time.

On the eve of battle, the mind thinks of a thousand things forgotten or regretted. On the eve of battle, neighbors become friends and friends become brothers. It goes without saying that every feeling is exaggerated to the highest degree. And it seemed the young men had similar feelings, because each sat in his end of the tent and began to write a letter on his knee.

The letters were long, at least four pages crammed with words, the writing growing successively smaller as the sheets were filled. Occasionally the young men looked up and smiled. Sensitive to each other's moods, they understood their feelings without saying anything.

Their letters completed, each put his in a double envelope, so no one could see to whom the inner envelope was addressed until the outer was unsealed. Then they approached each other and exchanged their letters, smiling.

"If I should suffer a mischance," said Bragelonne.

"If I should be killed," said de Guiche.

"Rest easy," they told each other.

They embraced like brothers, and then each wrapped himself in his cloak, lay down, and slept the deep and graceful sleep enjoyed by birds, flowers, and the young.

XXXVIII

A Dinner as of Old

The second rendezvous of the former musketeers was not as tense and threatening as the first. With his usual clarity and perception, Athos had recognized that meeting around a dinner table would make everyone more amenable to agreement. His friends, sensitive to his current dignity and sobriety, hadn't dared to suggest a repeat of the revelry of former days at the Pomme-de-Pin or the Heretic, so he was first to propose that they meet around some well-provisioned table, where each could set aside reserve and be true to his own character, resuming that easy camaraderie they'd had when they were known as the Inseparables.

This proposal was welcomed by everyone, especially d'Artagnan, who was eager to revisit the happy conviviality of his youth, as he felt that for far too long he'd had nothing but bad food and worse companionship. Porthos, on the verge of being made a baron, was delighted to have an opportunity to study the aristocratic manners of Athos and Aramis. Aramis wanted to hear the gossip from the Palais Royal from d'Artagnan and Porthos, and to stay on a good footing with friends as devoted as they, who formerly had supported his disputes with swords both ready and resolute. As for Athos, he was the only one who had nothing to gain from the others and was motivated solely by pure friendship and grandeur of soul.

They'd all agreed to exchange addresses, and that when they needed to meet it would be at the sign of the Hermitage, a famous caterer in the Rue de la Monnaie. The first rendezvous was set for the following Wednesday, at eight in the evening.

And so, on that day the four friends met at the appointed hour, each arriving on his own. Porthos came from trying out a new horse, d'Artagnan from his guard duty at the Louvre, Aramis from visiting one of his penitents in the neighborhood, while Athos, who had taken up lodgings in Rue Guénégaud, was already nearby. Unexpectedly, they all arrived at the door of the Hermitage at the same time, Athos coming by way of the Pont Neuf, Porthos by the Rue du Roule, d'Artagnan by the Rue des Fossés-Saint-Germain-l'Auxerrois, and Aramis by the Rue de Béthisy.

The first words exchanged between the four friends, whose manners were somewhat reserved, were rather stiff and formal. As the meal began it was apparent that d'Artagnan was forcing himself to laugh, Athos to drink, Aramis to talk, and Porthos to stay silent. Athos, noticing this mutual embarrassment, adopted the speedy remedy of ordering four bottles of champagne. Hearing this order, delivered with Athos's usual calm command, the Gascon's face brightened, and Porthos looked pleased. Aramis was astounded: he knew that not only did Athos no longer drink, but he even evinced a certain distaste for wine.

This astonishment redoubled when Aramis saw Athos pour himself a glass and drink it down with all his former enthusiasm. D'Artagnan immediately filled and emptied his glass, while Porthos and Aramis clinked their goblets together. In what seemed like no time, the four bottles were empty. Conviviality reigned, and the four guests seemed ready to renounce all their private agendas. Athos's excellent prescription had dissolved all the clouds that darkened their hearts. The four friends began to rattle on like old times, finishing each other's sentences and leaning casually on the table in their favorite postures. It wasn't long before the dapper Aramis actually undid the top two buttons of his doublet, which was Porthos's cue to open his entirely.

Old battles, desperate journeys, and blows given and received were the early topics of conversation, followed by memories of the grim conflicts waged against the man who was now called the Great Cardinal. "*Ma foi,*" said Aramis, laughing, "after these eulogies for the dead, shall we talk a bit about the living? I'd like to share some gossip about Mazarin. Is that allowed?"

"Always," said d'Artagnan, laughing in his turn. "Tell us your story, and we'll applaud it if it's good."

"There was a great prince with whom Mazarin sought an alliance," said Aramis. "The prince was invited by Mazarin to send him a list of the conditions under which he would honor the minister by allying with him. The prince, who was somewhat reluctant to deal with such an upstart, nonetheless compiled his list and sent it along. The list contained three provisions that Mazarin didn't like, so he offered the prince ten thousand crowns to drop them."

"Oh ho! The miser!" cried his three friends. "There wasn't much risk an offer that low would be accepted. What did the prince do?"

"The prince immediately sent Mazarin fifty thousand *livres,* begging him never to write to him again, and promising twenty thousand *livres* more if he'd agree never to speak with him as well. And what do you think Mazarin did?"

"He got angry?" said Athos.

"He beat the messenger?" said Porthos.

"He took the money?" said d'Artagnan.

"You guessed it, d'Artagnan," said Aramis.

And they all laughed so loudly that the host came over to see if they needed anything. He was afraid a fight was about to break out, but eventually their hilarity died down.

"Can we poke some fun at Monsieur de Beaufort?" asked d'Artagnan. "I'm in just the mood."

"As you will," said Aramis, familiar enough with the Gascon's spirit to know he'd never give up on something he was determined to do.

"All right with you, Athos?" asked d'Artagnan.

"I vow, faith of a gentleman, that if it's funny, I'll laugh," said Athos.

"Then I'll begin," said d'Artagnan. "Monsieur de Beaufort, talking one day with one of the friends of Monsieur le Prince, told him that during the early quarrels between Mazarin and the Parliament he'd found himself in a dispute with Monsieur de Chavigny, who'd attached himself to the new cardinal—so Beaufort, who held to the old ways, had cudgeled him soundly. This friend, who knew Monsieur de Beaufort was rather free with his fists, wasn't a bit surprised, and related the tale to Monsieur le Prince. The story spread rapidly, and soon everyone was snubbing Chavigny, who wanted to know the reason for such coldness, but no one would tell him. Finally, someone dared to say that everyone was surprised that a gentleman would allow himself to be cudgeled, even if Monsieur de Beaufort was a prince.

"'And who said the prince had cudgeled me?' asked Chavigny.

"'The prince himself,' the friend replied.

"Chavigny went back to the source and found the person to whom the prince made the remarks, who swore on his honor that's what he'd heard. In despair at this defamation, Chavigny, who couldn't understand it, declared he'd rather die than put up with it. So, he sent two emissaries to the prince to inquire if he really had said that he'd cudgeled Monsieur de Chavigny. 'I said it, and I repeat it,' said the prince, 'because it's the truth.'

"'Monseigneur,' said one of Chavigny's emissaries, 'permit me to say to Your Highness that blows from a gentleman degrade the giver more than the receiver. King Louis XIII was unwilling to have gentlemen as his *valets de chambre* because he wanted the right to beat his valets.'

"'Wait,' asked Monsieur de Beaufort, surprised, 'what's all this talk of beating, and who was beaten?'

"'But it was you, Monseigneur, who boasted of having beaten . . .'

"'Who?'

"'Monsieur de Chavigny.'

"'Me?'

"'Did you not cudgel Monsieur de Chavigny, or so at least you said, Monseigneur?'

"'Yes.'

"'Well, he denies it.'

"'Ha!' said the prince. 'I cudgeled him so well, I can give you the exact words,' said Monsieur de Beaufort with all the majesty he could muster. 'I said, "My dear Chavigny, I implore you not to heed this clown of a Mazarin."'"

"'Oh, no, Monseigneur—now I get it,' said the second emissary. 'You meant you were *cajoling* him.'

"'Cudgeling, cajoling, what's the difference?' said the prince. 'Really, our wordsmiths are such peasants! Or is that pedants?'"

Everyone laughed at the blundering speech of Monsieur de Beaufort, whose malapropisms were becoming proverbial, and all agreed that factionalism should be banished from their friendly rendezvouses: d'Artagnan and Porthos could mock the princes, and Athos and Aramis could cudgel Mazarin. "*Ma foi,*" said d'Artagnan to his two friends, "I assure you, you've got good reason to want to hammer Mazarin, as he certainly has it in for you."

"Bah! Really?" said Athos. "If I thought that clown knew me by name, I'd go and get re-baptized. Knows me, does he?"

"He not only knows you by name, he knows you by your deeds. He knows two gentlemen were particularly responsible for helping Monsieur de Beaufort escape, and I'm warning you, he's actively looking for you."

"For me? Who told him?"

"I did."

"What, you?"

"Yes, he sent for me this morning specifically to ask if I had any information."

"About those two gentlemen?"

"Yes."

"And what did you tell him?"

"That I didn't know who they were yet, but I was having dinner with two people who might tell me."

"That's what you said!" laughed Porthos, a broad smile spread across his face. "Bravo! But doesn't that frighten you, Athos?"

"No," said Athos, "it's not Mazarin looking for me that I fear."

"Oh?" said Aramis. "Tell me then what you do fear."

"Nothing—at the moment, at least."

"And in the past?" said Porthos.

"Ah, as to the past . . . well, that's another thing," said Athos, with a sigh. "In the past, and in the future . . ."

"Are you afraid for young Raoul?" asked Aramis.

"Bah! No one dies in his first action," said d'Artagnan.

"Nor in the second," said Aramis.

"Nor in the third," said Porthos. "At least, none of our kind do, and the proof is that here we are."

"No," said Athos, "it's not Raoul that most worries me, because he'll conduct himself, I hope, like a gentleman, and if he is killed, well then! He'll die bravely. But you know, if anything did happen to him, well . . ." Athos drew a hand across his pale forehead.

"Well?" asked Aramis.

"Well! I would regard such a misfortune as . . . an expiation."

"Ah!" said d'Artagnan. "I know what you're saying."

"As do I," said Aramis. "But don't think about that, Athos—the past is the past."

"I don't get it," said Porthos.

"The affair at Armentières," said d'Artagnan.

"What affair at Armentières?" said Porthos.

". . . Milady . . ."

"Oh, right!" said Porthos. "I'd quite forgotten that."

Athos gave him a grave look. "You'd forgotten that, Porthos?"

"My faith, yes," said Porthos. "It was a long time ago."

"So, the matter doesn't weigh on your conscience?"

"Well . . . no!" said Porthos.

"What about you, Aramis?"

"It does sometimes occur to me," said Aramis. "It's a case of conscience that's not completely unambiguous."

"And you, d'Artagnan?"

"I confess that when my mind dwells on that terrible affair, I think mainly about the icy corpse of poor Madame Bonacieux. Yes, yes," he murmured, "I have a thousand regrets for the victim, but none for her murderer."

Athos shook his head doubtfully.

"Consider," said Aramis, "that if you admit divine justice affects the events of this world, then that woman was punished by God. We were His instruments, that's all."

"But what about free will, Aramis?"

"How does a judge do it? He has free will and condemns without fear. What about the executioner? His arms swing the blade, yet he strikes without remorse."

"The executioner . . . ," murmured Athos. He appeared to start at the recollection.

"I know it's dreadful," said d'Artagnan, "but when I think that we've killed English, Spanish, Huguenot rebels, even Frenchmen, whose only crime was to meet us in battle and be too slow coming on guard, I'm not going to apologize for my part in that woman's murder—word of honor!"

"As for me," said Porthos, "now that you bring it to mind, Athos, I can still see the scene as if it were in front of me: Milady was there where you are"—Athos turned pale—"I was standing where d'Artagnan is. I had at my side a sword that cut like a Damascus blade . . . you remember it, Aramis, because you named it Balizarde,[102] right? *Eh bien!* I swear to the three of you that if it hadn't been for the executioner of Béthune—it was Béthune, wasn't it? By my faith, if it wasn't for him, I'd have cut off that monster's head myself in a heartbeat, or even quicker. She was a wicked woman."

"And, really," said Aramis, with that casually philosophical tone he'd assumed since joining the Church, a calculating philosophy in which there was more atheistic logic than trust in God, "why think of all this now? What's done is done. We'll confess this act in our final hour, and God will decide whether it was a crime, a minor misdeed, or a meritorious service. You ask, do I repent of it? *Ma foi*, no. On my honor and on the cross, I only regret the fact that she was a woman."

"The one good point of it all," said d'Artagnan, "is that there's no trace of the deed."

"She had a son," said Athos.

"Yes, I know—so you told me," said d'Artagnan, "but who knows what's become of him? Dead the serpent, and dead her brood? Do you think de Winter, his uncle, would raise such a son of a serpent? De Winter will have rejected the son as he condemned the mother."

"If so," said Athos, "then woe to de Winter, for the child had done nothing to him."

"The child is dead, or the Devil take me!" said Porthos. "There's too much fog and damp in that country, or so d'Artagnan says." And Porthos's conclusion might have restored the gaiety to their more-or-less worried faces, but there came the sound of footsteps on the stairs, and a knock on the door.

"Enter," said Athos.

"Messieurs," said the host, "there's a fellow below who's arrived in a great hurry to speak to one of you."

"Which one?" asked the four friends.

"The one who is called the Comte de La Fère."

"I am he," said Athos. "And what's this fellow's name?"

"Grimaud."

"Oh?" Athos turned pale. "Back already? What has become of Bragelonne?"

"Show him in!" said d'Artagnan. "Show him in!"

But Grimaud was already waiting on the landing. He rushed into the room and dismissed the host with a gesture.

The host went out and shut the door while the four friends turned expectantly to Grimaud. His agitation, his pallor, the sweat that bedewed his face, the dust that soiled his clothing, all declared him a messenger of important and terrible news. "Messieurs," he said, "*that woman* had a child, and the child has become a man. The tigress bore a tiger, and beware! For that tiger is stalking you."

Athos looked at his friends with a shrug and a rueful smile. Porthos reached to his side for his sword, which was hanging on the wall; from somewhere, Aramis had drawn a dagger. D'Artagnan arose. "Tell us what you mean, Grimaud," he said.

"I mean that the son of Milady has left England and is in France, on his way to Paris—if he's not here already."

"The devil!" said Porthos. "Are you sure of this?"

"I'm sure," said Grimaud.

A long silence followed this statement. Grimaud was so exhausted that he collapsed onto a chair. Athos poured a glass of champagne and gave it to him.

"Well, after all," said d'Artagnan, "so what if he lives, and so what if he comes to Paris? We've had enemies before, and he's just one more. Let him come!"

"Yes," said Porthos, looking longingly toward where his sword hung on the wall, "we'll be ready for him."

"Besides, he's just a boy," said Aramis.

Grimaud rose. "A boy!" he said. "Do you know what he did, this *boy*? Disguised as a monk, he discovered the whole story of Milady's death while confessing the executioner of Béthune, and after having learned everything he could from him, as absolution he planted his dagger in the dying man's heart. Here it is, still red and dripping, because it's no more than thirty hours since I took it from the wound."

And Grimaud threw on the table the dagger left by the monk in the executioner's chest.

In a spontaneous movement, d'Artagnan, Porthos, and Aramis arose and grabbed their swords.

Athos alone remained in his chair, calm and almost spellbound. "And you say he was dressed as a monk, Grimaud?" he asked.

"Yes, an Augustinian monk."

"What does he look like?"

"He's about my height, or so the innkeeper told me; slim, pale, with light blue eyes, and blond hair."

"And . . . he didn't see Raoul?" said Athos.

"On the contrary, they met. It was the viscount himself who brought him to the bed of the dying man."

Athos rose without a word and reached for his sword.

"Look at us, Messieurs," said d'Artagnan, trying to laugh, "acting like a pack of silly women! Us, four men who have stood before armies, trembling in the face of a child!"

"Yes," said Athos, "but this child comes in the name of God."

And they hurriedly left the hôtel.

XXXIX

The Letter from Charles I

Now we must ask the reader to follow us across the Seine, to the door of the Carmelite Convent on the Rue Saint-Jacques.[103] It was eleven in the morning, and the pious sisters were returning from a mass for the success of the arms of Charles I. Also leaving the church were a woman and a young girl wearing black, one dressed as a widow and the other as an orphan, on the way back to their cell. There, the woman knelt on a *prie-dieu* of painted wood, while near her the girl, leaning on a chair, stood and cried quietly.

The woman would have been beautiful, had she not been aged by sorrow. The girl was charming, and her tears made her even more so. The woman looked to be aged forty, the girl about fourteen.

"*Mon Dieu*," said the kneeling supplicant, "protect my husband, watch over my son, and take from me this life so sad and miserable!"

"*Mon Dieu*," said the girl, "preserve my mother for me!"

"Your mother is of no use to you in this world, Henrietta," replied the mournful woman. "Your mother has no throne, no husband or son, no money, no friends. Your mother, my poor child, has been abandoned by all the world."

And the mother, falling into the arms of the daughter who rushed to support her, burst into tears. "Have courage, Mother!" said the girl.

"Ahh! Kings are down on their luck this year," said the mother, resting her head on her child's shoulder. "No one spares a thought for us in this country, where everyone is caught up in their own affairs. So long as your brother was with us he sustained me, but now your brother is gone, and can't send news of himself to either me or his father. I've pawned my last jewels, sold all our clothes to pay the wages of your brother's servants, who refused to go with him until I made that sacrifice. Now we're reduced to living on the charity of these holy sisters—we are the poor, Henrietta, succored only by God."

"But why don't you address yourself to the queen, your sister?" asked the girl.

"Hélas!" said the weeper. "The queen my sister is no longer queen, my child, and another reigns in her name. One day you'll understand."

"Well, then, what about your nephew the king? Why not speak to him? You know how he loves me, mother."

"But my nephew the king isn't old enough to be king, and he himself, as La Porte has told us twenty times, has nothing of his own."

"Then let us turn to God," said the girl. And she knelt beside her mother.

These two women who prayed at the same prie-dieu were the daughter and granddaughter of Henri IV—Queen Henriette* and Henrietta, the wife and daughter of Charles I.

Just as they were finishing their double prayer, there came a gentle scratching at the door of their cell. "Come in, Sister," said the elder of the two women, drying her tears and standing up.

A nun respectfully opened the door. "Your Majesty will excuse me if I disturb her meditations," she said, "but in the parlor there's a foreign lord who's arrived from England, and who requests the honor to present a letter to Your Majesty."

"Oh, a letter! Did you hear that, Henrietta? Maybe it's a letter from the king with news from your father!"

"Yes, Madame, I heard, and I hope so too."

"And who is this lord, tell me."

"A gentleman of around forty-five or fifty."

"His name? Did he say his name?"

"Milord de Winter."

"Lord Winter!" cried the queen. "My husband's friend! Oh, let him come, let him come."

As he entered, the queen ran to meet the messenger and seized his hand eagerly. Lord Winter knelt and presented the queen a letter rolled up in a golden scroll case.

"Ah, Milord," said the queen, "you bring us three things we haven't seen in a long while: gold, a devoted friend, and a letter from the king, our husband and master."

Winter bowed again, but he couldn't answer, he was so deeply moved. "Milord," the queen said, taking the case, "you understand that I'm eager to know the contents of this letter."

"I will withdraw, Madame," said Winter.

"No, stay," said the queen, "and we'll read it to you. You must realize that I have a thousand questions for you."

Winter stepped back and remained, standing in silence. The mother and the daughter retreated to a window embrasure, where the girl leaned on her mother's arm as they avidly read the following letter:

> *Madame, My Dear Wife,*
>
> *We are at the end. All the resources God has seen fit to leave me are concentrated in our camp at Naseby,*[104] *from which I am writing in haste. Here I await the army of my rebellious subjects, and here I will fight them one last time. If the victor, I'll continue the struggle; if the vanquished, I'll have lost for the last time. I hope, in the latter case (alas, we must prepare for every outcome), to cross to the coast of France. But even if I can, will they welcome such an unlucky king to a country already in the throes of civil discord? Your affection and your wisdom must guide me. The bearer of this letter will inform you, Madame, what I dare not risk putting on paper. He will explain what action I expect from you. I also ask you to give my love to my children, and accept all my heart's affection for you, Madame and dear wife.*

The letter was signed, not "Charles, King," but "Charles, *still* King."

This sad reading, which Winter followed by watching the expressions on the queen's face, nonetheless brought some hope to her eyes.

"If he is no longer king," she cried, "defeated, exiled, proscribed, at least he still lives! Alas! The throne is too perilous a place nowadays for me to wish he were on it. But tell me, Milord," the queen continued, "and keep nothing from me: How do things stand? Is his position really as hopeless as he thinks?"

"Alas, Madame—even more hopeless than he thinks himself. His Majesty's heart is so good, he doesn't understand hatred; so loyal, he can't comprehend treason. England is caught in a kind of delirium, a fever that I fear can be quenched only in blood."

"But what of Lord Montrose?" asked the queen. "I've heard talk of great and rapid success, of a string of victories at Inverlochy, at Auldearn, Alford, and Kilsyth. I'd heard he was marching to the border to join his king."

"Yes, Madame—but at the border he encountered Lesley. He'd won victory by superhuman effort, until victory abandoned him: Montrose was beaten at Philiphaugh, had to dismiss what remained of his army, and flee disguised as a lackey. He's at Bergen, in Norway."

"God preserve him!" said the queen. "It's at least some consolation to know that a few of those who risked so much for us have reached safety. And now, Milord, since I see the king's position for what it is—that is to say, desperate—tell me what my royal husband asked you to say to me."

"Well, Madame," said Winter, "the king wants you to try to ascertain the feelings of the king and the queen toward him."

"Alas, as you know," the queen replied, "the king is still a child, and the queen, though a woman, is a weak woman—it's Mazarin who rules."

"Does he plan to play the same role in France that Cromwell plays in England?"

"Oh, no! He's a subtle and cunning Italian who might dream of a crime but would never dare commit it, the opposite of Cromwell, who does as he likes with the Houses of Parliament. In his battles with the French Parliament, Mazarin must stand at the side of the queen."

"All the more reason, then, why he should protect a king whom a parliament persecutes."

The queen shook her head bitterly. "From my experience, Milord," she said, "the cardinal will do nothing, or perhaps even oppose us. The presence of myself and my daughter in France already embarrasses him—imagine how he'd feel if we were joined by the king. Milord," Queen Henriette added with a melancholy smile, "I am sad and ashamed to say that we spent the winter in the Louvre without money, without linen, and almost without bread, often not getting up for lack of firewood."

"Horrible!" exclaimed Winter. "The daughter of Henri IV, the wife of King Charles! Why didn't you tell us, Madame, what had happened, what to expect?"

"You see the hospitality afforded a queen by this minister the king wishes to address."

"But I've heard talk of a marriage between His Highness the Prince of Wales[105] and Mademoiselle d'Orléans," Winter said.

"Yes, I had a brief moment of hope. The children loved each other—but the queen, who had at first approved of their love, changed her mind, and now the Duc d'Orléans, who had encouraged the beginning of their familiarity, has forbidden his daughter to think about such a union. Ah, Milord," continued the queen, without even bothering to wipe her tears, "better to fight, as the king did, and perhaps to die, than to live as a beggar as I have."

"Courage, Madame, courage," said Winter. "Don't despair. The interests of the Crown of France, even when preoccupied, must be opposed to the rebellion of the people in a neighboring realm. Mazarin is a statesman and will understand that."

"But are you sure," said the queen doubtfully, "that you haven't been preempted?"

"By who?" asked Winter.

"By Joyce, by Pride, or by Cromwell."

"By a tailor! By a carter, or a brewer! I should hope, Madame, that the cardinal would not enter into an alliance with such men as those."

"Well, what is he but such a man?" asked Madame Henriette.

"But for the king's honor, and that of the queen . . ."

"We'll have to hope he'll do something in their honor," said Madame Henriette. "With so eloquent a friend as you, Milord, I'm somewhat reassured. Give me your hand and let's go see the minister."

"Madame," said Winter, bowing, "you overwhelm me with honor."

"But if he refuses," said Madame Henriette, pausing, "and the king loses his battle—what then?"

"His Majesty might take refuge in Holland, where I've heard His Highness the Prince of Wales is."

"And can His Majesty, in flight, count on many such servants as yourself?"

"Alas, no, Madame!" said Winter. "But plans have been laid; I plan to search for allies in France."

"Allies!" said the queen, shaking her head.

"Madame," Winter replied, "if I can find the old friends I once had, I can answer for anything."

"Find them, then, Milord," said the queen, with that poignant doubt that afflicts the long-suffering, "find them—and may God hear our pleas!"

The queen went down to her carriage, where Winter, on horseback and followed by two lackeys, rode beside her window.

XL

The Letter from Cromwell

Just as Queen Henriette was leaving the Carmelite convent for the Palais Royal, a cavalier dismounted at the door of that royal residence and announced to the guards that he had something important to convey to Cardinal Mazarin.

Though the cardinal feared assassins, he nonetheless needed a great deal of information and advice, so he was relatively accessible. It wasn't the first door that was hard to pass, nor the second, but rather the third, where, besides guards and footmen, there stood the loyal Bernouin, that Cerberus whom no words could beguile and no golden bribe could subvert. It was at this third door that anyone who sought an audience would undergo a formal interrogation.

The cavalier, having tied his horse at the courtyard gate, climbed the grand stairway, and addressing the guards in the first chamber, asked, "Monsieur le Cardinal de Mazarin?"

"Go on in," the guards replied without even looking up from their dice and cards, as if to show they didn't consider it their job to act as ushers.

The cavalier entered the second chamber, which was guarded by musketeers and footmen, and repeated his question. "Do you have a Letter of Audience?" asked an usher, advancing to meet the visitor.

"I have one, but not from Cardinal Mazarin."

"Enter and ask for Monsieur Bernouin," said the usher. And he opened the door to the third chamber.

Either by chance or because it was his usual post, Bernouin had been standing behind the door and had heard everything. "I'm the one you're looking for, Monsieur," he said. "From whom is the letter you bear for His Eminence?"

"From General Oliver Cromwell," said the newcomer. "Please announce this name to His Eminence, and then let me know if he'll receive me." And he stood in that proud and somber pose favored by Puritans.

Bernouin, after taking a long look at the young man, went into the cardinal's study, where he repeated the messenger's words. "A man bearing a letter from Oliver Cromwell?" said Mazarin. "What sort of man is he?"

"A real Englishman, Monseigneur: blond hair, or rather red-blond, gray-blue eyes, more gray than blue, and puffed up with pride."

"See if he'll give you the letter."

Bernouin returned to the antechamber and said, "Monseigneur asks for the letter."

"Monseigneur must see the bearer to see the letter," replied the young man, "but to convince you of its bona fides, look here."

Bernouin looked at the letter's seal, and seeing that the letter really came from General Oliver Cromwell, turned to go back to Mazarin. "You may add," said the young man, "that I am not just a messenger, but an envoy extraordinaire."

Bernouin reentered the study and came out again a few seconds later. "Enter, Monsieur," he said, holding open the door.

Mazarin had needed the brief delay to get hold of his emotions upon hearing of the letter's origin. Meanwhile his shrewd mind was trying to figure out Cromwell's motive in sending the missive.

The young man appeared in the door of the study, holding his hat in one hand and the letter in the other. Mazarin rose and said, "Monsieur, you claim you have a letter for me?"

"Here it is, Monseigneur," said the young man.

Mazarin took the letter, opened it, and read:

Mister Mordaunt, one of my secretaries, bears this letter of introduction to His Eminence Cardinal Mazarin, at Paris. He has, in addition, a second, more confidential letter.

OLIVER CROMWELL

"Very well, Monsieur Mordaunt," said Mazarin, "give me this second letter and take a seat."

The young man drew a second letter from his pocket, gave it to the cardinal, and sat down.

However, the cardinal, having taken the letter, thoughtfully turned it over and over in his hand instead of opening it, and then decided to sound out the messenger with some questions, as his experience had convinced him that few men could hide their secrets if watched closely while interrogated. "You're very young, Monsieur Mordaunt, for the difficult job of ambassador, which taxes even veteran diplomats."

"Monseigneur, I am twenty-three, but Your Eminence shouldn't be fooled into thinking me young. In my way I am older than you, though I lack your wisdom."

"How is that, Monsieur?" said Mazarin. "I don't understand you."

"They say, Monseigneur, that years of suffering count double—and I have suffered for twenty years."

"Ah, yes, I see," said Mazarin, "a lack of fortune. You are poor, aren't you?" And he added to himself, "These English revolutionaries are all beggars and peasants."

"Monseigneur, I should have a fortune of six million, but it was stolen from me."

"So, you're not a commoner, then?" said Mazarin, astonished.

"If I bore my proper title, I'd be a lord; if I wore my real name, you'd know me by one of the most illustrious in England."

"What is your name, then?" asked Mazarin.

"I'm known as Monsieur Mordaunt," said the young man, bowing.

Mazarin saw that Cromwell's envoy wished to maintain his incognito. He paused a moment, considering the young man more closely than he had before. The young envoy was unmoved. "To the devil with these Puritans!" Mazarin said under his breath. "They're carved of marble." Then, aloud, he said, "But your noble relatives are still alive?"

"One of them is, yes, Monseigneur."

"And can't he help you?"

"I've presented myself three times to my uncle to implore his aid, and three times I've been driven from his door."

"Oh, Lord help us, good Monsieur Mordaunt!" said Mazarin, hoping to trap the young man with false pity. "*Mon Dieu,* your story moves me! So, you don't know the true facts of your high birth?"

"I have only recently learned the truth."

"And until you knew that . . . ?"

"I'd considered myself an abandoned child."

"So, you've never seen your mother?"

"I did, Monseigneur, when I was a child—she came three times to my nursery, and I remember the last time as if it were yesterday."

"You have a good memory," said Mazarin.

"Oh, *yes,* Monseigneur," said the young man, with a strange emphasis that sent a chill down the cardinal's spine.

"And who raised you?" asked Mazarin.

"A French nurse, who drove me away when I was five years old because she hadn't been paid, though she told me the name of the uncle my mother had spoken of."

"What happened to you?"

"I took to crying and begging on the highways, until a minister from Kingston took me in. He instructed me in the Calvinist faith, taught me everything he knew, and helped me in trying to find my family."

"And this research . . . ?"

"It was in vain. It was chance that finally led me to the truth."

"You discovered what had become of your mother?"

"I learned that she'd been murdered by my uncle with the help of four accomplices, and that I'd been expelled from the nobility and stripped of all my rights by King Charles I."

"Ah, now I understand why you serve Monsieur Cromwell. You hate the king."

"Yes, Monseigneur, I hate him!" the young man said. Mazarin was astonished by his diabolical expression as he uttered these words: unlike most complexions, which flush red, this young man's face was livid and suffused with gall.

"Your story is a terrible one, Monsieur Mordaunt, and touches me deeply; but fortunately, you now serve an all-powerful master who will help you in your quest. People in power have a great deal of information available to us."

"Monseigneur, offer the slightest scent to a well-bred hunting dog, and he'll follow the trail to the end."

"But this uncle you mentioned, would you like me to speak to him?" said Mazarin, who thought it would be useful to have an ally near to Cromwell.

"Thank you, Monseigneur, but I'll speak to him myself."

"But didn't you say he mistreated you?"

"He'll treat me better the next time I see him."

"So, you have a way to make him listen?"

"I have a way to make him afraid."

Mazarin stared at the young man but was met by such a fiery glare that he looked down. Unwilling to continue the conversation, he opened the letter from Cromwell. Gradually the young man's eyes returned to their usual glassy passivity, and he fell into a deep reverie. After reading the first few lines, Mazarin glanced up to see if the young man was watching him, and noticing his indifference, he shrugged slightly and said to himself, "To pursue your agenda by using those who are pursuing their own is one way to conduct affairs. Let's see what this letter is all about."

We reproduce it here verbatim:[106]

> *To His Eminence*
> *Monseigneur Cardinal Mazarini*
>   *I would like, Monseigneur, to know your intentions concerning current affairs in England. Our neighboring realms are too close for France not to care about our situation, or for us not to care about France. The English are almost unanimously opposed to the*

tyranny of King Charles and his supporters. Placed at the head of this movement by the public's trust, I appreciate more than anyone its nature and consequences. Today we go to war, and I will engage King Charles in a decisive battle. I will prevail, for the hope of the nation and the will of the Lord is with me. Once defeated, the king has no more resources in England or Scotland; if he is not taken or killed, he will try to escape to France to raise money, recruit soldiers, and buy arms. France has already received Queen Henriette, and thereby, unintentionally perhaps, contributed to sustaining the fires of civil war in our country; but Madame Henriette is a Daughter of France and is entitled to her hospitality. For King Charles, it is another story; if he receives refuge and aid, France would insult the English people and their government in a manner tantamount to open hostility . . .

At this point Mazarin, uneasy at the turn the letter had taken, stopped reading to glance once more at the young man. He was still lost in reverie, so Mazarin continued.

It is urgent, Monseigneur, that I know therefore the intentions of France; the interests of that realm and that of England, though seemingly different, are closer than they may appear. England needs domestic tranquility to complete the expulsion of its king, while France needs peace to secure its young monarch's throne; you, as much as we, need stability as we consolidate the power of our governments.

Your disputes with your parliament, your noisy quarrels with the princes who today are with you and tomorrow are against you, the popular uprising fomented by the coadjutor, President Blancmesnil, and Councilor Broussel; all this disorder, in short, which afflicts every level of government should make you wary of involvement in a foreign war—for then England, overexcited by enthusiasm for new ideas, would ally with Spain, who already desires such an alliance. So, I thought, Monseigneur, knowing your prudence and how affairs affect your personal situation, that you would prefer to focus your energies within the bounds of France and leave affairs in England to its new government. Such neutrality consists solely of denying King Charles entry to French territory, and all French arms, money, and troops, as he is a monarch entirely foreign to you.

This letter is confidential, which is why I send it to you by a trusted and devoted servant; it is intended to give Your Eminence forewarning of what measures I will take in certain events. Oliver Cromwell feels he can communicate better with an intelligence like that of Mazarini than with a queen who, though admirable for her firmness, is too susceptible to the privileges of royal birth and divine right.

Farewell, Monseigneur. If I receive no response within two weeks, I will consider that my overtures have been rejected.

OLIVER CROMWELL

"Monsieur Mordaunt," said the cardinal, raising his voice to arouse the dreamer, "my response to this letter from General Cromwell will be more satisfactory to him if no one else knows that I've made it. Wait for my reply, therefore, at Boulogne-sur-Mer,[107] and promise me you'll leave for there by tomorrow morning."

"I shall, Monseigneur," replied Mordaunt, "but how many days would Your Eminence have me wait for your response?'

"If you haven't received it in ten days, you may depart."

Mordaunt bowed.

"That's not all, Monsieur," continued Mazarin. "Your personal story deeply moved me, and in addition, Monsieur Cromwell's letter names you an ambassador. So, tell me, I repeat, what can I do for you?"

Mordaunt thought for a moment, and, after some visible hesitation, had opened his mouth to speak, when Bernouin rushed in, leaned toward the cardinal's ear, and spoke softly. "Monseigneur," he whispered, "Queen Henriette, accompanied by an English gentleman, has just entered the Palais Royal."

Mazarin started in his chair, a movement that didn't escape the notice of the young man, and he suppressed the confidence he was about to share.

"Monsieur," said the cardinal, "I hope you understand that I picked Boulogne because I assumed any city in France would suffice for you, but if you prefer another, name it; however, you can see that, surrounded by the inquisitive whom I can escape only by discretion, I'd prefer no one know of your visit to Paris."

"I depart, then, Monsieur," said Mordaunt, turning toward the door through which he'd entered.

"No, not that way, Monsieur, please!" said the cardinal quickly. "Exit through this gallery, which will take you to the vestibule. I wish no one to see you leave, as our interview must remain secret."

Mordaunt followed Bernouin, who led him into an adjoining chamber, where an usher showed him the way out.

Then Bernouin hurried back to his master to admit Queen Henriette, who was already crossing the window gallery outside.

XLI

Mazarin and Queen Henriette

The cardinal stood up and hurried to receive the Queen of England, joining her in the middle of the gallery that led to his study. He was all the more respectful of this queen who came without servants or jewelry because inside he was ashamed of his own avarice and lack of heart. As for the queen, supplicants learn to keep careful control of their expressions, and the daughter of Henri IV smiled as she went to meet a man she hated and despised.

"Oh ho!" Mazarin said to himself. "What a pleasant smile! Is she coming to ask me for money?" He gave a worried glance toward the door of his strong-room, and even turned the bezel of his magnificent diamond ring around to the inside of his palm. Unfortunately, this gem didn't have the power of Gyges's ring,[108] which when turned could render its wearer invisible.

And Mazarin would have liked to be invisible at that moment, because he guessed that Madame Henriette came to ask for something. When a queen he'd treated so poorly came with a smile on her lips instead of a threat, she wanted something.

"Monsieur le Cardinal," said the august visitor, "it occurred to me to talk first to the queen, my sister, about the affair that brings me to you, but then I thought that politics is really the province of men."

"Madame," said Mazarin, "Your Majesty overwhelms me with this flattering distinction."

He's being very gracious, thought the queen. *Can he have guessed why I've come?*

They'd arrived in the cardinal's study, and once he'd seated the queen in his own armchair, he said, "Now give your orders to this most respectful of your servants."

"Alas, Monsieur," the queen replied, "I lost the habit of giving orders when I had to turn to prayer. I've come now to pray to you, and will be only too happy if you hear my prayers."

"I'm listening, Madame," said Mazarin.

"Monsieur le Cardinal, it concerns the war that my husband wages against his rebellious subjects. You might not be aware that there is fighting in England," said the queen with a sad smile, "and that there will soon be a decisive battle."

"I had no idea, Madame," said the cardinal with a slight shrug. "Hélas! Our own conflicts absorb all the time and energy of a poor minister as infirm and incapable as I am."

"Well, Monsieur le Cardinal," said the queen, "I must inform you that my husband, Charles I, is about to make a final effort. In the event of his defeat"—Mazarin gave a start—"for we must prepare for anything, he wishes to retire to France to live here as a private individual. What do you say to this idea?"

The cardinal listened without a line on his face betraying his innermost thoughts and feelings; his expression was mild and pleasant, as usual, and when the queen had finished, he said in his softest voice, "Do you think, Madame, that France, agitated and unruly as it is now, is a safe harbor for a dethroned king? The crown already rests uneasily on the brow of King Louis XIV; how could he support a double burden?"

"The weight of a crown hasn't been so heavy as far as I'm concerned," interjected the queen with a sad smile, "and I ask no more for my husband than has been done for me. You see that we're very modest monarchs, Monsieur."

"Oh, but you, Madame!" the cardinal said hastily, to forestall this subject before it could turn to reproaches. "You are another matter entirely, a daughter of Henri IV, of that great, of that sublime king . . ."

"Which doesn't prevent you from refusing hospitality to his son-in-law, does it, Monsieur? You should nonetheless recall that that great, that sublime king, when threatened much as my husband is now, asked for aid from England, and England granted it—although Queen Elizabeth wasn't his niece."

"*Peccato!*" said Mazarin, finding it hard to contradict such simple logic. "Your Majesty doesn't understand me; she misjudges my intentions, doubtless because I express myself poorly in French."

"Speak Italian then, Monsieur; Queen Marie de Médicis, our mother, taught us that language before the old cardinal, your predecessor, sent her off to die in exile. If that great, that sublime King Henri of whom you spoke just now is watching us, he must be astonished at how you combine such profound admiration for him with such scant regard for his family."

Sweat began to bead Mazarin's forehead. "My admiration is, on the contrary, so great and so real, Madame," said Mazarin, declining the queen's offer to change language, "that if King Charles I—whom God protect from all misfortune!—were in France, I would offer him my house, my own home, though sadly that would be no safe haven. Someday the people will burn my house as they burned that of Marshal d'Ancre. Poor Concino Concini! All he ever thought of was the good of France."

"Yes, Monseigneur, just like you," said the queen ironically.

Mazarin pretended not to understand the double meaning behind this remark and continued to look sorry about the fate of Concino Concini.

"So, then, Monseigneur le Cardinal," said the queen impatiently, "what do have to tell me?"

"Oh, Madame," cried Mazarin, as if deeply moved, "Madame, will Your Majesty permit me to give you some advice? Please understand that before I do anything so bold, I place myself entirely at Your Majesty's feet to serve your desires."

"Speak, Monsieur," replied the queen. "The advice of a man as prudent as you must certainly be good."

"Madame, believe me, the king must defend himself to the bitter end."

"So he has, Monsieur, and in the coming final battle he'll commit all his resources, though they're less than those of his enemies, to show that he's determined not to give up without a fight—but then what? What happens if he's defeated?"

"Well, Madame, in that case, my advice, though I know it's presumptuous to offer it, is that His Majesty shouldn't leave his own realm. Absent kings are soon forgotten; if he comes to France, his cause is lost."

"But then," said the queen, "if that's your advice and you really support his best interests, send him some money and troops! I can do nothing more for him, I've sold everything down to my last diamond, I have nothing left, as you know better than anyone, Monsieur. Had I still any jewelry, I'd have bought firewood to warm my daughter and myself last winter."

"Oh, Madame," said Mazarin, "Your Majesty doesn't know what she's asking. From the moment that foreign aid enters a conflict to keep a king on his throne, it's an admission that he no longer has the loyalty of his subjects."

"In fact, Monsieur le Cardinal," said the queen, impatient with following his subtle mind through the maze of his words, "in fact, tell me yes or no: if the king stays in England, will you send him any help? If he comes to France, will you give him hospitality?"

"Madame," said the cardinal, in a voice of utmost sincerity, "I'm going to show Your Majesty just how devoted I am, and how dedicated I am to resolving this heartbreaking affair. After that, I think Your Majesty will have no cause to doubt my eagerness to serve."

The queen bit her lips and shifted impatiently in the armchair. At last she said, "Well, what are you going to do? Show me. Speak!"

"I shall go this instant to talk to the queen, and we shall take the matter up with parliament."

"With whom you're at odds, are you not? You'll put Broussel in charge of it, perhaps. Enough, Monsieur le Cardinal, enough. I see how things stand. Go indeed to parliament—for it's only from parliament, that enemy to kings, that the daughter of the great, the sublime Henri IV, whom you so admire, received enough charity to avoid dying of cold and hunger last winter."

And with these words, the queen arose in majestic indignation.

The cardinal extended his clasped hands to her. "Ah, Madame, Madame, how you misunderstand me! *Mon Dieu!*"

But Queen Henriette, turning her back on those hypocritical tears, crossed the study, opened the door herself, and, marching through the guards and retainers of His Eminence, and past the courtiers waiting their turns, went and took the hand of Lord Winter, who stood waiting unattended. Poor queen, already fallen, before whom all still bowed from etiquette, but who had, in fact, only a single arm upon which she could lean.

"That's done," said Mazarin, when he was alone. "It was an ugly scene, and I had to play a difficult role, but still I managed to commit to nothing whatsoever. Hmm! That Cromwell is a cruel enemy to kings—I pity his ministers, if he has any. Bernouin!"

Bernouin came in. "Find out if that short-haired man in the black doublet, who was here before the queen, is still in the palace," said Mazarin. Bernouin went out. The cardinal spent the time waiting for his return in turning the bezel of his ring back out, polishing the diamond, admiring its clarity—and as a lingering tear in one eye was interfering with this, he shook his head to make it drop.

Bernouin returned with Comminges, who was on guard duty. "Monseigneur," said Comminges, "I was conducting that young man out as Your Eminence requested, but as we passed the door to the window gallery he stopped and stared as if astonished at something beyond—probably that big Raphael painting. He stood spellbound for a moment, and then hurried down the stairs. I think I saw him mount a gray horse and ride out of the courtyard. Is Monseigneur on his way to visit the queen?"

"To what end?"

"Monsieur de Guitaut, my uncle, just told me that Her Majesty has had news from the army."

"Excellent. I'll go."

At that moment Monsieur de Villequier appeared, having been sent by the queen to find the cardinal.

Mordaunt had behaved just as Comminges had reported. While crossing the hall across from the window gallery, he had seen Lord Winter where he was awaiting the outcome of the queen's negotiations. The young man had stopped short, not in admiration of the Raphael, but as if fascinated by the sight of some terrible object. His eyes had dilated, a shudder had run through his body, and he looked as if he wanted to burst through the glass wall that separated him from his prey. If Comminges had seen the young man's face, hatred burning in his eyes as they fixated on Winter, he would have had no doubt but that the English lord was his mortal enemy.

But Mordaunt stopped himself—pausing, no doubt, to think. Then, instead of following his first impulse, which was to launch himself straight at Milord Winter, he went slowly down the stairs, head lowered. In the courtyard he got into the saddle, rode no farther than the corner of the Rue Richelieu, and there, eyes fixed on the gate, he waited for the English queen's carriage to leave the palace.

He didn't have long to wait, as the queen spent no more than a quarter of an hour with Mazarin—but that quarter hour seemed like a century to he who waited. Finally, the heavy coach they termed a carriage at that time appeared, the gates groaned open, and out it came, with Winter, still mounted, riding once more at Her Majesty's window. The horses went into a trot and made their way to the Louvre and through its gates. Before leaving the Carmelite convent, Queen Henriette had told her daughter Henrietta to wait for her at that palace, where they had lived so long, and which they'd only left because their poverty seemed harder to support while inside its still-gilded halls.

Mordaunt followed the carriage, and when he saw it pass under the dark arches of the Louvre gates, he took a position in the shadow of the walls, sitting astride but immobile against the background of Jean Goujon's moldings, like a bas-relief of an equestrian statue. And there he waited as he had outside the Palais Royal.

XLII

How Those in Need Sometimes
Mistake Blind Luck for God's Will

"Well, Madame?" Lord Winter asked, once the queen had sent away the servants.

"Well, it turned out just as I'd foreseen, Milord."

"He refused?"

"Didn't I say he would?"

"The cardinal refuses to receive the king? France refuses hospitality to a refugee prince? That's never happened before, Madame!"

"I didn't say France, Milord, I said the cardinal—and the cardinal is by no means French."

"But the queen—have you seen her?"

"Useless," said Madame Henriette, shaking her head sadly. "The queen will never say yes if the cardinal says no. Don't you know the cardinal rules the Court, inside and out? Furthermore, as I told you, I wouldn't be surprised if he'd been forewarned by Cromwell—he was embarrassed while speaking to me, but firm in his refusal. Plus, did you see how busy the Palais Royal was, all those people hurrying through its halls? Do you think there's been some news, Milord?"

"It's not news from England, Madame; I worked hard to make sure we arrived before we could be forestalled. I set out three days ago and passed by a miracle through the Puritan army. I rode post horses with my servant Tony, and the horses we ride now were bought here in Paris. Besides, before risking anything, I'm sure the king will await a response from Your Majesty."

"You'll tell him, Milord, that I can do nothing," said the queen in despair. "I've suffered as badly as he has, or worse, obliged to eat the bread of exile and to beg hospitality from false friends who laugh at my tears. Now he must sacrifice himself and die like a king. Would that I could die by his side."

"Madame, Madame!" cried Winter. "Your Majesty gives in to despair, but we may still find some hope."

"I've no more friends, Milord, no other friends in the world but you! Oh, *mon Dieu*!" cried Madame Henriette, raising her arms to heaven, "have you taken, then, all the generous hearts from the world?"

"I hope not, Madame," Winter replied fervently. "I told you I still knew four men."

"What do you think you can do with four men?"

"Four devoted men, four men willing to die for a cause, can do much, believe me, Madame—and the men I speak of have done a great deal in their time."

"And these four men, where are they?"

"Ah, now that I don't know. I've lost touch with them for almost twenty years, and yet every time the king was in danger, I've thought of them."

"And these men were your friends?"

"One of them held my life in his hands and returned it to me; I don't know if he's still my friend, but since that time at least I've always been his."

"And these men are in France, Milord?"

"I think so."

"Tell me their names—maybe I've heard of them and could help in your search."

"One of them was called the Chevalier d'Artagnan."

"Really! Unless I'm mistaken, your Chevalier d'Artagnan is a lieutenant of the musketeers, or so I've heard. But be careful, because I'm afraid he's a cardinal's man."

"If true, that would be the final blow," said Winter, "and I'd begin to believe that we're truly cursed."

"But the others," said the queen, clinging to this final hope like a shipwrecked sailor to floating debris, "what of the others, Milord?"

"The second—I heard his name by chance, because before fighting a duel with us these four gentlemen told us their names—the second was called the Comte de La Fère. As for the other two, the habit I had of calling them by their assumed names made me forget their real ones."

"But it's urgent that you find out," said the queen, "if you think these worthy gentlemen might be able to aid the king."

"They're just the men for the task," said Winter. "Think back, Madame— do you recall how Queen Anne of Austria was saved from the greatest threat any queen ever faced?"

"Yes, during her romance with Monsieur de Buckingham—some affair involving her diamond studs."

"That's right, Madame—and these are the men who saved her. The sad and shameful truth is that if these gentlemen's names aren't known to you, it's because the queen has forgotten them, when she ought to have made them Peers of the Realm."

"Well, then, Milord, they must be found. But what can a mere four men do? Or rather three, for I warn you we mustn't count upon Monsieur d'Artagnan."

"At a minimum, it's three valiant swords, four if you count mine. Four devoted men near the king to guard him from his enemies, to surround him in battle, to aid him with advice, and to escort him in his flight, that would be enough, if not to give him victory, then at least to save him if he's defeated. Four men to bring him across the sea—and no matter what Mazarin says, once he's ashore on the coast of France, your royal husband will find as many safe havens as a seabird on a storm-girt cliff."

"Seek them, Milord, seek out these gentlemen, and if you find them, and if they agree to go with you to England, on the day we regain the throne I'll give each one a duchy, and enough gold to pave the floors of Whitehall. This is the task I charge you with, Milord—find them!"

"I'll seek them, Madame, and I'll find them," said Winter, "but time is running out. Has Your Majesty forgotten that the king is anxiously awaiting a reply?"

"Then we are lost!" cried the queen, in a despairing tone.

At that moment the door opened, and young Henrietta appeared. The queen, with that supreme effort that heroism provides to mothers, buried her grief in the depths of her heart, and made a sign to Baron Winter to change the subject.

But her efforts, though bravely taken, didn't escape the notice of the young princess. She stopped on the threshold, sighed, and said to the queen, "Why do you hide your tears from me, Mother?"

The queen smiled, and instead of replying to her, turned to Winter and said, "Hear that, Baron? I've gained one thing at least by being but half a queen—my children call me mother instead of madame." Then, turning to her daughter, she continued, "What do you want, Henrietta?"

"*Ma Mère*," said the young princess, "a cavalier, who has just entered the Louvre, begs leave to pay his respects to Your Majesty. He comes from the army, he says, and has a letter to deliver to you from Marshal Grammont, I think he said."

"Ah!" the queen said to Winter. "He's one of my faithful. But do you notice, my dear Baron, that we're so poorly served here that my daughter has to act as usher?"

"Madame, have mercy on me," said Winter. "You're breaking my heart."

"And who is this cavalier, Henrietta?" asked the queen.

"I saw him from the window, Madame; he's a young man who looks barely sixteen years old and is called the Vicomte de Bragelonne."

The queen nodded and smiled, the young princess opened the door, and Raoul appeared on the threshold.

He took three steps toward the queen and knelt down. "Madame," he said, "I bring to Your Majesty a letter from my friend, the Comte de Guiche, who's given me the honor of doing you a service. This letter conveys his respect and contains important news."

At the name of the Comte de Guiche, a flush rose to the cheeks of the young princess, which the queen saw with disapproval. "But you told me the letter was from Marshal Grammont, Henrietta!" said the queen.

"I thought so, Madame . . . ," the young girl stammered.

"That's my fault, Madame," said Raoul. "I did announce myself as coming from Marshal Grammont, but as he was wounded in the arm, he couldn't write, so his son the Comte de Guiche served as his secretary."

"So, there's been a battle?" said the queen, gesturing for Raoul to rise.

"Yes, Madame," said the young man, handing a letter to Winter, who'd advanced to receive it, and who passed it to the queen.

At this news of a battle, the young princess opened her mouth as if impelled to ask a question, but then closed it without saying a word, as the roses gradually faded from her cheeks.

The queen noted all this, and no doubt her maternal heart understood it, for she asked Raoul, "Has anything happened to the young Comte de Guiche? For he's not only one of our faithful servants, as he told you, Monsieur, he's also a friend."

"No, Madame," Raoul replied. "On the contrary, he gained great glory that day, and had the honor of being embraced by Monsieur le Prince on the battlefield."

The young princess clapped her hands together, but then, ashamed of having allowed herself to be carried away to such an expression of joy, she turned away and leaned over a vase of roses, as if to sample their scent.

"Let's see what the count tells us," said the queen.

"As I had the honor to say to Your Majesty, he was writing in his father's name."

"Yes, Monsieur." The queen unsealed the letter and read aloud:

Madame and Majesty,

Not having the honor to write to you myself due to a wound suffered in my right hand, I write to you by way of my son, Monsieur le Comte de Guiche, who serves you as I do, to inform you that we have just won the Battle of Lens, and that this victory will bring power and prestige to Cardinal Mazarin and the queen, and influence in European affairs. I pray Your Majesty, if she will accept my advice, will take advantage of this occasion to seek favor for your august husband from the royal government. Monsieur le Vicomte de Bragelonne, who will have the honor of presenting this letter to you, is the friend of my son, whose life he almost certainly saved; he is a gentleman in whom Your Majesty may confide entirely, in case she has any verbal or written commands to send me.

With respect, signed in the name of . . .

Maréchal de GRAMMONT

When the marshal mentioned the service Raoul had done his son, the viscount couldn't help turning to glance at the young princess, and saw in her eyes a look of infinite gratitude—so Raoul knew, beyond doubt, that the daughter of Charles I loved his friend.

"The Battle of Lens is won!" the queen said. "Here they're happy, for here they win their battles. Yes, Marshal Grammont is right, this will improve their situation, but I fear it will do nothing for ours, if it doesn't actually make it worse. Your news is timely, Monsieur," continued the queen. "I'm grateful to you for having brought it to us so diligently; without you, and this letter, I wouldn't have heard it before tomorrow, and might have been the last person in Paris to know."

"Madame," said Raoul, "the Louvre is only the second palace to receive this news; no one else knows it. I'd sworn to the Comte de Guiche to deliver this letter to Your Majesty before even going to see my guardian."

"Is your guardian a Bragelonne as well?" asked Lord Winter. "I once knew a Bragelonne—is he still alive?"

"No, Monsieur, he's dead, and it's from him that my guardian, who was a close relative, I believe, has inherited the land whose name I now bear."

"And your guardian, Monsieur, what's his name?" asked the queen, who couldn't help taking an interest in this handsome young man.

"Monsieur le Comte de La Fère, Madame," replied the young man, bowing.

Winter started in surprise, and the queen looked at him, alight with joy. "The Comte de La Fère!" she cried. "Isn't that the name you mentioned?"

As for Winter, he couldn't believe what he'd heard. "The Comte de La Fère! Oh, Monsieur! Answer me, I implore you: is the Comte de La Fère a noble I once knew, handsome and brave, who was a musketeer under Louis XIII, and must now be about forty-seven or forty-eight?"

"Yes, Monsieur, that's quite right."

"And who was serving under an assumed name?"

"Under the name of Athos. I recently heard his friend, Monsieur d'Artagnan, call him by that name."

"That's him, Madame, that's him. God be praised! And is he in Paris?" continued the baron, addressing Raoul. Then, returning to the queen, "Hope still—hope! Providence protects us, since it moves to help me find that brave gentleman in such a miraculous fashion. Where is he to be found, Monsieur, please tell me?"

"The Comte de La Fère is staying in Rue Guénégaud, at the Grand Charlemagne Hôtel."

"Thank you, Monsieur. Ask this worthy friend to remain at home, and I'll come to see him shortly."

"Monsieur, I obey with pleasure, if Her Majesty will give me leave to go."

"Go, Monsieur le Vicomte de Bragelonne," said the queen, "go, and be assured of our affection."

Raoul bowed respectfully to the two princesses, saluted Winter, and departed.

Winter and the queen continued to converse for a while in voices so low the young princess couldn't hear them—not that it mattered, as she was lost in her thoughts.

Then, as Winter was about to depart, "Listen, Milord," said the queen, "I had preserved this diamond cross, which comes from my mother, and this plaque of Saint Michael, which came from my husband; together they're worth about fifty thousand livres. I had vowed to die of starvation before selling them, but now that these two pieces might be useful to the king or his defenders, I must sacrifice everything to that hope. Take them, and if you need funds for your mission, sell them without hesitation. But if you can find a means of preserving them, know, Milord, that I'll regard you as having rendered the greatest service a gentleman can do for a queen, and that on the day of my prosperity he who can bring me this plaque and this cross will be blessed by me and my children."

"Madame," said Winter, "Your Majesty will be served with true devotion. I go now to put in a safe place these objects that I wouldn't have accepted in the days of our good fortune; but our property has been confiscated, our income is dried up, and we must succeed by making use of whatever we have. After that I'll go visit the Comte de La Fère, and tomorrow Your Majesty will know where we stand."

The queen extended her hand to Lord Winter, who kissed it respectfully, and then indicating her daughter, said, "Milord, you were charged with delivering to this child something from her father."

Winter looked astonished; he wasn't sure what the queen was talking about.

But young Henrietta stepped forward, smiling and blushing, and said "Tell my father that, king or fugitive, victor or vanquished, powerful or poor, he has in me the most loyal and affectionate of daughters." And she presented her forehead to the gentleman.

"I know that, Mademoiselle," replied Winter, brushing Henrietta's brow with his lips.

Then he departed, going unescorted through those grand echoing chambers, now deserted and gloomy, wiping away those tears that, jaded though he was by fifty years of court life, he couldn't help shedding when faced with the sight of such deep and profound royal misery.

XLIII

The Uncle and the Nephew

Lord Winter's horse and lackey were waiting for him at the gate. Pensive, he rode toward his lodgings, looking back from time to time toward the dark and silent façade of the Louvre. It was then that he saw a cavalier detach himself, so to speak, from the wall and follow him at a distance. He remembered having seen a similar shadow behind him on the way from the Palais Royal.

Lord Winter's lackey, who followed him a few paces behind, had also been watching this cavalier anxiously.

"Tony," said the gentleman, beckoning his valet to approach.

"I'm here, Milord." The valet rode up beside his master.

"Have you noticed that man who's following us?"

"Yes, Milord."

"Who is he?"

"I don't know. I only know he followed Milord from the Palais Royal, waited at the Louvre for you to come out, and then left when we left."

"Some spy of the cardinal's," said Winter. "Pretend not to notice his surveillance."

And, spurring on, he plunged into the maze of streets that led to his hôtel in the Marais quarter. Long ago he'd lodged in the Place Royale, and now Lord Winter had returned to his former neighborhood.

The unknown follower put his horse into a gallop.

Winter reached his inn and went up to his rooms, where he hoped to see the spy from his windows, but as he put his hat and gloves on a table he glanced in a mirror and saw a figure appear in the doorway behind him.

He turned, and Mordaunt stood before him.

Winter turned pale and froze. As for Mordaunt, he stood in the doorway, cold, threatening, like the statue of Don Juan's Commander.[109]

There was a moment of icy silence between the two men. Then Winter said, "Monsieur, I thought I'd already made it clear that your harassment is tiresome. Withdraw, or I'll have you driven off as I did in London. I'm not your uncle, and I do not know you."

"Dear Uncle," replied Mordaunt in his hoarse, mocking voice, "you're quite mistaken—you won't drive me away as you did in London. You don't dare. As for denying that I'm your nephew, think again, as I've learned many things I didn't know a year ago."

"What does it matter to me what you've learned?" said Winter.

"Oh, I'm quite sure it will matter a great deal, Uncle, as I believe you'll agree," Mordaunt added, with a smile that sent a shiver down Winter's spine. "When I first presented myself at your house in London, it was to ask what had befallen me. The second time I introduced myself, it was to ask what had tainted my name. This time I stand before you to ask a question far more terrible than those before, to ask you, as God said to the first murderer, 'Cain, where is thy brother Abel?' Milord, where is your sister, that sister who was my mother?"

Winter recoiled from the fire in those ardent eyes. "Your mother?" he said.

"Yes, Milord—my mother," replied the young man, nodding savagely.

Though battered by the memories such fierce hatred stirred up, Winter made an effort to get hold of himself, and snapped, "What's become of her? Ask for her in Hell, wretch, and maybe Hell will answer you."

Mordaunt advanced into the room until he was face-to-face with Lord Winter and crossed his arms. "I already asked the executioner of Béthune," the young man said in a hollow voice, his face livid with grief and anger, "and the executioner of Béthune told me."

Winter fell back on a chair as if struck by a thunderbolt and tried in vain to reply.

"Oh, yes," continued the young man. "At his words all was explained, for they were the key that unlocked the abyss. My mother inherited from her husband, and then you assassinated my mother! My name would have given me my paternity, so you denied my name—and when you denied my name, you robbed me of my fortune. I no longer wonder why you refused to acknowledge me. When one is a thief, it's unseemly to call the one you robbed 'nephew'—when one is a murderer, it's inconvenient to recognize the one you've orphaned!"

These words produced an effect contrary to what Mordaunt had expected, as they only served to remind Winter what a monster Milady had been. He rose, calm and grave, and his severe look disconcerted the furious young man. "Do you want to know the whole truth of this horrible secret, Monsieur?" Winter said. "Well, then, let me tell you about the woman of whom you come today to call me to account. This woman had in all likelihood poisoned my brother, and in order to inherit from me, planned to assassinate me in my turn; of that I have proof. Now what do you have to say?"

"I say she was my mother!"

"She took a man formerly just, good, and pure and seduced him into stabbing the Duke of Buckingham to death. Of that crime I have proof. Now what do you say?"

"She was my mother!"

"Returned to France, at the Augustine convent in Béthune, she poisoned a young woman just because she loved one of her enemies. Will that crime persuade you of the justice of her punishment? For of that crime, I have proof!"

"She was my mother!" the young man cried, even louder than before.

"At last, filthy with murder and debauchery, abhorrent to all, still as menacing as a bloodthirsty panther, she was captured by five men she'd driven to despair, though they'd never caused her the slightest harm. She was found and judged for her appalling crimes. This executioner with whom you spoke, whom you said told you all—if he'd really told you everything, he must have told you that he trembled with joy when he avenged the shame and suicide of his debauched brother. Perverted daughter, adulterous wife, unnatural sister, poisoner, assassin, an abomination to all who knew her, to every nation that received her—that's what that woman was."

An involuntary sob tore from Mordaunt's throat and brought the blood mounting back to his pallid face. He clenched his fists, his face streamed with sweat, his hair bristling on his head like Hamlet's, and trembling with fury, he cried, "Silence! Silence! She was my mother! These quarrels, these vices, these crimes—I don't know them! What I do know is that I had a mother, and that five men, conspiring against one woman, killed her secretly, silently, vindictively, like cowards! What I know is that you were one of them, Monsieur, and that it was you, Uncle, who said, loudest and most fervently, that she must die! So now I warn you: listen to these words and engrave them on your memory so you'll never forget them—this murder that drives me mad, this murder that has taken my name, this murder that has impoverished me, this murder is what's made me corrupt, wicked, and implacable! I demand an accounting for it, first of all from you, and then, when I find them, from your accomplices."

Hatred in his eyes, froth rimming his mouth, his fist outstretched, Mordaunt took a terrible and menacing step toward Winter.

But the latter put his hand on his sword, and said, with the smile of a man who has gamed with death for thirty years, "Would you try to assassinate me, Monsieur? Then I'd have to acknowledge you as my nephew, for you'd reveal yourself as your mother's son."

"No," replied Mordaunt, exerting an iron will and forcing all the muscles of his face and body back into their usual slackened state. "No, I won't kill you—at least not now. For I need you to lead me to the others. But when I find them, Monsieur, you may then tremble . . . for I'll treat you as I did the executioner of Béthune. Him I stabbed to the heart without pity or mercy, and he was the least guilty of all of you."

At these words, the young man departed, descending the stairs so quietly he was unnoticed, even by Tony, waiting on the landing for a call from his master. But Winter didn't call; shaken, near fainting, he stood frozen, listening hard until he heard hoofbeats as a horse rode away. Then he collapsed in a chair, whispering, "I'm thankful, dear God, that he knows only my name."

XLIV

Paternity

While this terrible scene was playing out at Lord Winter's, Athos, seated by the window of his chamber, his elbow resting on a table and his head resting on his hand, listened rapt as Raoul recounted the events of his journey and the details of the battle. The gentleman's handsome and noble figure almost glowed with joy at the recital of the youth's first adventures; he drank in the sound of that youthful voice, so fresh and pure, as if listening to harmonious music. He forgot everything dark in the past, and everything cloudy in the future, as if the return of the beloved child had turned even fears into hopes. Athos was happy, as happy as he'd ever been.

"And you saw and took part in this great battle, Bragelonne?" said the former musketeer.

"Yes, Monsieur."

"And it was fierce, you say?"

"Monsieur le Prince personally led the charge eleven times."

"He is a great man of war, Bragelonne."

"He's a hero, Monsieur—I didn't lose sight of him for a second. Oh, it's a grand thing, Monsieur, to bear such a name as Condé!"

"Brilliant, and yet calm, is he not?"

"Brilliant as if at a party and calm as if on parade. When we approached the enemy, it was on the double; we were forbidden to fire first, and marched at the Spaniards, who awaited us on a crest, musketoons at the ready. At a range of thirty paces, the prince turned to our soldiers. '*Enfants*,' he said, 'you're about to withstand a furious volley; but afterward, believe me, they'll pay the price for it.' There was such a hush that the soldiers on both sides heard every word. Then raising his sword, he cried, 'Sound the trumpets.'"

"Well, well! . . . When the time comes, you'll do the same thing, won't you, Raoul?"

"Absolutely, Monsieur, for I found it both grand and moving. At a range of twenty paces we saw their muskets glint as they lowered them on us, for the sun gleamed on the barrels. 'At a walk, *mes enfants*, at a walk,' said the prince, 'now's the time.'"

"Were you scared, Raoul?" asked the count.

"Yes, Monsieur," the young man said naïvely, "I felt a chill grasp my heart, and as the word 'Fire!' echoed down the enemy ranks, I closed my eyes and thought of you."

"Did you indeed, Raoul?" said Athos, taking his hand.

"Yes, Monsieur. At that moment there was such an explosion you would have said that Hell had opened its gates, and those who weren't killed felt the heat of the flames. I opened my eyes, astounded at not being dead, or at least wounded; a third of the squadron was lying on the ground, bloody and mutilated. At that moment I met the prince's eye and thought of nothing except that he was looking at me. I drove in both spurs and found myself amidst the ranks of our enemies."

"And the prince was pleased with you?"

"He told me so at least, Monsieur, when he asked me to ride to Paris with Monsieur de Châtillon, sent to bring the queen the news along with our captured banners. 'Go,' said the prince. 'The enemy won't regroup for a fortnight. Until then I don't need you. Go and embrace those you love and who love you, and tell my sister de Longueville that I thank her for the gift she gave me in sending you.' And so, I came, Monsieur," added Raoul, looking at the count with a loving smile, "for I thought you'd be glad to see me again."

Athos drew the young man to him and kissed him on the forehead as he would a young girl. "And so," he said, "you are launched, Raoul. You have dukes as friends, a Marshal of France for a godfather, a Prince of the Blood as your captain, and in one day you've been received by two queens. Not bad for a novice."

"Oh, Monsieur!" said Raoul suddenly. "You've reminded me of something I forgot to say, I was so eager to recount my adventures: in the Queen of England's chamber was a gentleman who, when I mentioned your name, gave a cry of surprise and joy. He said he was a friend of yours, asked me your address, and said he's coming to see you."

"What was his name?"

"I didn't dare to ask him, Monsieur; but, though he spoke quite well, based on his accent I think he's English."

"Ah!" said Athos. He bent his head as if searching his memory, but when he looked up, the memory was before him, as a man was standing in the half-open doorway and looking at him fondly.

"Lord de Winter!" cried the count.

"Athos, my friend!"

The two gentlemen embraced for a long moment. Then Athos, taking him by the hands, looked at him and said, "What's the matter, Milord? You seem as sad as I am happy."

"Yes, dear friend, it's true—and moreover, the sight of you redoubles my fears." And Winter looked around as if seeking something. Raoul understood that what he wanted was privacy and left the two old friends without hesitation.

"Now that we're alone," said Athos, "let's speak of you."

"While we're alone, we must speak of both of us," replied Lord Winter. "*He* is here."

"Who?"

"The son of Milady."

Athos, struck again by this name that seemed to pursue him like a fatal echo, hesitated a moment, frowned slightly, and then calmly said, "I know."

"You know?"

"Yes. Grimaud ran into him between Béthune and Arras, and returned at the gallop to warn me of his coming."

"Grimaud recognized him, then?"

"No, but he stood at the deathbed of a man who did."

"The executioner of Béthune!" cried Winter.

"How do you know that?" said Athos, astonished.

"From the son—I just saw him," Winter replied, "and he told me every-thing. Ah, my friend, what a terrible plight! We should have buried the child with the mother!"

Athos, like all noble natures, didn't inflict his painful feelings on others; instead he swallowed them, and tried to replace them by emanating hope and encouragement. It was as if he transformed his personal griefs into shared consolation. "What are you afraid of?" he said, understanding the need to address that instinctive terror he had also felt at first. "Is this young man a trained assassin who murders in cold blood? He slew the executioner of Béthune in a mad rage, but now his fury is sated."

Winter smiled sadly, shook his head, and said, "Don't you know whose blood he shares?"

"Bah!" said Athos, trying to smile. "Such ferocity would be diluted in younger generations. Besides, friend, Providence has warned us, so we're on our guard. All we can do is wait, so let's wait. But as I said before, let's talk about you. What brings you to Paris?"

"Some important matters I'll get to eventually. First, what's this I hear from Her Majesty the Queen of England that d'Artagnan is one of Maza-rin's men? Pardon my bluntness, my friend—I have nothing against the cardinal, and I trust your judgment completely, but are you by any chance also with his party?"

"Monsieur d'Artagnan is in the service," said Athos, "and as a soldier, he obeys the constituted authority. D'Artagnan isn't wealthy and needs his lieutenant's salary. Millionaires like you, Milord, are rare in France."

"Alas!" said Winter. "I'm now as poor or even poorer than he is. But let's return to you."

"So, you want to know if I'm with Mazarin? Well, pardon my bluntness, Milord, but no—a thousand times no."

Winter rose and pressed Athos in his arms. "Thank you, Count," he said, "thanks for this wonderful news. I rejoice and am rejuvenated! You're not with Mazarin—what great good luck! Of course, you couldn't possibly be one of his minions. But, pardon my asking, are you at liberty?"

"What do you mean, at liberty?"

"I'm asking if you're married."

"Oh, as to that—no," said Athos, smiling.

"I wondered: that young man, so handsome, so elegant, so gracious . . ."

"He's a child whom I raised, and who doesn't know his father."

"Ah, very good. You're still the same, Athos, grand and generous."

"Come, Milord, why do you ask?"

"You're still in touch with your friends Messieurs Porthos and Aramis?"

"And d'Artagnan as well, Milord. We are four friends who are as devoted to each other as always—but when it comes to serving the cardinal or opposing him, as Mazarin's men or Frondeurs, we are in two camps."

"Monsieur Aramis sides with d'Artagnan?" asked Lord Winter.

"No," said Athos, "Monsieur Aramis does me the honor to share my convictions."

"Can you put me in touch with your charming and witty friend?"

"Indeed, whenever you like."

"Has he changed?"

"He's become an abbot, that's all."

"Now that worries me—for surely that's made him give up on adventures."

"On the contrary," said Athos with a smile, "he was never more of a musketeer than he is since becoming an abbot—you'll find him a veritable Galaor.[110] Do you want me to send Raoul for him?"

"Thank you, Count, but he might not be instantly available. But if you think you can answer for him . . ."

"As much as for myself."

"Then would you engage to bring him at ten o'clock tomorrow morning to the Louvre drawbridge?"

"Oh ho!" said Athos, smiling. "Do you have a duel arranged?"

"Yes, Count, a fine duel, a duel of which you'll approve, I hope."

"Where shall we go, Milord?"

"To see Her Majesty the Queen of England, who has charged me with bringing you to her."

"Her Majesty knows of me, then?"

"No, but I know you."

"A conundrum!" said Athos. "But I agree nevertheless, and you have my word on it—I don't need to know more. Will you do me the honor of dining with me, Milord?"

"Thank you, Count," Winter said, "but that young man's visit, I must confess, has robbed me of my appetite, and will probably rob me of my sleep. Why did he come to Paris? It wasn't to track me down, because he didn't know I was here. That young man terrifies me, Count; he has a future of blood ahead of him."

"What has he been doing in England?"

"He's one of the most ardent followers of Oliver Cromwell."

"What brought him to that cause? His mother and father were Catholics, I believe."

"The hatred he bears for the king."

"He opposes the king?"

"Yes, the king declared him a bastard, deprived him of his property, and forbade him to use the name of Winter."

"What name does he go by now?"

"Mordaunt."

"A Puritan, disguised as a monk, traveling alone on the roads of France."

"A monk, you say?"

"Yes, didn't you know?"

"I know only what he told me."

"It's true, and by that imposture—may God pardon me if I blaspheme—he was able to hear the confession of the executioner of Béthune."

"Then I think I understand at last. He's an envoy sent by Cromwell."

"To whom?"

"To Mazarin. And the queen had guessed rightly: we were forestalled. Everything is clear to me now. Adieu, Count, until tomorrow."

"But the night is pitch black," said Athos, seeing Lord Winter anxious and trying to hide it. "Have you any lackeys with you?"

"I have Tony—a good lad, but green."

"Holà! Olivain, Grimaud, Blaisois—get your musketoons and go with Monsieur le Vicomte."

Blaisois was a big fellow, half servant, half peasant, whom we glimpsed at the Château de Bragelonne announcing that dinner was served, and whom Athos had baptized with the name of his province.

Hearing these orders, Raoul came in. "Viscount," said Athos, "you will escort milord to his inn, and not allow anyone else to approach him."

"Really, Count," Winter said, "what do you take me for?"

"For a stranger who doesn't know his way around Paris," said Athos, "so let the viscount lead the way."

Winter shook his hand. "Grimaud," said Athos, "place yourself in the vanguard of the troop, and watch out for the monk." Grimaud started and then nodded, caressing the stock of his musketoon with eloquent silence.

"Until tomorrow, Count," said Winter.

"Yes, Milord."

The little troop made its way toward Rue Saint-Louis, Olivain trembling like Sosia[111] at every shadow, Blaisois confident because he was unaware of what risks they were running, and Tony looking left and right without saying a word, since he didn't speak French. Winter and Raoul marched side by side and spoke together. Grimaud, at Athos's orders, preceded the band with a torch in one hand and his musketoon in the other, leading the way to Winter's inn, where he knocked on the door with his fist. When they came to open it, he bowed to the lord without a word.

They followed the same routine for the return. Grimaud's piercing gaze saw nothing suspicious until he spotted a strange shadow at the corner of the quay and Rue Guénégaud. It seemed to Grimaud that he'd seen this shadow before, and he darted toward it, but before he could reach it the shadow disappeared into a dark alley where Grimaud didn't think it would be prudent to pursue.

Athos was informed of the expedition's success, and as it was ten in the evening, everyone retired to their rooms.

The next morning, upon opening his eyes, the count found Raoul waiting at his bedside. The young man was fully dressed and was reading a new book by Monsieur Chapelain.[112] "Up already, Raoul?" said the count.

"Yes, Monsieur," replied the young man, after a slight hesitation. "I slept poorly."

"You slept poorly—you, Raoul? Was something bothering you?" asked Athos.

"Monsieur, you'll say I'm too eager to leave you again when I've only just arrived, but . . ."

"So, you had only two days' leave, Raoul?"

"On the contrary, Monsieur, I had ten; I wasn't planning to go back to camp yet."

Athos smiled. "To where, then, if it's not a secret, Viscount? Having fought your first battle, you're almost a man, and have earned the right to go where you like without telling me about it."

"Never, Monsieur," said Raoul. "So long as I have you as my guardian, I wouldn't think of it. I was just thinking I'd pass a day or two at Blois. Wait, are you laughing at me?"

"No, not at all," said Athos, suppressing a sigh. "No, I'm not laughing at you, Viscount. If you want to visit Blois, that's entirely natural."

"Then, you'll let me go?" Raoul said happily.

"Certainly, Raoul."

"And in your heart, Monsieur, you have no qualms?"

"Not at all. Why should I be concerned by what pleases you?"

"Oh, Monsieur, how good you are," cried the young man, who went to embrace Athos, then stopped out of respect. But Athos opened his arms to him.

"Then I can leave right away?"

"Whenever you like, Raoul."

Raoul took three steps toward the door, then stopped and said, "Monsieur, there is one thing: it was thanks to the Duchesse de Chevreuse, who was so good to me, that I owe my introduction to Monsieur le Prince."

"And you owe her some gratitude—is that it, Raoul?"

"So, it seems to me, Monsieur . . . but it's up to you to decide."

"Send to the Hôtel de Luynes, Raoul, and ask if the duchess can receive you. I'm very pleased that you remember your manners. Take Grimaud and Olivain with you."

"Both of them, Monsieur?" asked Raoul, astonished. Athos nodded, so Raoul bowed and went out.

Watching him close the door and hearing him call out in a joyful voice to Grimaud and Olivain, Athos sighed. *All too soon he leaves me*, he thought, shaking his head, *but it's only to be expected, for it's Nature's law to look forward. He certainly loves that child in Blois; but must he love me less for loving others?* Athos admitted to himself that he hadn't expected such a speedy departure, but Raoul was so happy about it, that swept away any concerns.

By nine o'clock everything was prepared for the departure. As Athos watched Raoul mount his horse, a footman arrived for him from Madame de Chevreuse. He'd been sent to tell the Comte de La Fère that she'd heard of the return of his young protégé, as well as of his conduct at the battle, and that she'd be very glad to congratulate him in person. "Tell Madame la Duchesse," replied Athos, "that the Vicomte de Bragelonne is mounted and on his way to the Hôtel de Luynes."

Then, after giving Grimaud some instructions, Athos made a sign to Raoul that he could depart.

It occurs to me, Athos thought, remembering his own appointment, *that maybe it's best for Raoul to be away from Paris at just this moment.*

XLV

Once More the Queen Asks for Aid

In the morning, Athos had sent a message to Aramis by way of Blaisois, his only remaining servant. Blaisois found Bazin donning his beadle's robe; it was his day of service at Notre Dame.

Athos had ordered Blaisois to try to speak to Aramis personally. Blaisois, a brawny but simple lad, who knew only what he'd been told, had asked for the Abbé d'Herblay, and despite Bazin's telling him he wasn't at home, had insisted so persistently that Bazin had lost his temper. Blaisois, seeing Bazin dressed as a man of the Church, wasn't bothered by his anger and tried to go around him, assuming the man he was dealing with possessed the virtues of the cloth, that is, patience and Christian charity.

But Bazin, still the valet of a musketeer when the blood rose to his round face, grabbed a broomstick and struck at Blaisois, saying, "You've insulted the Church, you lout—you've insulted the Church!"

At this unaccustomed commotion, Aramis finally appeared, cautiously opening the door of his bedchamber. Bazin respectfully grounded one end of his stick, as he'd seen the Swiss Guards do at Notre Dame, while Blaisois, with a glare at the rotund Cerberus, drew his letter from his lapel and presented it to Aramis. "From the Comte de La Fère?" said Aramis. "Very good." He took it and went back into his room without even asking the reason for all the noise.

Blaisois returned sadly to the Grand Charlemagne Inn, where Athos asked him for a report on his mission. Blaisois told his story. "Idiot!" said Athos, laughing. "Didn't you tell Bazin that you'd come from me?"

"No, Monsieur."

"And what did Bazin say when he learned you were mine?"

"Ah, Monsieur, he made all kinds of apologies, and forced me to drink two glasses of very good Muscat with him, in which we dipped three or four excellent biscuits. But he's still a brutal devil. A beadle, acting that way!"

Well, thought Athos, *since Aramis has received my letter, then unless he's forestalled, he'll be there.*

At ten o'clock, Athos, with his usual punctuality, stood on the bridge of the Louvre. There he met Lord Winter, who arrived at the same time. They waited about ten minutes, until Winter began to worry that Aramis wasn't coming. "Patience," said Athos, who was looking toward the Rue du Bac. "I see an abbot clouting a man and bowing to a woman: that must be Aramis."

It was him, in fact. A lad chasing birds had splashed him as he passed, and with a blow of his fist Aramis had sent him reeling. Then he met one of his congregation, and as she was young and pretty, Aramis had bowed to her with a most gracious smile. A moment later he arrived in front of the Louvre.

At his reunion with Lord Winter, there were several hearty embraces, as one might imagine. "Where are we going?" Aramis asked. "Is it a fight? If so, *sacre bleu*, I'll have to run back to my house for my sword."

"No," Winter said, "we're paying a visit to Her Majesty the Queen of England."

"Ah, very good," said Aramis, and added in an undertone to Athos, "and what's the purpose of this visit?"

"My faith, I have no idea. Some evidence needed from us, perhaps?"

"I hope it's not about that cursed affair of the son," said Aramis. "If it is, I'm not eager to be reproached about it. I give reprimands to others, and don't like receiving them myself."

"If that were the case," said Athos, "we wouldn't be conducted to Her Majesty by Lord de Winter, as he was one of us, and shares the blame."

"Yes, quite so. Let's go, then."

Upon entering the Louvre, Lord Winter went in first. There was just a single usher at the door, and in the cold light of day Athos, Aramis, and the Englishman couldn't avoid seeing the awful destitution of the lodging a miserly charity afforded the unlucky queen. The grand halls were stripped of furniture; the cracked and faded walls were enlivened only by bits of gold molding that hadn't fallen yet; windows, which no longer shut properly, were missing panes of glass; and there were no carpets, no guards, and no servants. This sad dilapidation hit Athos hard, and he silently pointed out the worst of it to his companion, nudging him with his elbow and indicating with his eyes.

"Mazarin lives a good deal more grandly than this," said Aramis.

"Mazarin is nearly a king," said Athos, "and Madame Henriette is almost no longer a queen."

"If you'd only made the effort to be witty, Athos," said Aramis, "I believe you'd have outdone even Monsieur Voiture."

Athos smiled.

It seemed the queen was waiting impatiently, for at the first movement she heard from the hall outside her chamber, she herself came to the doorway to receive the witnesses of her misfortune. "Come in and be welcome, Messieurs," she said.

The gentlemen entered, and at first they stood, but at a gesture from the queen, who invited them to be seated, Athos set the example of obedience. He was grave and calm, but Aramis was angry; this insult to distressed royalty infuriated him, and he glared at the signs of misery around him.

"You've noticed my luxurious lodgings?" Queen Henriette said, with a sad look around the room.

"Madame," said Aramis, "I beg Your Majesty's pardon, but I can't contain my indignation at seeing how the Court of France treats the daughter of Henri IV."

"Monsieur is not a cavalier?" asked the queen of Lord Winter.

"Monsieur is the Abbé d'Herblay," he replied.

Aramis flushed. "Madame," he said, "I am an abbot, it's true, but it's not my preference, as I've never had a vocation for the cloth. My cassock is held on by a single button, and I'm always on the verge of doffing it and becoming a musketeer once more. This morning, unaware that I was to have the honor of addressing Your Majesty, I donned my clerical outfit, but I'm nevertheless a man Your Majesty will find utterly devoted to her service, should she wish to command me."

"Monsieur le Chevalier d'Herblay," added Winter, "was one of those valiant musketeers of His Majesty King Louis XIII of whom I've spoken to Your Majesty." Then, indicating Athos, he continued, "As for Monsieur here, he's the noble Comte de La Fère whose reputation is so well known to Madame."

"Messieurs," said the queen, "just a few years ago I was surrounded by wealth, soldiers, and loyal gentlemen who would obey my command at a gesture. Today as you look around me you might be surprised by my situation, for now, to accomplish a plan that will save my life, I have only Lord Winter, a friend of twenty years, and you, Messieurs, whom I've just met for the first time, and know only as my compatriots."

"That will be enough, Madame," said Athos, bowing deeply, "if the lives of three men can redeem yours."

"Thank you, Messieurs. Now hear me," she continued, "I'm not only the most wretched of queens, but the unhappiest of mothers and the most desperate of wives. Two of my children, the Duke of York and Princess Elizabeth,[113] are far from me, exposed to the attacks from our enemies and ambitious opportunists; my husband the king is trapped in England, enduring a life so painful that death might be better. Here, Messieurs, is the letter he sent me by Lord Winter. Read it."

Athos and Aramis tried to decline, but, "Read it," said the queen.

Athos read aloud from the letter, the contents of which we know, in which King Charles asked to obtain refuge in France. "Well?" asked Athos, after he'd finished reading.

"Well!" said the queen. "Mazarin has refused."

The two friends exchanged smiles tinged with contempt.

"And now, Madame, what is to be done?" asked Athos.

"Then you can have compassion for so much misfortune?" the queen said, moved.

"I have had the honor to ask Your Majesty what Monsieur d'Herblay and I can do in her service; we are ready."

"Ah, Monsieur, you truly have a noble heart!" the queen burst out, her voice choked with gratitude, while Lord Winter gave her a look that seemed to say, *Didn't I tell you so?*

"And you, Monsieur?" the queen asked Aramis.

"Wherever the count goes," he replied, "I follow without question, Madame, even unto death—but when it comes to the service of Your Majesty," he added, with a look as ardent as in his youth, "I go before even Monsieur le Comte."

"Well, Messieurs!" said the queen. "If that is so, and you're willing to devote yourself to the service of a poor princess whom the rest of the world abandons, here is what you can do for me. The king is all alone, except for a few remaining gentlemen whom he expects to lose any day, and is among the Scots, whom he mistrusts, though he's Scottish himself. Since Lord Winter left him, I scarcely dare breathe. Well, Messieurs, though I'm in no position to ask, please: go to England, join the king, be his friends and his guards, march by his side in battle, and stand next to him in his house, where there are dangers even greater than the risks of war; and in exchange for this sacrifice I promise, not to reward you—for I think you would find that insulting—but to love you like a sister, and to regard you above all others but my husband and my children, so swear I before God!"

And the queen slowly and solemnly raised her eyes toward heaven.

"Madame," said Athos, "when shall we depart?"

"You agree, then?" said the queen with joy.

"Yes, Madame, though Your Majesty goes too far, it seems to me, in offering a friendship that is beyond our merits. We serve God, Madame, by serving such an unhappy prince and virtuous queen. We are yours, body and soul."

"Oh, Messieurs," said the queen, moved to tears, "this is the first moment of hope and joy I've felt in five years. Yes, you serve God, and as I'm too weak to recompense your efforts, it's from him your reward will come, from him who reads in my heart all the gratitude I feel for you and yours. Save my husband; save the king; and though you may never receive what you deserve for it here on Earth, at least I can hope to live long enough to thank you in person. Until then, I wait. Is there anything I can do for you? For now that you're my friends, and involved in my affairs, I should do whatever I can."

"I have nothing to ask of Her Majesty but her prayers," said Athos.

"And I," said Aramis, "am alone in the world, and have no one to serve but Your Majesty."

The queen offered them her hand, which they kissed, and then whispered to Winter, "If you're short of money, Milord, don't hesitate for a moment to break up that jewelry I gave you, and sell some of those diamonds to a moneylender—they ought to be worth fifty or sixty thousand livres. Sell them if necessary, but make sure these gentlemen are treated as they should be, in other words, like kings."

The queen had two letters ready, one she'd written herself, and one written by her daughter Princess Henrietta. Both were addressed to King Charles. She gave one to Athos and one to Aramis, so that if they became separated, each would still have an introduction to the king; then they withdrew.

At the base of the stairs, Winter paused. "Let's each of us go to our own lodgings, Messieurs, so as not to arouse suspicion," he said, "and then meet tonight at nine at the Saint-Denis gate. We'll ride on my horses as far as they'll take us, and thereafter travel by post-horse. Once again, I thank you, my dear friends, both in my name and in the name of the queen."

The three gentlemen shook hands, then Baron Winter went down Rue Saint-Honoré, leaving Athos and Aramis, who remained together. "Well!" said Aramis, once they were alone. "What do you think of this affair, my dear Count?"

"It's bad," replied Athos, "very bad."

"But you took to it with such enthusiasm!"

"As I will always come to the defense of such an important principle, my dear d'Herblay. Kings aren't great without their nobility, and the noblesse is only as great as its kings. In supporting the monarchies, we support ourselves."

"We're going to get murdered over there," said Aramis. "I hate the English—they're coarse, like all folk who drink beer."

"Would it be better to stay here and serve a sentence in the Bastille or the dungeon of Vincennes, since we helped Monsieur de Beaufort to escape?" said Athos. "*Ma foi*, Aramis, believe me, there's nothing to regret about this. We stay out of prison and get to be heroes—it's an easy choice."

"True enough, *mon ami*. But at the beginning of every affair, we face the same question, vulgar though it may be: do you have any money?"

"Around a hundred pistoles, which my tenants had sent me before leaving Bragelonne, but I must leave fifty for Raoul, as a young noble must live with dignity. That leaves about fifty for me. And you?"

"If I go home and turn out all my pockets and search in all my drawers, I'm sure I can turn up ten *louis d'or*. Fortunately, Lord de Winter is rich."

"Lord de Winter is ruined, for the moment, because Cromwell has confiscated his revenue."

"This is where having Baron Porthos with us would be handy," said Aramis.

"I also regret not having d'Artagnan," said Athos.

"What a bulging purse!"

"What a proud sword!"

"Let's recruit them."

"This secret isn't ours to share, Aramis. I don't think we should take anyone into our confidence. Besides, recruiting our friends would seem like we doubted ourselves. Let's regret their absence, but privately, and say nothing."

"You're right. What are you doing for the rest of the day? I must postpone a couple of matters."

"Are they matters that *can* be postponed?"

"*Dame!* They have to be."

"What are these matters?"

"First, I owe a sword-thrust to the coadjutor, whom I saw last night at Madame de Rambouillet's, where he made some remarks about me in an offensive tone."

"What? A duel between priests! A fight between allies!"

"What would you have, *mon cher*? He's a swordsman, and so am I; he's a rabble-rouser, as I am; his cassock weighs on him, as mine does on me; I sometimes wonder which of us is Aramis and which the coadjutor, we're so alike. This doppelganger business vexes me and makes me feel like a shadow. Besides, he's a bungler who will ruin our faction. I'm convinced that if I hit him hard enough, as I did with that lad who splashed me this morning, it would change the face of affairs."

"And I, my dear Aramis," Athos replied calmly, "think it would just change the face of Monsieur de Retz. Besides, it's best to leave things as they stand; he belongs to the Fronde as you now do to the Queen of England. Now, if the second matter you must postpone is no more important than the first . . ."

"Oh, it's much more important."

"Then get it over with quickly."

"Unfortunately, it's not something I can do whenever I please; it must be done at night, late at night."

"I see," said Athos, smiling. "At midnight?"

"Thereabouts."

"Well, my friend, these affairs must be postponed, all the more because you'll return with such a good excuse for having postponed them."

"Yes—if I return."

"If you don't return, what does it matter? Be reasonable. Come, Aramis, you're no longer twenty years old."

"To my great regret, mordieu! Ah, if only I were!"

"Indeed, I think you'd involve yourself in some grand follies!" said Athos. "But we must part; I have one or two visits to make myself and a letter to write. Come to my place at eight o'clock—unless you'd rather dine with me first at seven."

"All right," said Aramis. "Though I have to make about twenty visits and write about that many letters."

They took their leave of each other. Athos went to visit Madame de Vendôme, had a word with Madame de Chevreuse, and wrote the following letter to d'Artagnan:

> *Old friend, I'm going off with Aramis on a matter of importance. I'd prefer to bid you farewell personally, but don't have time for it, so I'm writing to remind you of how fond I am of you.*
>
> *Raoul has gone to Blois and doesn't know of my departure. Watch over him in my absence as best you can, and if you haven't heard from me in three months, tell him to open a sealed packet he'll find in my bronze coffer there, the key to which I'll enclose with this letter.*
>
> *Embrace Porthos for Aramis and for me. Farewell, and perhaps goodbye.*

And he sent Blaisois off with the letter.

Aramis arrived at the appointed hour. He was on horseback and had at his side that trusted sword that he'd drawn so often, more often now than ever. "*Ah çà!*" he said. "I think it's a mistake to go off like this without notifying Porthos and d'Artagnan."

"I took care of it, my friend," said Athos, "and sent them both our embraces."

"You're an admirable man, my dear Count," said Aramis, "and you think of everything."

"Well, then! Are you ready to set off on our journey?"

"Absolutely—and the more I think about it, the happier I am to be away from Paris at this time."

"And I, as well," replied Athos. "I regret not saying goodbye to d'Artagnan in person, but he's such a clever devil he'd have guessed what we're up to."

As they were finishing supper, Blaisois returned. "Monsieur, here's the reply from Monsieur d'Artagnan."

"But I didn't tell you to wait for a reply, you imbecile!" said Athos.

"Well, I started to leave without waiting for one, but then he called me back and gave me this." And he held out a little leather purse, round and jingling.

Athos opened the brief note, which read as follows:

> *My dear Count,*
>
> *When one travels, especially for three months, one never has enough money. Now, I remember our times of hardship, so I'm sending you half my money in this purse. It's cash that I managed to sweat out of Mazarin, but don't use it poorly on that account.*
>
> *As for the idea that I might not see you again, I don't believe a word of it. A man with your heart—and your sword—can pass through anything.*
>
> *Farewell and not goodbye.*
>
> *It goes without saying that from the day I met Raoul I've loved him as if he were my own; but believe me when I say I sincerely pray to God to keep me from becoming his father, no matter how proud I'd be of a son like him.*
>
> *Your D'ARTAGNAN*
>
> *P.S.: Of course, the fifty louis I'm sending you are as much Aramis's as they are yours.*

Athos smiled, and tears welled up in his eyes. D'Artagnan, whom he'd always loved, still loved him, even if he was allied with Mazarin.

"And, my faith, here they are—fifty louis," said Aramis, emptying the purse on the table, "each one with Louis XIII's face on it. Well, what shall we do with this money, Count—keep it, or send it back?"

"We keep it, Aramis, though we won't have it for long. What is offered so nobly should be nobly accepted. You take twenty-five, Aramis, and give the other twenty-five to me."

"It's a timely gift, and I must say I agree with you. Now, then, shall we be off?"

"Whenever you like . . . but aren't you bringing any lackeys?"

"No, that fool of a Bazin had the bad judgment to become a beadle, and now he can't leave Notre Dame."

"Well, you take Blaisois, then, whom I don't need, since I already have Grimaud."

"Willingly," said Aramis.

At that moment, Grimaud appeared on the threshold. "Ready," he said, laconic as usual.

"Then let's go," said Athos.

Indeed, the horses were saddled and waiting, and the lackeys were prepared.

They rode into the night, but at the corner of the quay they encountered Bazin, who ran up to them all out of breath. "Ah, Monsieur!" he huffed. "Thank God I caught you in time."

"What is it?" said Aramis.

"Monsieur Porthos stopped by the house and left this for you, saying it was very urgent and you had to have it before you left."

"What's this?" said Aramis, taking a purse from Bazin.

"Wait, Monsieur l'Abbé, there's a letter too."

"You know I warned you that if you called me anything other than *chevalier* that I'd break your bones. Let's see the letter."

"How are you going to read it?" said Athos. "It's as dark as the bottom of a well."

"Wait," said Bazin. He took out a flint and lit a taper of the kind used to light church candles. By its light, Aramis read the following:

> *My dear d'Herblay,*
> *I hear from d'Artagnan, who embraces me on your behalf and that of the Comte de La Fère, that you're leaving on an expedition*

that may last two or three months. Since I know you don't like to ask aid of your friends, I offer this so you don't have to: here are two hundred pistoles you can use as you think best, and which you can repay if it's ever convenient. Don't worry about putting me in hardship; if I need some money I'll just send to one of my châteaux: at Bracieux alone I have twenty thousand livres in gold. So, I could have sent more, but I was afraid you wouldn't take it if I sent too much.

I address this to you because you know the Comte de La Fère always intimidates me a little, although I love him with all my heart. But you understand that what I offer to you, I offer equally to him.

I am, as you should never doubt, your devoted
DU VALLON DE BRACIEUX DE PIERREFONDS

"Well!" said Aramis. "What do you say to that?"

"I say, my dear d'Herblay, that it would be sacrilege to doubt in Providence when one has such friends."

"And so?"

"And so, let's share out Porthos's pistoles as we did d'Artagnan's louis."

They split the money by the light of Bazin's taper, and then resumed their journey. A quarter of an hour later they were at the Saint-Denis gate, where Lord Winter was waiting for them.

XLVI

In Which It Is Shown That the First Impulse
Is Always the Right One

The three gentlemen took the road to Picardy, that road so familiar to them, reminding Athos and Aramis of some of the most colorful adventures of their youth. "If Mousqueton were with us," said Athos, as they arrived at the spot where they'd fought with the road workers, "he'd tremble as we rode past. Do you remember, Aramis? This is where he took that famous musket ball."

"And I'd let him tremble, by my faith," said Aramis, "for he's not the only one to shiver at this place: there, beyond that tree, is a little spot where I thought I was a dead man."

They went on their way. Soon it was Grimaud who was taken by a memory. As they arrived before an inn where he and his master had dined so long and so well, he approached Athos, pointed at the cellar door, and said, "Sausages!"

Athos began to laugh, as amused by this recollection of his youth as if hearing a mad tale told about someone else.

At last, after riding two days and a night, they arrived, in magnificent weather, at Boulogne. At that time, it was still a small town, lightly populated, and built up on the heights; the district now known as the lower town didn't yet exist. But behind its walls, Boulogne had a formidable position.

Arriving at the gates of the city, Lord Winter said, "Messieurs, let's do as we did in Paris, and separate to avoid suspicion. I know an inn that is little frequented, but where the host is entirely devoted to me. I'm going to go there, because that's where letters will be waiting for me. You should go to one of the city's leading inns, such as the Épée du Grand Henri, and briefly

419

rest and recuperate. Then meet me on the jetty in two hours, where our boat will be waiting for us."

They agreed. Lord Winter followed the road around the walls and entered the city by another gate, while the two friends went in through the gate in front of them. A few hundred paces inside they came upon the large inn Winter had recommended.

The horses were fed and rested, but not unsaddled, and the lackeys were sent to supper. It was beginning to grow late, and the two masters, impatient to embark, told their lackeys to meet them on the jetty, and meanwhile to speak to no one. Of course, this latter instruction applied only to Blaisois; the silent Grimaud needed no such orders.

Athos and Aramis went down to the harbor. By their dust-covered clothes, and by a certain easy manner that always indicates a man accustomed to travel, they attracted the attention of several dockside loiterers. There was one on whom their arrival had made a definite impression. This man, whom they'd noticed for the same reasons others had noticed them, was walking morosely up and down the jetty. However, once he saw Athos and Aramis he stared, and seemed taken with a sudden need to speak with them. This man was young and pale, with eyes of such a light variable blue that they seemed, like a tiger's, to change to reflect his mood. His walk, though slow and wandering, was stiff and determined; he was dressed all in black and wore a long sword at his side with the ease of familiarity.

Stepping onto the jetty, Athos and Aramis paused to look at a small boat moored to the pier and equipped as if ready to go. "No doubt that's ours," said Athos.

"Yes," Aramis replied, "and that sloop at anchor out there is probably the one intended for us. Now, if only de Winter won't keep us waiting; there's no amusement to be had here, and not a woman in sight."

"Hush!" said Athos. "Someone might be listening."

In fact, the pale loiterer, who, after staring at the two friends, had resumed walking up and down, paused at the name of *de Winter*—but as his face showed no emotion upon hearing this name, he might just have paused by chance. Turning, the young man bowed to them and said politely, "Messieurs, pardon my curiosity, but I see that you've come from Paris, or are at least newcomers to Boulogne."

"Yes, we have come from Paris, Monsieur," Athos replied just as politely. "What can we do for you?"

"Monsieur," the young man said, "could you please tell me if it's true that Cardinal Mazarin is no longer prime minister?"

"That's a strange question," said Aramis.

"He is, and he isn't," Athos replied. "By which I mean that half of France opposes him, but by balancing intrigue with promises, the other half supports him. That situation might continue for quite a while."

"Then, Monsieur," the stranger said, "he's neither fled nor in prison?"

"No, Monsieur—not for the moment, at least."

"Messieurs, my thanks for your courtesy," said the young man as he walked away.

"What do you think of this inquisitive fellow?" said Aramis.

"I think he's either a bored provincial or a nosy spy."

"And that's the answer you give to a spy?"

"I could scarcely have replied otherwise. He was polite to me, as I was to him."

"But if he's a spy . . ."

"What's a spy going to do to us? We're no longer in the reign of Cardinal Richelieu, who could close the ports on a mere suspicion."

"Nonetheless, it was a mistake to answer him that way," said Aramis, watching the young man as he disappeared among the dunes.

"And you," said Athos, "forget that you committed an imprudence of your own when you mentioned the name of Lord de Winter. Didn't you notice that that's what attracted the young man?"

"All the more reason, when he spoke to you, to tell him to move along."

"And start a quarrel?" said Athos.

"Since when are you afraid of a quarrel?"

"I'm always afraid of a quarrel when I'm on a mission that a quarrel might endanger. Besides, to tell the truth, I wanted a close look at this young man."

"Why's that?"

"Aramis, you're just going to laugh at me, tell me I'm seeing things, and am obsessed with a single idea."

"Let's hear it. What, then?"

"Who do you think that man looks like?"

"In ugliness or in beauty?" asked Aramis, laughing.

"In ugliness, insofar as a man can resemble a woman."

"Ah, pardieu!" said Aramis. "Now you've set me to thinking. No, of course you're not seeing things, *mon cher ami,* and now that I think about it, you're right: that thin, narrow mouth, those eyes that take orders only from the mind and not from the heart. It's Milady's bastard, of course!"

"You laugh, Aramis!"

"From habit, that's all. For I swear to you, I'd hate to encounter such a serpent in our path as much as you would."

"Ah, here comes de Winter at last," said Athos.

"Good, then there's only one thing lacking," said Aramis. "Now we need only our servants."

"No," Athos said, "I see them, they're about twenty paces behind milord. I recognize Grimaud with his cocked head and long legs. Tony is bringing our carbines."

"Are we going to embark at night, then?" asked Aramis, glancing toward the west, where the sun was just a golden haze sinking into the sea.

"It seems likely," said Athos.

"The devil!" replied Aramis. "Even by day I don't like the sea, and it's worse at night—the slap of the waves, the whine of the wind, the dreadful shifting of the deck—I'd much rather be in the monastery at Noisy."

Athos smiled his melancholy smile, for though he seemed to be listening to his friend, it was clear he really was thinking about something else. He made his way toward Winter, and Aramis followed him. "What's wrong with our friend?" Aramis said. "He looks like those damned in Dante who had their necks twisted by Satan to turn backward. What the devil is he looking for behind him?"

Noticing them, Winter doubled his pace and reached them in no time. "What's wrong, Milord?" said Athos. "You're out of breath."

"Nothing," said Winter, "nothing. Only, passing by the dunes, it seemed to me . . ." And he turned and looked anew.

Athos gave Aramis a look.

"But let's depart," Winter continued. "Here's the boat waiting for us, and our sloop is at anchor—do you see it there? I wish I was already on it." And he turned again and looked back.

"*Ah çà!*" said Aramis. "Did you forget something?"

"No, I'm just distracted . . ."

"He saw him," Athos whispered to Aramis.

They arrived at the gangway to the boat. Winter first sent down the lackeys carrying their arms, next the porters with their trunks, and then began to follow them. As he did, Athos noticed a man who was hastening along the shoreline parallel to the jetty, as if trying to reach the opposite wharf across from where they were embarking. He thought, through the descending twilight, that he recognized the young man who'd questioned them. "Oh ho!" he said to himself. "Is he a spy after all, and planning to block our departure?"

But if that was the stranger's plan, it was already too late to put it into action. Athos, in his turn, went down the gangway, but without losing sight of the young man, who went out upon the breakwater. *He seems to be angry at us*, thought Athos, *but let's just depart. Once we're on the open sea, he can be as angry as he likes.* Athos leapt into the boat, the ropes were loosed, and it began to pull away due to the efforts of four brawny rowers.

But the young man began to follow the boat along the breakwater, or rather precede it. The boat had to pass between the end of the jetty, where the harbor lighthouse had just been lit, and a boulder at the end of the breakwater. The man could be seen climbing the boulder so as to tower over the boat as it passed.

"See there?" said Aramis to Athos. "That young man is definitely some sort of spy."

"What young man?" asked Winter, turning to look.

"That one, who spoke to us earlier, followed us, and now awaits us. See!"

Winter looked where Aramis was pointing. The lighthouse clearly illuminated the little strait they were about to pass through, and the boulder where the young man stood waiting, head bare and arms crossed.

"It's him!" Lord Winter cried, grabbing Athos by the arm. "It's him. I thought I'd seen him, and I was right."

"Him? Who?" asked Aramis.

"Milady's son," Athos replied.

"The monk!" cried Grimaud.

The young man heard these words, and perched over the water on the edge of the boulder, he looked like he was ready to pounce. "Yes, Uncle, here I am. I, Milady's son; I, the monk; I, the aide and friend to Cromwell—and I recognize you and your companions."

There were three brave men in that boat, men of whom no man could dispute the courage—but at that voice, in that tone, they felt a shiver of terror run down their spines.

As for Grimaud, his hair was bristling on his head, and sweat poured from his brow.

"Ah!" said Aramis. "So, this is the nephew, the monk, and Milady's son—that's him, is it?"

"Alas, yes," murmured Winter.

"All right, then," said Aramis. And he picked up, with that terrible sangfroid he displayed in extremity, one of Tony's muskets, loaded it, and took aim at the man standing on the rock like an angel of malediction.

"Fire!" cried Grimaud, beside himself.

Athos knocked aside the musket barrel before Aramis could shoot. "The devil take you!" Aramis exclaimed. "You ruined my shot just when I was about to put a ball into his chest."

"It's quite enough to have killed the mother," said Athos gruffly.

"The mother was a monster who hurt us and those dear to us."

"Yes, but the son has done us no harm."

Grimaud, who had risen when Aramis took up the musket, fell back discouraged, wringing his hands.

The young man burst out laughing. "Ah, it is you, for sure—and now I know you." His harsh and menacing laughter rang out over the water, fading as the boat rowed on into the darkness.

Aramis shuddered. "Calm down," said Athos. "What the devil! Are we men, or aren't we?"

"We are," said Aramis, "but him—he's a demon. Just ask the uncle if he thinks I'd have done wrong to rid him of his nephew."

Winter's only response was a sigh.

"I could have finished this," Aramis went on. "Agh! I'm afraid, Athos, that your restraint has led you into folly."

Athos took Winter's hand and said, changing the subject, "How long will it take to reach England?" But Winter wasn't listening and didn't answer.

"Look, Athos," said Aramis, "maybe it isn't too late. Look, he's still in the same place."

Athos turned with an effort, as the sight of the young man seemed painful to him. Indeed, he still stood on the rock, the glow from the lighthouse making a halo around him. "But what is he doing in Boulogne?" asked Athos, who, being reason incarnate, sought the cause for everything, little caring for the effect.

"He followed me, he followed me," said Winter, who this time had heard Athos, since the words echoed his own thoughts.

"To follow you, my friend," said Athos, "he would have had to know we were leaving; and besides, it seems probable he was here ahead of us."

"Then I can't understand it!" said the Englishman, shaking his head like a man who sees no use in battling the supernatural.

"Decidedly, Aramis," said Athos, "I think I was wrong not to let you do it."

"Oh, hold your tongue," Aramis replied. "You'd make me weep, if I was the sort of man who could weep."

Grimaud just uttered a deep, mournful groan.

At that moment, a voice hailed them from the sloop. The pilot, who was seated at the rudder, answered the call, and the boat approached the vessel. Within minutes, the gentlemen, their servants, and baggage were all aboard. The captain waited only for the porters to return to the boat; as soon as they were clear, he set a course for Hastings, where they were to land.

Meanwhile the three friends, anxious despite themselves, peered back toward the breakwater, where, on the boulder at the end, the menacing shadow that pursued them was still visible. A voice echoed across the water with a final threat: "We'll meet again, Messieurs—in England!"

~ The Story Continues in Book Four, *The Son of Milady* ~

Dramatis Personae: Historical Characters

ANNE: *Anne of Austria, "Anne d'Autriche," Queen of France* (1601–66). Eldest daughter of King Philip III of Spain and sister to King Philip IV, Anne was wed to King Louis XIII of France in a political marriage at the age of fourteen. A Spaniard among the French, unloved by the king, proud but intimidated, and vulnerable to manipulation by her friends, she wielded very little influence until she finally gave birth to a royal heir, the future Louis XIV, in 1638. After Louis XIII died in 1643, with his heir still a child, Anne was declared Queen Regent and thereafter came into her own, holding France together against threats both internal and external until Louis XIV was old enough to rule. Anne was intelligent and strong-willed but not a skilled politician; in that she was aided by her close association with her prime minister, Cardinal Mazarin. Were they lovers? Anne's level of intimacy with Mazarin is a matter of conjecture; Dumas the novelist prefers the juiciest possible interpretation.

ARAMIS: *Aramis, Chevalier/Abbé René d'Herblay,* is based loosely on Henri, Seigneur d'Aramitz (1620?–1655 or 1674), as filtered through Courtilz de Sandras's fictionalized *Memoirs of Monsieur d'Artagnan.* Though Sandras had made Aramis the brother of Athos and Porthos, the historical d'Aramitz was a Gascon petty nobleman, an abbot who spent at least the first half of the 1640s serving under his uncle, Captain de Tréville, in the King's Musketeers. Sources disagree as to the date of his death.

Artagnan see D'ARTAGNAN

ATHOS: *Athos, Comte de La Fère,* is based loosely on Armand, Seigneur de Sillègue, d'Athos, et d'Autevielle (c. 1615–1643), as filtered through Courtilz de Sandras's fictionalized *Memoirs of Monsieur d'Artagnan.* Though Sandras had made Athos the brother of Aramis and Porthos, the historical d'Athos was a Gascon petty nobleman who joined his cousins, Captain de Tréville and Isaac de Portau (Porthos) in the King's Musketeers in 1640. Little is known of his life; he was killed in a duel in December 1643.

BEAUFORT: *François de Vendôme, Duc de Beaufort* (1616–69). Beaufort was the grandson of King Henri IV and his mistress Gabrielle d'Estrées, which made him a Prince of the Blood because his father, César de Vendôme, though illegitimate, was an acknowledged royal bastard. After the death of Louis XIII, the popular Beaufort expected to be a leading member of the Regent's Court, but when his rivalry with Mazarin came to a head the queen sided with the cardinal, and Beaufort was imprisoned in the royal Château de Vincennes. After his dramatic escape from Vincennes in 1648, he cast his lot with the Fronde, but rejoined the Court in 1653 after the Fronde sputtered out, and thereafter behaved as a loyal subject of Louis XIV.

BERNOUIN: *Monsieur Bernouin* or *Barnouin*. Little is known about Mazarin's premier *valet de chambre* Bernouin, except that he may have been a Provençal who came north to Paris with his master when Mazarin became a protégé of Richelieu's.

BRAGELONNE: *Raoul, Vicomte de Bragelonne*. The young viscount is almost entirely Dumas's invention, based solely on a single reference in Madame de La Fayette's memoir of *Henriette d'Angleterre,* which mentions that in Louise de La Vallière's youth in Blois she had once loved a young man named Bragelonne. Raoul's relationship with Louise—and her relationship with King Louis XIV—will be central to all the volumes of the Musketeers Cycle that follow *Twenty Years After.*

BROUSSEL: *Councilor Pierre Broussel* (1575?–1654). A popular and influential councilor in the *Parlement de Paris* during the Fronde, Broussel was a persistent voice opposed to the steep rise in royal taxes, leading to his arrest on Mazarin's orders on August 26, 1648, an act that precipitated the Day of the Barricades. Released two days later, he was hailed as a hero by the Parisians, and continued to lead the anti-Mazarin faction in parliament as long as the Fronde continued. He was a canny politician, and if Dumas portrays him as a bit of a fool, this was probably due to Broussel's depiction in the memoirs of his rival Cardinal de Retz (the former coadjutor), who called him "senile."

Cardinal see MAZARIN or RICHELIEU

CHARLES I: *Charles Stuart, King Charles I of England* (1600–1649). Charles was a complex man who led an eventful life, not easily summarized. Born in Scotland, his father inherited the throne of England in 1603, and thereafter Charles was raised as an Englishman. But he wasn't trained to wear the crown, as he had an elder brother, Prince Henry, who was the heir to King James. When Charles was twelve Henry unexpectedly died, and suddenly Charles was the heir. He came under the influence of a royal favorite, the first Duke of Buckingham, who was an appalling role model, arrogant and authoritarian. By the time Charles assumed the throne in 1625 he was determined to rule by divine right, an attractive program to a monarch who just wasn't very good at politics. He was almost immediately married to the sister of Louis XIII, Princess Henriette of France, a controversial match because of her ardent Catholicism. It was a stormy marriage at first, but after Buckingham was assassinated in 1628 Charles seems to have reassigned his affections to his wife, who thereafter bore him nine children. Charles's preference for direct rule led him into protracted conflict with the English Parliament, which led to open warfare in 1642. The king was detained or placed under arrest several times, the last in November 1648; he was tried in January 1649 in London under Cromwell's military control, and beheaded on January 30. For the purposes of his story Dumas depicts Charles as noble and sympathetic, even sentimental, but this is a grave oversimplification.

CHAVIGNY: *Leon Le Bouthillier, Comte de Chavigny* (1608–1652). Like Mazarin a protégé of Richelieu, and a minister of state for foreign diplomacy late in the reign of Louis XIII. When Louis died Chavigny, like Mazarin, continued as a member of the King's Council under the regency of Queen Anne. Chavigny and Mazarin were rivals on the council, but Chavigny was outmaneuvered by the cardinal and forced out, though he retained his role as the governor of the Royal Château of Vincennes. Loyal to the Court during the first half of the Fronde, he later allied himself with the Prince de Condé and was himself arrested on the orders of Cardinal Mazarin.

CHEVREUSE: *Marie-Aimée de Rohan-Montbazon, Duchesse de Chevreuse, "Marie Michon"* (1600–79). One of the most remarkable French women in a century that abounded in remarkable French women, Marie de Rohan was a vector of chaos who challenged every social convention of her time with wit, cheer, charm, and unshakable self-confidence. Throughout the reign of Louis XIII, she was a steadfast friend and ally to Anne of Austria when the queen had few of either. Brilliant, beautiful, free-spirited, mischievous, adored, and adorable, she had a long list of lovers on both sides of the English Channel, many of whom ended up dead or in prison thanks to her habit of involving them in plots and conspiracies against the French Crown. She first came to prominence in 1617 when she married Albert de Luynes, Louis's former falconer and first favorite; when Luynes fell from favor in 1621 and almost immediately died, Marie avoided obscurity by marrying the Duc de Chevreuse, a wealthy Lorraine noble and perennial ornament of the French Court. Marie and her second husband had what nowadays would be called an "open marriage," leaving Madame de Chevreuse free to pursue her own interests, which were romance and treason in equal measure, mixing the two whenever possible. She was involved in every notable conspiracy of the reign of Louis XIII, was an inveterate enemy of Cardinal Richelieu, continued to make trouble for his successor Cardinal Mazarin during the Fronde, and will continue to play a prominent part in the rest of Dumas's Musketeers Cycle.

COADJUTOR: *Jean-François Paul de Gondy* or *Gondi, Bishop Coadjutor of Paris* (and later *Cardinal de Retz*) (1613–1679). The Gondis were a family of Florentine bankers who were introduced to France in 1573 by Queen Catherine de Médicis and had quickly associated themselves with the high nobility. As a third son Jean-François was destined for the military, but the death of his elder brother meant he had to change his uniform for a cassock and go into the Church to maintain the family's hold on their clerical appanages, which included part of the Bishopric of Paris. A thorough Parisian, Gondy was educated at the Sorbonne and tutored in religion by St. Vincent de Paul. During the reign of Louis XIII, he was ambitious for appointment to the position of Bishop Coadjutor of Paris, but in his youth he had written some political essays with republican leanings that probably caused Cardinal Richelieu to suppress his advancement. After Louis XIII died, Queen Anne finally granted him the appointment; he immediately began currying favor with the citizens of Paris, speaking up on their behalf when it seemed in his interest to do so, and when the Fronde broke out in 1648 he seized the opportunity to put himself at its forefront. During the chaotic ending of the civil war in 1652 he was finally awarded a cardinal's hat, but then arrested shortly thereafter and imprisoned for two years before he escaped and left the country. In 1662 the young Louis XIV restored him to favor; he returned to France, where he was active in Church politics and diplomacy, and once more took up writing. His lively but not entirely dependable memoirs, which had been reprinted in France in 1837, were one of Dumas's primary sources. They're a good read, even today: Retz was nearly as snarky and caustic as his great rival La Rochefoucald (see Marcillac below).

COMMINGES: *Gaston-Jean-Baptiste, Comte de Comminges, lieutenant* (later *captain*) *of the Queen's Guard* (1613–1670). Comminges was brought up at Court, and served in the Queen's Guard under his uncle, the Sieur de Guitaut (see below), eventually replacing him upon his retirement. He was far more loyal to Mazarin than Dumas makes out: Comminges arrested the Duc de Beaufort in 1643, and was named a Marshal of France in 1649 and Lieutenant-General of the King's Armies just two years after that. The wars over, he was appointed French Ambassador to England after the Restoration of Charles II, serving in London from 1662–1665.

CONDÉ: *Louis de Bourbon, Prince de Condé, "Monsieur le Prince," later "The Grand Condé"* (1621–1686). One of the most celebrated military commanders of his time, when he was still the Duc d'Enghien he won two signature victories in the long war against Spain, those of Rocroi in 1643 and Nordlingen in 1644. Upon the death of his father in 1646 Louis became Prince de Condé, First Prince of the Blood and third in line for the throne, but he continued his role as France's leading general, further cementing his military reputation with the victory at Lens in 1648. This was followed by his successful leadership of the royal troops in the first half of the Fronde, when he commanded at the Battle of Charenton. After that he appeared to resent deferring to Cardinal Mazarin, and in 1650 seemed to be preparing to claim a broader role in the government, possibly even the regency, when Mazarin had Condé, his brother Conti, and his sister the Duchesse de Longueville arrested, which triggered the Second Fronde. In the confusion that followed, Anne was forced to release Condé and his siblings, but Monsieur le Prince was now her sworn enemy, and after the Fronde ended he actually left France to fight for Spain. After the long Franco-Spanish war finally ended in 1659, Condé was rehabilitated by Louis XIV and welcomed back to France, where he served with distinction until his death.

CONTI: *Armand de Bourbon, Prince de Conti* (1629–1666). Younger brother of the Prince de Condé and the Duchesse de Longueville, the completely inexperienced Conti was named a leader of the Parisian forces in early 1649 solely because he was the ranking Prince of the Blood among the princes and peers supporting the Fronde. During the Second Fronde he was briefly imprisoned by Mazarin along with his siblings, but Conti was more interested in religion than politics, and after the end of the Fronde he was reconciled with Cardinal Mazarin and ended up marrying one of his nieces.

CROMWELL: *Oliver Cromwell, Lord Protector of the Commonwealth* (1599–1658). A towering and divisive figure whose character and deeds are still controversial, Cromwell was a Puritan and member of Parliament who rose to prominence as a commander of the parliamentary forces against King Charles's supporters early in the English Civil War. He gradually emerged as both a political and military leader, and used the power of his loyal soldiery to enforce the purge of parliament that enabled the trial and execution of the king. Dumas depicts Cromwell as a calculating mastermind in the mold of Richelieu and Mazarin, but his success was probably due more to relentless determination and force of will than to wits and cunning. As Lord Protector he ruled England, Ireland, and Scotland for almost ten years, brutally crushing all opposition. He died of natural causes in 1658, and the Restoration of the monarchy came two (eventful) years later—as we'll see in *Between Two Kings*, later in the Musketeers Cycle.

D'ARTAGNAN: *Charles de Batz de Castelmore, Chevalier (later Comte) d'Artagnan* (c. 1611–1673). The historical d'Artagnan was a cadet (younger son) of a family of the minor nobility from the town of Lupiac in Gascony. Like so many other younger sons of Gascony, he followed his neighbor Monsieur de Tréville to Paris to make his fortune, and by 1633 was in the King's Musketeers at a time when Tréville was a lieutenant. D'Artagnan spent the rest of his life in the musketeers, except for the periods when the company was briefly disbanded and he soldiered with the Gardes Françaises. He gradually rose through the ranks until he became captain-lieutenant (in effect, captain) of the musketeers in 1667. During the Franco-Dutch War of 1673 he was killed at the Battle of Maastricht. Dumas, of course, borrowed d'Artagnan from Courtilz de Sandras's highly fictionalized biography, *The Memoirs of Monsieur d'Artagnan,* but his personality and character in the novels of the Musketeers Cycle are entirely the product of the genius of Dumas.

D'Orléans see GASTON

GASTON: *Prince Gaston de Bourbon, Duc d'Orléans, "Monsieur"* (1608–1660). Younger brother to Louis XIII and first heir to the throne, favorite son of Marie de Médicis, Gaston seems to have had no redeeming characteristics whatsoever. Proud, greedy, ambitious for the throne but an arrant coward, he was the figurehead in one conspiracy after another against the king and cardinal. These plots failed every time, after which Gaston invariably betrayed his co-conspirators in return for immunity from consequences—because as the healthy heir to a chronically unhealthy king, he knew his life was sacrosanct.

Gondy see COADJUTOR

GRAMMONT: *Antoine III, Duc de Gramont* or *Grammont, Marshal of France* (1604–1678). In 1640, when he was still just the Comte de Guiche, Antoine was the arrogant and lecherous villain we see in Rostand's *Cyrano de Bergerac.* A capable military commander, he was made a marshal in 1641, and for his victories—and because he was married to one of Richelieu's nieces—he was elevated to the peerage and became Duc de Gramont in 1643. He served Louis XIV as a diplomat.

GUICHE: *Guy Armand de Gramont, Comte de Guiche* (1637–1673). Armand de Guiche, son of the Duc de Gramont, was one of the leading playboys of the Court of Louis XIV; as Raoul de Bragelonne's closest friend, we'll be seeing a lot more of him in the subsequent volumes in the Musketeers Cycle. He was only eleven to thirteen years old during the Fronde, and his depiction in *Twenty Years After* is entirely fictional.

GUITAUT: *François de Pechpeyroux de Comminges, Sieur de Guitaut, captain of the Queen's Guards* (1581–1663). Guitaut, a crusty old relic of the Wars of Religion, was famously loyal to Anne of Austria, and served her for decades.

HENRI IV: *Henri de Bourbon of Navarre, King Henri IV, "Henri the Great"* (1553–1610). A complex and towering figure, a warrior king and at the same time a beloved man of the people, Henri IV ended the Wars of Religion, united France, and made it one of the great powers of Europe.

HENRIETTE: *Henriette Marie de Bourbon, Queen of England* (1609–1669). Daughter of Henri IV and sister of Louis XIII, Henriette was married by proxy to England's Charles I shortly after he assumed the throne in 1625. Haughty, entitled, and fiercely Catholic when to be Catholic in England was a major liability, Henriette's relationship with Charles was stormy at first, but eventually they proved to be well matched, and she bore him nine children. (The youngest, named after her mother, this editor has chosen to call *Henrietta* to differentiate the two.) During the English Civil War she was forced to flee to France, where she lived in poverty until the Restoration.

Herblay see ARAMIS

King see CHARLES I or LOUIS XIII or LOUIS XIV

La Fère see ATHOS

LA PORTE: *Pierre de La Porte, Cloak-Bearer to the Queen* (1603–1680). La Porte entered Queen Anne's service in 1621 and became one of her most trusted confidential servants, assisting the queen in her petty intrigues and conducting her correspondence with the Duchesse de Chevreuse. Richelieu finally had him thrown in prison in 1637, though he was freed in 1643 after both king and cardinal had died. The 1839 edition of La Porte's *Memoirs* was one of Dumas's primary sources. La Porte will reappear in an important (albeit nonhistorical) role in the final book in the Musketeers Cycle, *The Man in the Iron Mask*.

LA RAMÉE: *Jacques-Chrysostome La Ramée, Deputy Governor of Vincennes.* Contemporary accounts of the escape of the Duc de Beaufort from the Château de Vincennes mention that his primary guard was an Exempt (royal officer) named La Ramée, but that's all we know. Everything else in the novel about him, including his first names, is an invention of Dumas.

LA VALLIÈRE: *Françoise-Louise de la Baume Le Blanc de La Vallière* (1644–1710). Louise de La Vallière was raised in Blois at the court of Prince Gaston, and after coming to Versailles in 1661 became the first long-term mistress of King Louis XIV. Louise is introduced in *Twenty Years After* to set up the love triangle between Louise, Raoul de Bragelonne, and the king that is one of the major plot elements of the succeeding volumes of the Musketeers Cycle.

LONGUEVILLE: *Anne-Geneviève de Bourbon Condé, Duchesse de Longueville* (1619–1679). Though mostly offstage in *Twenty Years After,* the sister of the Grand Condé was a key player in the politics of the Fronde, and one of Mazarin's most determined foes. A child of rebellion, she was born in the dungeon at Vincennes during the imprisonment of her parents, the elder Prince de Condé and Charlotte de Montmorency, who'd been jailed by Queen Marie de Médicis for opposition to her regency during the youth of Louis XIII. Lively, witty, and beautiful, she was an ornament of the salons of Madame de Rambouillet in the 1630s, until she was married in 1642 to the Duc de Longueville, a widower twice her age. It was not a happy marriage, and she turned her energy to love affairs and politics. A friend and ally of Coadjutor de Gondy, she threw herself into the turmoil of the First Fronde, attracting to the cause her younger brother de Conti and even her husband, though she was conducting an open affair at the time with another noble Frondeur, the Prince de Marcillac (see below). After the Parisian Frondeurs were defeated militarily by her other brother, the Prince de Condé, she persuaded him to conspire against Mazarin, and in 1650 he had all three siblings jailed in the prison where Madame de Longueville was born. After the

Fronde came to a messy end, she retired from public life and devoted herself to religion, becoming an important patron of the Jansenist movement.

LOUIS XIII: *King Louis XIII, His Most Christian Majesty of France, "Louis the Just"* (1601–43). Dumas wrote a great deal about Louis XIII and his reign, most of it quite accurate, in part thanks to the research of his assistant Auguste Maquet. Dumas had a good grasp of the melancholy king's character and portrayed it well, especially in the previous book in the Musketeers Cycle, *The Red Sphinx.*

LOUIS XIV: *Louis de Bourbon, King of France* (1638–1715): The only Frenchman of his century more important than Richelieu, the Sun King consolidated all power in France under royal control, thus ending centuries of civil strife, but creating a political structure so rigid it made the French Revolution almost inevitable. *Twenty Years After* begins Louis's relationship with d'Artagnan, which will evolve for the rest of the Musketeers Cycle until it achieves resolution in *The Man in the Iron Mask.*

MARCILLAC: *François IV de La Rochefoucauld, Prince de Marcillac or Marsillac,* later *Duc de La Rochefoucauld* (1613–1680). The author of the *Maxims* (1665) was a firebrand in his youth, enticed early into conspiracy against the throne by Madame de Chevreuse, and continued the practice into the Fronde as the lover and co-conspirator of Madame de Longueville. He was seriously wounded twice during actions in the Fronde, first at Lagny in 1649 and then at the battle of the Faubourg Saint-Antoine in 1652, after which he retired from cabals and conspiracies. Though Dumas revered the major French literary figures of the 17th century, his admiration did not extend to the cold and calculating La Rochefoucauld, whose arid cynicism was the polar opposite of Dumas's hearty romanticism.

MAZARIN: *Cardinal Jules Mazarin,* born *Giulio Raimondo Mazzarino or Mazarini* (1602–1661). In 1634 the Italian-born diplomat became a protégé of Cardinal Richelieu and in 1639 was naturalized French and entered the king's service. Through Richelieu's influence he was made a cardinal in 1641 and brought onto the King's Council. After Richelieu and Louis XIII died, Mazarin made himself indispensable to the regent, Anne of Austria, and basically stepped into Richelieu's shoes to become France's prime minister. He was probably intimate with Queen Anne and functioned as her co-ruler until Louis XIV attained his majority. He was an extremely able diplomat, negotiating an end to the Thirty Years' War, maintaining royal authority through the chaotic years of the Fronde, striking an alliance with Cromwell, and maneuvering the fractious French nobility back into compliance with the crown in time to hand an intact and flourishing state over to King Louis XIV. He was widely disliked for being a foreigner and *arriviste* who presumed to place himself above the native nobility, feelings basically endorsed by Dumas, who preferred men of heart to men of mind. We saw the beginning of his career in *The Red Sphinx* and will see the end of it in *Between Two Kings.*

PORTHOS: *Porthos, Baron du Vallon,* based loosely on Isaac de Porthau (1617–1712), as filtered through Courtilz de Sandras's fictionalized *Memoirs of Monsieur d'Artagnan.* Though Sandras had made Porthos the brother of Aramis and Athos, the historical de Porthau was a minor Gascon nobleman who joined his cousins, Captain de Tréville and Armand d'Athos, in the King's Musketeers in 1642. When his father died in 1654 he left the musketeers and returned to Béarn, where he served as a parliamentarian and local magistrate until his death in 1712. His character and personality in the Musketeers novels are entirely the invention of Dumas.

Retz see COADJUTOR

RICHELIEU: *Armand-Jean du Plessis, Cardinal de Richelieu* (1585–1642), Louis XIII's incomparable prime minister. One of the two most important Frenchmen of the 17th century, exceeded only by Louis XIV, Richelieu has been the subject of scores of biographies (including one by Dumas), and his life and works have been analyzed in excruciating detail, starting with his own *Memoirs*. His deeds were momentous, but it was his character and personality that interested Dumas, who loved historical figures who were great but also greatly flawed. After deploying Richelieu in *The Three Musketeers* as the worthy antagonist of his most enduring heroes, Dumas couldn't resist revisiting him as a protagonist for *The Red Sphinx*. Though gone from the Musketeers Cycle after *The Red Sphinx*, Richelieu nonetheless casts a long shadow over the rest of the series, all the way through *The Man in the Iron Mask*.

ROCHEFORT: *Comte Charles-César de Rochefort*. The dangerous intriguer who appears in *The Three Musketeers* and *Twenty Years After* is a composite of two of Courtilz de Sandras's characters, the Comte de Rochefort from the 1689 pseudo-biography *Les Mémoires de M.L.C.D.R.* (1689), where M.L.C.D.R. stands for Monsieur le Comte de Rochefort, and the villain Rosnay from *The Memoirs of Monsieur d'Artagnan*, the result then brought to vivid life by Dumas. It's difficult to identify Dumas's amoral adventurer with a single historical figure; for one thing, *Rochefort* is a common place-name in France, and a Comte de Rochefort could have come from any of several noble French families. The agent of Richelieu in Sandras's story has been speculated to be from the Rocheforts of Saint-Point in Burgundy, and might have been based on Claude de Rochefort d'Ailly, Comte de Saint-Point, who was active in the first half of the 17th century. Another nominee is Henri-Louis d'Aloigny, Marquis de Rochefort (born 1625), who was one of the lieutenants of Marshal Turenne. At this remove, it seems impossible to be sure who he was.

SCARRON: *Abbé Paul Scarron* (1610–1660). A prolific author, renowned for his wit, Scarron was a Man of the Robe (his father was a member of the Parlement of Paris) who spent the early part of his life in Le Mans. In his late twenties he was stricken with a painful wasting disease, most likely polio, and spent the rest of his life in a wheelchair. He moved to Paris in 1640 and established himself as a presence among the *literati*. During the Fronde he wrote essays opposing Mazarin, but other than cutting off his pension there wasn't much revenge the cardinal could take on an invalid. In 1652 Scarron married the brilliant and beautiful Françoise d'Aubigné, who in later years, as the widow Madame de Maintenon, became Louis XIV's final mistress and secret second wife.

TREMBLAY: *Charles Le Clerc, Marquis du Tremblay, Governor of the Bastille* (1584–1671). Charles du Tremblay was the brother of François du Tremblay, known better under the name Father Joseph, the confidant and spymaster of Cardinal Richelieu, and Charles owed his appointment as governor of the Bastille to this connection. He was relieved of the position when the Parlement of Paris took control of the fortress in 1649, and thereafter retired.

TRÉVILLE: *Jean-Arnaud de Peyrer, Comte de Troisville* or *Tréville, Captain of the King's Musketeers* (1598–1672). The archetypal poor Gascon who came to Paris to find success by joining the King's Musketeers, he worked his way up through the ranks, finally becoming captain-lieutenant in 1634. He was certainly present at both the Siege of La Rochelle, depicted in *The Three Musketeers,* and the Battle of Susa Pass recounted in *The Red Sphinx.* He was associated with (but not complicit in) the Cinq-Mars conspiracy of 1642 and was briefly exiled, and then restored to favor when Queen Anne assumed the regency. She elevated him to the rank of count in 1643, but he didn't get along with Mazarin, who forced his retirement in 1646 by temporarily disbanding his company of musketeers. He was reconciled to the Court in the 1660s, possibly due to the influence of the historical d'Artagnan with the young Louis XIV.

Vallon see PORTHOS

Notes on the Text of *Twenty Years After*

1. **THE PALAIS CARDINAL, OR PALAIS ROYAL:** As early as 1629, Louis XIII's prime minister Cardinal Richelieu began planning a grand palace on Rue Saint-Honoré not far from the Louvre. Construction on the Palais Cardinal started in 1633 and was completed in 1639. When Richelieu died in 1642 he willed his Paris residence to the king, and it was renamed the Palais Royal. Upon the death of Louis XIII, Queen Anne moved her family—including Cardinal Mazarin—from the Louvre into the more modern Palais Royal.

2. **ASSASSINATED AND DISMEMBERED CONCINI:** Concino Concini, Maréchal d'Ancre (1575–1617), was a handsome Italian courtier who was a favorite of Queen Marie de Médicis. During Marie's regency after her husband King Henri IV was assassinated, the arrogant Concini was showered with posts and preferment; he lorded it over the French nobility, and they cordially hated him for it, no one more than the youthful King Louis XIII. Luynes, the young king's favorite, engineered Louis's rise to power (and his own) when he orchestrated Concini's public assassination in 1617.

3. **THE EARL OF ESSEX:** Robert Devereux, Second Earl of Essex (1565–1601), was a favorite of Queen Elizabeth I and was rumored to have had a romantic relationship with her. Ambitious and dissatisfied with taking second place, he staged an abortive coup and was executed.

4. **RING CONSECRATED BY A VOW IN THE PALAIS ROYAL CHAPEL:** It was widely rumored that Queen Anne and Cardinal Mazarin had been secretly married in a private service, but there is no solid historical confirmation of this.

5. **PARLIAMENT:** Unlike in England, where the Parliament was a house of representative legislators, in France the *parlements* were deliberative bodies of magistrates and legal officials, the so-called Men of the Robe, whose positions were largely passed down from one generation of attorneys to the next. Local parliaments ratified decrees and ordinances, settled legal conflicts, and decided issues of boundaries and privilege. The Parliament of Paris, because it ratified royal decrees that affected the entire realm, was the most important of these bodies, and the *présidents* of the Parisian Parliament considered themselves on par with the *Grands* of the nobility. (The nobility disagreed.)

6. **PRESIDENT BLANCMESNIL:** René Potier de Blancmesnil (?–1680) was one of the senior *présidents* in the Grand Chamber of the Paris Parliament, and a frequent ally of Broussel during the Fronde.

7. BARRIÈRE DES SERGENTS, THE QUINZE-VINGTS, AND THE BUTTE SAINT-ROCH: Three strategic checkpoints in the streets around the Palais Royal, extending west along Rue Saint-Honoré.

8. SWISS GUARDS: From the Renaissance onward, Swiss mercenaries served as royal guards in a number of European courts, most notably France and Spain. The *Cents Suisse*, or Hundred Swiss, were guards at the Louvre and other royal palaces such as Fontainebleau; in wartime entire regiments of mercenaries were raised from the cantons of Switzerland.

9. KING'S MUSKETEERS: A company—later two—of elite soldiers, the musketeers were the personal guard of King Louis XIII and after him Louis XIV. They were founded in 1622 when a carbine-armed company of light horsemen was upgraded and given the new, heavier matchlock muskets as primary arms. Though their function was mainly ceremonial and to serve as royal bodyguards, they were sometimes deployed on the battlefield, where they fought either mounted as cavalry, or dismounted and relying on their muskets. They are often depicted wearing their signature blue tabards with white crosses, which were adopted sometime in the 1630s. At the time of *Twenty Years After,* the King's Musketeers had been temporarily disbanded by Mazarin in favor of guard companies loyal to the cardinal rather than to Tréville (see Dramatis Personae), but that didn't suit d'Artagnan's character arc, so Dumas conveniently ignored the fact.

10. TRÉVILLE'S: Jean-Arnaud de Peyrer, Comte de Troisville or Tréville (1598–1672) was captain-lieutenant of the King's Musketeers from 1634 to 1646, but had been forcibly retired by Mazarin when the cardinal temporarily disbanded the elite company.

11. THE MUSKETEERS ARE BETTER SOLDIERS THAN THE GUARDS: This continues the theme of rivalry between elite guard units established in *The Three Musketeers,* with its clashes between the Cardinal's Guards and the King's Musketeers. In 1648 the elite units guarding the royal family were selected companies of the *Gardes Françaises* plus the company of Cardinal's Guards, which Mazarin had inherited from Richelieu.

12. THE CATHOLIC LEAGUE: In the previous century, during the French Wars of Religion (roughly 1562–1598), the hardline Catholic members of the nobility, who wanted to crush the Protestant (or Huguenot) faction, were often held in check by the more moderate Catholics, the *Politiques*, who were usually allied to the then-current Valois king. In 1576 a powerful and ambitious Catholic peer, Henri I, Duc de Guise, founded the Catholic League to organize opposition to the Huguenots and to King Henri III, who was regarded as too conciliatory toward the Protestants. The League was heavily

armed, and more than a few battles were fought before Henri III had the Duc de Guise assassinated in 1588.

13. A DUC DE GUISE: See note 12. Henri I, Duc de Guise (1550–1588) was a powerful and ambitious Catholic *Grand* charismatic and canny enough to rouse and organize other nobles to the anti-Protestant cause.

14. FRONDE: A number of social and political conflicts combined in France to cause the messy and intermittent revolution of the Fronde from 1648 to 1652. King Louis XIV, still in his minority, was too young to rule, and the realm was ruled by a queen regent and her foreign-born prime minister, a leadership regarded as weak by the opportunistic *Grands* of the high nobility. Worse, the country was locked in a seemingly endless war with Spain, an existential conflict that was ruinously expensive, so much so that taxes had more than doubled in the decade leading up to the Fronde. This ever-increasing tax burden had alienated the country's business interests and infuriated the commoners and peasantry, upon whom the burden fell (nobles were exempt). The people were outraged at the excesses of the royal "tax farmers" who collected the imposts, and were (rightfully) regarded as enriching themselves at the expense of both citizens and the monarchy. The King's Council, at Mazarin's behest, had also alienated the parliaments, the Men of the Robe of the legal profession, by creating and selling scores of new judicial positions that added to the treasury but diluted the value of the existing offices. In protest, treasurers stopped collecting taxes, parliaments refused to ratify decrees, and councilors and attorneys—the sinews of government—began taking up the cause of the troubles of ordinary citizens. Incidents of resistance to authority occurred in several major cities, but the center of unrest was Paris, where the neighborhood militias, organized to maintain order, instead became the instruments of rebellion. *Twenty Years After* is set during the so-called First or Parliamentary Fronde of 1648–49, a conflict resolved, albeit temporarily, when the Court and parliament came to terms after a year of struggle.

15. HÔTEL DE RAMBOUILLET: The Marquise de Rambouillet's literary and society salons at the Hôtel de Rambouillet are justly celebrated as the crucible of modern French art and manners. Her kindness and generosity were boundless, especially to penniless writers, and in a society in which character assassination was a spectator sport, no one ever had a bad word to say about her. It is not too much to say that, by respecting French artists, she made French art respectable.

16. AT THE SIEGE OF LA ROCHELLE, AT SUSA PASS, AT PERPIGNAN: D'Artagnan's exploits at the Siege of La Rochelle are detailed in the second half of *The Three Musketeers*, and the

forcing of Susa Pass forms part of the climax of *The Red Sphinx*. At Perpignan in 1642, after a protracted siege, French forces supporting Catalan rebels drove out a veteran Spanish force, winning the province of Roussillon to France.

17. THE BASTILLE: This hulking fortress, built at the eastern entrance to Paris during the 14th century to protect the city during the Hundred Years' War, served a second function as a royal prison starting early in the 15th century. Its eight cylindrical towers, connected by tall curtain walls, housed prisoners of all ranks in lodgings befitting their differing social conditions. Many prisoners who disappeared into the Bastille were never seen again.

18. FATHER JOSEPH: François Leclerc du Tremblay, known as Father Joseph (1577–1638), Capuchin monk, Christian mystic, politician, diplomat, and Richelieu's spymaster, was one of the most fascinating men of his age. The phrase *eminence grise,* for a shadowy adviser, derives from his role: he was the Gray Eminence to the cardinal's Red Eminence.

19. MARSHAL BASSOMPIERRE: Maréchal François de Bassompierre (1579–1646) was a gentleman of Lorraine, a suave and adaptable chevalier successively a favorite of Henri IV, Queen Regent Marie de Médicis, and Louis XIII, and one of the leading ornaments of their Courts—especially by his own estimation. His lively memoirs of the period are among Dumas's primary sources.

20. CLOAK-SNATCHING ON THE PONT NEUF: Dumas found this incident in Courtilz de Sandras's *Mémoires de M.L.C.D.R.,* his pseudo-memoir of the Comte de Rochefort. Parisian cloak-snatchers, known as *tire-laines,* were a sort of mugger who specialized in seizing nobles' expensive cloaks and running off with them. At several points in medieval and early modern times, this practice was indulged in as a prank by drunken young gentry.

21. KING HENRI'S BRONZE HORSE: The Pont Neuf crosses the western, downstream end of the Île de la Cité, and on the very point of the island, halfway across the bridge, is a small square dominated by a tall pedestal atop which is an equestrian statue of King Henri IV. Destroyed in 1792 during the French Revolution, it was restored in 1818 after the Bourbon restoration, and you can see it there today.

22. WHEN I MET YOU AT MEUNG: In the very first chapter of *The Three Musketeers*.

23. PLANCHET: Like his counterparts who serve the three musketeers, d'Artagnan's doughty lackey appears throughout the novels of the Musketeers Cycle, eventually becoming less servant to the Gascon than friend and partner.

24. THE SEVENTEEN SEIGNEURS: A group of Louis XIII's high-ranking Court cronies, who, late in his reign, adopted this pompous sobriquet for themselves.

25. A SECRET PASSAGE: Secret passages are a staple of the swashbuckling genre, and Dumas was as responsible for this as anyone: they show up in *The Three Musketeers* and *The Red Sphinx*, in several places in this novel, and recur most famously in *The Man in the Iron Mask.*

26. QUINTE CURCE'S *HISTORY OF ALEXANDER*: Curce's *History of Alexander the Great* first appeared in 1639, and though we don't know if the young Louis XIV read it, we certainly know that it was the sort of thing he *would* read: the boy king was fascinated by military history.

27. THE OPERA *THISBE*: This most likely refers to Théophile de Viau's *Les Amours Tragiques de Pyrame et de Thisbé,* first performed at Court in 1621 and at the Hôtel de Bourgogne thereafter, though it was a court ballet rather than an opera. There's no record of an opera titled *Thisbe* before Leveridge's *The Comickal Masque of Pyramus and Thisbe* in 1716, itself based on the play-within-a-play in Shakespeare's *A Midsummer Night's Dream.*

28. QUEEN MARIE DE MÉDICIS: The Italian heiress Marie de Médicis (1575–1642) was the second queen to France's King Henri IV, who married her in 1600 in a desperate quest for an heir after the infertile Queen Marguerite was set aside. A nasty piece of work, Marie inherited all the ambition, pride, greed, and ruthlessness of the Medici, but none of their brains or finesse. However, she did give King Henri the royal heirs he wanted. The plot of *The Red Sphinx* turns, in part, on the question of her complicity in the assassination of King Henri IV.

29. MADAME DE GUÉMÉNÉE: Anne de Rohan, Princesse de Guéménée (1604–1685) was sister-in-law to Madame de Chevreuse, and while she didn't have her relative's taste for politics, she was a thorough connoisseur of romantic intrigue.

30. WHO LOVED ONE OF MY WOMEN: A reference to Constance Bonacieux, the queen's onetime linen maid who served, in *The Three Musketeers,* as her go-between with the Duke of Buckingham. Constance and d'Artagnan shared romantic adventures and fell in love, an affair that ended in tragedy.

31. THE ASSASSIN OF CHALAIS, OF MONTMORENCY, AND OF CINQ-MARS: Three French nobles, all of whom went to the execution block for supporting Prince Gaston in conspiracies against the throne. The rebellion and capture of the Duc de Montmorency is central to *The Dove,* the final section of *The Red Sphinx.*

32. MONSIEUR DES ESSARTS: François de Guillon, Sieur des Essarts (?–1645) was a captain of a Royal Guards regiment, and d'Artagnan's commander before he joined the King's Musketeers.

33. PISTOLES: *Pistole* was a French word for a gold coin of the 16th and 17th centuries, usually Spanish in origin. The leading European states liked to mint their own coins, but gold was hard for them to come by—except for Spain, which flooded Europe with gold from its possessions in the New World, making the Spanish escudo the de facto base currency of European trade for two centuries. When Dumas's characters refer to pistoles, they are mostly Spanish escudos. One pistole is worth about ten livres or three French crowns (écus).

34. RUE TIQUETONNE: A street in the middle-class neighborhood of the Rue de Montorgueil north of Les Halles, it had just changed its spelling in 1647 from Rue Quiquetonne, which had been named after the establishment of a prosperous 13th-century baker.

35. THE CAMPAIGN IN FRANCHE-COMTÉ: Dumas embroiders; there was no campaign in the eastern province of Franche-Comté until Louis XIV wrested it from the Spanish in 1668.

36. CEMETERY OF THE INNOCENTS: The oldest and largest municipal cemetery in the capital, in central Paris off the Rue Saint-Denis on the Right Bank, dated back to medieval times, but the walled compound was no bigger than a large city block.

37. THE FIRST A *GRAND SEIGNEUR* . . . THE SECOND A SOLDIER . . . AND THE THIRD A REFINED ABBOT: In the French nobility, if a family had multiple sons, this order of careers was their usual destiny: the eldest would inherit the title and estate, the second joined the military, and the third entered the clergy. Many a melodrama begins with a son who isn't satisfied with his predestined fate.

38. SIEGE OF BESANÇON: More embroidery: Besançon, the capital of Franche-Comté, wasn't besieged until 1668 (see note 35).

39. THAT THESIS HE DISCUSSED SO EARNESTLY AT CRÈVECŒUR WITH THE CURATE OF MONTDIDIER AND THE SUPERIOR OF JESUITS: In Chapter XXVI of *The Three Musketeers,* "The Thesis of Aramis."

40. BAZIN: Just as the scheming Aramis is the least sympathetic of the musketeers, his servant, the pompous and selfish Bazin, is the least likable of the lackeys, mainly serving as a butt for Dumas's jokes about churchmen.

41. BATON THAT CONDÉ THREW—OR DIDN'T THROW—INTO THE ENEMY'S LINES AT THE BATTLE OF FRIBOURG: According to popular tradition, at the Battle of Fribourg (1644) the young Duc d'Enghien, not yet the Prince de Condé, threw his marshal's baton into the ranks of the enemy to induce his soldiers to charge and recover it.

42. HIPPOCRAS: A drink made by mulling wine with sugar and spices, a process that took at least twenty minutes.

43. HE WENT TO NOISY: Dumas later makes it clear that he means the town of Noisy-le-Sec, a few miles northeast of Paris. However, he has confused it with Noisy-le-Roi, the town southwest of Paris where Cardinal de Gondy had a château that became a gathering place for Frondeurs.

44. AN AFFAIR WITH COLIGNY: Madame de Longueville's affair with the Comte de Coligny led to his celebrated duel with the Duc de Guise in the Place Royale on December 12, 1643—a duel referred to several times in *Twenty Years After* due to Aramis's relationship with the duchess. Coligny was badly wounded, and died of his injuries.

45. LAFOLLONE: Père Mulot de Lafollone, one of Cardinal Richelieu's cronies, famous for his appetite. He appears in Chapter XXVI of *The Red Sphinx*.

46. *PAS DE DEUX*: Dumas's title for this chapter was "The Two Gaspards" ("*Les Deux Gaspards*"), a reference to the popular 1817 play of the same name, in which two con men, Gaspard l'Avisé and Gaspard Simplet, banter humorously while trying to cheat each other at cards. This pop culture reference would have made sense to Dumas's Parisian readers in 1845 but is lost on 21st-century Anglophones like us. Not coincidentally, *gaspard* was also Parisian street argot for a rat or weasel—but titling this chapter "The Two Weasels" just seemed a bit too disrespectful to our dashing musketeers.

47. MONSIEUR VOITURE: Vincent Voiture (1597–1648) was the most popular poet among the habitués of the Hôtel de Rambouillet, a favorite of the ladies and an intimate crony of Prince Gaston. Voiture was arguably more successful as a courtier than he was as a versifier; a master of sly innuendo and the poetic in-joke, he knew just how far he could go in lampooning his patrons among the Great Nobles.

48. MONSIEUR DE BOIS-ROBERT: François Le Métel de Boisrobert or Bois-Robert (1592–1662) was one of Cardinal Richelieu's famous Five Poets. A diligent aide in all Richelieu's literary pursuits, he was the prime mover in the founding of the Académie Française. After Richelieu's death he attempted to transfer his loyalty to Mazarin, but the minister didn't care for him.

49. MARQUIS DE CARABAS: The fictional nobleman whose name Puss uses with abandon in Charles Perrault's fairy tale "Puss in Boots," which wouldn't be published until 1697.

50. MADAME DE MOTTEVILLE: Françoise Bertaut, Madame de Motteville (1621–1689), longtime maid of honor to Anne of Austria, wrote several volumes of memoirs after the queen's death in 1666, which were republished in 1823 and 1838; they were among Dumas's primary sources about internal affairs at the French Court.

51. MADAME DE FARGIS: Madeleine de Silly, Madame de Fargis (?–1639), was sponsored by Richelieu to join Queen Anne's household to replace the Duchesse de Chevreuse when the latter was temporarily exiled after the scandalous affair in the garden of Amiens. Smart, talented, irreverent, and mischievous, Fargis quickly gained Anne's trust and transferred her loyalty from the cardinal to the queen.

52. MOUSQUETON: As related in *The Three Musketeers,* the birth name of Porthos's Norman lackey was Boniface, but his master renamed him with the more martial French word for musketoon, a large-caliber musket cut down to the length of a carbine. Further on in the story he will be renamed again, this time at his own behest.

53. BACK TO PHARAMOND, OR CHARLEMAGNE, OR AT WORST HUGUES CAPET: In other words, bloodlines that go back to France's earliest rulers: Pharamond in the 5th century, Charlemagne in the 8th, and Hugues Capet in the 10th.

54. NO PESKY JUSSACS: In *The Three Musketeers,* Claude de Jussac (1620–1690) was an officer in the Cardinal's Guard with a penchant for meddling in the musketeers' business.

55. DUEL WITH THE ENGLISH AT THE LUXEMBOURG: This refers to an incident in Chapter XXXI of *The Three Musketeers* in which the four comrades fought a duel against Lord Winter and three other Englishmen. In Dumas's original manuscript this line erroneously places the duel at the *enclose de Carmes,* confusing it with the duel with the Cardinal's Guards in Chapter V.

56. GRIMAUD: Like the other lackeys, Athos's servant Grimaud appears throughout the Musketeers Cycle, and eventually one gets the impression that this stoic but caring and utterly reliable man is Dumas's favorite of the four.

57. BLOIS: Old medieval city on the Loire River about 120 miles southwest of Paris. The large Château de Blois was a royal castle occupied by Prince Gaston from about 1620 until his death in 1660.

58. CHAMBORD: The largest château in the Loire valley, built for King François I early in the 16th century as a hunting estate. Still stunning today, it's one of the finest examples of French Renaissance architecture.

59. RAOUL: Athos's son Raoul, the Vicomte de Bragelonne, who at this point is not yet aware that the Comte de La Fère is his father, is an invention of Dumas, based on a single reference to a young man whom Louis de La Vallière loved in her early youth. Raoul, who embodies all of Athos's noble virtues, even those unsuited to a less chivalric age, will be a major character throughout the rest of the novels of the Musketeers Cycle.

60. DUCHESSE D'ORLÉANS: Marguerite of Lorraine, Duchesse d'Orléans (1615–1672) was the second wife of Prince Gaston, who secretly married her in 1632 against the wishes of his brother Louis XIII, who annulled the marriage when he learned about it from the Duc de Montmorency (on the eve of his execution for rebelling on Gaston's behalf). On his deathbed in 1643 Louis forgave Gaston and gave his permission for the marriage, and Gaston and Marguerite renewed their vows.

61. MILADY: "Milady" Clarice de Winter, the fictional agent and assassin for Cardinal Richelieu who bedeviled d'Artagnan and company in *The Three Musketeers*.

62. KING HAS SPILLED STRAFFORD'S BLOOD: To be accurate, King Charles reluctantly agreed to allow parliament to spill the blood of Thomas Wentworth, 1st Earl of Strafford (1593–1641), and it had actually happened seven years earlier than Athos implies. After Buckingham's assassination, Wentworth gradually stepped into his shoes to become Charles's new chief advisor, eventually being made an earl. His rule as Lord Deputy of Ireland was tyrannical and bloody, and moreover parliament blamed him for advising the king to treat the body in the haughty and cavalier manner that led to open conflict. Parliament made Strafford the scapegoat for the nation's ills under Charles, and condemned him to death under a bill of attainder. Backed into a corner, Charles agreed to allow the execution to go forward, a decision he bitterly regretted later.

63. BENVENUTO CELLINI: One of the greatest artists of the Italian Renaissance, the Florentine Benvenuto Cellini (1500–1571) was a sculptor, goldsmith, musician, artist, and writer, practically defining the term *Renaissance Man*.

64. THE BATTLE OF MARIGNANO: The first great military victory for King François I took place in 1515, when the French and their German mercenary allies finally defeated the Swiss, who had been kicking the French around Northern Italy for a generation.

65. TASSO OR ARIOSTO: Two Italian authors of chivalric romances: Torquato Tasso (1544–1595) wrote *Jerusalem Delivered* (1581), an epic poem of knightly exploits, and Ludovico Ariosto (1474–1573) wrote the even more celebrated *Orlando Furioso* (1516).

66. URBAIN GRANDIER: A French priest burned at the stake for witchcraft in 1634 at Loudun after the nuns of the Ursuline convent there accused him of summoning a demon to force them to have sex with him. Though Grandier was a notorious libertine, his prosecution was mainly political, as he'd written some strongly worded tracts criticizing Richelieu.

67. THE PREDICTION OF A MAN NAMED COYSEL: Coysel, Goisel, or Goiset was an astrologer who predicted that the Duc de Beaufort would escape Vincennes during Pentecost (Whitsunday) in 1848. (Spoiler: he did.)

68. THE CHÂTEAU DE VINCENNES: This grim 14th-century royal fortress just east of Paris was used by the French monarchy as a refuge in wartime and as a prison for their enemies in times of peace; Henri IV himself, when he was still Prince Henri de Navarre, had been held there during the Wars of Religion in the late 16th century.

69. BARON DE BLOT: Claude de Chauvigny de Blot (1605? 1610?–1655) was a French poet and satirist who was an early supporter of Mazarin. When the cardinal failed to reward his support with a pension, Blot turned his pen against the minister.

70. IGNATIUS LOYOLA: Íñigo López de Loyola (1491–1556), the Spanish priest and later saint who founded the Society of Jesus, aka the Jesuits.

71. A BAYARD OR A TRIVULCE: Legendary knightly warriors: Pierre Terrail, Chevalier de Bayard (1473–1524) was a paragon of French chivalry; Jacques de Trivulce, or Gian Giacomo Trivulzio (1440–1518) was a conquering Lombard knight who joined the French; both served King Louis XII.

72. PUYLAURENS, MARSHAL ORNANO, AND THE YOUNGER VENDÔME: Three opponents of Louis XIII and Richelieu who were imprisoned in Vincennes for their rebellion, and died there of its unhealthy conditions. Marshal Jean-Baptiste d'Ornano (1581–1626) and Antoine de l'Age, Duc de Puylaurens (1602–1635) both conspired on Prince Gaston's behalf; Alexandre, Chevalier de Vendôme (1598–1629)—the Duc de Beaufort's uncle—was likewise jailed for his involvement in Gaston's so-called Chalais Conspiracy.

73. MADAME DE MONTBAZON: Beaufort's mistress was Marie d'Avaugour de Bretagne, Duchesse de Montbazon (1612–1657), second wife of the Duc de Montbazon (and thus stepmother to the Duchesse de Chevreuse, who was twelve years her senior). She was a great beauty, but notoriously avaricious and self-centered.

74. ASTRAEA: A vast novel of pastoral romance by Honoré d'Urfé published in installments from 1607 through 1627, this tale of the endless tribulations of the shepherdess Astrée and her beloved shepherd Celadon was probably the most popular literary product of 17th-century France, spawning countless imitations.

75. THE MUSHROOMS OF VINCENNES FOREST ARE FATAL TO MY FAMILY: The duke's uncle, Alexandre de Vendôme, was said to have died of eating poisoned mushrooms while imprisoned in Vincennes (see note 72).

76. PONIARDS: A poniard was a long, lightweight dagger, all point and little or no edge, used for thrusting through chainmail or light armor, or for parrying when held in a swordsman's off hand.

77. CHOKE-PEAR: A *poire d'angoisse*, or pear of anguish, was a bulbous metal gag and/or torture device that, once inserted in the victim's mouth, could be gradually expanded by turning a screw.

78. A FOLLY THAT HAD DEPRIVED THE CROWN OF AN HEIR: On March 14, 1622, when the young Queen Anne was pregnant, the Duchesse de Chevreuse persuaded her to run with her along the great hall of the Louvre. The queen fell and suffered a miscarriage, and the duchess was banished from Court, the first of many such exiles.

79. A SERVANT OF HERS, NAMED KITTY: Kitty was introduced in *The Three Musketeers,* where she was initially the maid of the villainous Milady de Winter. After falling in love with d'Artagnan and helping him intrigue against her mistress, she fled from Milady and was found a new home, by Aramis, with the Duchesse de Chevreuse.

80. *11 OCTOBER 1633*: The actual flight of Madame de Chevreuse to Spain while in male guise took place in 1637, but Dumas fudged the date so Raoul could be fifteen in 1648.

81. MONSIEUR ROTROU: Jean Rotrou (1609–50) was one of Cardinal Richelieu's Five Poets. Rotrou, like Pierre Corneille, was a bourgeois from Normandy who came to Paris to make it as a playwright; both appear in *The Red Sphinx*.

82. MADEMOISELLE PAULET: Angélique Paulet (1592–1651), "The Lioness," was a singer, musician, and actress who was a favorite of Parisian high society, and well known at the salons of Madame de Rambouillet.

83. *SI VIRGILIO PUER AUT TOLERABILE DESIT HOSPITUM, CADERENT OMNES CRINIBUS HYDRI*: From Juvenal's *Satires*: "If Virgil hadn't had a decent place to stay, the Fury would have lost her hair of serpents."

84. MADEMOISELLE DE SCUDÉRY: Madeleine de Scudéry (1607–1701) was a celebrated French novelist who wrote under the name "Sappho," and was best known for *The Grand Cyrus* (1648–53) and *Clélie* (1654–61). Her elder brother Georges de Scudéry (1601–1667) was a writer as well, though a lesser light than the brilliant and witty Madeleine, and often collaborated with his sister.

85. MADAME LA PRINCESSE, THE MARÉCHAL D'ALBRET, MONSIEUR DE SCHOMBERG: Respected nobles of high rank: the Princesse de Condé; César Phoebus d'Albret, Comte de Miossens (though not a marshal until 1654); and Charles de Schomberg, a leading Marshal of France in the previous reign.

86. *THE DUKE OR PÈRE VINCENT?*: The Duke of Buckingham or Vincent de Paul—in other words, romance or religion, sin or sanctity.

87. MADEMOISELLE FRANÇOISE D'AUBIGNÉ: Though it seems like Dumas is introducing a potential romantic foil for Raoul here, the author is really just digressing to briefly bring on stage the extraordinary Françoise d'Aubigné (1635–1719), who in 1652 would marry Paul Scarron, and then much later, as the Marquise de Maintenon, become Louis XIV's final main mistress and secret second wife. Raoul seeing something in Françoise that reminds him of young Louise is Dumas foreshadowing and being ironic, as both would later become mistresses of the Sun King.

88. GRAND CHÂTELET: A medieval keep in central Paris on the Right Bank at the Pont au Change, the Grand Châtelet contained the offices of the Provost of Paris and the city's

civil and criminal courts. The Châtelet's dungeons, which were below river level, were notorious for their unhealthy dampness.

89. THE OLD BASILICA: By the time the Basilica of Saint-Denis was built in the 12th century, the site had already been the burying place of French kings for two hundred years, and it would continue to fulfill that function well into the 18th century. It was a popular pilgrimage destination.

90. THE LAST KING: That is, Louis XIII, whom Athos doesn't name, just as he doesn't name Richelieu, in order to elevate his fable of the monarchy above the mundane reality of individuals.

91. IF YOUR HAND IS NOT YET STRONG ENOUGH TO WIELD IT: Athos's father's weapon is probably a 16th-century broadsword, heavier than the nimble rapiers Raoul would have trained with, but arguably a better weapon for battlefield purposes.

92. AS HANDSOME AS ANTINOUS: Antinous (c. 111–130) was a Greek youth revered by the Emperor Hadrian for his perfect beauty. After his untimely death in Egypt, Hadrian deified him and founded a cult to worship his new god.

93. DROPPED, LANDING HARMLESSLY ON HIS FEET: The escape of the Duc de Beaufort from Vincennes occurred very much as Dumas describes it here, with the exception of the invention of the fabulous pie and the involvement of his fictional characters.

94. THE NOVEL *DON QUIXOTE* WAS THEN IN VOGUE: Cervantes's great classic was published in Spain in 1605, and first appeared in French in 1614 (Part I) and 1618 (Part II). The novel was immediately popular in France and proved extremely influential.

95. MONSIEUR LE DUC DE LONGUEVILLE: Henri II d'Orléans, Duc de Longueville (1595–1563) was a lower-ranking Prince of the Blood of the Orléans branch of the royal Bourbon family. After his first wife died in 1637, in 1642 he wed the much younger Anne Geneviève de Bourbon, sister of the Grand Condé and one of the great conspirators of the Fronde. A diplomat who had served Queen Anne and Mazarin in the negotiations that led to the Treaty of Westphalia that ended the Thirty Years' War, the duke probably would have stayed out of the Fronde were it not for the influence of his brilliant and fiery young wife.

96. THE PLACE ROYALE: This handsome and perfectly square plaza was built from 1605 to 1612 during the modernization of Paris by King Henri IV, a program that also included laying out the Place Dauphine and completing the Pont Neuf. All the matching town-houses lining the square were built to the same plan, a first for Early Modern Europe, and it was a fashionable address throughout the 17th century. Surrounded by covered arcades and planted with trees, it was a popular place for nobles to promenade and show off their finery. It was also the notorious site of a number of deadly duels. Cardinal Richelieu had a house there from 1615 to 1627, and in *The Three Musketeers* it was also the home of Milady de Winter.

97. LA GRANDE MADEMOISELLE: Just as the king's younger heir was always called "Monsieur" at Court, his daughter was always called "Mademoiselle." Anne Marie d'Orléans, Duchesse de Montpensier (1627–1693), the daughter of Prince Gaston, was known as "La Grande Mademoiselle" for the swath she cut at Court in a long life of romantic and political intrigue. Having been raised at Court with Madame de Longueville, when Anne-Geneviève threw herself into the chaos of the Fronde, Anne Marie followed, and as she was the wealthiest heiress in France, her considerable financial resources helped prop up the Fronde while the Condés were briefly imprisoned.

98. NON BIS IN IDEM: "Not twice the same," the legal doctrine that says a defendant can't be tried twice for the same crime ("double jeopardy").

99. HIS FATHER, HENRI DE BOURBON: Henri II de Bourbon, Prince de Condé, born in 1588, had died in 1646, elevating his son the Duc d'Enghien to become the new Prince de Condé.

100. AGL' OCCHI GRIFANI: The exact quote from Dante's *Inferno* is "*Cesare armato cogli occhi grifagni,*" or "Caesar, fully armed, with clear and falcon eyes."

101. COUNT FUENSALDAGNA, GENERAL BECK, AND THE ARCHDUKE: The high commanders of the Spanish army in the Netherlands, Captain-General Fuensaldagna, General Jean de Beck, and the archduke himself, Leopold Wilhelm of Austria, who was Governor of the Spanish Netherlands from 1647 to 1656, and the younger brother of Emperor Ferdinand III of the Holy Roman Empire.

102. BALIZARDE: In Ariosto's *Orlando Furioso* (1516, revised 1532), the hero Orlando (Roland) had an invincible sword named "Balisardo"—or "Balizarde" in the popular French translations.

103. THE CARMELITE CONVENT ON THE RUE SAINT-JACQUES: Not to be confused with the humble Carmelite convent in the Faubourg Saint-Germain where the duel between the

King's Musketeers and Cardinal's Guards took place in *The Three Musketeers*, this Left Bank edifice was the grand headquarters of the Carmelites in Paris.

104. *NASEBY*: Dumas's chronology of the English Civil War is far less dependable than his account of the Fronde: King Charles's defeat at the battle of Naseby took place in 1645, not 1648.

105. HIS HIGHNESS THE PRINCE OF WALES: Prince Charles, who would become King Charles II (1630–1685) at the Restoration of the Monarchy.

106. WE REPRODUCE IT HERE VERBATIM: Dumas's assurances to the contrary, all the diplomatic correspondence in *Twenty Years After* was invented by the author.

107. AT BOULOGNE-SUR-MER: That is, at Boulogne on the French coast of the English Channel, an important port dating back to Roman times. In the early 17th century it was known as a haven for smugglers.

108. GYGES'S RING: In Plato's *Republic*, the magical ring than grants invisibility to its wearer, enabling Plato's hypothetical tests of morality.

109. LIKE THE STATUE OF DON JUAN'S COMMANDER: In most of the tales of the lover and rogue Don Juan, the Commander is a Spanish noble slain by Juan, a crime that eventually comes out. Molière's *Dom Juan* (1665) began a tradition of the Commander being represented by an ominous statue.

110. A VERITABLE GALAOR: One of the heroes of *Amadis the Gaul*, a Spanish chivalric romance of the late medieval period that was told and retold in many versions, rather like the English tales of King Arthur. Translated into French, the stories were nearly as popular in France as in Spain. In *The Red Sphinx*, the Comte de Moret's young sidekick is named Galaor.

111. TREMBLING LIKE SOSIA: In classical tales, Sosia was the fearful servant of Amphitryon —though Dumas is doubtless referring to the character in Molière's play *Amphitryon* rather than the classical stories.

112. A NEW BOOK BY MONSIEUR CHAPELAIN: Jean Chapelain (1595–1674) was an author, critic, and one of the founding members of the Académie Française. Since his poetry was not yet widely published in 1648, Raoul would have to have been reading one of Chapelain's works of literary criticism—not a likely choice for a fifteen-year-old lad, no matter how romantically inclined.

113. THE DUKE OF YORK AND PRINCESS ELIZABETH: James, the Duke of York and eventual King James II (1633–1701) and his sister Elizabeth (1635–1650), whom Dumas had mistakenly called Charlotte.

Acknowledgments

The cover painting, usually titled "The Game of Cards," is by the great 19th-century genre painter Adolphe Alexandre Lesrel. The interior illustrations are by Louis Marckl and Frank T. Merrill; many thanks to good friend Mathew Weathers for digitizing and formatting the old engravings.

Thanks also to Philip Turner, my ever-wise literary agent, for all his help in guiding this series to publication.

And many thanks, as ever, to the redoubtable Claiborne Hancock and his loyal musketeers at Pegasus Books, especially Sabrina Plomitallo-González, whose clean and modern designs nonetheless evoke the classic look and feel of the books of a century ago.

For your benefit, reader, I want to acknowledge and welcome you to my website, Swashbucklingadventure.net, where you'll find news and information about this book and others, plus additional related matters of interest. Check it out!